For *Suitcase City*

"[T]he telling is masterful . . . Sit back and enjoy Watson's latest. It's better than bourbon on the rocks." —*Kirkus Reviews*, starred review

"Hypnotically beautiful novel . . . Paranoia has been defined as 'seeing too much pattern.' Author Watson can make us sweaty victims of that madness, partaking of it, suffering from it, and loving every minute." —*Booklist*, starred review

"Watson's magic is in pacing and taut prose . . . *Suitcase City* is an absorbing thriller, a vivid adventure in a bright, humid, perilous underworld . . . [A] tense, bloody thriller with a strong sense of place and a soft heart."
—*Shelf Awareness*, starred review

"A noir gem . . . A deeply contemplative and darkly poetic prose style comple-ments the well-crafted plot." —*Publishers Weekly*

"A solid revenge tale . . . There is plenty of action to be had in this suspense tale, but it is the examination of the characters' motivations that really makes it shine. For fans of Lee Child and Nicci French." —*Library Journal*

"Watson weaves . . . questions about race into a plot that takes one bloody turn after another, a crescendo of violence that ends with a day at sea that might be the most chilling of all." —*Tampa Bay Times*

"[An] irresistible earworm of a novel . . . With its airtight atmosphere of im-pending, life-sinking doom, and taut language evoking palpable Gulf Coast Florida seediness, *Suitcase City* duly takes its place alongside the best works of former Floridian Pete Dexter, and the brilliant Tampa novels of Dennis Lehane . . ." —*Paste Magazine*

"Gripping . . . As [Watson] spins additional threads within the plot, deepening our interest in even minor characters, his grip remains steady. . . . Peeling back the layers of Tampa society to reveal a crosshatching of race and class—the country club scenes are particularly fine—Watson stealthily heightens the suspense." —Barnes & Noble Review

"The novels of Sterling Watson are to be treasured and passed on to the next generation." —Dennis Lehane, author of *Mystic River*

"*Suitcase City* [is] such a damn great book, a too-rare (and sometimes nearly too real) depiction of the wildly different worlds that exist side by side in the city by the bay . . . Events uncoil with an unflashy confidence and understated poetry, drawing in diverse characters whose deep inner lives give the wire-tight plot a thumping, nervous heart." —*Creative Loafing Tampa*

NIGHT LETTER

NIGHT LETTER

BY **STERLING WATSON**

AKASHIC
BOOKS
BROOKLYN, NEW YORK

Published by Akashic Books
©2023 Sterling Watson

ISBN: 978-1-63614-063-6
Library of Congress Control Number: 2022933225
First printing

Akashic Books
Brooklyn, New York
Instagram, Twitter, Facebook: AkashicBooks
E-mail: info@akashicbooks.com
Website: www.akashicbooks.com

Also by Sterling Watson

The Committee
Suitcase City
Fighting in the Shade
The Calling
Blind Tongues
Sweet Dream Baby
Deadly Sweet
Weep No More My Brother

For Kath, again

. . . every form of refuge has its price.

—Glenn Frey and Don Henley

ONE

"You've never opened up with me, Travis, not really. You're good at saying what you think I want to hear, and I have to admit you've been pretty convincing on a couple of occasions, but the simple truth is we've been wasting our time, and we both know it."

I pull on my Thoughtful Smile, and Dr. Janeway pushes back in his green leather swivel chair and holds his tortoiseshell fountain pen level in front of his chin. He holds it perfectly parallel to the floor and rolls it with his thumbs and forefingers. It's a thing he does, but not the only thing. When his legs are crossed, he picks at the little diamonds on his argyle socks. When I say something that surprises him, he pretends to take notes while he gets over being pissed off at me or thinks of what to ask me next. He has a lot of little habits, and I've learned to read them. It's valuable knowledge. I can tell when he's angry, when he thinks I'm making progress, when I'm getting to him, and when I'm putting him in doubt. I think he's an obsessive-compulsive personality.

He rolls the pen and watches me, and I have to admit I'm surprised. This is our last session. I'm leaving next week, and I didn't think he'd break what I call our COB, Contract of Bullshit. He's telling me the truth, now that it's too late for the truth to do either of us any good. Too late for me to give him back some of the same. For years, he's waited for me to break down and cry and tell him some deep dark secret. The real reason I did what I did. The thing that's not in any court record or file or disciplinary report. Maybe it's my mother. Maybe I'll suddenly remember that she accidentally stuck my pee-pee with a diaper pin when I was a baby or that she couldn't show her love to me like she should have. Maybe that's why I did what got me sent here.

One of the things Dr. Janeway doesn't know is I've been reading up on psychology in the library and learning how he thinks and how to dance with him. How to get in step with the sick music he hears in his head and do the therapy bop with him—make him happy and stay pretty happy myself. As happy as you can be in a place like this. This is my last miserable hour with him, and he's telling me I haven't fooled him and we both know it. Well, maybe I have and maybe I haven't, but the simple truth is my time is almost up. I'm eighteen, and they can't hold me any longer. The law made them choose: send me to a real prison or let me go. A judge said they had to let me go. Six years was enough of my life for them to take.

I tighten my Thoughtful Smile a little, add some Wrinkles of An-guish to my forehead, and say, "I don't know, Dr. Janeway. I think a lot of our sessions have been very helpful. And you might think this is a little strange . . ." He perks up here, his eyes widening, his chin rising an inch above the tortoiseshell horizon. ". . . but I've come to think of us as, well, friends. I mean in a limited sort of way . . ." I let this trail off like I don't really understand it myself. Like it's a good thing for me to leave here today still puzzled about the exact nature of the friendship between a therapist and a fucked-up kid with homicidal tendencies.

Maybe I've gone too far. It's not exactly angry, the way he puts the pen down on the polished desktop. His pale-blue eyes get smaller, cooler. His hair is gray now, but his eyes haven't changed like some eyes do. I used to think they reminded me of my Grandpa Hollister's eyes. Police eyes. Eyes that always expect the worst.

"Travis," he says, "I want you to know something. It's something I wouldn't ordinarily tell a . . ." It stops him. He doesn't know what to call me. He doesn't like the word "patient." I'm not a client because I don't pay him. The state of Nebraska does that. He can't call me an inmate, and "boy" doesn't quite capture the sorry nature of my stand-ing. *Underling*, I'm thinking. ". . . tell someone like you, but I'm going to tell you. I recommended that the judge release you, yet I had my doubts."

He raises his hand to stop me from objecting. (I wasn't going to object.) "Not about your violent tendencies. I think you've conquered those. What I'm worried about is the possibility that you've become an institutionalized personality. In some ways, I think you've accommodated yourself too well to . . . this setting. Here all of your needs and many of your wants have been taken care of in a very structured way. I'm worried about what will happen to you on the outside, away from this . . ." Dr. Janeway looks at the windows of the little office where we meet. All I can see from my side of his desk is the water tower with *Bridgedale School for Boys* written on it in big black letters. The guys joke about those words: *Crime School for Boys*, they say when they're sitting around bullshitting about the best ways to hot-wire a car. *Bridge to Hell School*, they call it. Outside the windows, beyond the tower, a couple of turkey buzzards ride the hot currents. There are always two or three of them up there, insolently wheeling, looking down. I've envied them.

Dr. Janeway looks back at me. ". . . away from the routine and the support you have here. It's a different world out there now, Travis. There's a lot going on nobody ever expected when you came here." He stops. He seems a little embarrassed, like he's letting me see his own fears, not describing mine. I know what he means. I hear it on my illegal radio. Lyndon Johnson's president now, and there's a lot of bad news, and the music's different than when I came here. It's still sexy crazy, but there's an evil edge now too. There's a war in Vietnam and a lot of the guys have left here for the army.

Sometimes I just watch Dr. Janeway's mouth move. Now I photograph him with my eyes and count the ways he's changed in six years. First of all, he wasn't supposed to stay here. We used to meet in Mr. Bronovich's office because it was all temporary, and Dr. Janeway was this Ivy League guy who looked like the Hathaway man doing research on very bad boys, and he always let you know in little ways that he was just passing through your shitty world of deviance and dead-end time servers like Mr. Bronovich. Now Dr. Janeway is permanent and has his own office about the size of a closet. Three years ago, Mr. Bronovich went on to be the head of the State Division of Corrections.

I used to examine Dr. Janeway's tweeds and his Cordovan shoes and his tortoiseshell glasses that match his fancy fountain pen and try them on in my mind. You have to do *something* when you're stuck with him for an hour making progress. I used to sit here imagining myself in his job and his life and in his head, then I'd go look him up in the library. Sometimes I'd find him in magazines, sometimes in the novels I'd read. You know the kind, by guys like Marquand and O'Hara, only you can't get all of O'Hara in here. Not the sexy ones. Guys like Janeway go home to women like Emily, Thomas Harrow's second wife. They have kids at Choate or Phillips Exeter. They drink martinis on the terrace and look down on their servants in amused and gentle ways (the servants never get this, of course). I've learned from Dr. Janeway all the little put-downs I'm not supposed to understand. The ways he has of telling me that even before I was a deviant and a criminal I wasn't cut from his kind of cloth.

This morning Dr. Janeway looks old and tired. His tweeds don't seem so stylish. I wonder if he's noticed that the cool guys aren't dressing like the Hathaway man anymore. He isn't brisk and in a hurry anymore, just stooped and annoyed. It's been a long time since he let anything slip about his research or the book he's writing about violent boys, and the position he's going to have on the faculty of some college in leafy New England. This morning Dr. Janeway looks like the beginning of one big failure, and I'm happy to see him, even though he's telling me I'm an institutionalized personality, and I won't make it on the outside because I'm used to the comforts the State of Nebraska provides for me. I could tell him a thing or two about survival, but I won't, not even on our last day. Today I'll be just like always. I'll walk out of his life leaving him wondering about progress. Wondering if some people don't change no matter how many hours they spend with guys like him and their good intentions and their theories.

Dr. Janeway's eyes narrow like they sometimes do, and he says,

"Travis, I'm sorry you chose not to write about your problems. You're a good writer. You've got some talent in that direction. It would have been good for you to put down some of your thoughts about what you did and why you did it. About who you were then and who you are now."

I play my part, slowly shake my head, sincerely puzzled about why I haven't used my talent for writing. I wonder if he knows I would kill him if I could for stealing the Delia Book from me. For having my locker tossed and for ripping open my mattress and finding the Delia Book I wrote and the drawings I drew and all the letters I sent only in my heart. I'm sure of one thing: in this last hour, we won't talk about that.

I came back one night from my job in the furniture factory, high as one of those turkey buzzards from sniffing varnish all afternoon, and the Delia Book was gone and I was expecting a DR and time added to my stay and maybe some shitty work detail like cleaning out the grease trap in the mess hall, but nothing happened. I was only fourteen at the time, and at first I was relieved. Two days passed, and I didn't get called in by Mr. Bronovich, and the counselors (that's what they call the guards here) weren't staring turds at me. Then Friday came, time for my appointment with Dr. Janeway, and I saw it immediately. It was in his eyes. He was excited. He had the Delia Book. He'd asked me to write about my case, my progress, why I stabbed Jimmy Pultney, and I'd told him I would. But I didn't. I only wrote about Delia. So he had them take the book, and he wasn't going to say anything about it. It was a test, a setup. He wouldn't mention it unless I did. Well, you already know what I did. I'd let them rip my tongue back to its root before I'd ever mention the Delia Book to Dr. Janeway.

So I swallowed what I saw in Dr. Janeway's eyes and what I could have done to him for it, and we had our session as usual that day, and on and on, for all the days. And he never mentioned it, and I never did either. That's therapy for you, that's medical science of the mind. The Janeway variety.

I had a week of sleepless nights thinking he might burn the Delia Book, but, finally, I knew he wouldn't. Just like I knew who took it and why, I knew he'd keep it. He'd read and reread it, and knowing that hurt deep like a broken bone, but there was nothing I could do about it.

Now I square myself up in my chair and look him straight in the eyes and say, "I know it's going to be tough out there, Dr. Janeway. You can't stay in a place like this for six years and miss everything that's happened outside and not have some . . . difficulty adjusting. But I'm going to make it. I know I am. I've learned a lot in here . . . about myself, about what to do and not to do when I get out." I'm Travis Making Progress with Wrinkles of Anguish on my forehead and a Not-Too-Assertive Smile fitted firmly to my lips. I say, "I've learned a lot from you, Dr. Janeway, even if you don't think I have. And I want to thank you for it."

The few other times I've thanked him, he's let me go early. He likes a good ending. But this time I know he won't, and I don't want him to. We'll stay till the last minute turns. I know I'm going to miss our sessions. There's not a lot you can control in this place. There's a lot that's unpredictable, mostly in the lives of the other guys and the things they can do to you if you're not careful. But I've learned to control Dr. Janeway. Except for the time he stole the Delia Book, and I know what to do about that.

TWO

Back in the dormitory, it's hot like it always is when it's not cold. The last of the summer afternoon light is the color of ginger ale at the west windows. The place smells like piss, sweat, and the laundry soap they use on our denim uniforms. There are a few guys lying around reading, two intellectuals playing chess, a few lost fools drooling in their sleep. One fool has his knees pulled up to his chin and his hands between his legs, and I know what he's dreaming about. When the bell rings, the sleepers will rise, the chessmen will put away their knights and pawns with their usual superior air, the readers will mark their places, and we'll all shuffle out for dinner. And I'll eat my next-to-last meal in this shitty place. Now I have to pack my things.

We don't have much here. A bed (older guys and hard cases in the lower bunks), a footlocker, a chest of drawers, some books, and pictures cut out of magazines. When my release papers came through, I was measured for a pair of gray wool slacks, a white shirt, and a cheap blue blazer. Nebraska will try to cover up what I am, but when I walk out of here tomorrow morning, I'll be wearing state-issue underwear, the old life closest to my skin. In here, they preach about the difference between what you want and what you need. They say it's what we wanted that got us into trouble.

They say we have only three needs: physical, spiritual, and mental. For the body, we get food, clothes, a toothbrush and soap, vaccinations, and our teeth fixed by a student dentist who isn't too careful about pain or the cosmetic side of his craft. For the spirit, we get plenty of chapel and the Holy Bible, free from the Gideons. Which makes interesting reading sometimes if you ask me. Our needs are mental too, and that, as old Prince Hamlet says, is where it rubs. We go to school in the mornings here at six. After lunch, we work, then there's an hour of recreation before dinner. The library's open then, and after dinner until ten o'clock, and that's where I've spent most of my free time.

It rubs you hard when you can only read what they tell you to read for school, and the library shelves are full of crazy gaps where books somebody thought would warp your already twisted mind have been removed. We find ways. Things get smuggled in here, in spite of the Christian vigilance. Some guy's flat-chested sister stuffed two copies of *Lady Chatterley's Lover* into her brassiere. Either the counselors didn't notice she was suddenly and strangely stacked, or they thought she was just like her brother, growing up in unusual directions. The books got passed around until they fell apart. The pages were so greasy from a thousand sweaty hands and God knows what else that the books were twice their normal size before they finally got dismembered. Pieces of them, the good parts I guess, are still around, hidden here and there. Some guy used a razor blade to cut out the center of *Frazer's Concise Bible Commentary* and that's where we keep the best of *Chatterley*. Sitting at my table in the library, I see the guys who never read anything but Captain Marvel come shuffling in to pull down the Frazer. That's our word for jerking off. Frazering. The librarian, Mr. Hale, hasn't caught on yet.

I've got the education they serve up bland in the classrooms here, American history, English grammar, algebra and geometry, biology, and even a little physics. They think they know I'm smart but unmotivated. A classic underachiever. I got mostly B's without busting my ass or kissing anybody else's. I got my real education in the library and writing the Delia Book and from the other guys. I've spent a lot of time inside my own head where the space stretches on and on like the wheat fields outside these fences. In there, anything can happen, and I can be anybody I want to be, even when I'm listening to Dr. Janeway's theories or turning out spindles on a lathe in the furniture factory.

The education I got from the guys, like all good things, is divided into three parts: stand up for yourself, pick your friends, and bide your time. I didn't have much trouble when I was new here because people thought I was crazy, and crazy scares even the toughest guys. I didn't act all that crazy, but somehow word got around that I stabbed a guy with a bayonet and he nearly died from loss of blood and he lost the use of his right arm, the one he used to shoot the arrows at me. I'm not sorry about that. Jimmy Pultney dragging around one dead arm only means a lot less trouble will happen in the world. I've had a few fights here, won some and lost some, and got in trouble for some. We keep things secret here. If you settle your problems without ratting to the counselors, you get respect along with your bruises and chipped teeth.

I never played team sports because those guys look to me like a bunch of performing seals (clap-clap-arf-arf, swallow that mackerel), even if they do get trips outside to play against other reform school kids and sometimes even public school kids. I could have played baseball. I was pretty good before I came here, and I still toss it around with some of the guys on the team. But I never wanted the rules, the coaches telling me what to do, the stupid code of humility and team spirit. I'm my own team, and that's the way it is with most of the guys I respect in here. Be everybody's buddy and nobody's friend. That'd be our motto, if mottoes weren't stupid.

It's midnight, and I can tell by the sounds of their breathing that most of the guys are asleep. I'm listening to my illegal radio, hearing the sounds of the world I'm going back to. Learning from the songs how people think now and what they do. Getting ready. I'm up late to see the last day come in. When the sweep second hand on my watch passes twelve, Del Rio, Texas, says, "Well, folks, it's midnight. A new day has dawned, and I've heard the cock crow as he did once a long time ago for our precious Lord and Savior, and as I put this gospel hour of the airwaves to bed, I put this question to you: how will you use this new day to glorify your sweet suffering Jesus?"

You get these guys late at night on a radio made from winding stolen copper wire around a toilet paper roll. It's the atmosphere up there or something, bouncing signals and frequencies around until they come in clear as a bell at midnight in a shithole reform school in Nebraska. I've listened to the radio preachers for years, late at night when I'm as alone as I ever can be, and their sweet, crazy, sobbing voices come into my ear like they're lying here next to me and they're so sure about how I ought to live my life and about how easy things will be for me once I've taken their Jesus into my heart.

They've got one thing right. They know about evil. They know it lives in every human heart. They know it can't be fixed by doctors, lawyers, cops, or any other earthly power. They know evil, and they're good enough to be sorry for you if you have it big in you, scared for you if you can't control it. What they don't know is human love. They don't know it can save you, at least in this world. And they don't know what it can make you do.

I look at the radium dial of my watch, and enjoy the first minute of my last full day in this place. I say goodbye to the Reverend Somebody-or-other out there in the land of the sagebrush Jesus (the only pulpit west of the Pecos). I switch off my illegal radio (I'll give it to one of the younger guys tomorrow morning, or maybe just stick it in some lucky fool's locker for him to find after I'm gone). I get up quietly and get my little kit from where I've hidden it behind the radiator and walk through the silent bay of bunks and cheap metal furniture, through the weather of all their breathing and all their sad dreams.

The dormitory isn't locked at night on account of fire regulations, but there's a silent alarm rigged to the exterior doors. It activates a buzzer in the counselors' office down at the main entrance. I go up one flight of stairs, down the hallway to the door that leads onto the fire escape. In my kit for tonight, I've got some adhesive tape and two razor-thin steel plates with three feet of copper wire soldered to them. I figured out if you slide the two plates between the door and the frame with the loop of wire in front of you, you can open the door without breaking the electrical circuit that sets off the silent alarm. I step out onto the fire escape, carefully rotate the plates, close the door, and pull the plates out by the length of wire.

Dr. Janeway's third-floor office door is a cinch, a simple screw-driver job. Getting into the building is the problem. The exterior doors are double locked. I've made a plan, and I think it will work, but it depends on Dr. Janeway's habits. Like I told you, he has a lot of them.

He hates the smell of printer's ink from the print shop on the floor below. They print state paychecks down there, and that's one reason the building has tough locks. Dr. Janeway complains about the ink, it gets to his sinuses. His habit is to open his office window a little when he leaves to let in the fresh air. The night security man travels a regular circuit, and I'm timing my visit so that he'll be far away, but there's always the possibility that he'll close Dr. Janeway's window.

I make it to the roof without any trouble. There's an incinerator at the back of the building and the brick smokestack has a ladder. It's a long jump from the ladder to the roof, but I can do it. I made a dry run three nights ago, and the rope I left on the roof (liberated from some old gymnastics equipment in the rafters of the gym) is ready for me. I read up on knots in a library book on marlinspike seamanship. I've adapted an old design for a boson's chair, except you stand in it. I've made hemp work like a pulley and block. There was no way to practice with it. Tonight's the night. It either works or it doesn't. I can succeed or fail, fall or be found in the morning hanging helpless from some weird harness outside Dr. Janeway's window.

I throw my rig over the side, crouch at the edge of the building, and fit my shoes into the sling, then I swing down into the dark. I scrape my forearms a little going over, but that's all right. I pay out a little rope and there's a groan and some bumpy slippage though it seems like my pulley knot is working. Going down is the easy part, of course. It'll be heavy hauling coming up, but I've been doing push-ups for years and climbing to the gym rafters (where I got my rope idea), and I've got the upper-body strength of a pole vaulter.

I hang for a few seconds, swinging with a soft, groaning sound and feeling the cool night wind on my sweating face. I'm four stories up, and a fall will kill me. I look out over the tarred rooftops of this way station for guys whose young years went wrong. I think of guys I've known, a few worth the effort, a few who've died here, and some who've been shipped on to prison. And here I am committing a crime that could get me sent to Lincoln, where boys become men fast, or die. But I have to do it. I'm not going back without what I came for.

Twenty feet down, outside Dr. Janeway's window, I see my bad luck: the window's shut. If the security man shut it, he locked it too. I've got my kit tied to my belt, and I could try to pry up the sash with a screwdriver, but it probably wouldn't work, and if it did, it would leave the kind of evidence that could get me stopped at the front gate tomorrow morning. I can't risk that.

I swing there in the cool night. My arms are getting tired and my feet are hurting where the rope pinches my shoes. I try to think, but nothing comes. I'm getting tired. Soon I'll be too shaky to make it back up. I dangle, and when I know I have to give up, hot tears start in my eyes. I start pulling up, and my block knot is working. The pulling's hard, and I'm breathing like I've already done fifty push-ups, and that's when I hear it, a little rustle of something soft, something near my face, something alive. I don't know why, but I reach out toward the side of the building, toward a dark space between a ledge and a drain-pipe. And something moves against my hand. And I know what it is.

They fly down from Canada. They fly fast and low like bullets across the wheat fields, and when I first came here, I could look through the fences sometimes and see men shooting them in the sunset fields. They're called mourning doves because the sound they make is so sorrowful. I know she's a mother. I know she's on her nest, warming her eggs, or maybe her chicks. I strain to see her in the dark, and maybe I do, a lighter shape in the deep moon shadow. She's a fierce little thing and won't leave her nest even though I'm close and I'm danger. My hand darts out before I even know what it's doing.

With the strangled dove inside my shirt, I let myself back down. I punch the screwdriver handle through the glass just above the latch. The glass breaks with a loud pop, but there's no one around to hear. I reach inside my shirt for the bird and toss her through the hole. Dr.

Janeway will find her in the morning, artfully arranged in the pile of broken glass on his office floor.

It's not hard getting into Dr. Janeway's file cabinet. Reform school is crime school and a furniture shop is a hardware store. The techniques and tools for picking a simple lock are easy enough to learn. I find the Delia Book at the back of the bottom drawer. I knew he'd keep it. Maybe for his research, a curiosity of crime like the shivs guys make here, or maybe it's his proof that I deserved what I got, the six years they took from me. Well, I did deserve what I got and probably more, but not for what I did to Jimmy Pultney with a bayonet.

I get one surprise in Dr. Janeway's office. Before I stuff the Delia Book into the waistband of my pants and swing out on my harness and lock the window, I find my file. My surprise is the good doctor's "recommendation."

"On balance," he wrote, "it seems to me that Travis Hollister is too conflicted and unstable a personality to represent an acceptable risk at this time. He should be sent on to the adult facility at Lincoln for continued observation and rehabilitation." Well, maybe I'll see Dr. Janeway again sometime, and we'll talk about truth and falsehood.

I'm a liar. I learned it from Delia, and I'm good at it. I lied to Dr. Janeway because he had all the power, and he could destroy me with a line or two of writing from his fancy fountain pen. In the game we played, that was my part: I lied. He could have told me the truth, but he wasn't man enough. I don't know what Dr. Janeway will do when he discovers the Delia Book is gone. I had to have it back. It's the story of the most important thing in my life. If they come after me for taking it, I'll just have to deal with that.

My last morning in hell and I'm scared and trying not to show it. All through breakfast and later back in the dorm, changing into my release clothes and then walking with my pasteboard suitcase to the administration building to get the state seal on my release papers, my hands are shaking and my knees feel like they're coming out of joint. I'm afraid they'll search my things. I've talked to guys who left and came back, and nobody said anything about tossing suitcases, but anything's possible. So I shuffle down the long sidewalk to the gate with my heart banging around my chest, and lights going on and off in my head like a pinball machine. It's only when I'm finally outside and hear the gate closing behind me and know the gate guard, Mr. Sowers, is watching my back with his cold blue eyes and thinking he'll get me back someday or somebody like him will get me . . . only then that I feel the freedom driving up from the earth into my legs, pouring into my chest, and falling out of the sky into my eyes. It's in the earth and in the light. Somehow, I don't know, it's brighter outside the fence, and the breeze is cooler and the wind smells of Canada geese flying down to Louisiana. It's just one step from inside that gate to the outside, the world, but the distance is forever and everything.

I stand on that one spot, one stride outside the gate, breathing deep, clenching my suitcase hard against my thigh, and looking up into the vast blue sky. I want to scream as loud and as long as I can, one endless cry that's the name of freedom, but I can't. I won't. The habit of carefulness, of holding in what I feel and what I want, is too strong. I start to walk, and I haven't gone fifty steps when the sadness starts.

Even though I knew it wouldn't happen, it couldn't, a little part of me, maybe the weakest part, thought somebody might meet me here. The thing is, I don't know who that somebody would be. Things change in six years, and people change more than things. I stand in the parking lot, looking down the long dirt road into the wheat and wondering what to do. Should I wait here for a while?

And I wonder if they even know I'm out. If they know anything about me now. That I'm a high school graduate with B's, know how to operate a lathe, have some secret skills I don't tell anyone about, have learned to stand up for myself, pick my friends, and bide my time.

The parking lot holds only the cars that belong to guards or teachers or maintenance personnel. I've seen them all come and go a thousand times. The road that leads straight off into the wheat is empty. I could wait until the shift changes and hitch a ride with a counselor or a teacher, but I decide against that. I don't want to take my first step into the future with somebody from back there behind me.

I shift the suitcase from one hand to the other and start walking fast into my new life.

THREE

'm heading west, in a Buick going sixty, and I'm thinking about how much I don't know. I only know things from books, movies, the radio, and the stories of guys who were outside and came back to tell about it. Clifton Ames, the guy driving this big Roadmaster, is a vacuum cleaner salesman from Omaha. He's just starting what he calls his "swing" through the small towns out on the western edge of the state. He talks a mile a minute, and he'd sell me a vacuum cleaner if he thought I owned a scrap of floor. I only had to wait twenty minutes for him to stop, and standing there with my thumb pointing into the future didn't feel like begging.

I felt like a beggar every time they gave me something at Bridgedale, even a mouthful of greasy meatloaf. But standing there by the road in the morning sunlight asking the world for a ride, I was smiling big enough to crack the corners of my mouth. The cheap blazer and slacks the state gave me fit pretty well, so I slanted my hip out a little like William Holden and tilted my head to the side and before too long this guy named Clifton Ames pulled up in the Buick. He reached over and swung open the door. "Get in, man," he said, and it sounded good to me. I'm a man, and the rest of my life is out there waiting for me to find it.

Clifton talked for a while, and for a while I gave him back my best, all about how the weather's a little cooler than usual for this time of year and, no, I haven't been waiting long, and how I'm on my way home from a trip east to stay with my brother in boarding school where he's captain of the lacrosse team and going off to Cornell to study medicine next fall (thank you, John O'Hara), and I'm just hitching rides for the fun of it, meeting people and seeing the country. Aren't I missing some school? Naw, I go to private school out in San Francisco where my parents live. They let us go early out there.

Clifton Ames looks over at my cheap coat and the state socks falling down around the tops of my round-heeled black oxfords. He raises his eyebrows, lights a Chesterfield, and concentrates his mind on the vast, fascinating future that waits for him in vacuum cleaners. He finishes the Chesterfield, flicks the butt out the window, and checks the rearview, satisfied to see a shower of sparks.

I excuse myself into my own head. It's only late morning, but I'm tired. I used up a lot of nervous energy leaving Bridgedale. The steady hum of Clifton's big V-8 and the burr of the asphalt under his tires and the warm breeze coming from the vents invite me to sleep, but before I accept, Dr. Janeway knocks at the door of my mind. He smiles with concern and asks me for the deep dark secret, the real reason I did it. He always hinted it was my mom. I pull the Wrinkles of Anguish onto my forehead for the last time and I lie to him.

But it is my mom, I guess, along with a lot of other things, some of which I understand and some I don't. When I had to tell Dr. Janeway something, I always said my mother loved me fine but there were just things she couldn't carry anymore so she had to leave. And the way she left was in her mind. She just went away in there and wouldn't come out. I understand that, at least some of it, and now I'm going to California to find her and ask her to tell me about the things I don't understand. I won't ask her for a place in her life, but if there is one we'll both know it.

The beer truck stops on Market Street. My driver, a big Italian named Gino LaVeccio, says, "Here it is, buddy. The best street in the best town in the world." I smile and thank him. It's been a long, strange trip, but I'm here. I jump off Gino's running board, set my suitcase down, and watch him drive his steam truck on up the hill. In Frisco, Gino told me, beer is called steam.

The street is crowded. People are leaving office buildings, going home from work. They walk with a purpose, they look happy and well-dressed. I back up against the window of a store called I. Magnin. I lean against the glass to get out of the way and take it all in. For a week, my life has been highways and truck stops and people talking through the night to keep from falling asleep. The talk has been boring and crazy and sometimes full of the secret truth people only tell at four in the morning when they know they'll never see you again.

I've seen America and I've seen the people who are seeing America. I lost my blue blazer near Tucumcari when I got picked up by some Zuni Indians and slept in a truck bed with their two sheepdogs. When I woke up, one of the dogs was sleeping on my coat and looked like she needed it more than I did. It was falling apart anyway from getting rained on and used as a blanket under a bridge in Denver. How did I get from a bridge in Denver to sleeping with sheepdogs in Tucumcari? Hitching rides, you go where people are going, and you take their word for that, and sometimes their word's no good, or their sense of direction is worse than yours, or you're just too damned tired to care as long as you're going somewhere and it's warm and dry.

On Market Street there's a big-city excitement I've never seen before. It's been building since I helped Gino unload the last of his steam in some little towns out in the desert and we came into Oakland and I could smell the sea air, and it started to go from hell-hot to bearable and finally almost cold, and then I could see a big bridge out ahead and I asked Gino if it was the Golden Gate and he said, "Naw, buddy, that's the Bay Bridge, but it's a good bridge, ain't it?"

"Sure it is," I said, feeling kind of high on all the driving and the new smells and the closeness to what I've been waiting for. "It's a great bridge."

I turn around and look into the I. Magnin window. Six women wearing evening gowns and diamonds look back at me. They're supposed to be at a dance or something and they have wineglasses wired to their hands. Inside the store, a real woman watches me like I might be soiling the window, or I might break it and grab a mannequin and run off down the street to some dance of my own. I smile and step away and see my reflection in the glass. I guess I'm pretty scary. My black hair is gray and stiff with dust, and my skin feels crusty. My white shirt is gray, stained under the arms, and there's a six-inch rip behind the left elbow. My pants are bagged, and they've shrunk so much from rain that my bare ankles show where my socks slop down around my shoes. There's a big, red, infected deerfly bite on my forehead. I lost my left shoe heel running for the back of a truck full of hop pickers just outside of Sacramento. Later on, a guy saw me limping past his house in Fairfield. He said, "What's a matter kid, you got a gimpy leg?" I said, "No sir, I just walked my heel off."

He invited me in, gave me half of the liverwurst sandwich he was eating for lunch, and took me out to his garage. He cut some tread from an old tire, shaped it to fit, and nailed it onto my shoe. It looks like hell, especially here on Market Street, but it went fifty miles and never hurt me. I wave to the lady watching me from behind the six plastic debutantes. She frowns, and I pick up my suitcase and move on up the sidewalk, weaving through the rushing people.

You get a lot of funny looks walking up Market Street with a varnished pasteboard suitcase. People see you don't know where you're going. Their eyes say they want you to keep moving, or they want to give you directions, or they wonder where you've been. You're a mystery when you carry a suitcase. I'm a mystery all right. All I've got in my suitcase is the Delia Book, some paperback novels, my release papers, and the boy clothes I had on when I went to reform school six years ago.

In Chinatown I pass a laundry, and there's a little booth in front with an old lady sitting behind a sewing machine. Steam pours out through the laundry transom and clothes hang in racks behind the counter inside. A Chinese lady comes from the back and stands behind the counter. Her black hair is bunned on her head with shiny combs, and she's wearing a black skirt and a blouse with white cherry blossoms embroidered on it. She looks at me through the window and frowns.

I go inside and tell her I want to get my clothes cleaned. She looks at my pants and shirt, at my face. I smile. She frowns. "No good. Not worth it. Throw away." She pinches her nose with her thumb and forefinger. I don't know why I think it's funny. I wait. She says something in Chinese to the old lady at the sewing machine. The old lady answers but doesn't look up from her work. Her tiny brown fingers move the needle and thread like she's talking to the cloth in sign language. The lady behind the counter says, "You got money?" She raises her left hand, rubs her fingers together. I dig into my pockets for the last of my State of Nebraska cash. I pull out a ten-dollar bill. She frowns, mutters something, then says, "You come."

I follow her to a little room in the back where clothes with tags on them hang in racks. They smell clean and some of them look pretty cool. She says, "Nobody come for these. Long time." It takes me a second, then I get it: unclaimed freight. She walks out and pulls the curtain shut behind her. I'm in a little room with a curtain between me and the old lady, and on the other side there's a door. I can smell food from the room beyond the door. It smells good. A man in that room says something in Chinese, and a child answers in a voice as high and light as a piccolo.

I pick a pair of chino slacks and a white shirt. It takes awhile to find things that fit. I know from traveling that the blazer was all wrong, so I choose a windbreaker with a zip-up front and a flannel lining. I'm bending over bare-assed, pulling the pants up, when the lady comes back through the curtain. I jump to cover myself, but she doesn't look at me. She keeps her eyes on the door where I heard the man's voice. "You need," she says, and holds out a pair of cotton underwear and two pairs of black socks. I have to hop over with the chinos half up my shins to take them from her. I say, "Thanks," but she's leaving again. I take off the chinos, and I'm about ready to pull on the used but clean underwear when she comes back in with a bucket of water, a washcloth, a bar of soap, and a towel. "You wash," she says, and holds her nose again. "Pooh!" she says and leaves.

So I wash standing there in the room with unclaimed clothing and the sewing machine whining on and off out in front. The warm water feels good, and I do a pretty good job, even kneeling down and dunking my head in the bucket. When I'm finished, the white towel is gray and the water in the bucket has half of Route 66 in it. I wonder what the lady's gonna think. I put on the used new clothes and go out and stand at the counter. She's waiting on a customer, a businessman in a fresh gray suit with gold cuff links and a blue silk tie. He pays her, takes his laundry wrapped in brown paper, and says, "Thank you, Mrs. Hawn." She frowns and says, "You come again." The man smiles and walks out into the crowded street.

I step up to the counter and put down my ten-dollar bill. I'm hoping there's enough left for some food. I haven't eaten since noon yesterday, pickled eggs and crackers at a gas station in the desert. Mrs. Hawn takes my ten, goes to the cash register, comes back, and counts out eight dollars. I look at the money, look up at her, and I can't help smiling. I say, "Thank you, Mrs. Hawn." She looks at me for a long time, frowns, and says, "You wait."

I wait, watching the old lady sew. Her brown fingers move like quick spiders around the edge of a torn pocket in an alpaca sport coat. Mrs. Hawn comes back through the curtain holding a blue bowl. She sets it on the counter. It's full of rice and some kind of meat, chicken maybe. She lays chopsticks beside the bowl. It smells so good, it makes me dizzy. She says, "You sit," and points at the little bench where customers wait for their laundry. I say, "Thank you, Mrs. Hawn," and sit. She frowns, folds her arms across her narrow chest, and watches me try to eat with chopsticks. It's funny at first, but I start to get the hang of it. It is chicken, and I've never tasted anything like it. We only got salt and pepper in reform school and this chicken has flavors I've never met. I've been on short rations for a week, and my stomach has shrunk. I can feel my belly warming up and stretching around this strange, good food.

Mrs. Hawn watches me the whole time I eat, and the strange thing is I'm this dirty, hungry guy who walked in off the street and she seems to care what I think of her chicken. I'm good at faking appreciation, but I don't have to now. I grin and make happy noises as I eat, and Mrs. Hawn's frown deepens the lines on her forehead, and I know she's happy. When I finish, I put the bowl on the counter and thank her, and she looks at me like I'm a puppy she isn't going to pet anymore because it might follow her home. She says, "You go now," and I do. I could offer her money for the food, but I know she doesn't want it. Just like she wants me to go now. I walk out and don't look back.

FOUR

Out on the street it's a new world because I'm clean and my clothes are new, and it's still morning and I'm seeing things I've never seen before. The streets are narrow, and they all seem to go uphill and every other doorway opens into a restaurant, and inside there are Chinese men in starched white coats, moving fast laying out white plates and silver and napkins folded into shapes like birds. And everything is painted bright red and there are a lot of dragons with wild eyes and big black teeth. Big brass lamps hang from the ceilings with rows of red tassels dangling from them. On the street, the people move fast and don't look at you and everywhere you can hear people talking and arguing in their strange musical language. Men pass me on bicycles with racks bolted to them full of loaves of bread and pans of steaming food.

There's an old man on the sidewalk cutting out paper profiles of people's faces with a pair of scissors. He stares at their faces and goes into a trance, and he works as fast as the old lady sewing. I watch him do a family of tourists. Mom, Pop, little Buddy, and little Suzie. They stand in a row and stare their goofy faces at him, and the old man gets them all pretty right. There's an argument when they pay him, though, because they say he raised the price. Pop gets red-faced and pushes his hat back on his forehead and shoves his fists into the fat at his sides and says, "But you said two bucks, not two bucks a *person!*" The old man starts yelling, and his voice is high like a woman's, and a crowd gathers fast, all of them looking hard at Pop and Mom and Buddy and Suzie, and they get embarrassed and pay the eight bucks and hurry away. I stay around long enough to see the old man's anger disappear as fast as he cut with his scissors. He smiles and pockets the money. I walk on down the street looking for a phone booth.

I don't know where my mom lives. I don't know if the Japanese people live with the Chinese, but it seems like a pretty good guess. So I'm in Chinatown looking up Kobayashi in a phone book. There are thirty-seven of them, but I'm not too worried. My mom's brother is named Hiroshi, and I think she's staying with him. That's what my dad wrote to me in his last letter three years ago. There are three H. Kobayashis. I write down all of the addresses and numbers, and I go out on the street to ask directions. A cabdriver tells me how to find the first address, and it's only six blocks from Mrs. Hawn's laundry.

It's an apartment on the second floor and when I knock, an old man answers. He's about eighty, and he's holding a newspaper in his hand, and he squints at me through wire-rimmed glasses. When I say, "Hello, sir, does Miko Kobayashi live here? She's my mother," he just bows and closes the door. I don't think my mom's brother is that old.

The second address is a restaurant, and it's Chinese not Japanese, and I'm about to leave when I see a sign on the wall with an arrow pointing into an alley too narrow for a car. It says: *H. Kobayashi, DDS*. That's all. Maybe my mom's brother is a dentist. I don't know. I go down the alley, and there's a little courtyard between the buildings and a doorway with a blue china pot of daisies on either side of the door. That's when my knees get a little shaky and my heart starts to drum. I'm remembering my mom's household god, the little blue china altar she kept in her bedroom with my dad. It was the same color.

I could simply go in and ask, but suddenly I don't feel like it. Or maybe I just can't. There's a window, so I look in. The office is small, and I see a woman behind a counter writing and beyond her a Japanese man in a white smock working on a man sitting in a dentist's chair. The doctor steps back and the patient leans over and spits, and then another woman passes between them and hands the doctor something. I can't see her face very well, but there's just something about her. Something I remember. Maybe it's the way she moves, the shape of her head. How much does your mother change after shock treatment and five years in San Francisco?

I jump back from the window when a Japanese man comes down the alley. He's got a white bandage wrapped from his chin up across his head and his hat pushed down over it. He's walking carefully with one eye shut and his right hand holding the side of his face. He stops and looks at me, and I don't know what to do, so I bend down and smell one of the pots of spicy daisies and then smile at him. He goes into the office.

I decide to wait across the street. It's almost noon, and I figure maybe they'll close the office for lunch and I'll see them leave and I'll know for sure if it's my mom. There's a restaurant across the street with a booth in the window, so I walk over there and sit in the booth. It takes me awhile to explain to the Chinese lady that I only want tea. I talk and talk and point across the street and say I'm waiting for someone and we'll have lunch here when she comes out of the dentist's office, but (I hold my hand to the side of my face) you never know how somebody's going to feel after a trip to the dentist. The lady looks at my suitcase, not at me, and says she wants me to eat or leave, not just drink tea, but finally she gives in and brings a blue teapot and a cup. I smile at her, but she frowns and I know her frown doesn't mean what Mrs. Hawn's meant.

I wait all through the lunch hour. The streets fill up with people and the restaurant does a pretty good business. About every five minutes the lady comes over and asks me if I'm ready to eat. She puts a menu down in front of me, and I just ask for more tea. She points at some people waiting for a booth, and I point across the street at the alley and tell her my lunch partner is coming any minute. Finally, I can't do it anymore. The clock behind the cash register says one thirty. I get up and pay for the tea, and the lady takes my fifty cents and shakes her head like I've made a mess in her restaurant and now she has to clean it up. When I leave, she's muttering in Chinese to some people in a booth by the door, and there's nothing for me to do but stand around on the sidewalk.

I wait another half hour and a cop with a billy stick comes up the street. He goes into the restaurant, talks to the Chinese lady, then comes out and says, "What you doing around here, kid? You live in this neighborhood?"

I say, "No sir. I'm just waiting for a friend to come out of the dentist's office."

It's not that I don't like cops. Some are okay, just guys doing their jobs, but some like to push people around, and some will play with you the way kids throw rocks at a stray dog. Just to see what you'll do. It's easy for them if you're nobody. I'm nobody from no-where with a pasteboard suitcase and seven dollars and fifty cents in my pocket.

"What kinda friend?" the cop says.

I'm not going to tell him it's my mother. That I haven't seen her for six years. That I can hardly even remember her face. That the last time I saw her, she was standing with both hands over her mouth and that dying look in her eyes watching the cops take me away for stabbing Jimmy Pultney. I say, "Just a buddy of mine."

The cop says, "You got Japanese buddies, kid?" He thinks he's got me.

"Yeah," I say, "I do. My mother is Japanese. My dad's a marine, and he met her when he was in the occupation forces. Now he's an attorney down in Florida. I'm here on vacation to see my mom's relatives."

My face is a mystery. It puzzles people and I get searching looks, double takes from blue-eyed blondes and brunettes. I could be any-thing—Mexican, black Irish, part Cherokee. My color could be a dark tan from working in the sun. My hair is black like my mother's, and my eyes are my father's, round and brown. To my face, people have called me *mixed*. *Mixed up*, I used to say as a joke.

This cop's a jukebox, and I've got a quarter in him now. The gears are grinding, and I can see the song of confusion playing in his eyes. He looks back at the restaurant window where the Chinese lady stands with her hands on her hips watching me dance with the police department. I can see in the cop's eyes that he doesn't like the lady inside any more than he likes me, and now that I've told him I'm half Japanese, he puts us in the same category. He pushes his cap back, rubs his forehead with a big, pale hand, and says, "Well, you're bothering Mrs. Chen, so move on down to the corner, why don't you? You can wait down there just as good as here."

I say, "Yes sir," and start walking. I glance back over my shoulder, and the cop looks at Mrs. Chen, touches his nightstick to the bill of his cap, and walks back in the direction he came from. It's a victory. Every time you don't get pushed around, it's a victory.

I wait another hour and it's almost three o'clock and the woman I saw in the office of H. Kobayashi, DDS, comes out of the alley across the street and she's my mom. She's older and smaller and thinner, but it's her. I can tell by the way she holds herself so carefully when she walks, and the way she looks up at the sky suddenly like something's coming at her and she doesn't know what it is. My knees go to water watching her, and my heart throbs in my neck. Everything around me seems larger, brighter, louder, and full of things I need but can't reach.

I've waited for this a long time. I lean against the building and try to get my breath. My mom looks around, pulls her purse up under her arm, and starts up the street in my direction. Once, she looks right at me before I turn away and pretend to inspect some shoes in the window of a cobbler's shop. She doesn't recognize me, and it hurts but maybe it's good too. In the store window, I see her move up the other side of the street. She's weaving through the crowd with her head down. I turn from the window just as a man passes her and looks back at her legs moving under her white skirt. I remember how nice her legs were and how she always kept the seams of her stockings straight. The man smiles and moves on and I want to kill him.

I follow her, all the time telling myself to cross the street and touch her shoulder and say, *Hello, Mom, it's Travis, out of reform school and ready for my life.* But somehow I can't. I've dreamed this moment a hundred times, a thousand times. Some of the dreams were good and some were bad, but I never dreamed I wouldn't be able to cross a street and speak. I don't know what's stopping me. I know I don't want to scare her. I know if I keep following her, I'll learn something. Maybe I'll learn how to talk to her again, or I'll learn why I can't do it.

We walk about six blocks, me keeping a half block behind her. She's easy to follow. She doesn't feel me behind her like some people would. She turns off this street of shops and restaurants and starts uphill into a neighborhood of neat, pretty houses. I can tell by the way the shrubs are cut and the brass bells on the doors in the shapes of temples and Buddha that this is where Japanese people live. We come to a big building that's not a house, and there's a crowd of women, all Japanese, standing around in front. My mom stands with them, but she keeps her distance too. She listens and nods her head, though she doesn't speak.

One of the women looks across the street at me. She elbows another woman and points. I turn away and pretend to examine the front of a house. There's nowhere to hide. I shift my suitcase from one hand to the other. I look back over my shoulder and see the two women talking about me. I don't know what to do. Pretty soon I'll have to leave or knock on the door in front of me and pretend I'm looking for a Mr. Smith about a used car. Is he home? I look back and now three women are watching me. A bell rings.

There's a moment of silence after the bell stops, and then the door flies open and kids pour out screaming their heads off like all kids do when they get out of school. I watch as the mothers take their kids into their arms and hug them, put them down, and straighten their collars or their little school caps with that concerned look mothers give their kids when they've been apart for a while, and they start off down the street, some of them giving me hard looks as they walk by. A few cars come up the street and the doors open and kids crawl in and they drive away. My mom waits with the women and pretty soon two kids come running out. A boy about eight, I guess, and a little girl who is six or seven. I try to remember what grade you're in when you're their ages, but I can't. I can't remember anything much. My mom bends down and takes them in her arms, one under each arm, and hugs them, and when their little faces are buried in her white blouse, she looks up at the sky and closes her eyes, and I can see how happy she is, and it's not like things are coming at her now. She's got what she wants and nothing can hurt her.

She walks back down the street the way she came, and as she passes with the two kids holding her hands and both talking a mile a minute and the little girl holding some pink construction paper with a crayon drawing on it, my mother looks over at me and smiles at a stranger and keeps on walking down the street.

I follow them, staying back but not really worried about my mother seeing me. Holding the two little hands, my mother turns into the narrow alley and walks past the dentist's office. She turns again and I see the back porch of the house behind the dentist's office. A Japanese woman, younger than my mother, is waiting on the porch looking at the watch on her wrist. She's pretty and everything my mother is not—confident, easy in her motion, and anything but fragile. The children see her and both squeal the same word in Japanese, and it's one of the few words I know in that language. It's *Okasan.* Mother. They let go of my mother's hands and run to the woman who's coming down the porch steps. I see the trouble flare again in my mother's eyes as she watches the woman kneel to the children.

I see it now. These are Dr. H. Kobayashi's children, this is his wife, and my mother walks their children home. I have seen her hug the children and they her, I have seen her protect them, and I have also seen the thing in her eyes I first saw when I was younger than these children, a thing she tried hard to keep from my father and me. She could never love us like this.

Watching, half-hidden by the corner of the building, in the fear of being recognized as a threat or a lost son, I am paralyzed by a sudden, exterminating sadness. After all I've done, the good and the bad, I thought I'd felt everything there was to feel, but never this. My mother is not the sovereign of her own home. She helps good people and they give her a living in exchange for the few things she can be trusted to do. There is no place for me here.

Carefully, I step away from this scene of reunion. In the narrow alley, I press my hands to my eyes until the light leaves them, and the words come from somewhere: *A guy like you could only make this worse.*

FIVE

The front door swings open and a family of tourists steps into the noise and hustle of Big Sam's Shrimp and Slaw. They look around, smiles breaking bright, noses rising to the high, heady odors of fried shrimp, coleslaw, and french fries. They've seen our red and blue neon sign. They've found Big Sam's, famous for miles. They've cut from the stream of cars on Highway 98, and stopped for dinner here in Panama City Beach before motoring on to a motel in Pensacola or Mobile. Tonight they'll sleep with the Gulf of Mexico blowing its warm, wet breath against their door.

In the morning, who knows? A romp on a blinding-white beach, a swim in surf warm as a bowl of chowder? Then more black asphalt highway and beach towns strung like pearls along the blue coast? A happy hearth and home somewhere? Anything is possible. This is America. Lyndon Johnson is in the White House. We're the Great Society. Much is right with the world and some things are wrong.

I'm a busboy and invisible. I'm here like a potted plant is here. I like it that way. My nights are all right, my days fair as the weather when it's fair. I work hard, and sometimes things get so crazy that hours pass in minutes, but I'm never too lost in the weeds to search the faces, the rows of chewing mouths and grabbing greasy hands. I look for Delia. I have no idea what I'll do or say if she walks through that door. I will not find her tonight.

In San Francisco I found my mother and knew she was better off without me. Delia was my second quest, so I was back on the road. Traveling broke, I worked. Truckers paid me to wash their rigs. Restaurants hired me for a few bucks and a place to sleep. I washed dishes, burned garbage, waxed floors at four in the morning, killed and plucked chickens, and even helped slaughter a hog. I was road trash and trash does the dirtiest work. I slept in storerooms, on a pool table, and in a dead collie's doghouse. The collie was gone, but the fleas welcomed me.

Now I'm back in Panama City, a place I left six years ago under suspicious circumstances. It's Friday night, and Big Sam's is roaring busy. Friday nights are all-you-can-eat—fried mullet, hush puppies, french fries, and, of course, slaw. We serve what the local fishermen catch—redfish, grouper, flounder, and shrimp. We serve Apalachicola Bay oysters, the best in the world.

The first night I worked here, a week ago, I turned a corner too fast with a sixteen-ounce water glass on the edge of my bus tray. The glass pitched right into the crotch of a guy in a business suit treating his wife and kids to the crab-stuffed flounder. He was good about it after he got over the surprise. I didn't know what to do. I was about to swab his crotch with a bus towel when he cleared his throat, and we looked carefully at each other. LeLe, head witch of the waitresses, shouldered me out of the way and started mopping to save her tip. Later, she grabbed me by the collar coming out of the kitchen. Her candy apple–red fingernails raked skin from my chest. She leaned close, smiled, and said through her teeth so the tourists wouldn't hear, "You miserable little prick, get some forks out here. You're taking food out of the mouths of my children."

She tried to get me fired that night. Big Sam came over after she had a talk with him back in his office. "Look, kid," he said, "didn't anybody tell you to put the tilty stuff in the middle of the tray?"

"Naw," I said, "they didn't tell me anything."

I got hired on a Friday night when the old busboy came in too drunk to work. They just handed me a tray and shoved me into the dining room. Nobody told me about the different tubs for knives, forks, and spoons. I was dumping everything in one tub. The dishwasher tore off his apron and backed me up against a row of fryers full of hot lard. He's a mean little peanut farmer named Jimmy Danes with *FUCK YOU!* tattooed on his hands, one letter to each knuckle (exclamation on the last). He was drawing back his fist when Emil, the fry cook, shoved a smoking-hot spatula between us. "You white boys want to fight, take it outside. I ain't gon' have you ruckin' around in here with all this hot fat." He looked hard at both of us. I didn't want to find out what he could do with that spatula.

Jimmy Danes pointed his finger at me. "Later, shithead."

Emil took me aside and told me how dangerous it was for Jimmy if I mixed steak knives with the spoons and forks. He told Jimmy it was just my ignorance. Jimmy and I haven't had any more trouble. We're not exactly friends, though.

I get minimum wage here, a buck fifty an hour, plus a share of the waitresses' tips. At the end of the night, they leave on the bar whatever they can spare for busboys. Strictly voluntary. The way I live is to save my paycheck to pay rent and buy a car, skip breakfast, use my tip money for lunch, and eat what I can from my bus tray on the dinner shift. It's called garbage mouth. It's not so bad, really. People order stuff they never touch. If Emil's not too busy he'll yank tinfoil from the big roll that hangs over his head, wrap my choice leftovers, and warm them in the oven. "Come get your leavin's, white boy."

Emil keeps a jar of white corn whiskey in the storeroom, and sometimes when I stay late and help him clean up, we sit out back and smoke his Camels and drink white corn from those little silver cups we use for drawn butter. Emil likes it that way, says it's classy. Good things in small doses.

I think Emil likes me. I don't know why. Maybe there's no reason why people like each other. Why did I like Delia the moment I saw her, and then love her so much? She was beautiful, fun, smart, good to me, and she did crazy things. Things nobody else dreamed of doing, not at that time, six years ago, in a small town called Widow Rock twenty miles from here. It's just a mystery. People like each other or they don't, like me and Jimmy the dishwasher.

Maybe Emil likes me because I'm at the bottom of the heap. I don't come from around here, at least he doesn't think I do. I live in a tourist cabin owned by a drunk widow that costs thirty dollars a week, with no air-conditioning or phone, mildew on the bathroom ceiling, and a mattress so broken down it's more like a hammock slung between two trees. Emil knows I'm interested in what he has to say, and I think he knows I've got a secret, even though I've lied to him about my past.

Maybe Emil likes me because I work hard, keep my mouth shut mostly, and don't give him any crap. You can give a Black man a hard time in Panama City if you're white, but Emil falls into a special class because he turns fried shrimp into gold for Big Sam, and Big Sam is on the county commission and owns half the waterfront property from here to Mexico Beach. Big Sam is big, but Emil's bigger, and he isn't fat like Big Sam, though Big Sam was once lean and can prove it with the football pictures that hang on the dining room walls. Big Sam standing lean and hard with other Gator notables before he blew out his knee and came home to take over the family business.

Big Sam likes Emil and rests his hand on his shoulder and squeezes the muscle there when they put their heads together and talk business, but Emil walks a line. In the kitchen he's king, nobody crosses him, and even Big Sam stays out of his way. Times I've seen Emil out on the streets of town, he's been different. Not exactly meek, but smaller seeming, blinking in the sun, a look in his eyes that says he's never as comfortable as he is working at his hot fryers.

It's late and the dining room is dark and empty. Big Sam is in his office counting the night's receipts. The only lights are Big Sam's and ours out here on the loading dock behind the kitchen where Emil and I sit drinking and smoking. I never buy cigarettes because I don't really smoke. I think Emil likes to give them to me, even though he makes all the old jokes about a kick in the chest to get me started. The cigarettes and whiskey are his way of thanking me without saying anything. He has to deal with a lot of trashy white people, phony surfers, bikers, and rednecks, a lot of them young and already drinking or smoking reefer, and he appreciates anything that's a cut above the usual sorriness.

We drink and look up at a sky full of stars. With the traffic easing up on 98, you can hear the surf across the road. It's never exactly cool in the summer in Florida, but on nights like this the breeze makes you forget the hot kitchen, and you can almost feel the dew coming on in the sea oats on the dunes along the beach. I like it when there's a riptide. You can hear the waves breaking far off, getting louder, rising to a high froth, then seething off into the darkness. They sound like truck tires on a rainy road in winter.

In reform school, I used to stand at the far fence during the recreation hour and look out at the wheat fields and watch the world coming closer. My first year, there was nothing, just wheat. Sometimes I'd see men shooting pheasants in the fields and farmers driving tractors and combines, throwing up clouds of dust and chaff. The third year, they were building houses out on the horizon, some wheat land giving way to bricks and shingles and people. A town coming closer to the place where I was because they wanted me far away from people. It felt good and it felt bad.

Wheat fields are beautiful in a way, and you hate to see them go, but the people coming toward you are exciting. I used to reach my fingers through the fence and hope to see a house close enough for the people to have faces. To see a man get up in the morning and drive off to work, his wife hanging out the wash, his kids riding bikes and tossing a ball around. Normal life.

The fifth year they built a highway, and late nights in winter I could hear the high cold whine of the tires and the big trucks going by in the rain with a seething sound like I knew waves on a beach would sound when I finally heard them again. That highway made it hard. All those people going places and me with my fingers reaching through the fence and the big questions in my mind: *What is she doing now? Right now? This very minute, what is Delia doing? Who is she with? Is she thinking of me now, like I'm thinking of her? What does she look like now? Why didn't she answer my letters?* That's when I'd have to leave the fence and promise myself not to go back and never to think of her. But try that. Try it sometime, never thinking of something or someone you care about.

Emil tilts back his little silver cup of white corn, sips it, licks his lips, and twitches his Camel back to the center of his mouth. He inhales a big drag, blows the smoke out through his nostrils. He raises the little silver cup and turns it in his hand. "My young friend," he says, "this is made by people who know what they doing. It's run through a clean copper coil. Some of them fools make it with an automobile radiator. You don't want to drink none of that. You go blind."

"You ever know anybody who went blind, Emil?"

He draws back and looks at me through slit eyes with the Camel streaming smoke up the middle of his face. After he lights a cigarette, he never touches it. He smokes with his lips, and he can move a butt from one corner of his mouth to the other without wetting it. When he's standing over the fryers, he whips his head to the side to keep the ashes from falling into the food. I look back at him, showing that my question is innocent. I just want to know.

"Boy," he says, "I known them that had everything happen. Legs cut off by a ploughshare, razor-slashed, shot, died of infected rat bites, hit by a diesel train sleeping drunk on the tracks, punctured they colon with a store-bought enema, and that's just what I can think of late at night when I'm tired."

We sip and smoke for a while, and he says, "Colonel" (short for Colonel Numbnuts, don't ask me why), "what you gon' do with your miserable white-boy life? You gon' just stay around here and work in restaurants and wake up one day old and weary and can't do nothing but keep on doing what you doing?" Emil and I talk about the kitchen, about the people who work here, about his life (mine's not interesting enough to bother with), and about what I call philosophy, although I'd never use that word with Emil.

I look over at his big, brown face. He's good looking for a guy over thirty, and they say the ladies on his side of town can't resist him. They say he's got the love wounds to prove it. He wears a white starched chef's hat, always a little crushed and pushed back to where the ruff of black hair starts on his half-bald head. His starched cotton smock begins the night snow white, just like the apron he wears over it. Now it's gray with sweat and brown with grease, and he smells like fried mullet. He rolls his sleeves up over his grapefruit-sized biceps, and you can see the navy tattoos on his forearms. Crossed anchors on the left and *USS Coral Sea* on the right. Emil learned his cooking and what he calls personnel management (which means terrifying people into doing what you want) in the navy. You can't do one without the other, he says, at least not in a place like Big Sam's where you got so little to work with. And he doesn't mean the fish.

I say, "Hell, I don't know. I'm just barely making it right now, economically, I mean." This is philosophy.

He laughs, "Huh," when I use the big word.

I go on: "I haven't had time to think about what I'd like to do when I can rub two nickels together. You know how it is, man."

He chuckles again, letting me know who's the man. I've tried cussing a little with him, but he doesn't like it. He's got some idea that I'm quality white people. Dr. Janeway said I'm an institutionalized personality. Sometimes I feel like I could tell Emil about that, like he wouldn't mind it, he'd understand, even though I'm not sure I understand it myself.

We're sitting there smoking, drinking the little cups that don't add up to enough to make Emil want to go poontanging until dawn, and he's telling me I ought to go finish my education and get myself as far away from fish guts and hot lard as I can, and I'm telling him it takes money to go to college, and they don't give scholarships to guys who got B's. A girl walks up the alley behind the restaurant. She stops and looks at us, punching her weight from one leg to the other. She's got on a white dress that's supposed to have a belt but is missing, a pair of cheap red sandals that show her red-painted toes, and a shoulder bag that's imitation black patent leather. Even I can tell she doesn't match. She's got sort of honey-brown hair and, when she licks her lips, the prettiest white teeth I've seen in a long time. She can't be more than sixteen, and she's a knockout.

She looks at us for a long time, first at Emil, then at me. She finally settles her eyes on me. "Y'all seen Jimmy Danes?" Her eyes are like little blue birds looking out from a cage.

Jimmy, the dishwasher. When she mentions his name, I can feel Emil going cold beside me. I take a William Holden drag on my Camel and flick it into the alley.

She watches the sparks dance, then go out. "You wouldn't have another one of them cigarettes, would you?" She comes closer into the light. She's got a nice shape, but I know some girls get that before they've got the brains to know it's dangerous. Not that anybody ever gets that smart.

I hook my thumb at Emil and say, "I'm bumming from him."

This disappoints her a little, but she stands in front of Emil with an expression on her face that says she'll wait until he hands over a Camel. He shakes one out of the pack for her, and she leans forward and touches his hand while he lights it, and he says to me, "She ain't getting none of this corn. That's trouble, you understand me."

When Emil says, *You understand me*, it's not a question. You understand him. I nod. "Sure, Emil. I'm just being polite."

Behind us, Big Sam cranks the handle on his calculator, and we both look back over our shoulders at the light in his office.

"You all seen Jimmy?" she says again in that sleepy, blinky country-girl way that makes you think she forgot she already asked.

Emil purses his lips and looks up at the sky full of cold white stars. "Jimmy done gone, sweetheart. What you want with that shiftless thing? He ain't got no future. Not like my young friend here."

I can't help it. My neck gets thick, and I can feel the red blush flooding up into my cheeks. The girl looks at Emil like he's my owner and I'm up for sale. Then she does me with her eyes from my feet all the way to the top of my head. She says, "I told Jimmy I'd meet him out here after he got off work. I guess I'm a little late, huh?"

"Huh," Emil agrees with her, then says to me, "Ask her where she lives, fool."

So I say, "Do you live around here? I haven't seen you on the beach or anything." There aren't that many people permanent in the summer. You get to know who's around.

The girl looks at me and then at Emil like she's trying to decide if she should divulge her whereabouts. She smokes like a thirty-year-old woman sitting on a barstool waiting for her future to walk in the door in a Palm Beach suit. (I've seen a lot of pickups at the bar in Big Sam's.) She sticks her cigarette hand out, turns the palm up, and examines the red polish that's chipping off her nails. "Naw, I live out to Ebro. My daddy carried me in with him this afternoon, but he met some people and went off, and I met Jimmy and we said we'd meet."

Emil shakes his head at this evidence of transience. He says, "Whole lot of meetin' goin' on. How you planning to get home, sweetheart?"

The girl thinks about it. She doesn't seem worried. Maybe the world is a welcoming place for a girl with thirty years of personality on a sixteen-year-old frame. Emil gets up, stretches, throws away his Camel, and picks up the mason jar of white corn. He says, "Travis here'll walk you on down to the Aces. Jimmy might be down there playing pool with some of them boys he hangs out with." The girl and I look at each other. Nobody asked me if I want to walk her anywhere. "Good night, colonel," Emil says. He looks into the kitchen. The light goes out in Big Sam's office. Emil looks back at me, then at the girl-woman. He says to me, "Mind your manners," and I know exactly what he means.

SIX

An hour later, the girl-woman and I are standing under the bare light bulb on the front porch of my tourist cabin. Everywhere we've been, Jimmy just left. The whole town is closed down for the night. More walking around is sure to get us an interview with law enforcement. I've had enough of cops to last me the rest of my life. What I haven't had much of is standing right here in front of me in a white dress and red shoes. She sees the way I'm looking at her and says, "Boy, don't you know jailbait when you see it?"

I feel the red creeping up my neck. I'm glad it's only a forty-watt bulb hanging from the wire over my doorstep. I say, "Of course I do. I told you why I brought you here. We can't keep walking around looking for Jimmy or waiting for your daddy to come back."

She smiles. "Just don't get any ideas." She looks over her shoulder at the lights still on in the cabin where the Widow lives. "And open the door. I'm tired of standing out here."

I bite on the words I'm about to say (something like, *Well, if you got a better offer . . .*) and stick my key in the lock. I turn and tell her, "Don't come in yet. I've got to check on something."

Down here, they call them palmetto bugs, but they're really cockroaches and they're really big. They stink when you step on them (revenge of the dying insect monster), and if you see just one running for the baseboard when you turn on your light, that means you've got six million under your sink. Unless you can afford to have the place exterminated.

When I complained to the Widow, she just said, "Kid, if you want to live at the Fontainebleau, haul your ass to Miami." So I developed a system. Once a week, I buy a bag of potato chips. When I go to bed at night, I put some chips in a bowl in the middle of the floor and spray them with bug bomb. The roaches like potato chips so much they're willing to put up with the poison. Every morning I throw out a bowl of chips with ten or fifteen belly-up palmetto bugs in it. It's disgusting, but it keeps them from eating my eyebrows while I'm asleep.

The girl waits in the doorway while I pick up the bowl and take it to the bathroom and flush the contents. I come back, flip on the light, and invite her in. She stands in the middle of the room looking around at the first place I've ever called my own. She's not impressed. Why should she be? The floor is sagging pine painted gray. The walls are plywood with six different paint jobs bleeding through one another to make a vomity yellow-green. There's a single bed under the front window, a kitchenette across from it, a desk and chair, and a bathroom indecently close to the kitchen. There are framed drawings of seaside scenes on the walls. The Widow drew them herself back before her husband died and she started drinking. They aren't bad to my eye, but what do I know about art? One of them is a view from the seawall where I sometimes go fishing. Things haven't changed much in this part of Panama City since the Widow was a girl.

In my bathroom there's a toilet, a sink, a mirror, and a shower with one of those rings that hang above your head holding a plastic shower curtain—mine has smiling purple fish on it. If you studied ballet, you can turn around inside that plastic circle. My kitchenette has a refrigerator that leaks water into a pan that has to be emptied every day, a hot plate with frayed wiring inside that electrocutes two or three roaches every time I turn it on. Try that smell along with your grilled cheese. There's a table and two chairs made of chrome tubes. Home sweet home.

The girl walks over to the bathroom, turns on the light, and I hear some rustling in there, then the sound of pee hitting water. Women make a hissing sound; it's different from men. I move over to the open front door and watch the world outside until she comes back without washing her hands. Her name is Dawnell Briscoe. She had to spell it for me, first and last. Her daddy makes a living dragging cypress logs out of the swamps. He cuts up the cypress in his own sawmill and sells it to farmers for fences and sheds. I can think of easier ways to make a living.

Walking around town, I learned a lot from Dawnell and didn't let on much about myself. She talks pretty much nonstop and doesn't seem to care what she says. With her, talking is like peeing with the bathroom door open and not washing your hands. She's a free spirit, I guess, country style.

I step out of the doorway and close the door. I don't know what the Widow would do if she caught me with Dawnell, and I don't want to chance it. It might be complicated. Sometimes the way the Widow looks at me after she gets up in the morning at ten thirty and has her first vodka and grapefruit juice, I think she'd like to show me some things about mature women. She isn't so bad, either, just a little on the flouncy side and a lot over thirty. I watch Dawnell walking around my kitchen opening drawers and cupboards, inspecting what's in the refrigerator. "How long you been here, boy, and you ain't got beer in your icebox?"

She's already acting like she's older than me. I say, "You have to be twenty-one to buy beer in this town, or didn't you notice? I'm only eighteen."

She tilts her head to one side and looks at me like a cat watching a hole where a mouse might be hiding. "Hang around me for a while, boy, and I'll show you how to get beer without even paying for it."

"You're a real child criminal, aren't you?" I say it to be funny and to get her thinking, maybe, but saying it makes me think about my own past. I don't like the thoughts. I close my eyes against the pictures that start to come.

She takes my carton of milk from the refrigerator and drinks from it, giving herself a milk mustache. She looks at me and laughs. "Wanna lick it off?"

I swallow. "What about Jimmy?"

Jimmy would love to have more than steak knives in the spoon tub against me. Not that I'm afraid of some dumb puke with *FUCK YOU!* tattooed on his knuckles.

"Oh, him," she says. "He was just a ride home. He's got a pretty cool car."

I've seen Jimmy's '59 Ford with two whitewalls, two blackwalls, and red lead primer daubed all over it. The windshield is cracked where some girl threw her shoe at him, and there's a rebel flag in the back window. "Some ride," I say. "He left you stranded."

She tilts her head again like she's trying to understand me. "I didn't say Jimmy was a *career*, son. I said he was a ride. *Fun*, you understand?"

I don't know. Maybe I don't understand fun, not like she means. We didn't have much of it where I've been. She licks the milk from her upper lip and frowns at me like I've missed my big chance. Big chance to go to jail, I'm thinking.

I say, "It's late, and I worked two shifts today. We better think about going to bed or something." We both look over at my single bed which is getting smaller by the second. She walks over and sits on it, bounces a couple of times, then flops over onto the foot of the bed and says, "We'll sleep head to foot. That ought to be safe. Or else you can be a gentleman and sleep on the floor." She props her chin on her fist and looks at me like I'm her guest.

Well, I've seen this bit in the movies. There's usually an easy chair or a bathtub and somebody has to sleep in it. The man tells the woman it's his house, thank you very much, and he's by golly not giving up the bed. Then they cut to morning and the man is waking up in the tub with a backache. Tonight the scene's not funny. If I don't get the light off soon, the Widow will get curious. Sometimes she walks around late at night nursing her tenth vodka and grapefruit juice, humming to herself songs about bygone days, and wondering what's going on in the lives of her tenants. I move over to the bed and prop a pillow under Dawnell's head.

She says, "Thank you, sir. Now tell me a bedtime story."

I go to my closet and get my windbreaker and wrap it around two pairs of jeans and lie down with the bundle under my head. I don't take off my clothes, and of course Dawnell doesn't either. It won't be comfortable sleeping in the clothes I worked in, and I don't know what I'm going to do with her in the morning. The three thimbles of white corn I drank with Emil are wearing off, and my rational mind is knocking at the door of my libido, as Dr. Janeway might say. And what's her daddy going to say, if she really has one, about where she's been all night? What's going to happen when she gets home? Is somebody going to stripe her legs with a belt for being a bad girl? Did her daddy already wake up somewhere from his skirmish with alcohol and call the sheriff about his lost girl?

She says, "Aren't you even going to turn off the light?"

"Jeez," I mutter, "I guess that *would* be conducive to getting some sleep."

"What's *conducive*?" She giggles. She doesn't care what it is. She's just making fun of me for sounding like I come from higher in the tree of life than Jimmy.

I say, "Never mind. Go to sleep."

She says, "No bedtime story?"

I say, "Not tonight, I'm too tired. Good night, now, hear."

She says out of the dark, "I hear. You stay down there at your end of the bed, boy, and don't be smelling my toes."

I make sniffing noises. "They're as sweet as roses, now good night."

She says good night and yawns, and then she giggles and says, "Toe roses," and giggles again. Then she says, "Salute the fleet and smell my feet," and that's the last I hear from her until almost morning.

As I pull to the surface from the deep water of oblivion, I feel something move on my arm, and I tense, and all the strange information from the night before floods back into my mind. I'm in bed with a girl named Dawnell Briscoe, and I don't know her age, and this is not her toes. I feel her warm cheek in the little dip between my shoulder and my chest. She takes a deep breath and yawns and says, "You had a dream, boy. I came up here to hold you still."

"Did I kick around?" The dream is coming back to me now. Things that happened six years ago, things I don't want anyone to know about.

She says, "You kicked me a good one right upside my head." She reaches out and presses her hand to my chest, feeling my heart. "You're better now. What was you dreaming about?"

"I don't know," I say. "I don't remember anymore." But I do. It was the fire, all the roar and heat and hell of the flames, and the dancing inside the barn. The mad dancing and the last black flying of a boy I once knew. A boy who was my age now when he died. A boy who lived somewhere not far from here. I reach out and take her hand and lift it from my hammering heart. "Maybe we better go back like we were. I'm sorry I kicked you awake."

I don't know how I can tell, but I know she's smiling in the dark. She says, "I'm more comfortable like this. Why don't you let me stay?"

I say, "I don't think that would be a good idea."

So she groans, and moves back down to the foot of the bed and whispers, "Toe roses," again, and we try to sleep. I listen to her breathing, and after a while I know she's asleep, but it's a long time before I get back out to the deep water.

SEVEN

When I wake up again, the first dawn light is falling through the blinds, and I'm alone in the bed. It's not until I smell her hair on the pillow near my face that I remember I had a bed companion. Dawnell Briscoe. I push up in the bed and look around. It's dim inside my cabin. I get up and check the bathroom, but I know she's not there. I strip off my rancid restaurant clothes and throw them into the corner.

Before I even pee, I go to the front door and look out and almost run into the Widow standing there with a vodka in one hand and the other raised up to knock. We pull back and grin surprise at each other. Finally, she says, "Well, aren't you going to invite me in?" We both look down at my underwear.

I say, "Just a minute," and close the door.

I pull on some clean jeans and come back to let her in, but she's already pushing through the door. She has a key anyway, and sometimes I think she's been in my cabin when I'm at work. She's got on her bedroom slippers (she wears them outside all the time) and a big yellow tent she calls a muumuu. It's supposed to be Hawaiian or something and has red hibiscus blossoms on it. She's wearing red lipstick and two spots of red rouge on her cheeks, and her hair is up in curlers under something she calls her "gardening hat." It's yellow straw with blue plastic cornflowers woven into the white band. If there's a garden around, I haven't seen it. Once, after I first moved in, I walked by her cabin coming home from work and her blinds were open and I saw her getting out of the shower. I mean I *saw* her, just a glimpse. I kept on walking. I'm not a window-peeper. If the Widow took a little care of herself, she wouldn't be bad looking.

She stands in the middle of the room peering at my unmade bed, still warm from me and Dawnell Briscoe and my bad dream, and then she looks at me from under her eyebrows. "Boy, what're you looking so guilty about? You haven't been drinking here underage, have you?" She sips her vodka and grapefruit juice. There's a little rim of red syrupy stuff floating on top, and she sticks her finger in it and licks it. She sniffs the air and smiles at me. "Or maybe you've been smoking some of that marijuana? I hear that stuff's getting popular with all you little beach rats."

I try to stop looking guilty, which probably has the opposite effect. I say, "No ma'am, I haven't been drinking or smoking, except Camel cigarettes."

She watches me over her vodka. The glass has blue parrots on it. "I get reports on you, you know. I keep track of my tenants. I heard about you and that cook, Emil Bontemps, sitting out on the loading dock late at night, so don't try to tell me you don't drink." She smiles like she's happy I drink.

Inside my head, I curse small-town life. You can't ever get away from what people see and talk about. I can try to convince her it's not true about me and Emil, or I can back up a little and hope the weird smile she's wearing at seven in the morning means she's not in one of her bad moods. I say, "I don't drink here because you told me not to. Look around. You won't find any booze." That's when we both notice the kitchen counter, and the bones melt out of my legs and my head goes light and swimmy. There's the Delia Book sitting open next to my hot plate.

The Widow does what I told her to do. She looks around the place in a playful detective way, for evidence of drug and alcohol activity. "You better believe I look around." She jingles the keys in the pocket of her muumuu. She pokes her head into my little clothes closet, comes out and says, "A friend of mine told me you little beach rats can't ever hide that marijuana because of the seeds. There's always . . ." her voice goes up higher, and she makes a little pinching motion with her thumb and forefinger, "a little seed lying around somewhere."

I try to be casual, walking over to the counter and closing the Delia Book, imprisoning inside it the note that Dawnell Briscoe left for me:

I found this in your desk. I couldn't sleep after you kicked my head. Ha Ha. I had to do something to past the time. Interesting reading. You didn't tell me you're a writer, Mr. Hemenway. Thanks for taking care of me last night. See you soon . . . Dawnell.

When people who don't read much talk about writing, they always mention Hemingway because everybody's heard of him. Just once, I'd like to be sitting on a bus next to somebody who finds out I write a little and calls me Mr. Marcel Proust (and doesn't rhyme it with joust).

I could pick up the Delia Book and put it in the cupboard or something, but that would call attention, so I just turn my back to it and lean against the counter. My head is still a little tilted, and I'm trying to focus on the Widow playing detective over by the bed, but I'm seeing Dawnell getting up in the dark just before morning and rifling through my desk for the Delia Book. That sneaky little shit.

The Widow comes over and stands in front of me. She notices the puddle of water on the floor beside my left foot. She says, "I got to get that refrigerator fixed. You're paying good money for rent, and you shouldn't have to worry about a leaky refrigerator."

I almost say I don't worry about it, I just pour my pan of leak water on the half-dead azalea bush outside and mop up what spills over. I smile at her, trying to get my eyes completely into focus. She takes another step closer to me and shifts the vodka from one hand to the other and pokes a finger at my bare chest. I look down at it. She touches her ice-cold fingertip to the little line of man hair that runs down the center of my belly. A drop of very cold vodka slips down that line of hair into the waistband of my jeans. We both watch it, then we look at each other. She reaches up and for a second it's like she's going to touch my face, but her hand floats away to the curlers sticking out from under her straw hat. She gives one curler an uncertain little twist.

She says, "I guess the refrigerator's not the only thing I ought to take better care of. Did you know I was homecoming queen at Escambia County High? Of course, that was before . . ." She shifts the vodka back to her cold hand and takes a sip.

She never finishes the sentence. It's like if she doesn't say it, it never happened or something. I guess we all have things we don't want to talk about. If she does mention him, she always cries. They got married real young, like a lot of people do around here if they don't go off to the university after high school, and her husband was killed in some freak accident on a shrimp boat. She used the insurance money to buy this place, the Wind Motel, and she's been running down with it ever since. It's the cheapest place to live anywhere near the beach, and that's why I'm here with a drop of vodka from her cold fingertip in my belly button.

I say, "Mrs. Reddick, you know you shouldn't be getting onto that subject." I feel sorry for her. All of us who live here do, and I figure mentioning her husband's death in a roundabout way will move her back a step or two. I see sudden tears in the corners of her eyes.

She drinks some vodka and says, "You look a little bit like him. Especially with your chest nekkid like that. He was a very handsome boy. He played football with Big Sam and all them."

All the men around here played football with Big Sam, and the older they get, the better they used to be. To hear them talk, the team dressed out two hundred players for every home game and every one of them scored a touchdown every Saturday night, even the defensive tackles. I smile thin to let her know I appreciate the compliment in a limited way.

She smiles back, and the red in her cheeks is not just rouge. She turns away and says, "I don't know what got me up so early this morning. I thought I heard somebody walk by my bedroom window, maybe six o'clock or so, and I know you work late and like to sleep in. Did you hear anything?"

I look up at the ceiling, close one eye, and try to remember what I heard early this morning. I try very hard, but I don't come up with much. Except Dawnell Briscoe sneaking off to God knows what new adventure. "No," I say, "but there's been a couple of raccoons messing around the garbage cans over by the washhouse." The Widow has her own little coin-operated laundry for our convenience here at the Wind Motel. We call it the washhouse.

She turns back around and looks at me, then down into her half-finished first vodka of a very long day to come. "Well, all right. I'll see what I can do about that fridge. You behave yourself now, hear, and stop drinking with that Emil Bontemps, or he's going to get you in trouble." She gives me what a writer would call a wan smile and turns to go. I want to tell her that Emil is one of the few people I've met so far in this town who has the natural good sense to mind his own business and stay out of trouble, but that would be like trying to tell her Jesus wasn't blond, Elvis isn't going to win an Academy Award, and vodka doesn't become a breakfast food when you mix it with grapefruit juice.

EIGHT

Emil and I are riding in his big Lincoln on our way to buy me a car. He knows a guy out near Ebro who's selling one for a hundred dollars. It's a 1950 Plymouth with a flathead six-engine. Emil says it's not pretty, but it's good transportation. He says those old flathead sixes go on forever. He knows a guy at a local marina who uses one in a forklift, and it's been pulling like a plow horse for eight years since it quit being a car. I'm so high about having my own transportation that I'd buy the thing sight unseen on Emil's word that his friend wouldn't cheat me. My wallet is fat with fives and tens I've saved by eating cold fried shrimp standing over a garbage can in Big Sam's kitchen. When Emil told me about the car, I lay awake most of the night thinking about myself with wheels under me and the freedom to go as far as gas money can take me. But where I need to go is Widow Rock.

When I was hitchhiking across America, I had plenty of time to think. Standing beside the road with hours between rides or spending a night under a highway overpass, you think. Riding with somebody who's taking Benzedrine and can't stop talking, your voice goes on saying "yes" and "uh-huh," but you're thinking. Sometimes in my mind I'd just get off a bus in Widow Rock and stand on the street greeting people and telling them I'm Travis Hollister, son of Lloyd Hollister, local attorney at law, and I'm back to claim my life. I never got very far into that story, *The Return of Travis Hollister*, before the plot got too thick to flow.

What would I say when somebody asked me where I'd been, why my dad didn't know I was coming back, and where my mother is? I'd start lying, and since I'm good at it, I'd get along by making things up and answering questions with questions and letting people tell me what they knew by letting them think I was telling what I knew. But finally, the lying has to stop. You can't just get off a bus in your father's town after six years away. Your father might not like it. It might damage his position, and you don't want to do that. But before I see my father, I need to see Delia. I need to know who she is now, and I need a car to do that.

It's all country road to Ebro, and the land gets low and swampy with cypress trees and tea-dark water in the ditches and flooded fields with cows clustering knee-deep in mud on the high ground. You see ponds and sinkholes and abandoned houses with scrub oak trees growing up through rooms where people talked and dreamed and planned. As you speed along, rolling from side to side on the curves, you see gopher turtles pulling their heads in and clamping their houses shut as you pass and the carcasses of armadillos and possums that didn't make it across the road the night before. You hear bobwhite quail calling from the palmetto scrub and see a red-shouldered hawk banking back and forth above the hot blacktop searching for rabbits and mice in the ditches. It's beautiful country if you like Florida, and I do.

Out west, I got rides with people who said there's nothing like the desert scenery of Arizona and New Mexico, and they're right. There's nothing like it, but Florida has a beauty that gets into you after a while, and I'm not talking about the beaches. There's an inland Florida the tourists don't see that I love just as much as the beach. I don't know why. Maybe it's the down-and-out craziness of things, like the ten-foot-high rusting steel statue of the Michelin Man that stands for no reason beside a country road with his arms outstretched and that idiot grin on his face, or the farmer who took an old Cessna airplane and perched it on tree stumps in the corner of his field, or the abandoned gas station we just passed where somebody climbed up on the roof and painted a picture of Jesus riding the big red-winged horse that sells Mobilgas and wrote, *Jesus is coming. Are you ready?*

Who did that? What kind of person climbed up there with a brush and buckets of paint to proclaim the second coming on a secondary road? What kind of person imagines Jesus riding the Pegasus of Mobil Oil back into this world? I think Florida gets the crazies, good and bad, because it's the last place you can go in one direction and still be American. California gets them too. It's the last place west, but it's the same kind of crazy.

Emil and I ride along listening to a Tallahassee gospel station turned down low (*"Just a closer walk with thee, grant it, Jesus, it's my plea"*). The wind from the vents cools our faces, and we don't talk much. I look over at him, and he seems thoughtful, content. He told me he's from the country around here, and he likes to get back out where he can see horses and cattle and smell the country air. He served twenty years in the navy and retired as a chief petty officer. He lives on his pension and what Big Sam pays him. He says he's scrambled eggs on everything from a destroyer escort to the aircraft carrier USS *Coral Sea*.

I don't know how old Emil is; you can't tell. He could be forty or sixty. His dark-brown skin is smooth over his high hard cheekbones, and his half-bald head shines with health. His teeth are straight and white, and he can lift a ten-gallon lard can with one hand from a high shelf and not even catch his breath. He steers the Lincoln with his long, burn-scarred index finger. He's wearing a starched white shirt, collar buttoned, black suit trousers, and black suspenders with a thin purple stripe running up them. Shiny black shoes with pointy toes. He looks like he just took off his coat and tie after church, except he doesn't go to church. He looks over at me and clears his throat. "You an' that little white girl ever find Jimmy Danes?"

So I tell him the story of my night with Dawnell Briscoe. Of course I leave out some things: sleeping head to toe, Dawnell sneaking into the Delia Book, and the Widow searching my place for marijuana seeds. Emil listens, squinting at the sun that jumps into our eyes from the long black hood of the Lincoln. Finally he shoots me his this-fish-is-too-old-to-fry look and says, "I hope you ain't gon' take up with that girl, colonel. She can't be more than sixteen, and that ain't all the trouble about her."

Emil says he talked to some people out around Ebro where she lives, and what he learned isn't good. I listen because it's Emil, but I kind of don't want to hear it. I don't know why. Maybe because it's the kind of thing people probably said about me after I stabbed Jimmy Pultney and left my neighborhood in handcuffs. Anyway, Dawnell lives with her father and an older brother, and Emil says, "That brother of hers is crazy as a run-over dog. He helps the father drag cypress logs out the swamps, but his real interest is hunting at night with a flashlight taped to his rifle. He shoots what he finds, in and out of season, possums, rabbits, deer, gopher turtles, anything that'll stand there dumb with light in its eyes."

"What does he do with them?" I ask.

"Nothing. Just throws them away, I reckon. People I talk to say he hangs around a gas station out here drinking Royal Crown Cola and looking at you out of red, swollen eyes 'cause he's been up all night sighting down a rifle barrel. Say it's enough to give you the fantods."

I don't ask him what they say about Dawnell. I know he'll get around to her. He looks out the window at a pasture where some Appaloosa horses stand scratching their necks on the top strand of barbed wire and watching us pass.

"That girl just runs wild, they say. Say it's a shame. She don't go to school but half the time, and the daddy and brother don't seem to care what she does."

"What happened to her mother?" I ask.

"Up and run away, they say. Didn't give no reason. Just one morning the family gets up expecting breakfast, and she's gone with her clothes stuffed in the pillowcase she snatched from the bed where that little girl's daddy was sleeping drunk. The daddy's been a running-around fool ever since, not that he wasn't already."

I thank Emil for sharing with me what he knows. I know people didn't just tell him. He found it out for me, to warn me away from Dawnell, as if I had any intention of seeing her again. Emil looks over at me, expecting more than thank you. He wants me to tell him I won't see her. I just look out at the hot sun jumping from the simonized hood of the Lincoln. Emil keeps his car as clean as his kitchen.

We pull up in front of a neat little country house with shutters and a tin roof painted the same dark green and a ditch of cypress-stained running water in front of it. We rumble across the ditch on a little log bridge and stop under a tall live oak, and I see it. The car I'm going to buy is nothing to look at, but I love it anyway. It's a big gray, humpbacked turtle of a thing with a missing hood ornament and rust patches coming through the cloudy gray paint. Emil and I get out, and I'm standing there with two Black men twice my age looking sternly at me, their eyes asking if I know a good thing when I see it. I know this is no time for horse-trading.

I walk around the car like I know what I'm doing, stub my toe on some pretty good rubber, open the door, get in, and kick over the engine. There's a hole in the floor near the master cylinder sump, and the brown headliner sags in spots, but the engine hums like a Singer sewing machine. I get out and start peeling greenbacks from my wad until I'm the owner of a 1950 Plymouth, and my wallet's as thin as it was the day I hitched into Panama City Beach. The best weight I've ever felt is those car keys in my hand.

Emil and his friend talk awhile, and I listen to be polite, but I'm itching to get in that car and go. Finally they laugh at me, and Emil says, "Colonel, you think you can find your own way back to town?"

I tell him I can. I thank the man, Mr. Storrow. He's short, with skin the color of saddle leather, and thick through the chest with thin legs in Sunday trousers just like Emil's, and he looks at me kind of stern again and says, "You treat her good, boy, and she'll do the same to you."

I promise to take good care of the flathead six, and Emil says, "Get on now. I've got some things I need to talk to Mr. Storrow about." They grew up together around here, I guess. I'm also guessing Mr. Storrow has a whiskey still somewhere back in the cypress hammock. He makes the white corn Emil and I drink from the mason jar.

I back off from their stern faces and get into my own car and fire her up again and feel her come to life under me—it's the best feeling I've had since I stood outside the Bridgedale School my first morning of freedom.

I back my new Plymouth out of Mr. Storrow's sandy driveway, across the log bridge, and point the big turtle-humped, ornamentless hood straight down the narrow secondary road. I crank the shifter down into first and give her some gas. I'm not going to scratch out, that would make Emil and Mr. Storrow doubt me. I ease her into a long slow glide, and I know my future's coming faster than ever.

NINE

At first I take the same road Emil and I took coming out here, but roads branch off, so I turn just to turn and drive just to see what happens. Every road seems to end out there ahead of me in a dark wall of trees. That darkness, well, it calls to me. It's like the water you see on hot asphalt a long way off that always dries up before you get there. It's an illusion. The road always curves and moves on, and before you know it there's another place far off where it seems you'll crash into the dark if you don't stop.

A lot of people would think my life right now is dull and has no promise in it, but they've never been locked up. Standing at a garbage drum in Big Sam's kitchen scraping scooped-out baked potatoes and fish scraps, I feel free. I know I can just drop the plate I'm holding, hand Big Sam the apron I'm wearing, and walk out the back door, down the sandy alley and keep on going to Mexico Beach or Pensacola or New Orleans and look for what's next. Now I've got a car. If I decide to go, I can do it on my own wheels. I'm free of everything except Delia.

I cruise the blacktop, drinking in the sunshine that falls onto my hood between the stripes of shadow from the tall pines and cypress trees. I breathe deep the swamp-spicy air. I've traveled five miles of I-don't-know-where before it even occurs to me to turn on the radio. My heart beats hard when I think of riding with Delia in her white '54 Chevy and how she used to play the radio and sort of dance to it from the waist up, and she was all wiggles and smiles and eyes that promised fun. I'm scared my radio won't work. I turn it on, and the little light winks red, and I hear the scratchy sound of a Dothan station playing Otis Redding, "*She may be weary. The young girls, they do get weary, wearing that same old shaggy dress. But if she's weary, try a little tenderness.*" I throw my head out the window to sing with Otis, loving that raggedy-raspy sob he puts into his voice just at the turn between *weary* and *try*. I try, but I can't sing like Otis. I can't sing at all, but the pines and cypress trees don't mind, and then I stop wailing and pull my head in because there's someone up ahead. Someone walking the roadside all alone in the middle of this strange, gorgeous nowhere.

I pass her, glancing over quick as she rushes by, then catch her up in my rearview. I'm almost a half mile gone before I make up my mind to U-turn. As I come up on her in the other lane, I see she's walking with her head down, pressing a transistor radio to her ear and holding a cherry popsicle in her other hand. Either she's pretending she doesn't see this big old gray Plymouth drifting toward her on this lonely road, or she's really that lost in music and red-painted sugar. I stop with the empty lane between us, and the heat rushes into my windows, and I feel the flathead six running smooth under me, and I see the heat in her flushed cheeks and in the dark spots under the arms of her white dress. It's the same white dress. She makes like she's going to walk on by, so I turn down the radio with Otis just finishing *("... try a little tender-neeeeess"*), and then I hear the same thing, Otis I mean, coming from the tinny little radio pressed to her ear. I say, "Where you going on such a hot day?"

She looks over at me. "Oh, it's you, boy."

You were expecting . . . ? I just smile. My question hangs in the hot air.

I say, "Get in. I'll take you where you're going." It feels so good to say that. She watches me over the red nub of the popsicle, and I can see where it's dripped down over her knuckles and stained the corners of her mouth. Her eyes are almost closed like she could fall asleep standing up in this heat. She looks off down the road like maybe there's a better offer coming any minute. She cocks her head to the side and considers me and my car, and *"You know you make me want to shout"* starts up on both our radios. The Isley Brothers. She licks the popsicle and says, "All right. I'll ride with you awhile, but you can't take me where I'm going."

I want to ask what that means, but I don't, not yet. I reach over and push the door open, and she walks in front of my new old car looking it over carefully. What's she got to compare it to, I'm thinking, Jimmy Danes's spavined Ford? I watch her pass in front of me and listen to the engine humming like Emil said it would, reliable and even, no valve clatter or misfire, and it seems like Dawnell's walking motion gets in synch with the pistons and the push rods, and she and the car are one lovely little performance for me alone. Just for a second or two, and then she slides across my upholstery and closes the door, and it's suddenly very quiet in my Plymouth even with all that you-make-me-want-to-shouting.

I take my second U-turn and start off in the direction she was walking. She turns off the cheap radio and rests it in her lap. Looking straight ahead with the stripes of sunlight and tree shadow dappling her face, she offers me the last of her popsicle. I take it, swallow it in one bite, toss the stick out my window, and look over at her. She's licking her red knuckles, very serious, like a cat cleaning itself after a big bowl of milk.

There's nothing out here, nowhere to go, so we just ride along. I don't ask her where, because I figure she'll say something eventually. She reaches out with her newly licked hand and turns the radio dial to Pensacola. We get the last few seconds of Jay and the Americans, "This Magic Moment." It's a song I like. Dawnell says, "Where'd you get the wheels?"

"Just bought her," I say. "Emil helped me find her. What do you think?"

She purses her lips and slits her eyes like some kind of horse trader. "It's all right." She puts her hand out flat on the seat between us. "It runs . . . I guess."

It bothers me, but I don't show it. "I guess it does," I say, "so far."

She points to something up ahead. "See that fence post with the coffee can nailed on it? That's where I'm going."

I slow. The rusting red Hills Brothers coffee can comes into view. Out here, farmers nail them onto fence posts so that rainwater won't rot the posts. It's ugly as hell, but it works, I suppose. You can't tell there's a road at the red marker until you're right up on it. I start to turn in, but Dawnell says, "Don't. I said you can't take me there."

I straighten the wheel. Fresh tire tracks run from the asphalt across a ditch with about a foot of tea-colored water in it, then cut back sharply into a stand of cypresses hung with kudzu vines. Dawnell slides toward the door and opens it. "Wait a minute," I say. "Where you going?"

She points at the curtain of vines. "Home. That's where I live."

"Why can't I take you there?" I think I know, but I want to hear her say it. I want to know if Emil was right about her.

"My daddy wouldn't like to see me ride up with you. My brother, he'd like it even less. He's pretty mean sometimes."

I want to tell her I'm pretty mean sometimes, too, but that's the kind of tough-guy talk I try to stay away from. An old guy I met hitching out in the desert west of Tucumcari told me, "Kid, all the tough guys are in the jailhouse and the graveyard." The imprint of a set of human teeth was bitten permanent into his left ear. I didn't tell him I'd been in the jailhouse. I think he knew it. I think he'd been there himself. He called himself the Last of the Hoboes. He spent a lot of time explaining to me the difference between a hobo and a bum. It seemed to mean a lot to him. We hitched together for a while, but we didn't get rides, and I knew it was because of him, so I ditched him when he fell asleep outside of Flagstaff. He passed me later that night, shooting a bird from the front seat of a brand-new Cadillac.

Dawnell just sits with the Plymouth singing under us. I'm thinking she's right. I probably shouldn't go to her house, or anywhere near it. She swings her knees back toward my radio, though she doesn't close the door, and all her little-girl-on-a-grown-woman frame seems to go soft. Suddenly there's only little girl. She says, "All right, there's a place you can take me." She points straight down the road. She closes the door, and I drive. We turn off the asphalt onto a sand road, and off that onto another, narrower one, and finally we stop in front of an old falling-down farmhouse on some cleared land that used to be a working farm. There's a shed with a few moldy bales of hay stacked next to it and a salt lick and a trough with a standpipe dripping water into it. Off in a field beyond the rusted tin roof of the house, the wheel of a tall windmill still turns with a rusty groan. I'm guessing we're about a half mile from the two ruts where Dawnell wouldn't let me take her home. She looks around her, blinking. She says, "I come here sometimes to get away from . . . my family. I walk through the woods. There's a path nobody knows about but me."

Somehow I doubt that, but I nod and wait. She opens the door, slides out, stretches, and pulls the skirt of her white dress down over her legs. I look off into the trees. Abandoned houses are sad places, if you ask me. You can't help thinking about who lived in them and what they wanted and whether they got it and if they left happy or sad, for a better place or a worse place or no place at all.

She stands in the forlorn dooryard scratching her knee with the edge of the radio. "Come on, boy, I'll show you something." But before we move, she gives me a look that's dead serious. "You won't tell, will you?"

Immediately I say, "I won't. I promise." I take promises seriously, and it occurs to me that I just promised too fast. So I think about it while her scared blue eyes watch me. "I mean it. I won't tell."

She walks toward the house, and I follow.

TEN

It's a mess inside. The roof leaks in the front room, and the pine floor is rotted out. Big oily-looking mushrooms grow up out of the punky wood. We walk close to the walls so we don't fall through. Somebody stuffed wadded newspaper into a hole in the window glass above the kitchen sink. There's no water in the toilet, just a rusty ring, but there's still half a roll of paper on a twelve-penny nail sticking in the wall. In one bedroom, there's an old plaid coat and a stack of *Life* magazines on the floor, and a bird's nest on a closet shelf. I can't shake the feeling that something bad happened here, or will. I follow Dawnell Briscoe to the second bedroom.

Even before I go in, I can see it's different. Someone has made a crude latch of nails so that the door can be locked. I don't know who or what the latch would keep out, but it comforts somebody, I guess. Dawnell stops in the middle of the small bedroom, hands on her hips, looking around her. I stand behind her. Along one wall under a window painted white, there's a single bedstead with a pallet rolled up on it and sheets and a blanket folded across the roll. Pictures cut out of magazines are pinned all over the walls. Men mostly, movie stars. Men kissing women. Troy Donahue. Martin Milner and George Maharis, the light guy and the dark guy, partners on *Route 66*. Men in tuxedos holding glasses of champagne. Men in trench coats aiming pistols straight at you. Do the pictures, the way they're arranged, tell any story? I can't make it out. They're just there.

There's an old record player in one corner with a pile of 45s next to it, but no place to plug it in. Spaced around the floor, colored candles, new and half-burned, rest on coffee can lids and cracked saucers from the farmhouse kitchen. It smells like somebody splashed perfume all around to kill that mildewy mushroom smell that comes from the other rooms. If there's a surprise, it's not the stack of magazines (*Seventeen* and *Screen Idol*), but the small collection of paperback novels. They could have fallen off the back of a bookmobile for all the care that went into their selection, but I see some interesting things among the trash romances and gory murders. She's got *A High Wind in Jamaica*. Maybe she thought it was a romance (hell, maybe it is, in a way). She's got *Little Women*, *Peyton Place* (my eyebrows jump at that one—not easy to come by), and there's even a worn and water-stained copy of *A Farewell to Arms*. Dawnell shoves her hands onto her hips to prove she has them, sighs like she's suddenly dissatisfied with something, me maybe, and turns around. "So," she says, and a sly little smile curves her lips, "who's Delia?"

The name. Two syllables out of her mouth ("Deel-yuh") in the air between us, and I reach out to steady myself against the doorjamb. I try to control my eyes, know I'm not hiding what's in them. *Delia*. No one has said it aloud, not even Dr. Janeway, since I left Panama City six years ago. Maybe I've said it aloud in my dreams, but how would I know?

Dawnell puts the transistor radio down on the floor next to one of the candles and a book of matches. She turns it on, and we hear Dickey Lee singing "Sweet Dreams of You." It's a beautiful song. Patsy Cline did it first and best, but Dickey's got a pretty good version and it's climbing the charts. Dawnell rolls down the mattress, spreads a sheet on top of it, sits, and pats the place next to her. "Sit down here, boy, and tell me about Delia."

Dickey sings, "*Why can't I face the truth, start loving someone new, instead of having sweet dreams of you.*" I turn away from her, to the wall where a man in a tuxedo with a black eye patch smokes a cigarette.

"Stop calling me *boy*. I'm older than you are." I'm surprised by the anger that comes out with it. The truth is, I feel just . . . strange. When I woke up that morning with Dawnell gone and the Widow walking around in her flowered muumuu sipping vodka and pretending to bust me for pot, it felt really strange to see the Delia Book open on the kitchen counter. For the first time since Dr. Janeway stole it from me, somebody had read it, or part of it, and for the first time I thought it might be all right someday if other people did. Maybe I didn't write it just for myself and Delia.

I look down at Dawnell Briscoe and say, "Don't you have a room at home?"

Her face shades red. She lifts her chin an inch and turns away from me. She reaches under the bed and pulls out a pack of Chesterfield cigarettes, an ashtray, and a Zippo lighter. She shakes a cigarette out like one of the actresses on the wall would do it, casual, sure of her little hands, and stabs it into the corner of her mouth. She lights it, takes a deep drag, and blows gray smoke through her nose. She dips her chin, turns her pretty face in a tight half circle, and locks her eyes onto mine. "Of course I have a room. Did you think I sleep with my daddy?"

Now my face gets red. I didn't want her to think that. I guess I wanted to get us off the other subject, at least until I knew what I wanted to say about it. We just look at each other, getting over being mad or surprised or embarrassed or all of them. She sucks on her cigarette and examines the air above my head where a cloud of smoke is canceling out the smell of perfume. She holds the Chesterfields out to me, and I take one. She hands me the lighter. I take it, light a Chesterfield, and drop the Zippo on the mattress next to her.

I smoke for a while. I don't really like Chesterfields. They have an odd taste if you ask me. Camels are best and after that Luckies if you're going to smoke without a filter. I guess my favorite filtered cigarette is a Winston. I sure as hell can't take anything with menthol. My experience of smoking is about as small as it is of girls and whiskey—of just about everything outside the walls of Bridgedale School. The walls of Dawnell Briscoe's secret room in the woods remind me of how I used to paw through every magazine I could borrow or steal for pictures, searching for women who looked like Delia.

Most of them didn't. Which I guess means she's some kind of original. When I found one that came close, I'd clip and paste it in the Delia Book. They let us keep a few pictures of family on our chest of drawers, so I put the two best Delias there in frames I made in the furniture factory. I'd take them to bed with me at night, hold them close to me with a little flashlight, squint my eyes and slant the light and make the faces change until they were Delia. But there were times when I lost my memory of her face. I'd panic then. I'd go half crazy thinking I'd lost her face forever, but she always came back to me. She always came back in a dream, true and beautiful, and I'd wake up remembering.

I sit down on the saggy little bed beside Dawnell, thinking how much we're alike in some ways. We both have rooms for the first time in our lives, rooms of our own. We both have secret places, real and inside us, where we hide the things we want the most. We don't know much about each other. We haven't told what we want. But we know. We know we will.

It makes me think about fate. I'm afraid of it, but it pulls me too, like the water out there in the gulf that's pushed in through the narrow channels by the moon and passes miles and miles inland before it's pulled back out again by that same big glowing circle in the sky. I look straight ahead, drawing on the Chesterfield, and adding my own to the shimmery rim of smoke that floats up along the ceiling. I can feel Dawnell beside me, looking straight ahead too.

"You talked in your sleep the other night. You said her name. That Delia."

I can't keep my heart still when she says the name. "So what?"

"I got up and turned on the light, and you didn't even wake up. You were too far gone." She sings the last three words like they come from a song.

"So what again?"

"So who is she? How come you dream about her so angry and sweaty, and how come you wrote a whole book about her?"

I stand up fast and take a few steps toward her wall of pictures where all kinds of magazine love stares back at me. "How come you don't mind your own business? How come you go rooting around in other people's things and looking at what they don't want anybody to see?" I've said too much, but I can't help it. I pull the liar's look onto my face and add this: "You called me Mr. Hemingway. Well, you got it right. Bingo. Bull's-eye. I'm a writer." Her books are stacked in neat rows at the foot of the bed. "You're a reader," I say, "or else you just tear out pages when you go to the outhouse in the woods. If you've read them, you know writers dream about their characters."

Her dark-blue eyes lighten a little. "She's just made up then, that Delia?"

"Sure," I say, remembering who taught me to lie. Remembering how Delia said it was one of life's essential skills.

"I want to read the rest of it." Dawnell says. She pulls on her sophisticated face. "Maybe I can help you with it. Give you the woman's point of view."

I want to ask how much of it she read. How long she was at it while I was asleep, riding my dream of fire like a boat in a storm. But I don't. I can't. So I say, "I'll think about it. I have to finish it first—the first time through, I mean."

I turn away to the door that leads out into a hallway and the other, ruined bedroom and the little bathroom with the waterless toilet bowl. I'm thinking about how I wrote the Delia Book. How it started out as letters I didn't send after I never heard from her. Then how it become a diary—me telling myself exactly what had happened, writing it all down as clearly and truly as I could remember it, so I'd never lose it. Because already time was doing what time does. Blurring the edges of the sharpest things, changing the order, rubbing holes in what happened.

I turn back to the here and now, to Dawnell. "Do you want a ride back to . . . the other place?"

She stands and smooths her skirt. "I'll walk through the woods." She's disappointed in me and jealous of my made-up Delia.

"Show me the way?"

She shakes head. She's keeping her secret because I have mine.

The path won't be hard to find if I want to.

ELEVEN

I come out of Big Sam's kitchen in a cloud of dishwasher steam, carrying a bus pan full of clean knives, forks, and spoons on my way to restock the waitress stations. I get the usual evil glare from two waitresses hipping by with laden trays. They're running low on forks again. It only takes one movement in the side of my eye. A slant of the head up and to the side, tossing a wave of hair. It hits me like a sickness, like the first grip of nausea and bliss from a too-big swallow of Emil's atomic moonshine. I know it's her before I even know. My blood is heating, my bones are rolling in their joints, because it's her even before my mind cranks and churns and gives me the conscious thought. *Delia.*

Delia. Here in Big Sam's. Of course. I knew she'd come. I stand frozen five steps out of the kitchen with a fifty-pound tray of metal implements on my shoulder. The thinking part of me starts to work as the working part of me stops. My mind says, *That's not her. That hair is blond.*

The woman dips her head to her plate and lifts a fork of slaw and again, it's the motion. No one in the world moves like that. Only Delia. My mind says, *People dye their hair.* Then LeLe, head witch of the waitresses, hisses at me, "Damnit, Travis, get your thumb out of your ass and bring me some forks." LeLe's divorced with two kids and diabetic, so we make allowances.

Big Sam's is big. One big room, about the size of a high school gym. Low partitions with sick-looking ferns growing in them break up all that space. There's no place for me to hide. I'm completely exposed, but a busboy might as well be a fern—until something goes wrong, that is. I have to see the face of the blond woman before I can be sure, so I get the job done. I go from station to station, gliding fast and invisible, my hands flying with knives, forks, and spoons.

Along the way, I get under-the-breath waitress curses and impossible instructions ("Don't you let me run out again, you little *ass*hole!" "Get more napkins out here right now!"). I don't say anything. I don't explain that I can't manufacture clean silverware out of thin air. That it has to come from a dishwasher, and ours works as hard as it can all night long. When I've circled the room, passing close to the blond woman's table, chewing my own heart with nervous jaws as I move only inches behind her, keeping my back to the electric field of her being, I find a place to stand where I can melt into the background and get a good look.

I wipe off an already clean four-top, watching from under my brows as I bend over my rag. It's her all right. And now she's a blonde. And I'm thinking two things. One is that my senses, that weird radar of the heart, picked her up across this crowded, greasy, loud food riot of a room on the lift of a chin, the tilt of a head, a breaking wave of hair. The other is: Why didn't *her* radar work too? Why doesn't she know I'm here? She looks good blond. The last time I saw her, it was night, she was pale, she'd lost weight worrying about things I had to go fix. In the moonlight from the window of her bedroom, she looked almost blue, like a dead woman. I wanted to bring the light, the life, back to her eyes, her skin. And I found a way to do it.

Now I see her sitting with three other people, all about her age, two men and a woman, and I know which man is with Delia because he laughs, reaches up, and wipes a bit of something from her chin. She looks at him, smiles, lifts a cocktail, whiskey I guess, and takes a sip. She makes a kissing motion (*So what if I had half a shrimp hanging from my chin?*) at the whole table and goes back to eating. Same old Delia: *Screw you* to the world. I keep the beams of my eyes moving, lighting her up as they flicker across her table. I don't want the bright charge that's in my eyes to make her notice me. This is not how I want her to know I'm back.

The man with her is tall, handsome I guess, in a cool, Joe College kind of way. He reminds me a little of Bick Sifford, the boy who wanted Delia almost as much as I did. He doesn't look like Bick, he's not as handsome for one thing, and he shows a lot less of what's inside him for another, but he has that easy self-assurance Bick was learning. The thing that made Bick believe he could summon Delia Hollister late at night to a secret meeting place with a hand-scrawled note left in the front seat of her car. It's the way a man looks, I guess, when he knows that what he wants to happen probably will. You don't see a lot of that at Bridgedale School. (At Bridgedale it was knowing they'd do to you exactly what *they* wanted.) I suppose Dr. Janeway had that Bick Sifford look for a while. It was one of the things that kept me interested in my sessions with him. Bick Sifford was there somewhere in Dr. Janeway's Ivy League eyes.

The man with Delia looks at his watch, looks at the other couple, smiles, lifts his scotch or bourbon, and takes a trim sip, surveying the room from behind his glass. Very cool, and somehow careful too. He wants to know who's around, how much they're worth maybe, what they think of him and his. When his eyes swing across me, they register absolutely nothing. Which is exactly what I am in Big Sam's. So, fine.

Delia raises her left hand, reaches out for a glass of water, and I see it, big and sparkling and worth Emil's yearly wage at least: a diamond the size of a rifle bullet. Resting next to it, bathing in its glow, is a wedding band.

Delia's party is almost finished eating, but I have to play potted fern for at least another half hour. I spend as much time as I can in the kitchen, making up jobs. I take two plastic bags full of garbage out to the big bin in the alley, and when I come back, Emil looks up from his fryers, sweating like Vulcan at his forge, and says, "What you doing, colonel? Slop the hogs later. We got people *eating* out there."

I'm out in the dining room when the four finally leave. The man with Delia, her husband I guess, pulls her chair out for her and doesn't look stupid doing it like I would. He makes it as natural as putting a shrimp in your mouth. Delia gets up a little unsteadily and gives a bourbon giggle and smiles over her shoulder into his eyes. The other couple rises too, and they're almost as well dressed and almost as happy with themselves as Delia and her man. I don't know much about clothes, especially women's, but I know expensive when I see it, and the dumbest guy in the room can see how big the pieces of gold are that droop from ears and wrists and necks.

People stop eating to watch the four head out. My heart swims in a storm when I see Delia walking. That walk. Nobody else has it. Sexy but not slutty, movey but not too loose, controlled and out of control and controlling the eye of the beholder. Me. Actually, a lot of guys look at her, then look back at the women they're with and go shy in the eyes and suddenly start inspecting their shrimp for plumpness and richness of color.

I turn when Delia's gone, and there's LeLe standing behind me, hands on her hips, sweat pooling in the hair at her temples, red lipstick seeping into the cracks at the corners of her mouth. She reaches up and swipes a hank of damp, mouse-brown hair from her eyes. She's watching the royal exit too. I can tell by the mean squint of her eyes. I take a risk: "Hey LeLe, who's that guy?"

She doesn't look at me, just watches the door close behind the Delia party. "What guy?"

I don't know what to say. "The, uh, the guy with that woman in the white dress. They just left your section."

LeLe looks at me with reluctance. In her eyes I could be something crawling in the sand under the surf we can hear sighing across the street. A sand flea. She decides to answer, but with chilly disdain: "That's Temp Tarleton. He's on the county commission."

"He's a politician?" I don't know what's in my voice, but it convinces LeLe I'm stupid.

She rolls her eyes, snatches at a bead of sweat that breaks from her right temple and rolls down her cheek. "No, dumbass. He's a lawyer from Widow Rock who happens to serve on the Choctawhatchee County Commission. He's the youngest man ever elected to it."

I can tell who LeLe was looking at during the awesome rite of serving dinner to the commissioner and his . . . and Delia. I say, "So, what kind of lawyer is he? Do you know?"

She looks over at me like I've just eaten the surf and turf and don't have a dime to pay for it. "What do you care what kind of lawyer he is?"

This means she doesn't know there's more than one kind of lawyer. At least I got something out of her that wasn't exactly abuse. I say, "Thanks, LeLe," and head back to the kitchen for another bus pan of forks and spoons.

TWELVE

The phone book tells me where Mr. Templeton Tarleton lives in the new housing development in what used to be the pine and cypress forest that sloped down to the river, then up to Widow Rock. Maybe I've had one too many of those little cups of Emil's white shine, or maybe I'm high on something else, my own backed-up, stuffed-in necessity, six years of it, but I'm sliding to a stop at the curb in front of a house two down from Temp Tarleton's imitation of an English country estate. I get out of my humpbacked, primer-splotched Plymouth and look around at the moonlight on the blue-green lawns, and at the hedges clipped into such sharp corners they could cut you, and the cars that snicker at mine, Lincolns and Cadillacs and Chrysler Imperials. A dog barks at the rusty squeal of my door hinge. He has a big, deep-throated bark, the kind of dog I don't want to meet in the dark, but a frustration deep in his throat tells me he's fenced.

I stop and catch my breath when an air conditioner cycles on in somebody's bedroom window across the street. Some guy sleeping with his country-club bride in the cool weather of an air-conditioned dream. The houses all have galleries and porches, some of them with chairs and porch swings, but nobody's out and not just because it's so late. Air-conditioning has robbed the summer night of its charms. I remember when the ten degrees of difference between a sleeping porch and a bedroom could keep half the town of Widow Rock out after midnight, swinging, rocking, sipping iced lemonade, and eating homemade ice cream. Tonight I'm glad for this change. The air conditioners that hum and chuff help me sneak down this street.

I stop at Temp Tarleton's driveway. The milky stream of new concrete flows to his shadowed doorway where the wrought-iron numbers *928* confirm his presence, and Delia's too. 928 Brandywine Lane, an English country estate on a night so hot and humid even the moonlight seems to melt and drip from the hood of Temp's creamy white Continental. There's a curbside mailbox, but not the ordinary tin kind with the red metal flag you raise and lower. This one is made of the same light-brown fieldstone as Temp's big house. It's a little version of the house, in fact, with tiny turrets of stone in each of the four corners, and tiny battlements atop the turrets. A lot of attention to give a mailbox, and a lot of expense. But it had to be, I guess, because I look up and down the street and there they are, all of them, curbside mailboxes cutely repeating the houses they stand for. It's some law of this neighborhood. A little ship stands on a wave of blue-painted plywood in front of a house with a big schooner prow, and next door to it, in front of the modern split-level, a mailbox is a rolled blueprint standing on an I beam. The man who gets news from it must be a builder of modern designs. Or maybe he's just telling his sentimental seafaring neighbor that he'll stand for no phony nostalgia.

I make my way to the backyard of Temp Tarleton's castle where there's a flagstone patio with a barbecue grill the size of some people's kitchens. Yes, the grill is a castle too, with little stone chimneys that will belch real smoke when Temp Tarleton is pumping out Perfect-burgers for family and friends. There's even a tiny flagpole at the top of the castle grill, but Temp's Perfectburger banner isn't flying tonight. There's a sliding glass door, but I can't see into the dark house. A curtain blocks my eye. The trusting couple did not lock the door. It's easy enough for me to slide the door open, slip through, and stand just inside the living room, like old Polonius behind the curtain. I stand there with the glass door at my back and the shock of Temp's air-conditioning on my sweating face. I wait for my eyes to get used to the darkness. I don't want to stumble into a heraldic coffee table or do some noisy dance with a life-sized knight in a suit of armor, but the truth is my thoughts are complicated. This is a criminal act. The guys at Bridgedale called this B-and-E.

I reach up and touch my face, feeling the sweat evaporating into Temp Tarleton's cold, sweet-smelling air, and I notice that my hands are shaking. And I notice that I'm angry. I don't know when I've been so angry, and I don't know why it's happening now. My face feels like someone else's to me. I rub my shaking hands across my forehead, down the sides of my face, and wipe them on my shirt. *You've got to think. Don't take another step until you think. Didn't you learn anything those six years in the warehouse of unclaimed youth?* Then I hear a sound, a body shifting, fabric rubbing, textures colliding. I hear a groan and lips smacking, then a long breath.

Silence. It's Hamlet out there. Temp Tarleton can't be more than three steps from me, and my luck is that he's sleeping. My dumbass Polonius, man behind the curtain, prince of good advice and bad behavior, isn't going to get a rapier in the heart. Not yet, anyway. *Think. Think. What are you doing here?* I have to see her again. Even if she's asleep. Even if she's not, I have to see her. *What if he wakes up? What if he was awake when you slid that glass door just the few inches you needed to slip through and stand behind the curtain? What if there's a revolver in the drawer by the couch?* What if . . . what? You can't live your life by *what if.* You have to live by what *is.* You have to try to know what is, and sometimes it's risky to find out. *What are you going to do now?*

I don't know?

Don't do anything until you know.

I can't live that way.

I slip from behind the curtain with the strange idea in my mind that Dr. Janeway would be proud of me now. He was all about boys who acted on impulse and the trouble they got themselves into. He was all about calculating your actions and taking responsibility for the consequences. I stand three feet from Temp Tarleton asleep on the couch. The movie scenes and the old jokes play around in my head: *Temp Ole Boy, is this a sofa or the doghouse?* What did you do, Ole Temp, to earn this exile? Where is your wife, my Delia? Why did she, the knight's reward, boot you out of the nuptial bedchamber? Surely you haven't been married long enough to establish this dry accommodation.

I get a whiff of Ole Temp's breath. It's ninety proof bottled in bond, with some rank shrimp and french fry accents. He smells like a wino in an alley. (I know. I spent a cold night with one under a highway overpass in Denver. You don't forget that breath.)

I stand there looking down at Temp Tarleton who isn't quite snoring, but whose breathing sounds a little like an old cat purring. My face has cooled, and my hands are quiet now, and I like watching him, thinking about what I could do to him. Not that I would. Not now. Not yet. I move to the head of the sofa and examine his face. He's the real American Dream Guy all right. He's all the Joes rolled into one (Joe College, G.I. Joe, Joe Friday, Joltin' Joe, it goes on). Sort of a sandy-haired John Derek type. Could have been in the movies type but had more important things to do. He's got some "aw shucks" at the corners of his mouth and around his eyes, still young but a real Old Southern Charmer in the making. He's got the square jaw, of course, but there's just the hint of a double chin starting, and I can see a little of his middle age on him. When he gets there, he'll be more of the Gig Young, a little fleshy, a little corruption flavoring the boyish charm. Then I see the piece of paper and the pen on the coffee table.

Temp's right hand falls from his lap. It dangles, and he groans as though he's lost it for good. I tense, but his eyes stay shut. He just keeps blowing stale bourbon into the cold weather of this room. He looks as though he just finished writing his whiskey testament, just put down the words on the paper beside the still-uncapped fountain pen (a good, masculine Parker, gold or gold-plated).

Carefully, I pick up the paper and move to a spot by the front door where the moonlight slips through a leaded Tudor window.

Dear Delia Baby,

Well, of course, all of a piece, Delia is this man's baby. They are two hip young marrieds and this is, of course, what they will call each other. Out by the patio barbecue or with friends at Big Sam's, and in bed: Delia holding a cigarette to her plum-ripe lips (*Give me a light, Temp, baby*). The two lovers in the knight's bedchamber (*Oh, baby, yes, baby, oh, baby, baby, baby*). The note goes on:

> *I'm sorry I made you angry at me. I didn't mean to, I promise. And I promise never to do it again. So, when you wake up in the morning and I'm gone off to work, will you please, baby, read this and think of me as your loving Ole Temp, and*

My God, there it is! I clap a hand over my mouth to keep from retching laughter. He is, the man is, after all, her Ole Temp. And the note finishes:

> *let's not fight like this anymore. It wears us out. It makes me worry, and, baby, I'm strong, I'm strong for both of us, but I don't want to worry like this so much. I want us to be happy like we used to be, and I know you want that too, no matter what you say when you're mad at Ole Temp and you've had maybe a little too much of Ole Mr. Barleycorn.*

It's signed, *Your ever-lovin' daddy, Temp.* I put the note back where I found it. I stand there in the dark watching the sleep-twisted face of the fool who wrote it. Well, he's not the first knight made foolish by love, and he's not the first to write down some of his foolery. There's a whole volume of my own called the Delia Book. I picture tomorrow morning. Ole Temp rising with a head the size of a July watermelon and going about his getting ready as quietly as he can so as not to wake the princess sleeping in the master bedroom. He doesn't want her awake before he goes out a-lawyering. He wants her to find the note, his love offering, and think about him for a while before they meet again, when, by the way, Delia will have shrunk her drunken head too, and will have perfumed and powdered and painted on her

Dream Girl face for Ole Temp, the captain of this Dreamboat. So, they'll meet again at the end of the day for the suburban cocktail they will laughingly call the hair of the puppy (*Just a small one; let's not overdo it tonight*), and maybe they'll eat Perfectburgers, and Ole Temp's love note will have done its work. The pox that was in their love idyll will be cured by a puppy martini, a patio kiss and cuddle, and a wink (hers) and a smile (his) that promise they'll be sleeping in the same room later on.

But that's just my imagination and Emil's white corn whiskey running away with me. Who knows what this is about? Who knows what they'll do at dawn's early light? I've never been in a house like this before. All I know about how people live here is what I've read in the John P. Marquand novels and in *Architectural Digest*, and seen in movies like *The Courtship of Eddie's Father*.

There's one more thing I have to do before I leave here tonight. I say goodbye to the sleep-twisted, dream-sorry face of Ole Daddy Temp (ever-lovin'), and back away into the shadows, looking for the hallway that will take me to the master bedroom. I see it, but before I move again, I suffer a magnificent afterthought. I swipe Temp's fountain pen from the coffee table.

I grope down a hallway in the dark, quietly opening doors. First there's a linen closet full of what I learned from a novel by Jane Austen is called a trousseau. I can't see what's inside, except in my imagination, but I can smell the lavender sachets tucked in among the embroidered sheets and pillowcases. The next door opens to a bathroom, and a little night-light glows from the socket above the sink where Temp plugs in his electric razor. I'm a Gillette Blue Blade man (at Bridgedale, they gave us two a month, so we learned to sharpen them by rubbing them around the inside of a drinking glass). The bathroom is tiled in some kind of happy light green and, surprise, there's no tub. Instead, there's a big shower stall with a glass door like out on the patio and a green tile bench built into the corner. Plenty of room for two.

When I step out of the bathroom, heading for the last two doors,

I can hear Delia breathing, and I pass through a door that's not here at all into a world of memory. At the end of the hallway, I stand and listen. It's my first night in Widow Rock. I'm twelve years old, a little boy in a storm, a little boy who wants to be called a man, or if not that, a guy. The boy-man stands at Delia's doorway in flashing lightning from a black howler of a Gulf of Mexico squall, straining to hear the sound of his Aunt Delia weeping in her bed. *Weeping for someone lost.* Six years ago.

I try to remember if Delia's door was closed that night or partly open. I decide it was not closed. The little boy would not have dared open a closed door. But it was not wide open. That would have invited the house, the whole house, to investigate the sounds of grief. It was partly open, keeping out the house and inviting the boy's courage. So he entered. So he walked to the bed to comfort the weeping sixteen-year-old, the aunt who had somehow already stolen his love from his mother.

I stand outside Delia's door in the dark again with a weird hard smile ruffling my lips, thinking about how quickly she did it, how powerful she was to do it so quickly. One embrace, an auntly hug standing in the front yard under the oaks, my boy's face hidden in the tent of her black hair, suddenly and completely besotted by the secrecy of us two there apart from everyone and everything else, then thrust away into laughter, the Delia conspiracy of fun and danger and, *Oh, to be included! Oh, to be invited in!*

I put my hand on Delia's doorknob, wondering if it's locked, wondering why the trouble between her and Ole Temp was so big and so bad that she had to shut the knight out of his own bedchamber. And I hear her breathing. I try to count the times, mornings, afternoons, and nights, that I lay beside her or sat near her, sleeping or waking, and listened to her breathing. There were not so many, not enough of them. The door isn't locked. Slowly, as slowly as a doctor might insert his forceps into a wound, I open the door, thanking the abyss of night for new door hinges that haven't learned to squeak. Before I push my head through into the sweet terrain of Delia's private sleep,

I draw a deep breath of the air that has been enclosed with her since she and Ole Temp had their tiff. God, how it smells of her! This hasn't changed, though I have forgotten the scent and recovered it a thousand times since the last night I looked in on her sleeping. That night I closed the door with no acknowledgment from her of what I'd done, of how I'd saved her.

In a big double bed, lying on her side facing the window, she is sleeping. The air conditioner hums. My heart moves when I see her pale arm thrown up, her wrist resting across her brow. How I remember this! I step inside and close the door. My hands are shaking again, the right one a fist holding Temp's fountain pen. Again, I am Polonius unrevealed, and the voice of my reason tells me, *Think. Still time to leave here without trouble. Still time to push your old Plymouth off to a silent rolling start, quit your job at Big Sam's, and leave this town forever. Start a new life, as they say in novels, somewhere else, a place where nobody knows you. Where you can be like so much of America, undiscovered, only raw possibility.*

I almost take that first step back, out of here, out of all this complication that is me and Delia. But she sighs, rolls in her sleep, and I see in a vagrant beam of moonlight from the window the gold cross at her neck. She wasn't wearing it at the restaurant earlier tonight. She was wearing her show-off jewelry. But now she's got it on, the cross, like some little girl's protection from the night, the dark, this house with Ole Temp sleeping in his exile. She sighs again, and rolls back toward the window, and the sound is too sad for someone so young.

There's a little desk in one corner, and I know from novels what will be in it. I move to it and open drawers until I find the stationery Mrs. Templeton Tarleton uses to write thank you notes and RSVPs for Perfectburger Parties. I take a leaf of the soft creamy paper with Delia's embossed name and address at the top, and I unscrew Ole Temp's Parker pen. I lean to write my night letter, but before I can put words on this paper, I remember the note that summoned Delia, and me too, to the top of Widow Rock and the death of Bick Sifford. These shaking hands. These hands holding Ole Temp's pen were the instruments of Bick Sifford's untimely death. I still don't know how I did it, or how I could have stopped myself—from becoming what I became, the blood-and-fur-footed boy who climbed the rock on all fours and struck in simple ancient rage. How does the bird learn not to fly, the cat not to eat the baby bird that falls from the nest in a storm? I don't know. I've thought about it forever, *my* forever, all those days and nights in the warehouse of unclaimed youth, and I still don't know how it could have been different.

My night letter comes to me and Ole Temp's pen scratches softly in the dark:

> *Aunt Delia,*
>
> *I'm back after six years in . . . remember what you said about hell, how you thought maybe it was Widow Rock? Well, I've been there and it's not here. Anxious to give you my report.*

For a long time, the pen hovers over the creamy pool of paper where I have made my violations. Why can't I commit my name? Is it simply that six years have made me criminal enough to hesitate before leaving this trace? Or is it that I don't know who I am? Who is the Travis that came here tonight? He is a boy nobody knows. Nobody but Delia has ever seen him. I stand in the dark room breathing Delia's sweet, secret air, and she turns so suddenly in the bed that I think I am discovered. The turning flings her arm out toward me and exposes her face, and I see that she is only dreaming, her lips speaking silent anxious words to someone behind the curtain of her closed eyes. Is it Travis she speaks to in her dream?

Her lips quiet, and her face calms, and it comes to me that I have no right to stand here writing to her about hell. This fine and fancy castle could be, most nights, a happy place. My hell was not a place; it was a being without. I fold my letter, put it in my pocket, and pad softly from Delia's bedroom, down the carpeted hallway, and past the sleeping knight. I leave the castle as I entered it, through Polonius's curtain.

Standing in the moonlight by the Perfectburger castle, I remember that I left Temp Tarleton's pen on the table in Delia's bedroom. I won't go back to make that right. It's not the surprise I planned for her tonight, but it will do.

She'll think Temp stood by her in the night.

THIRTEEN

My hand traps a slippery shrimp in the bait bucket floating next to me. I push my hook through the hump of its armor, twist, and thread it back up into the succulent tail where a snook will hit first. I cast out into the deep water near a channel marker. I've hooked my shrimp so he's still alive. Now my educated forefinger can feel him kicking his tail at the bottom of the channel. He's trying to escape that swift tidal water into the shallows under the mangroves. He knows that redfish and snook come prowling up the channel looking for what isn't looking out for itself.

I'm standing chest deep in the falling tide at the mouth of Wilson's Marina. The grease slick from my restaurant clothes chums the water. Little bait fish dart around intoxicated by the lard and cornmeal that bleed off me. It's Sunday morning, my day off. The sun is already high behind me, driving hot pins and needles into the back of my neck, and I can see through my shadow the glow of my bare feet on the sandy bottom. A warm breeze is blowing, and the world smells like salt and tar and last night's dust captured in the dew that steams from mangroves along the shore. I've been at it maybe two hours, and my stringer, pegged at the waterline with a piece of driftwood, holds a Spanish mackerel and a two-pound snook.

Once in a while, some Chris-Craft Captain Ahab goes by farting diesel smoke, and the wake rocks me pretty good, and the silt gets stirred up, and the fishing's no good for a while, but mostly this is a pretty good spot. To fish and think. With me it's about fifty-fifty. Sometimes I've been lost inside my own head for fifteen minutes before the line tickles my finger and I yank back hard to set the hook.

Something hits my shrimp, and I drive my rod up above my head. The pressure of the water on your line can fool you, but soon enough you know if you're robbed or connected through that throbbing line to something out there fighting for its life. This time I've been had. I reel in an empty hook. Up the channel a boat is just turning at the concrete breakwater. It's not the usual flashy sporter for a guy with two bikinis in the bow and a cargo of beer. It's a medium-sized, open fishing boat with a little center wheelhouse, the kind of boat people own who are serious about fishing, but not too far offshore. Blue exhaust smoke from a big Evinrude engine hovers over the flat morning water. The boat noses on down the channel at idle speed, circles the channel marker, and turns straight toward me. It comes on at me, making the thirty yards or so to where I'm standing chest deep before I can decide what's going on, what to do. I take a step back, then stand my ground. I hold my rod out in my right hand ready to chuck it if I have to dive. The white fiberglass bow edges up to me, and I hear the operator shift into reverse, then neutral, letting his bow wave wash up to my chest. The boat rests nearly motionless in front of me. A man comes up to the bow and looks over. He's tall and straight and facing into the morning sun. He says, "Travis, gather your things and get up in here." The man is my father, Lloyd Hollister.

I sit soaking wet on a green cushion in the stern with a locker under me and watch my father guide the boat, his boat I suppose, to the mouth of the channel then through the breakers into the gulf. Out past the white-capped breakers he turns south toward Mexico Beach. The water grows darker under us, and we ride some big blue rollers. What he's doing doesn't look that complicated to me, but I guess it is, and I guess that's why he just steers the boat and doesn't say anything to me. The quiet gives me a chance to look him over. He's still military—stiff, brisk, and like he's about to give an order— and I guess if it hasn't worn off by now it never will. His face is still square-jawed and lean with whiskers almost blue, and his hair is cut so short on the sides you see more skin than anything else. On top, it's black like mine but with some gray mixed in. Salt-and-pepper I guess they call it. His pale-blue eyes concentrate on the water ahead, and his hands are light and confident on the stainless-steel steering wheel. The strange, and maybe the neat thing about him is that he's wearing business clothes. He's got on black suit pants with what the novels call a subdued chalk pinstripe, black lace-up oxfords, and a starched white shirt. His one giving in to leisure is rolling up his sleeves. Does he always take his boat out dressed like this? Was he in such a hurry to collect me for this as-yet-undisclosed mission that he didn't change into his dungarees and seagoing hat? I ask myself what I feel about him right now, and the answer is, honestly, not much, except for a certain awe at how much he looks like Grandpa did six years ago. The resemblance gives me the feeling I've often had that some things are given to us, and there's nothing much we can do about them. I'm the criminal in the family, and somewhere in a scrapbook (or a mug shot) there must be an old bandit ancestor who looks a lot like me. The rascal that passed down to me my bad nature. But maybe it's resembling on the inside, not with face and hair and manner, that matters most. And maybe my dad and Grandpa Hollister are more criminal on the inside than anybody knows.

My father cuts the engine back, and the boat wallows into a trough. He slips a tether over the steering wheel, takes a last look around at a gulf that's empty except for a big party fishing boat about a half mile away heading for the deep water, and looks at me for the first time since his face appeared over the bow of this boat as I stood in Wilson's channel.

I look into his eyes: he always told me to do that. Sometimes it isn't easy with people. This time I get surprised. An angry voice in my head says, *You paid six years for what you did, and your dad gave up on you after two. That was your gift to him, four years of a quiet life without you in it.* Nothing in his eyes tells me he knows this. He's about to speak, but my words jump out first: "So what did you tell people happened to me?"

His mouth is open like a cartoon character's, and I can almost guess the sentence that's stuck in there (*Travis, how long have you*

been back? or *Travis, what do you plan to do, now that you've come back?*).
Whatever it is dies in his throat. His mouth shuts like a snapper's on
a shrimp, and his lips are just about as thin. His face colors so fast
it's like a red light switched on, and I watch his hands become fists. I
watch them until the fingers go from white to tan again. They're lawyer's hands, clean, smooth, and competent, but twenty years ago they
killed soldiers of the Empire of the Rising Sun.

He takes a deep breath, full of all his patience and whatever else
he thinks and feels about my question, and says, "I told people you've
been with your mother."

I remind myself that he tried, and maybe tried hard, when my
mom was sick and he was starting his law career, and we didn't have
much money, and I was giving him the small trouble we'd all like to
have back now. He was never a hugger, that's for mothers to do, but I
remember him putting his hand on my shoulder in a way that made
me feel like the tiller of a boat he was guiding to calm water. So he
tried, but here come my words again, with a mean life of their own,
spilling out like I've memorized them for this moment, should it ever
come: "So I've been out in San Francisco all this time living with
the Japanese side of the family? When people ask, do you give them
progress reports on my education and prospects?"

He says, "Your mother and I are divorced, son. Around here
people respect a man's privacy. They don't ask questions about a
divorce."

I can see him slipping out of anger into something else, maybe
hurt, and I'm a little surprised that I have this power. When I was
little, he had all the power, and I was proud of him for that. He was
once Widow Rock's favorite son, and maybe he's still got plenty of
pull. Which reminds me of my next question: "Did you just happen
along as I was fishing, or were you out looking for me?"

His eyes are cool. Whatever it was he was feeling a second ago, he's
back to thinking now. He's powerful at that too. He says, "I stopped
by the Wind Motel. Your landlady told me where to find you."

"How did you know I was in Panama City?"

"Bridgedale let me know you'd been released. A Dr. Janeway called me, do you know him?"

I nod.

My father gives me a thin smile, the look of a man with ways of knowing. It's a smile I saw a lot back at Bridgedale. It's the lawful smile of jailors and keepers and those who mean well. He says, "This Dr. Janeway said he thought you might show up here. I asked a friend at the Department of Motor Vehicles to look you up. It seems you recently applied for the title to an automobile."

He looks at me as though buying a car is a rare and clever act few persons my age could manage. But really the surprise for him is that I'm here, his half-Japanese son Travis, back from the dark walk of incarceration. His eyes say he wasn't expecting me. Did he think I'd just disappear?

My father sits on the locker across from me and rests his hands on the thighs of his pressed suit pants. "Who have you seen since you've been back?"

I say, too quickly, "Nobody. Who is there left to see?"

He doesn't like my answer, my tone of voice. He sighs, and his impatience blows out between us like he used to blow the smoke from a Camel cigarette. He thinks I sound smart-assy, and maybe I do. I don't mean to. I'm learning as I go here. I haven't had a father for six years, and the one I had was far away, if not in miles then in time: what could a thirty-five-year-old tell a twelve-year-old about how things are? I tell myself to tone it down. I don't have an enemy here, at least not yet.

My father says, quietly, "Your Aunt Delia still lives in Widow Rock. Did you know that?"

I don't know what to do, lie or not lie. I'm good at lying. I've had a lot of practice. But he's a lawyer and should be good at telling chicken salad from chicken shit. And his eyes are more like Grandpa's eyes than they used to be, police eyes. Should I go on the game or try the truth on him? As soon as I consider telling it, the truth dies. I can't say Delia's name here.

"Well how long *have* you been back?" my dad asks.

I can't lie about this. He can find out easily enough. I tell him two months.

He leans back and looks at the blue sky above my head, then he glances at the bow to make sure we're still putt-putting along straight with nothing to run into. His voice is low and careful when he says, "That's a long time to be here without contacting me. How long did you plan to wait before you let me know?"

It's a hard one, and not because I don't know the answer. The answer is I might never have contacted him. I didn't come back here to see him. But I can't tell him who I came to see. And it's hard for another reason. He honestly doesn't know that you survive six years in the warehouse of unclaimed youth by forgetting about the people who don't write and don't call. By forgetting what forgets you. By forgetting very hard.

I smile, and it's a smile of meanness. I try to twist it into a smile of some weird kindness. I say, "I don't know. I was working on answering that question myself. I wanted to get myself established, see what the world was like in . . ." I don't say *the free world*, ". . . before I got in touch. I just wanted to be on my own for a while. See if I could make it."

He nods, looks around at the empty, easy rolling ocean, then back at me, and maybe the light that flashes in his eyes is an understanding, maybe it's even respect. Maybe he can understand a young guy wanting to do what I just said.

I wait a long time for him to speak, but he just sits peering at me. Once he looks down at his hands, turns them over, and stares into the palms as if to say, *What hath Lloyd wrought?* Finally he shakes his head in amazement or disappointment or something, and says, "What do you plan to do here?"

I answer fast: "I don't know. Just what I'm doing now, I guess. For a while longer anyway."

He doesn't like it. In his world there's always motion toward a goal. We can't even sit in this boat and drift, the engine has to be running. That's what defines people like him and like me, if I'm still a Hollister. For him it was moving out of the Depression and that humiliating poverty, and into the marines, and rising to the standing of an officer and then college on the G.I. Bill and after that, law school and a legal practice, and now making money in real estate; and the sky, as they say, is the limit. I look up at the empty blue sky, exactly the same shade as the water, which even I know can change colors with the passing of a cloud across the sun.

My dad says, "I could give you . . ." then stops. Starts again, "Hadn't you better get into college, son? Dr. Janeway said you made good grades, and I didn't need him to tell me you're smart. You know there's a war out there, don't you, son? It'll take you if you're not careful. It may take you anyway."

"Do you want me to go?" I ask him. I guess Dr. Janeway didn't tell him in their famous phone call that a boy with my record might not be a prize catch for the United States military.

My father doesn't even stop to think. "No, son, I don't think this is your war. I don't think it's ours, this country's war. It's not like the one I fought. Hitler and Tojo wanted to conquer the world, and they would have if it hadn't been for us. This thing in Vietnam is so far away from us. I don't see it threatening America."

"But they say the dominoes will fall." I've read the newspapers. I know the sides of the question.

"Maybe they will," my dad says, "but I doubt it, and I don't think the domino to defend is Vietnam. You stay away from it if you can. I've seen jungle fighting, son, and I wouldn't wish it on anybody."

"Somebody has to do it," I say. I've gone too far. I'm talking to one of the somebodies who did it.

"But not you." His voice is final. The issue is closed, and I should do what he says.

I'm thinking there's more for us to say about this, but not now. I say, "I don't think college is right for me yet. What else do you think I should consider doing?"

He looks into my eyes now, and I meet him. It's hard, but I do it.

I've given him a lot of surprises, and he's not caught up yet. But he's trying. I can see something soft and maybe a little scared in his eyes, and it reminds me of those days when I'd wait in the car at the mental hospital and he'd come out after visiting my mom and stand in the harsh sunlight and light a cigarette and rub his eyes and look up at the high white sky. It's all there now. The years are gone from his face, and it's all there. How lost he was those days when the visits didn't go well and the doctors had nothing good to tell him, and my mother could not talk to him and only sang songs in Japanese. He says, "One thing you can do is come and live with me . . . and my wife, Eleanor. Get yourself out of that . . . tourist cabin. I don't know how you're supporting yourself, but . . ."

"I work in a restaurant. Big Sam's on the beach. I'm learning the restaurant business from the ground up. I bet you've eaten at Big Sam's. Everybody else has."

He searches my eyes briefly for the mean humor that might be in them, but I keep it back out of sight.

"Anyway," he says, "I can put you to work in my law office. You can learn the law from the ground up. You'll end up on higher ground eventually if you do."

I'm firm, clear when I say, "No thanks. I like living where I am. It's not fancy, and the palmetto bugs sometimes try to carry me off at night, but I like the independence."

He frowns. He wants to convince me. I don't get his reasons. Is some long-buried pain about me clawing its way to the surface? I hold up my hand before he can speak again. "And hey, you don't want an ex-felon living with you. I know that from experience." What I mean is that I know how people react to a résumé like mine. Good first impressions can dissipate when they get to the line that reads, *Six Years, Warehouse of Unclaimed Youth.* My father's wife, Eleanor, is no doubt a wonderful woman, but somehow I doubt she'd take to having the Bayonet Boy of Omaha under her roof.

My father thinks about what I've said. Trouble wrinkles his brow and makes his clean lawyer's hands wring each other a little, so I hasten to add, "Really, I'm fine where I am, and it's close to the water, and you can see how I like to fish." But we both know it's not really about my accommodations, and he isn't half mollified. The honest me, or whoever it is that doesn't naturally lie, wants to say, *Listen, my Father, your son is inventing a new life, and he can't do it under an old roof.*

The old soldier in him stands up, stretches high and straight, and goes to the steering console and untethers the wheel. He turns the boat back toward land, and the bow rises as we pick up speed. At Bridgedale I read up on the Pacific Island campaigns, and I know more about my father than he'd ever be willing to tell. All I knew about him when I was twelve was that he'd been to Guadalcanal and Okinawa and Japan and some other places in the Pacific and that he came home with bad dreams, a Japanese wife, and slept with a bayonet under his pillow. Now I know what that fighting was like, and words like *savage* and *brutal*, and phrases like *to the last man*, have no power to describe it. It was burning gasoline sprayed into caves where men crouched starved and naked but unwilling to quit, and it was repeated waves of night banzai charges that left the morning jungle strewn with corpses. I know these things only as you know them from books, but at least I've taken the time to know them that way.

There's a lot more I want to know about my father, but now is not the time to ask. I have to let him swallow what I've put on his plate today, and I have to keep my eye on Delia, my Delia.

I jump from the bow of my father's boat into the water where he found me. I'm up to my chest again in Wilson's channel. My stringer is still pegged there behind me, and I wonder if the blue crabs have been at my fish.

My father reverses his engine and aims the boat up the channel toward the marina. "I'll take you out fishing sometime, son," he says. He's standing above me again, tall and straight. Blue exhaust fumes rise up around him.

I'm thinking a lot of things. What would we have to say to each other out fishing? There's either too much or nothing at all to say. *What would you really want to know about me? You could never talk about the war, and you never will, and I'll never tell you about my prison.*

I answer him, "Yes sir, maybe we'll do that."

Before he shifts into forward, he says, "I can see your mother in your face, Travis. She was a beautiful woman when she was young." Then he looks away, up the channel, and pulls back on the throttle. "When we were *all* young," he says, and I'm looking at the back of him, tall and straight, steering away toward the breakwater.

I call out, "She's still beautiful," but it's lost in the noise of his engine.

FOURTEEN

My days drag at Big Sam's. I know the job now, and there's nothing new except the faces that come through the door, and the few small surprises I get like a moment of kindness from LeLe, or the customer who comes over to me and presses a five-dollar bill into my hand. "Take it, kid. I used to bus tables in here, and I know how they treat you." (A glance over at LeLe.) "Buy yourself a decent meal and let *them* wait on you." He slaps me on the back and, before I even have a chance to thank him, walks out with his wife and three stair-step kids.

There are bad surprises too, like the old lady who has a heart attack in the middle of her fried shrimp and throws up all over the booth. After she's taken away in an ambulance in the care of the guy who answered when Big Sam got on the intercom and boomed, "Is there a doctor in the house?" I have to spend the next thirty minutes swabbing her stomach contents out of the crotch between the seat and the backrest. I don't envy the next party that gets that booth.

Emil and I have settled into a routine. We work hard, mostly surrounded by people who don't or who won't be around long enough for us to worry about it. We watch each other, and sometimes we shake our heads and smile grimly at the world of the kitchen that stumbles and mumbles and rumbles around us. When Emil mumbles it's mostly about the incompetence of the world, and it makes me dig up a few lines of a poem I had to memorize back at Bridgedale: *They stood, and earth's foundations stay; . . . And saved the sum of things for pay.* He smiles and raises his eyebrows, lifts his chin a degree or two into the heat behind the steaming fryers. "Who wrote that?" he asks. I tell him I can't remember.

I like to watch Emil. He's a spectacle of efficiency and power and dignity. He's like a lot of good people in the web of this world, hidden away in a kitchen where nobody sees him, but he's making good things happen for the people out there in the dining room. Maybe it's just hot fryers full of shrimp, but it seems like more than that to me. It seems like the way everything ought to be and so few things are.

When Emil watches me, I don't know what he's thinking, but I have my guesses. He's glad I'm here, but he also wants me to use more of the brains he's pretty sure I have. And he's thinking I've changed lately and wondering why, when all I do is work at Big Sam's and go fishing and ride around in my car. A couple of times he's asked me if I have a girlfriend, and I've told him no. He raises his eyebrows at this, and once he said, "Boy, you could be a poontanging fool if you wanted to, but you'd be a fool to do it. Nothing good happens that way." I think I know what he means. We haven't talked more about Dawnell. I guess Emil thinks I took his advice and I'm staying away from her.

And, of course, I've never mentioned Delia, but every day when I come to work, I expect to see her and Ole Temp walk in alone or with friends from the suburb where all of the houses arrived from foreign parts. I expect to see her drinking and having fun and not expecting to see me. But what if my father told her where I work? Does that mean she'll stay away from Big Sam's, and how will she explain that to Ole Temp? Sometimes I think she must want to see me again, want to find a way for us to be together. That's what I want. Other times I think all I can ever be is a reminder of her bad-girl past.

"What's a matter with you tonight?" Emil sips his shiny little butter cup of colorless whiskey. He rolls the treat around in his cheeks before swallowing with an appreciative "Ahh." We're sitting out on the loading dock. Ground fog creeps up the alley toward us from the inland side. On the gulf side, we can hear the cars swishing by on Highway 98 and, beyond the road, the surf "sheew-sheewing" at the shoreline.

"Nothing," I say.

"Nothing can jump up my ass," Emil says, looking over at me sharply. "You sho' didn't have your mind on your work tonight. Skulking around my kitchen like you was afraid of the dining room. Is that LeLe on your ass again?"

LeLe's an excuse, so I say yes. Emil doesn't like her any more than I do, but he won't let me say anything bad about her. She's a good waitress, and Emil appreciates competence in all forms. Even in the form of LeLe. I sip my whiskey and ask him for a cigarette, and he says, "Colonel, when are you gon' start buying your own. You think I'm the river of all good things in this life?"

My face gets a little red, and I remember the beggars we all were in reform school, but I know this is just a game we play. Emil doesn't mind me bumming. And he doesn't want me buying. We light up and blow smoke out into the alley. There's no wind, and our smoke just hangs in the air, clouding the light that comes through the window of Big Sam's office. We can hear Big Sam in there pulling the lever on the hand-crank adding machine, cussing his mistakes, and scribbling in his account book.

I'm still trying to figure out how I feel about seeing Delia again. So far, the feelings are glad, bad, and numb. The glad is as big and as good as it ever was, and I guess that doesn't surprise me. The bad is all about Ole Temp and the way I know she's changed, even though she looks as good as I hoped she would. The numb is how you feel after you've been hit in the face by a guy twice your size and you go to sleep standing up, don't feel the ground when you hit it, and wake up in a place you've never seen before. That's numb, and it's happened to me a few times.

I take a drag and breathe some smoke out through my nose. "Emil, do you have a girlfriend?"

He yanks his face around to me like he would if I dropped a stack of dinner plates on the kitchen floor. "You ain't been talking to any of those gossips down on Third Street, have you?"

It's an answer, but I don't say so. I just smile and say, "Only wondering."

Emil takes a last drag and tosses his Camel into the alley. He finishes his whiskey and sticks the little silver butter cup into the pocket of his gray-checked chef's pants. He says, "Come on, colonel, I'll show you something."

Panama City is a beach town, all strung out along the water, but like most towns I've seen, it has a good section, a bad section, and a Black section. And the Black section is divided just like the white section is, into good and bad, but only the Black people know that. To the whites, the Black section is just part of the bad that's part of their town. Emil's taking me someplace I've never been before.

We drive past the rooming house where Emil rents the whole top floor. I've been up there. His car was in the shop, and I picked him up in the morning for work. He asked me in, and I sat in his living room while he finished dressing. Right away, I could see that we're alike. What the navy taught him, reform school taught me. To be neat, tidy, to keep things squared away, ready to hand. To own what you need and not much more, to take inventory and discard what's used up or useless. At first you do it because they punish you if you don't. Later on, for some guys at least, Emil and me for sure, it becomes necessity. I didn't know what I was doing was called philosophy until I read Henry David Thoreau, the part about the Indian tribe and how they had a ceremony once a year. They piled up everything they didn't need in the center of the village and burned it. They danced around the fire and considered themselves the most fortunate people in the world.

Emil turns down a dark street, then down an alley, and we go from small, neat houses with lighted windows and Black people rocking on the porches, their bodies moving with that tired grace you get from working a hard day and enjoying the slow motion of your evening. We break from the last thin scattering of houses and the alley becomes a sand road that heads off into the woods in a direction I've never been before, and we come to a lighted row of raw pine buildings. Emil rolls down the windows, and we hear music off in the distance, first the steady beat of a drum and then, as we pull up to the last building at the end of the line, the twang of a guitar and the sweet, high lament of a woman's voice. The music is loud now, and there's a strong smell of woodsmoke and pork barbecue in the air.

We park in a row of cars and pickup trucks that I can tell are owned by Black people, either because they're so run-down or so bright-colored. We get out and walk toward the open doorway of what I guess is a bar, and I look back at Emil's big black Lincoln snugged in among the bright-purple and yellow Cadillacs and Pontiacs. It looks like we got lost on our way to a funeral.

We push through the door into a room full of low light and loud music and laughing, murmuring, listening people. A few faces turn to us, all of them Black, then a few more, and then everybody in the room is looking not at us but at me, and all of the talking stops and there's only the music, a blues song, coming from a small stage shoved into a corner and crowded with a drum set, a bass violin, a guitar, a piano, and a lady singer in a blue dress covered with gold sequins that seem to flow down her body like water when she moves. The woman keeps singing, the band keeps playing, and nobody's listening but me. The whole room is wondering what this white boy is doing here. Emil steps over to a big Black man who sits at a table near the door and gives him two dollars for the cover charge. The man wears black suit pants, a black vest, a shiny purple shirt with garters on his sleeves, and a little white porkpie hat. Everything about him is big except the hat. There's an unlit cigar stuffed into a permanent socket in the corner of his mouth, and his left hand rests on a sawed-off baseball bat covered with the scars from encounters with various hard heads.

The big man puts the two dollars into a cigar box. "Good to see you, Emil."

Emil says, "Likewise, George. George, this is my young friend, Travis."

George smiles at me around the cigar, and I can't tell if it's really friendly or just business. Emil steps back from the table and looks at the silent room. When he sees everybody looking at me, he reaches over and puts his hand on my shoulder and pushes me toward a table. And with that touch, everything changes. Heads swivel back to the stage, first a few and then more, and finally the whole room is like it was before Emil and I broke in here.

We take a table in the back, it's the only one we can get, and a small Black woman with tight spit curls across her forehead comes over. She's wearing a short satiny red dress, and it's the first time I've ever seen a woman I'm pretty sure isn't wearing any underclothes. Emil says, "Gina, brings us two bourbons and two waters back."

The woman looks at me hard, then back at Emil, who nods, and she spins and disappears into the smoke that hides the small bar where a row of men without women sit on stools fondling cigars and eyeing the crowd as much as the stage.

When the woman in the red dress comes back with our drinks, we sip the strong, earth-tasting whiskey, and Emil says, "So, colonel, what you think of this place?"

I love it here. Without Emil, I wouldn't have made it past the man at the door, and I think that's what I love most about it. Being here with him. Seeing how the others took me in because of him. I say, "This whiskey is good, and I love that music." Emil smiles, and it's his older and wiser smile. He knows what's going on in my head right now, that I'm like a blind dog in a meat house. That I can't decide what to snatch at first. "Do you come here a lot?" I ask him.

He smiles, nods, sips his whiskey. "Yes, colonel, a lot, and you're about to see why." He checks his watch, and then settles into his chair, taking in the stage.

I don't know much about blues, except that it's got a certain kind of beat and the stories are mostly about trouble. And I know it's out of style right now with the younger Black people and the white kids who like Black music. I love Otis Redding, and Sam Cooke, and the Supremes, and I can hear the blues in the background of their songs sometimes, but they're the new Black music, Motown, and what I'm hearing tonight could have happened in a place like this twenty years ago.

We listen to the set, and the woman's voice can reach the high sky where she sounds like a Black angel in the choir of a country Baptist church, and it can grind low like anger and trouble coming up out of her belly, accusing and abusing. She sings about men who have left her with little children, and men who have cheated on her, and men who have loved her but not enough, and once or twice about men she's gotten back at with a broom handle or a wine bottle upside the head or with another man.

The band takes a break, and Emil orders us two more whiskeys, and I look over at the door. A white woman is standing there. She looks careful but comfortable too, and she's scanning the room for something or somebody. She's wearing the kind of clothes white women wear when they go grocery shopping in Panama City, a flower-printed shirtwaist dress with a little belt. She's applied her makeup to bring out what's natural in her face, and that's not the rule in this place where lips shine in the dark like cherries ready to be plucked from trees. She's not a pretty woman, she's what other women call pleasant or handsome and some men call homely. But there's a person in her face, somebody who tells you she won't put up with fools and she can't be led too far down the garden path. She pays George the cover in a distracted way, still appraising the crowd as she passes over the money. When her eyes find our table, and a sad, sweet smile comes to her face, I know why we're here tonight, and for the first time I'm a little scared.

The woman walks over to us, and Emil stands, and before I figure out that I should stand too, he reaches over and hoists me by grabbing a handful of flesh from between my neck and shoulder. There's no handle there, but he makes one and it hurts.

The woman says, "Why thank you, gentlemen," and she sits next to me, not Emil, and I can see it bothers him for a blink or two of his big eyes, but then he shakes his head and smiles at her cunning. Is she punishing him for bringing me here on the spur of the moment? The woman leans forward and puts her hands on the table in front of her but not her elbows (my grandmother used to say, "All joints on the table will be carved"), and says, "Emil, introduce me to your friend."

I like being called Emil's friend, but I don't think I am quite yet, and I may never be. It's more like I'm a project or a protégé. I don't know. Emil says, "Sarah, this is Travis. Travis is my right-hand man at the restaurant."

Sarah turns to me and gives me her full face and the heat of her large soft eyes. She holds out her hand, and I take it. She says, "Hello, Travis Right-Hand Man. How do you like the restaurant business?"

Her grip is firm and warm, taking the measure of mine, friendly but not clingy. I remove my hand from hers, promising myself to remember her touch, and say, "I like it fine, I guess. Emil makes things interesting."

She looks across me at Emil, who is pushed back in his chair watching us like we're a scene in a movie he's not sure he likes. Their eyes exchange messages from places only they know about. She says, "Oh yes, Emil knows how to make things interesting."

There are a lot of strange things here, but the strangest is that nobody seemed to notice this white woman when she walked in. She sure didn't get the reaction I got. She and Emil have been here together before, and maybe they come here a lot. Sarah's hands rest on the table in front of her again. She leans toward Emil while he leans toward the little Black woman whose naked body moves under the satiny red dress. Emil orders Sarah a dry martini, and I notice her left hand. There's no ring on it, though I can see the light-skinned trench where something was recently removed. I imagine the ring lying out there in the ashtray of her car, and in my mind's eye I follow the car along country roads or city lanes to a house somewhere, and a man she doesn't love, or who doesn't love her, or who is gone all the time, in the service maybe, off on a navy ship like Emil used to be, and I wonder what I've gotten myself into and why I'm here.

In the newspaper the other day, I read about riots in St. Augustine, some people protesting at the old slave market, a place right in the center of America's oldest city where human beings were sold on the auction block, and some other people, some of them Klansmen, starting a fight with them. Around here Black and white seem to live together without trouble, but you can feel the anger and the bitterness just under the surface, and it's hard to tell what's keeping it down there. Maybe it's the tourist trade, all the people coming and going, a river of humanity on US 98 pouring into the local mix, thinning it and washing the anger and the bitterness away into the Gulf of Mexico. But St. Augustine gets plenty of tourists, and they just had trouble that made the national news. And I'm sitting here in an establishment at the very edge of Black civilization (outside the back door of this place the piney woods stretch on all the way to Georgia), a mixed boy drinking underage with a mixed couple. I know Emil couldn't walk along Panama City Beach with this woman, no matter who she is. That would just be too much.

The woman in the red dress brings Sarah's martini, and we three settle into a mild discomfort, all of us straining our eyes through the smoke at the stage where the band tries to drag our emotions out of us, pull what we feel into their instruments and their voices, and send it all back out to us magnified so that we know more about what life and love are than we ever could alone. And it works. The whole room seems to bear down under the sound and the words, and we sing ourselves sometimes as one big sigh, sometimes as some kind of lost, vacant, inward sight, and sometimes as an anger that threatens to burst the walls and leave us all wearing the roof as a hat.

After a while, I excuse myself to the necessary room, and when I come back Sarah has taken my seat, and she's got her shoulder under Emil's big arm and her head on his lapel. Her eyes are closed, and she's listening to his heartbeat as much as to the music. She seems to wake up when I sit down. She opens her dreamy eyes and says to me, "Travis, what do you think of all this?"

I don't know how to answer. I don't want to say the wrong thing. I know Emil brought me here for a reason, but I don't know what it is.

So I say, "I love the music, and . . ." I glance at Emil, who looks back at me with eyes that say, *Be careful*. I go on, ". . . and I like you, Sarah."

Sarah smiles, closes her eyes, and says, "Are you going to talk about this to anybody? Any of your young friends at the restaurant?"

I'm too quick to say, "No." I take a breath and start over: "I don't think there's anything wrong with . . ." I stop again. I've gone in the wrong direction.

"With what?" Sarah says, her eyes still shut and dreamy, her head still lying on Emil's lapel. "With a Black man and a white woman being together in a place like this?"

I see now there's no good answer. If I say yes, agree with the way she just put it, then I leave her thinking I'm the only enlightened white boy in Panama City, one of two white people who are welcome in this country bar. If I say I meant something else, then what did I mean? Nothing wrong with a world that damns this kind of love? I don't understand what's going on here. So I say, "I'm sorry. I don't know what I was about to say." I'm miserable, and I look over at Emil for some kind of help, but I don't get it. He only gives me the look he'd give somebody who just dropped a three-foot stack of dinner plates, then he slides his eyes back to the band.

Sarah keeps that dreamy smile on her face, and sometimes she looks over at me with those soft warm eyes, and after a while it's not so much that I'm forgiven as forgotten. She's in the world of Emil, and I might as well be a chair. Emil doesn't forget, though. He never gives up the part of himself that is a sentry. There's always a glance at the horizon, at the door, in the rearview mirror, even when he's most relaxed. And so the evening goes that way. The drinks keep coming, and I keep thinking about what to say that will dig me out of the hole I've made for myself, and after a while the possibility of digging out gets lost in the whiskey, and I just don't care anymore.

When the band packs up to leave, and people begin to drift out, and Big George walks behind the bar with the cashbox in one hand and the cutoff baseball bat in the other, eyeing us like we're a job he has to do before he locks the doors, Emil stretches and Sarah seems to wake up from a long, dreamy sleep.

Emil says to me, "Come on outside, Travis. I need to talk to you."

Half the whiskey I've just drunk gets burned up in the adrenaline that starts to flow. He isn't saying, *Let's step outside,* is he? We walk out into the dark of after midnight with the dew dripping from the trees and the kind of quiet you hear only in the country when most of the world is sleeping. Emil walks to his car, and I follow, half expecting some kind of chastising, either by tongue or hand. I still don't know what I've done or might have done.

We get to his big black Lincoln, and he reaches into his pocket and gives me the keys. "Here, kid. Drive the car to the restaurant and leave it in the alley. Sarah will bring me home."

I take the keys and look up into his face. "Emil, I'm sorry if I—"

"Never mind, colonel. You didn't. It's just . . ." he waves his hand around at the quiet dark, "the way things are, I guess. Sarah didn't mean nothing. She's a good girl."

I want to ask a hundred questions, but I know I'm not allowed. I come out with only one: "Did you know she was coming tonight?" If he knew, then he brought me here to meet her. To see them together.

Emil glances off over my shoulder into the night, then over at the front door of the bar. Sarah's still in there. He says, "I wasn't sure. She comes sometimes, sometimes she don't."

We stand there looking at each other.

He says, "Don't worry about it, kid, but think about it. Think about it. You'll come up with something."

"Something interesting?" I remember what Sarah said about Emil.

He laughs. "Yeah, that's right. Something interesting. Now you get along home, and I'll see you tomorrow in the salt mine."

I turn and walk toward the Lincoln.

Emil says, "And take care of my ride."

FIFTEEN

I wake up to someone knocking, and even before I can swing my legs over the edge of the bed, the nausea is at the back of my throat. I choke out, "Just a minute," and try for the bathroom, but I can't make it. Halfway, I detour to the kitchen sink and gag out the muddy sludge of last night's whiskey. Behind me, there's knocking again. My head feels like a bucket somebody's beating with a length of pipe, and each gagging spasm tears me from belly to gaping mouth. After what little's in me is out, the dry heaves start. And the knocking doesn't stop. I call out, "Just a MIN-ute!" and turn on the water, washing away what I can of the mess I've made, then filling my mouth with cool, sweet relief. I rinse and spit, then I try a swallow, then another, filling the caustic hole in my middle and hoping to hold down the sweet clean water. I stand in the reek of myself at the sink, my face sweating and my eyes tearing from the strain, waiting to see if the big spit is going to happen again. The burning hole seems to be cooling, and the room tilts only about ten degrees, but the headache seems permanent, as permanent as my resolve: *I will never drink whiskey again.*

The Widow's voice comes through my door, "I can hear you in there, Travis. Who are you talking to?"

"My resolve," I mutter. "Only my resolve."

I lurch across the plunging deck to the door and pull it open. She's standing out there six steps from my front porch in full yellow muumuu, holding her plastic tumbler of vodka and grapefruit juice out in front of her with both hands like the sword she will swing at whatever demons fly from my den of evil. Her eyes, usually alcohol-dilated and slitted against the sun, jump to full round when she sees me. I am pain and anger. I must look a fright. And I'm thinking that even road trash like me has a right not to be jacked out of bed in the morning by the Women's Christian Temperance Union. Especially when the local delegate is herself a dedicated drunk. I say, "What?" Then, "WHAT DO YOU WANT?"

She takes another step back. She looks truly frightened. Have I lost my mind?

"Look," I say, "Jesus Christ, I'm not feeling very well. Can't you just . . ." Can't she just what? Stop being the pain-in-the-ass snoop and busybody she was born to become?

"Well!" she says, recovering her dignity and managing not to spill her drink. "There's no need to bring Him into this."

I push my hand straight up the middle of my face, hard, pushing lips and nose together, pressing nose toward forehead and forehead into hairline. The headache only persists. "Him?" I ask. "Him *who?*"

"Jesus," she says, turning Him into a four-syllable word with a dying fall at the end.

"Oh," I say. "Well, sorry. I didn't mean to . . ." This could go on forever, and I am feeling the need to return to my sink, or perhaps this time make it all the way to my bathroom. And I'm wondering how much longer the sink and the bathroom will be mine. I've never talked to the Widow this way before. The strange thing is that she hasn't already left to call the sheriff or whoever it is you summon to begin eviction proceedings.

She takes a step toward me, looks at the drink in her hand as though she needs some of it badly, and says, low and meek, "Travis, can I come in for a minute?"

I leave the door open and, both arms extended for balance, slide across the unsteady floor toward the bathroom. Inside the small, lurching locker, I terrify the toilet bowl for what must be only five minutes but seems like a crucified hour. When it's over, it seems to be over. I drink more water from the sink, splash some on my face, throw open the door, and there's the Widow at my sink with my can of Ajax in her hand cleaning up what's left of the mess.

She turns to me, purses her lips and flares her nostrils. "Pooh! It smells like an old drunk lives here. Travis, when did you start up with this kind of behavior?" She turns back to the sink and finishes cleaning. I free skate to the bed while she goes into the bathroom, waves her hand in front of her to dissipate the fumes, and says, "Well, I don't need to clean up in there."

I'm lying back in last night's whiskey sweat wondering if getting horizontal again is such a good idea. The Widow pulls a chair over and sits next to my bed, holding her drink in her lap. She watches me for a while, or I guess she does. My eyes are closed. Occasionally, I hear her sip and swallow. There's a crazy moment when I feel like I might drift off to sleep, but know I can't because she'll cut out my heart and pickle it in vodka distilled from orange peels. I fight both sleep and nausea for a while.

Finally, she says, "Travis, a man came here awhile back to ask about you?"

"Did he?"

"Yes, he did. A very nice man in a very nice car. A Cadillac, in fact. He was wearing a very expensive suit."

"Did he say what he wanted with me?" She's talking about my father, of course. The mood I'm in, which is known as Abandonment of All Hope, gives me the evil urge to play with her a bit. "Was he a policeman?"

She takes in a sharp little breath, and behind my closed eyelids I see her evaluating this possibility with a combination of distress and delight. Then she says, "No, I don't think so. Cops don't drive Cadillacs, and they wear checked sport coats from J. M. Fields. He didn't tell me what he did for a living, but he was very polite and said he just wanted to know where to find you. I told him where you go fishing when you're not working."

"Thank you."

"Thank . . . Travis, who *was* he?"

"How should I know? Why do *you* want to know?" This, of course, is the heart of the matter. I wonder if anyone else who lives here at the Wind Motel has ever asked her this question.

She seems prepared. She says, "I am naturally curious about my tenants and anything they might do that could reflect discredit on this establishment."

It sounds like something she memorized from an episode of *Perry Mason*.

I say, "And of course you are just as interested in anything a tenant might do that would reflect *credit* on this establishment. Such as having some kind of connection to a well-dressed man who drives a Cadillac?"

Silence. I want to ask her if she understands my question. I don't. I just lie there floating on sea swells of nausea, thanking the Widow's Jesus for the moments when the horizon behind my closed eyes seems to right itself and the possibility rises that I will not die today.

We sit in the quiet she blessedly provides for a while, and then I hear her stand and go to the door. "Travis, come over to my place. I know exactly what you need." And she's gone, leaving my door open.

After another little while during which things don't get better, I rise and, shielding my eyes from the blinding morning sun, zigzag like a convoy avoiding U-boats to the Widow's front door. Where she is waiting to let me in. Inside, things are unsurprisingly frilly and crowded but surprisingly clean. And air-conditioned. She takes me by the arm and leads me to a chair in her small kitchen and pulls a bottle of vodka from the freezer. She pours an ounce into a shot glass she plucks from a silver tray that holds many, many shot glasses. "Here," she says, "you'll get better if you don't do this, but not in time to go to work. You'll get better quicker if you drink it. Believe me, I know."

I look up into her eyes, and I believe her. I believe that she knows about such things. And I am desperate. And I need to go to work more or less on the level, for many reasons, not the least of which is that I don't want Emil to know that an evening in his company has so thoroughly sunk my boat. I reach out and take the ice-cold shot glass from the Widow's surprisingly steady hand and, sucking a deep breath, down it.

She hands me a glass of water. "Chase it with this," she says knowledgeably. I do.

After three shots I am in a glowing place where there are smiles, but they are wry, and they do not come with laughter. I am able to walk, talk, open my eyes to the light, and contemplate a future that contains, if nothing truly ambitious, at least an eight-hour shift at Big Sam's. Who knows what tomorrow will bring?

The Widow pours me a fourth and says, "Just sip this one, okay?" I nod.

She says, "So who was that man, really?"

"Really?" I ask her wryly.

"Yes," she says, "really. And don't be a smart-ass on the courage of my vodka."

I tell her this is not courage. I tell her she has not seen my courage yet, a luminous thing, but may someday see it. If she's lucky.

She frowns, shakes her head, then can't stop herself from laughing. She's got a breathy, girlish laugh, and this is the first time I've heard it. Her eyes grow stern again. "Really, Travis?"

Oh, all right. "He's my father."

She rocks back a little in her chair and nods the way women do in church when the preacher says something particularly scriptural. She knew it all along.

"He looks like you," she says.

"You mean I look like *him*. It can go the other way."

"You think you're very smart, don't you?"

"No, just smart enough . . . sometimes."

She nods as though this might be true. "Where does your father live?"

"In Widow Rock." I thought this might disappoint her, and I see that it does. Widow Rock is too country for the folks in Panama City (who are themselves considered denizens of the boondocks by the sophisticates of Tallahassee).

"What does he do? For a living, I mean."

"He's an attorney by trade, but I really don't know what he does. I haven't seen him in a long time."

She marvels at this, mostly by raising her tall drink and taking a long contemplative sip. "And he didn't even know where you were living." She says this to herself, but I answer anyway.

"Apparently not." But thinking: *He sure knew how to find out.*

"Is your father still married to your mother, Travis?"

"No," I say, "and he told me that folks around here were too polite to ask questions about his divorce."

The Widow gets my drift, and we are surely drifting. I put down the half-finished fourth shot glass, a nominal gesture at best. The feelings are still wry, but the day stretches on ahead full of smoky frying lard and the roar of the crowd in Big Sam's and overflowing garbage cans and bus pans full of dirties replaced by cleans. The Widow sees that I am about to rise and go, and I can tell she's calculating to keep me awhile longer.

She says, "How long has it been since you saw your father? Where did you live before you came here?"

I tell her I was in boarding school. I'm not sure she knows what that means, and I only know it approximately from reading *The Catcher in the Rye* and one or two things by John P. Marquand and John O'Hara. Holden Caulfield thinks boarding school is almost as bad as reform school, but what the hell does he know about incarceration?

The Widow only says, "Oh." She considers all of this for a moment, then says, "Does it cost a lot to go to boarding school?"

"Sure," I say in the offhanded manner of rich boys, which, it occurs to me for the first time, I may be, by some not-too-far-fetched calculus. I am, after all, the son of an attorney who is making money in real estate. But it was the State of Nebraska that paid for my room and board and my education, such as it was, and I remember reading somewhere that it cost the state a pretty penny per annum to keep a miscreant boy. The comparison was, I believe, to the cost of tuition at Harvard University. All I can say is that there must have been a lot of graft, a lot of money siphoned off along the way from the state purse to the poor penitent boy, because I never saw anything but bad food, piss-smelling mattresses, and deflated footballs.

I stand and wait to see if I am steady. I flex my knees and regard the door where the bright sun shines through the Widow's green-tinted jalousies. Her medicine is working. I tell her, "Well . . ." to indicate the imminence of my departure.

Her eyes tell me she'd like us to keep talking for a while. But sadly she rises and looks carefully into my face. "Are you sure you're all right to leave now?"

"I won't drive to work. I'll walk. It'll do me good."

At the door, she leans close and puts her hand on my shoulder. I can't tell if it's support she needs from me now, or something else. She says, "I always knew there was something different about you. That you weren't the usual road trash that comes through here."

I turn and our faces are very close and our breath mingles, vodka to vodka, confusion to confusion. I look into her widowed eyes at the long years of living alone here, defending herself from the usual trash, keeping the place in good enough order to keep the trash knocking at her door and asking, "You got a vacancy?" I stare deep into her eyes. She has a vacancy.

I stare blankly at the hand on my shoulder until she removes it. "Thank you," I say, and I mean it. "I'm glad you always thought well of me."

As I step out onto her porch into a sun that makes beads of pure vodka spring to my forehead, she says, "Well, I do, and I don't want you to break bad like a lot of young people around here do. Even the best ones can fall in with the wrong crowd."

I'm thinking: *So you gave me the vodka cure.*

I say, "I appreciate that very much. A guy on his own like me can use some guidance from time to time."

The sleeve of her yellow muumuu has slipped down onto her upper arm revealing a red brassiere strap. She reaches over and girlishly snaps it back up. Her eyes darken with a seriousness that is almost fear. "You won't . . ." She glances back behind her at the vodka dispensary where my condition was cured.

I shake my head solemnly. "Not a word." Then I draw my finger across my lips. "If you won't. Is it a deal?"

"It's a deal," she says and closes the door.

* * *

It's night, after ten o'clock, and I'm carrying my bucket of laundry to the Widow's washhouse. I'm wearing jeans and sneakers, but no shirt, and my pocket is full of quarters for the Widow's wheezy old Maytag. The night air feels good on my chest, and I stop for a few seconds and stand under the stars with the heavy bucket pulling my right arm toward the earth and just enjoy the cool and the quiet. I take a deep breath of clean, ocean-smelling air and let it out hard, expelling hours of the roar and smoke and drunken smiles and repeated necessary but brainless acts of Big Sam's, and then start walking again. As I step into the pool of light at the washhouse and the universe of madly flying night insects that spins around it, I peer off to my right at the old cracked sidewalk that leads to the oystershell parking lot in front of the Wind Motel. A tall man in a dark suit is walking toward me. He comes on straightlaced and broad-shouldered and almost marching, and I know even before his face resolves out of the darkness that it's my father. I stop and set my bucket down and wait for him.

When he stops in front of me, I see he's got something in his hand, an envelope. He holds it out to me. I wipe a wet hand on my Levi's and take it.

It's an invitation. I'm invited to dinner at my father's house on Saturday night. After I read it, I look up at him, and he smiles in a way that's almost embarrassed. He says, "I would have just called or come by to ask you, but Eleanor likes to do things this way." He means the fine parchment paper, the handwritten message (*The pleasure of your company is requested...*), the formality of it all.

Some kind of moment is happening here, and I'm not entirely sure what it is. Am I being invited back into the Hollister fold? Is this document a negotiable bond between the family and me, good for all future openings of my father's door? My smart-ass self almost goes off like a cheap popgun with something like, *Well, I'll have to check my social calendar to see if I'm free on that evening,* but judgment or luck prevails, and I just look into my father's embarrassed face and say, "Thank you."

He shifts his weight from one foot to the other. "Well, I see you've got some washing to do, so I'll just . . ."

And I nod and look down at my bucket and say, "Yeah, I . . ."

And he says, "So, we hope to see you Saturday."

And I say, "Yeah, I . . ." And he winces, probably because I'm not "yes sirring" him like a decent son would. "Well, see you later," I say, and start moving toward the washhouse.

My father says, "All right, son. Good night." And he turns and walks, tall and purposeful, back up the sidewalk toward the parking lot of the Wind Motel.

I'm sitting on the bench generously provided for those who wait for the old Maytag to work its miracle, rereading the invitation from the as-yet-unseen Eleanor, when the Widow pokes her head, eyes shaded by a pale shaking hand, into my little pool of light. "Was somebody here?" she asks.

What a question! The answer is always yes if the tense of the verb is past. But I don't want to talk to her about my father's visit. I fold the invitation and slide it into my Levi's and pick up a magazine someone has left on the bench. The magazine looks like it has spent time in the bottom of a birdcage. Before that it lived in a rack by the checkout line down at the IGA store. It's full of starlets and fully fledged movie luminaries and their strange fates. These people know no moderation. It's always either misery or ecstasy with them, a life of extremes. Someone else does their laundry.

The Widow comes on into the light of the washhouse, swatting at a big moth that selects her face as the luminous disk to orbit. She leans against the side of the pay telephone that serves all of her tenants, a drink in her hand. I pretend to read the magazine. She says, "I thought I heard somebody drive away from the lot. I thought maybe they was looking for a room."

I put down the magazine. For some reason, I don't want to lie to her. "It was my father."

She walks over and lifts the top of the washer and looks down suspiciously at my whirling load of clothes. She closes the lid and says, "This ole thing will live longer than I do." She means the May-tag. "What did he want?" She means my father.

"To invite me to dinner at his house on Saturday night." I wish I had a cigarette. I wish the Widow would produce another plastic tumbler from the folds of her muumuu and divide the big vodka and grapefruit into two portions. I wish.

She sits down next to me on the bench and sips. She says, "He's trying to reestablish contact with you, Travis. He's *trying!*" For a second, I think she's going to cry. I've tried not to think about what her life must really be like. She's alone, running this business, perpetually grieving, and surrounded by people like me, or people who are like what she thinks I'm like. Now she's revising her opinion of me because my father has been here twice in a good suit and a Cadillac. This is both good and bad for her, and I don't know what it is for me. It's good for her because I may not be a specimen of the usual riffraff (when I moved in, I thought about signing her guest book, *Travis Flotsam*, but didn't risk the joke). It's bad for her because now she thinks she has to treat me differently from the rest of what stops here, and she's not sure what the difference is going to be. I look over at her, and it's clear she's having a bad night with Mr. Vodka, or a good one, depending on how you look at it.

So I say, "Yes, he's trying. And I'm trying too. Maybe we're not trying for the same things."

She says, "I don't understand *you*," the way drunks do, with a weird emphasis on the wrong word. "Where have you been? Why is your father showing up here asking me how to find you?"

For a second my anger flashes. *Mind your own business*, or worse, is hot in my mouth, but I bite down. She wants me to have a family. Hers was taken away. A young husband is dead, and the babies they might have had are somewhere in a grave with him, and now she's married to a vodka bottle and a string of moldering tourist cabins. I say, "I've been away. With my mother. I finished school and decided to come back here, but I wasn't sure I wanted to see my father or he wanted to see me." I reach over and take hold of her big plastic tumbler, and her eyes get wild, and she holds on tight until I say, "I just want a sip. I'll give it back."

She watches me take a drink. It's pretty good, vodka and grape-fruit. We sit there for a while handing the plastic tumbler back and forth and me wishing I had a cigarette. It's a habit now, I guess, a bad one the Widow doesn't have.

She walks over to the edge of the light, stands there in the whirl-ing universe of night bugs. She looks out into the dark, then steps back toward me. "Travis, will you get me some of that marijuana?" Her face is a girl's again, her eyes alight with the adventures of sin.

I don't have to think about it. I shake my head. "That wouldn't be a good idea. They put people in jail for that." The Maytag stops, groans, then whines about starting its spin cycle.

The Widow's face falls. The wrinkles around her eyes reach down for a meeting with the deepening trenches at the corners of her mouth. Sin is Gravity. She says, "Well, if I get some, will you smoke it with me? I'd feel safe doing it with you."

I see the naked appeal in her eyes. She'd trust me to perform this crime with her, and her eyes ask if I'd return the favor. I keep my eyes empty and say, "You don't know the kind of people you'd be dealing with."

She thinks about it, looks into the bottom of the big plastic tum-bler I helped her empty. "Maybe I'm not as country stupid as you think I am."

I get up and open the washer and start separating my tangled gar-ments. "I don't think you're stupid, and I don't know where you come from. But I know people who sell drugs will sell other things when they have to, and one thing they'll sell is your name."

"How do you know that, Mr. Teenage Wisdom?" Her big soft chest heaves, and her eyes go small and dark in the cold white light. It's the closest to angry I've ever seen her. She says, "Where have you *really* been? Not off with any mother. You don't act like a boy who's been living with his mother."

"How do I act?"

She thinks for a minute. "Like a man who knows how to take care of himself. Like a man who's been around . . ." she pauses, looking off into the buzzing insect constellations, "around danger."

I laugh quietly and start dropping wet clothes into the closest dryer. She's right if you consider Bridgedale School dangerous. At times it was, and I've got some scars to prove it, and maybe some of the things that happened to me going west and coming back qualify.

I put two quarters into the slot on top of the dryer and shove it into the machine. I walk over and stand close to her, look into her eyes. "What I told you is true. I came here from being with my mother. Maybe I've seen some danger. I don't know what you mean by that, but I know I don't want anything to do with what will get you five years in Raiford. I think you're best advised to stay away from it too."

She looks at me, and I see her fighting the alcohol for some kind of vision that comes hard to her. Finally, she says, "I think you're a lost boy, Travis. You're lost like me, only you're different. Somebody came here to find you, your father did." She raises the tumbler, tries to drink, is surprised again when she finds it empty. "Let me tell you something you don't know, Mr. Wisdom, Mr. Smarter Than Your Years. People don't keep trying forever. After a while they just let you stay lost. It's easier that way, and sooner or later most people will do what's easy."

She gets up heavily and steps to the side to catch herself. She seems to walk by falling forward and throwing her feet out just in time to keep from going down. She's gone into the dark, and soon I hear her front door. Confusion rattles it open, and anger slams it shut. I sit for a while listening to the dryer turning and thumping, then I pull my father's invitation out of my Levi's and hold it in my hand. I don't know what it is. Maybe it's some kind of passport back into the human world. And I don't know what I'll do with it, but I'll do something.

There's a knock at my door. I quit folding laundry and open it. The

Widow stands under a bright, bare light bulb with a dry cleaner's clear plastic bag in her hand. She gives it to me. "Here," she says. "He was about your size. He only wore it a few times, to get married and when we went to church. We didn't go to church all that much."

I take the bag from her and smell the camphor of mothballs, feel the weight of it. The suit inside is dark gray, and I can see through the plastic a white shirt and a black tie tucked under the suit's lapels. I throw the ghost over my arm and look up to thank her, but she's gone into the night.

SIXTEEN

My father's house is in the best part of town. It's the old Williams House. The summer I lived in Widow Rock, old Doc Williams was still alive. I remember driving with Delia past this big white house with gables and dark-green shutters and watching men work in the yard, and a maid walk onto the long shaded gallery carrying a tray draped with a white cotton napkin and a silver pitcher of iced tea for old Doc Williams who sat out in the late afternoons reading medical journals in a gray seersucker jacket and a white shirt with a closed collar but no tie.

Now I park my Plymouth at the curb and look at what my father has done. A new dark-green canvas awning leans out over the long gallery, hoarding the cool shade. The green casement windows are new, and so are the cedar shakes that cover the steeply pitched roof. I know why my father is not out in one of the swank new suburbs that circle the town. I remember Delia saying that my grandparents had no money, but being the sheriff's wife, Grandma Hollister had a certain social position. I think she meant *un*certain. My father, Sheriff Hollister's son, is a success now, a professional man with money. This house is the heart of the town he left for war and marriage, and law school, and the Midwest. It's the prize and the proof of certainty.

I stand in the street smoothing my hands down the front of a dead boy's gray serge suit. I can feel the nervous moisture departing my fingers for the knot of a too-narrow black tie. One side of me hopes these clothes are right, that I will fit in, but the other side, the bad refugee from the warehouse of unclaimed youth, hopes I'm dressed all wrong. Wants to stand out like a wen on the nose of a bridegroom, or the bad cough that won't settle in the chest of the preacher at a funeral. I stand on the redbrick sidewalk listening for any sound from the house, any hum of happiness or groan of discontent from the old pine boards that were sawed long and straight when Taft was president and old Doc Williams was just a gleam in his father's eye. I don't hear anything. The party hasn't started yet. I walk up the redbrick path to the gallery and the wide golden oak door with a carved border of twining vines.

I pull an old-fashioned brass doorbell and hear the faint tinkling inside, and then I'm greeted by a smiling Black woman not much older than I am. She looks me up and down briefly with no conclusion in her eyes, then steps back, hauling open the heavy door. I move into a long foyer with wide, dark, linseed-smelling planks of heart pine and framed paintings of race horses in shady green paddocks. This maid might as well be the receptionist in a dentist's office. Her smile is cool and professional. She says, "Welcome, sir. You go straight ahead, then left into the parlor. Mr. and Mrs. Hollister are waiting for you." I nod, smile, look around for cameras, someone to snap wooden scissors in front of my face and shout, *Take One, Scene Three! The Prodigal Enters at the Front Door!*

I thank the woman and walk as directed. In the parlor, a room with high ceilings and a chandelier, my father and his wife sit—no, they are composed—in matching wing chairs in front of a fireplace so high I could stand inside it. What stands in it now is a tall crystal vase of yellow gladioli. A campaign table, the kind you lift by brass handles, rests between them, and two clear drinks, martinis I think, have been poured.

My father, in an open-necked blue shirt, blue blazer, and gray wool trousers, looks up from a pensive sip at his conical long-stemmed glass. "Travis! Good. Good. Welcome. This is . . . my wife, Eleanor." He stands and sets his drink on the tray, but Eleanor remains seated, as I guess she is supposed to do. I have no idea what I'm supposed to do. I step forward, trying to remember from reading novels if it is mine or my hostess's hand that should be offered first.

My father's wife reaches out slowly and, with a smile on her handsome face, takes the moist hand I did not have time to wipe on my borrowed trousers. She gives my hand a warm squeeze, then pulls me toward her gently, saying, "Oh, Travis, let's not be formal. Let's start this off right. Come and give me a hug."

I lean into a subtle perfumey warmth and hover my cheek near hers. My nose touches the wispy hair at her temple. I lightly rest my hands on her shoulders wondering if she will recoil from my criminal touch. I hold my breath, close my eyes, and . . . hold. Her cheeks have flushed, her eyes have misted, her hands tremble a little.

She says, "It's so good to finally see you. I've thought about you so often over the years and wondered . . . how you were doing."

Oh, the world of things we do not say. The things we think but cannot utter. This woman knows where I have been. Not even a man as private as my father could conceal such a thing from his second wife. It's clear, to me at least, from the way she sits composed before me, made up and yet so undone, that she has imagined me incarcerated and wondered what it was like. But of course she can't say so.

I set my feet a little wider and mumble, "Thank you for inviting me." I stand in front of them aware of my borrowed trousers bagged at the knees, my cuffs high and showing too much sock, the faint fish smell rising from my hands, a scabbed razor cut high on my right cheek where I tried too hard to square off a sideburn. I try to see me as they do now and fail completely.

My father clears his throat, a message. *Enough of this.* He did not foresee so much emotion at the starting line. He says, "Well, Travis, you can see what we're having. There's a martini for you, or Mary can bring you some iced tea or a Coke. Anything you'd like."

I see the half-full martini pitcher on the campaign table. I like the way the cold sweat runs down its crystal sides onto the napkin-draped silver tray. A long, glass stirring rod sticks out of it, looking vaguely medical. I say, "I'd like one of those, but you should know that I'm three years shy of the legal drinking age."

My father the lawyer, an officer of the court, gives me a complicated look. Is he a little insulted to be reminded of the age of his only child? Or is he wondering if he really ought to turn a felon loose on a pitcher of martinis? He says, "Son, I'm guessing this won't be your first encounter with alcohol."

Has he heard about me drinking with Emil out behind Big Sam's? The Widow knows about it. The warm wind that blows up and down US 98 carries messages. I look into my father's eyes, nod yes to his offer, and he pours me a martini, asking, "Olive or onion?" It's a long way from here to white moonshine with Emil at midnight on the loading dock.

I have no idea what is best. "Whatever's best," I tell him. He skewers an onion with a solid silver toothpick. Eleanor watches as though my father and I are unfolding some ancient sacred text in a room full of lighted candles and murmured prayers. *And Yea, they partook of the first martini.* I take the drink from my father's hand, look into his legal eyes again, sip, mull, swish, swallow, and know the revelation of one of life's very good things. My first martini is just plain damned good. I smile and say, "I like it."

My father nods, smiles gravely, and says, "The trick is to like it just the right amount."

It's a moral lesson, a chapter from my father's favorite book— *Moderation in Most Things.*

All three of us are touching martinis to our lips, and Eleanor is watching me across the rim of hers with an almost maternal interest, when we hear the old-fashioned pull bell tinkle at the front door. With the second rapturous sip of gin bathing my tongue, I reflect that my dinner invitation, the parchment my father brought me that night at the Widow's washhouse, said nothing about additional guests.

I can feel my face reddening with alcohol and fear. My buried senses know it before my mind tells me that Delia stands out on the gallery waiting for the maid to open the door. My mind doesn't have to wait long. Three rooms away, the rising lilt and teasing threat of Delia's voice sing out, and though we can't tell her words, her music affects us all. My father cocks his head to the side like a scout in the jungle. Something about his little sister's arrival puts him on alert. Eleanor sets down her martini as though it is an indiscretion and smooths the front of her white linen blouse. She arches both hands at the wrists and glances at her rings and bracelet like a woman steeling herself for a rival.

Delia enters the room like a butterfly looking for the single perfect place to perch in a rose garden. No, that's not right. A butterfly is a fast yellow flicker, and she's moving slowly, fanning herself with a hand as languid as a blossom on a broken daisy stalk. How glad she is to be out of the heat! I haven't moved. In this garden, I'm a weed. Delia sees me, and a slow, sweet smile takes over her face. She comes at me, arms aimed straight out. She grabs me hard, hugs and rocks me, reaching up and placing a hand too softly to the side of my face and pulling our two dizzy heads together. Our hug lasts too long. My eyes are closed tight. Inside my chest pressed to hers, I feel us as two mad, trapped creatures, not embracing but circling each other in a space that is too small.

She steps back, thrusts me roughly away, and, stormy-eyed, says, "Travis, it's been so long. And I've missed you. Did you know that?" I smile, my face raging red, my tongue stuck to the roof of my mouth. "Look at him," Delia says too loudly for just the four of us here. "All these years and he doesn't have a thing to say to his ole pal Delia, the girl who got him through one hell of a long summer when he was just a baby boy."

I know I have to speak. My father's eyes move gravely from my red face to Delia's and back again. So many messages, so many questions hover in the air. What does my father know about that summer six years ago? I'm guessing nothing, unless Grandpa Hollister spoke some word of caution about me or about Delia. Delia's message to me, the secret code beneath her entering words, is clear: *Protect me.*

"It's good to see you, Aunt Delia. Really good." Bootless, stupid words.

How can words measure such times as this? My Delia Book is full of words I have chosen carefully, words I have examined from every angle by an illegal flashlight under the covers of a bed in a penal institution, and I know they are inadequate too. I glance at Eleanor who seems to approve of my stopped-up mouth. I add, "I have wonderful memories of the summer we spent together."

"Well," Delia says, her face taking on a seriousness that sends me back to Sunday mornings when she was an angel faking piety in church, "some bad things happened that summer, but mostly we had fun, didn't we, Travis?"

When she mentions trouble, my father and Eleanor search deeply into the lucid pools of their martinis. We all know she means Bick Sifford's unfortunate accidental fall from Widow Rock, and maybe the town's leading attorney and his wife also remember the death of an obscure box factory worker in a fire on an old farm far outside of town.

We're all relieved when we hear a man's voice from the foyer. It's a musical, cordial drawl, pleasantries exchanged with the maid. There's a world of who he is in that voice, money from youth, a good if rascally college fraternity, never any worries about clothes or cars or invitations to the right places or his place among the right people. My father is smarter, burned hard in war, and willing to work long into nights when Templeton Tarleton is well into his cups at the country club, but still, I know that when Templeton finally comes through the parlor door grinning his first-tee-on-Saturday-morning grin, my father will be somehow at a loss. And probably even he won't know exactly why this man married to his sister always seems to have him at a disadvantage.

Templeton Tarleton stops not far from the door with a teasing reproach in his grin. "Well," he says, "I see y'all are already well into the principal pleasure of the evening. Anything left in that pitcher?" He does a loose-jointed, comic lean backward, then comes on at us, looking mostly at me. He stops outside our family circle, waiting to be introduced. I look at Delia, who looks into her martini.

My father does the honors. "Temp, this is my son, Travis. Travis, this is Temp Tarleton, Delia's husband."

SEVENTEEN

The hand I give Temp Tarleton contains the ancient potential to seize his throat and crush out his life. My smile and wide eyes tell him, *Look out, bastard!* but he doesn't notice. He gives me the surprisingly strong grip that I suppose comes from repeatedly seizing a five iron, smiles like a frat boy sizing up a pledge, and says, "Welcome back, Trav. It's good to meet you after all these years." Then he gets what I think he would call *really serious*, to let me know that all in him is not jest, and says, "Seriously now, Delia and I are looking forward to getting to know her long-lost nephew. But I guess she knew you pretty well when you were a boy, so I . . ." He seems to lose his way, then finds it. "We want to see you out at the house real soon."

And oh, the thoughts that whipsaw through my skull. I could tell him how well I know Delia. Speak of nights before she was his wife, nights when she was mine, even mention that I've already been "out at the house." For one crazy second, I almost say something, give him some evil hint, but my teeth clamp down. Temp Tarleton and I declare the handshake a draw and let go of each other. We step back, and my father's hand, holding a martini for Temp, intrudes between us. Temp reaches for the drink like it's a warm handshake from an old friend. He sips, nods at my father with appreciation, then turns to me and winks, the Conspiracy of the Confirmed Brotherhood of the Martini. Temp sips again, swallows, and sighs. "First one of the evening," he declares to any who will listen.

Eleanor looks at her watch, rises, and says, "I'll just go and check on things in the garden. Travis, why don't you come with me?"

Because I want to stay here and feast my eyes on my Delia. "Yes

ma'am," I say. Why didn't I see this coming? My stepmother, or whatever she is, and I are going to have a conversation. I look over at my
father. His embarrassment tells me that he did see this coming, that,
in fact, he and Eleanor have discussed it. Either she said, *Lloyd, at
some point during the evening, I want a moment alone with Travis, just
to let him know I have no desire to replace his mother.* Or he said, *Eleanor, at some point during the evening, I think it would be a good idea for
you and Travis to have some time alone together so you can let him know
you want to show him kindness, but you understand that he already has a
mother.* No, the last few words are too direct, crass even, and certainly
unkind to Eleanor. The sentence would have ended more in this vein:
. . . but that you understand he still has . . . feelings for his mother. So much
in that pause, my father letting silence intervene between himself and
the inadequacy of language.

I try for a last taste of Delia's eyes, some message from her about
the evening that stretches on before us, but she is looking only at
Temp with a kind of resolute attachment that I understand much
better than he does. So I follow Eleanor down a hallway, through
the formal dining room, through a set of French doors that let onto
a screened back gallery, and down some mossy redbrick steps to a
backyard half the size of a football field.

Eleanor walks quickly now. Back in the parlor she was a minor
player. Out here, she's in charge. Ahead of us under a live oak that
must be a hundred years old is a gazebo as big as a bandstand, and on
it, three steps up from the grass, is a round table set for five. Paper lanterns, unlit as yet, hang from the rafters under the gazebo's roof. They
move in a listless breeze, and so do the lacy points of the big white
cloth that drapes the table. Eleanor stops to let me catch up. When
I stand beside her on the brick path, she surveys the stage where our
dinner will be played and says, "What do you think, Travis? Is it too
hot to eat outside?"

I know this is a serious question. She could, if she wanted to, have
everything moved back inside, and she might if I tell her to. Not that
I would have the temerity. Another thought occurs to the busboy

standing beside this handsome and expensive woman. It's about the servants, whoever they are, huffing and sweating their way across the forty yards of lawn carrying food and drink to our party. I say, "No ma'am, I don't think it's too hot." I look over at her. Our short walk has caused little beads of sweat to sprout at her temples and upper lip.

She sighs. "Summers here are beautiful in so many ways, but being outside never feels as good as it looks, does it?"

She turns to me, tilting her head to the side the way cats do when they don't understand some human mystery.

"How did you meet my father?" I ask her.

She rights her head, taking the shock of my question. When she's over it, I can see she's glad we are onto something a little more purposeful than the weather. She says, "I met him at a tea dance in San Diego. That's where I grew up. Your father was at Camp Pendleton, and it was just before he shipped out for the Pacific Islands. The dance was at the Del Coronado Hotel. We liked each other, and exchanged addresses, but things being the way they were then, I thought I'd never see him again."

I say, "So he went off to war and met my mother in Japan, and that's how I happen to be standing here in your garden."

There's a little hardening around her mouth that's not unattractive (as Dr. Janeway would say), and she responds, "Yes, that's right. And later, after your mother went back to San Francisco to be with her people there, your father and I got back in touch." She names the year when they got back in touch. Her way of letting me know there was no unseemly haste, as old Hamlet would have put it.

I calculate a three-year interval between the time when my mom started singing in Japanese again and my dad and Eleanor got back in touch. I don't know what to say. Several things occur to me. *Well, you and my father seem well suited to each other. He and my mother certainly weren't. Well, my father was certainly not a man well suited to wartime romance. It looks as though the peacetime effort is the better of the two.* I look past Eleanor's delicately sweating face at the gazebo with its wafting tablecloth and paper lanterns slowly winding and unwinding on their strings. I turn and look back at the wealthy house, light pouring from its windows now that the sun has fallen below the rooftops across the street. I turn back to Eleanor. "You and my father have done very well for yourselves here. I think this is what he always wanted, and I don't think he could have ever had anything like it with my mother. She must have been something he did when he was a little crazy." I know she thinks I mean the war, and I do, sort of, but I also mean crazy in love, and I know what that means, and for the first time in my life I think it might be something I have in common with my father.

Eleanor isn't exactly pleased with what I've just said, but I can see in her eyes that it's acceptable. She and I will move on from here to someplace we can both at least tolerate. She says, "Your father and I get along very well. We have a stable and satisfying life here, though I am more used to the possibilities of a larger city than he is." She reaches out and takes my arm and turns me back toward the house. "And Travis, you might be surprised to learn how deep the affection can be between people who seem very old to you now. You'll be as old as we are someday, you know."

"If I make it," I say. I'm not sure where that comes from. Guys in reform school talk about dying young, and I knew a few who did.

Eleanor looks at me sharply. Maybe she knows I'm referring to my criminal past. She lifts her chin and narrows her eyes in a way that communicates certainty. "Young man," she says, "you'll live to a ripe old age and someday inherit all of this." She sweeps her hand out grandly at the house and yard.

"If I behave myself?"

"Possibly." She looks back at the gazebo. "It's too hot out here. I think I'll have the staff move us back inside. What do you think?"

I smile at her. "Fine with me either way. I'm adaptable. Where I've been you have to be."

"I think you'll find," she says in a tone not quite grim, "that's true of just about every place."

EIGHTEEN

We're all at the table in the formal dining room, contemplating bowls of something called She Crab Soup, a specialty of Charleston where Eleanor's cook, a dignified and austere Black man named Axel Timm, grew up and learned his trade. Around the table the faces glow in various pinkish hues, the result of settling into a good time, starting a second martini, the anticipation of the good wine to come, and, I suppose, some relief because Travis the Prodigal has turned out to be basically bearable. My hands rest in my lap, and I watch Eleanor to see if there will be a prayer before the first taste of soup, and if not that, to see which of several spoons she will lift from the embroidered tablecloth. Even my reading of novels about people who grew up on the Main Line, went to prep school, and joined eating clubs at Princeton, did not prepare me for so many spoons. When Eleanor forgoes prayer and selects a spoon from above her plate, I wait to see if all agree that she is correct, and thus I am the last at the table to taste Axel Timm's divine concoction of the meat and eggs of the female blue crab.

After tucking into the soup (and noticing that all but I dip the spoon away rather than dragging it forward), I lift my second martini and sip. I have decided to keep up with, or rather not to exceed, my father. My glass, about half empty now, matches his exactly. Setting it down carefully, I see that he is watching me, and I'm guessing that he knows exactly what I'm doing—playing the mimic and learning as I go. I don't know how he's taking it all. Not much, least of all approval, was ever very clear in his eyes.

Temp looks up from his soup. "My compliments to the chef," he says to Eleanor, making his brown eyes and grin big with apprecia-tion. I can hear Temp's second martini in the loosening of his voice.

Eleanor says, "Axel *is* a treasure. I can't tell you how many of my *good friends* have tried to steal him away from me."

Temp says, "I know what keeps him here. Aside from the fact that you appreciate him so much, he knows you have the most gas-tronomically sophisticated dinner guests in town." Temp surveys the table for our general approval. His eyes linger on me, and I see in them—it's unmistakable—how lucky he thinks I am to make this roster of wonderful guests.

Eleanor's smile is a little scolding. "I suspect it's my paying him exactly twice what he'd earn anywhere else that keeps him around. But I'll tell you, I watch him walk away from here some evenings, and I see the curtains moving in the front windows as he passes, and I'm just so scared that one of my neighbors is going to dash out with a handful of cash, and that will be the last I'll see of our Mr. Timm." El-eanor looks at my father, probably because it is he, not she, who pays Axel Timm. Her eyes are full of gratitude, but there's also the gleam of her own domestic vainglory. She's thinking, *None of this happens without me.*

And I feel very much like an actor in this family play, some com-bination of a lost boy who has stumbled upon the right path at last, a boy who could perform at least a passable role in this life, and a com-plete fraud, the impostor who will return after midnight to steal the silver. Hiding behind my soup spoon and a smile of she-crab appreci-ation, I look over at Delia. The last of the Saga of Axel Timm is play-ing out. She seems uninterested, unusually subdued, and I wonder if others notice, or if they are used to the mercury that is Delia. Six years ago, she was the life of every party. Is this new Delia the real one, or just a face she is showing, or unable not to show, because I am here?

She's wearing a sleeveless white cotton dress, low-cut, firm around her waist and breasts, but flowing full down her long legs. A single strand of pearls hugs her neck. As her head rises and falls, the lowest few gleaming pearls play with the valley between her breasts, and that's where my eyes go when they are not on her face. Her skin glows under the pinkish light from the chandelier above our heads, but really it seems to me that the light comes from inside her. Our eyes have only met twice since she gave me that first show-off family hug. Both times I have sent her Travis, all of him, but she's given back only her public Delia. She's with the others here, not me, mostly with the man I cannot yet bring myself to call a husband. As the talk goes around the table about the country club, my father's legal practice, Temp's adventures in local politics, I watch her hands. They rest in her lap, but rise above the table to manage fork or spoon, and sometimes to rest beside her plate an inch or two from Temp's arm or hand. She doesn't touch him. Never a pat or a reassuring glide of palm on forearm. I'm glad at first, and then I'm worried. I'm worried for her. It's terrible to be an impostor among the people who should love you, even if one of them is Temp Tarleton.

I haven't said much, didn't plan to. If I had a plan, it was to fit in, to learn, to see if there's really a place for me here, at least for a while. I lift my glass of red wine and take a long drink, and then notice my father's glass. Somewhere in the last half hour, I have passed him in the race to moderation. The wine feels warm in my belly, and the mysterious ruby fumes rise to the root of my tongue, and before I know it the words are out, "So, Temp, how did you and Aunt Delia happen to meet?"

I catch Temp with his mouth open, his front teeth slicing asparagus that drips yellow hollandaise sauce. He's listening to my father talk about an upcoming meeting of the zoning board and some deed restrictions under appeal. It's nothing I understand. There's a moment when all sound stops, and everyone acknowledges in one way or another that Travis the Prodigal has made a social error. I have interrupted my elders and betters. My father looks at me more puzzled than annoyed, then looks pointedly at my wineglass. Temp laughs, saving us all from further embarrassment. I glance at Delia. Her eyes burn holes in my face. *Don't.*

Temp says, "We met in college, Travis." He gives me his fraternity-boy grin. The grin is a little broader than might be proper, suggesting that Delia was really something to meet back in college. A knockout. He says, "She was the Sweetheart of Sigma Chi, just like the song says."

He's about to go on with this rhapsody, but I ask him, "Were you in Sigma Chi?"

He grins again, this time raffishly, and says, "No, I was a Deke." He looks around the table. We're all supposed to know what it means to be a Deke. The message I'm taking away is that even Temp wasn't quite good enough for the Sweetheart of Sigma Chi. Temp puts his hand on top of Delia's, rigid on the table. He squeezes, and she squeezes back, hard. I can see the effort in the tendons at her wrist. The smile on her face is phony nostalgia for the old college days. Temp says, "Your Aunt Delia was the prettiest girl at Chapel Hill."

I look at him. "Were you a dreamboat, Temp?"

"A what? A dream . . . ?" He looks at Delia, his eyebrows comically elevated.

I say, "It's a thing Aunt Delia used to say. It means a really good-looking guy. Like you . . . *Uncle* Temp." Calling him uncle is inspired. I don't know where it came from.

He looks at Delia again. He grins, inviting her to say he's a dream-boat. She's still holding his hand, hard. She says, "Travis, that's just old slang. Nobody says that anymore."

I say, "I guess I haven't kept up with what's cool."

Now that she's spoken to me, I can look into her eyes. I do, and they come back at me fierce, then fade out like signal lights on a black ocean. They've sent their message: *Shut up, Travis.*

I say, "What did you study in college, Aunt Delia?"

Her eyelids flutter as if she's trying to remember something from long ago. It wasn't that long ago. Her voice is tired when she says, "I just did general studies the first two years like everybody else." She looks over at Temp who nods at her, then at all of us, affirming the everlasting value of general studies.

I put some extra earnestness into my voice: "What about later?

What did you specialize in? Doesn't everybody have a major in college?" After all, I'm a guy who might go to college someday and further apply what I learned in reform school where I made furniture for state office buildings.

Delia looks down at her mostly uneaten portions of rib roast and asparagus, then back up at me, searching for the source of my questions, the destination I have in mind. She says, "Travis, honey, I dropped out of college after two years to marry Temp. He was already in his first year of law school. He needed me more than I needed to keep on grinding those old books. None of that meant anything to me anyway."

Before I can say anything, or Delia can go on about the uselessness of a college education compared to the joys of marriage to a young legal scholar, Temp puts his arm around her, pulls her close, and gives her forehead the kiss of a man who knows a sacrifice when he sees one and appreciates it. He says, "This ole darlin' gave up life as the heartbreaker of Chapel Hill and moved in with this poor ole addle-brained lawyer in the making, and we lived on tuna sandwiches and love until I finished the ole Juris Doctor. She sure did brighten up my dreary existence, but she cast a pall over the lives and prospects of thousands of my former fellow students." He grins again, just short of lascivious. "All those poor freshmen with no more Delia Hollister to long for."

Delia shrugs off his hug, turns and gives him a *you're impossible* frown. She says, "Prospects, my ass," then looks over at Eleanor, who only looks at my father. I expect him to come out with a *Now, Delia,* or something, to let us all know that Delia's posterior is not a proper topic for Eleanor's table, but he only looks at me, then again at my wineglass. The message is clear. I wouldn't be asking these questions if I hadn't gone a half glass over the line. I lift the glass and drink. Something's going on here, and I'm not in on it. Either it's not a good thing that Delia dropped out of college to marry, or there are elements of the tale, prospects, that nobody here wants to discuss. I'm on the outside, and for now that's where I want to be, but I know how discoveries are made. Delia and I will talk, alone.

I drink more wine. My glass is almost empty, and I know I won't get a refill. I'd ask, but it would be hard if I were turned down. My head feels a little loose on the stalk of my neck, and when I turn one way or another to see the faces around the table, it seems that my eyes slide in their sockets. Otherwise, I'm all right. In fact, I feel very good about things so far. I know now how Eleanor and my father met and later became a couple, and I know the College Idyll of Delia and Temp. Nobody here tonight seems to want to know anything at all about me.

The voice in my head is about to provide me with something else to say, something like, *Wouldn't anyone like to ask me a question about the last six years?* but before I can repeat what the voice says, Delia looks into my eyes and spills her wine. Dark red splashes into her plate, eddies over her uneaten roast beef, cascades onto the white tablecloth, and drips into Temp's lap. And Temp jumps like a rattlesnake has sunk its fangs into his crotch. He's dabbing at his gray slacks with his napkin, but I'm watching Delia slowly lower her head into her hands and begin to sob.

Instantly I am at her side with my napkin, mopping, dabbing, setting things right, my hands taking small liberties with Delia's shoulders, her upper arms, as I do what I have learned so well in the restaurant business. I clean.

Eleanor rises and stands beside me, behind Delia. She puts both hands on Delia's shoulders, her lips beside Delia's ear. "It's all right, dear. It's nothing. Just a little wine, and the tablecloth isn't anything special, so please don't worry about it." Eleanor speaks with a certain weariness, as though she has said just these words to Delia on other occasions.

Delia doesn't look up at her, or at anything else, it seems. She stares into her own hands as though to ask them why they blundered with a wineglass. I take one of her hands, dab it with my napkin, and place it into her lap. Then I press into her palm the note I have written. My invitation to her. I feel her hand close reflexively around the small square of paper. We all hear her frightened catch of breath, but only I know why.

My father stands, looks at the three of us as though we are some obscure legal principle that is the key to a case he is trying, and says, "Why don't we all move to the garden for coffee and dessert? I imagine it's cooled off enough out there for us to enjoy the stars." My father, the stargazer. Eleanor and I step back to let Delia rise. But Delia remains sitting.

Temp has recovered sufficiently from the insult to his crotch to notice that his wife is crying. I see first annoyance, then fear in his eyes. He leans over and says to her, almost fiercely, "You're all right, Delia. Come on now, honey. Don't worry about it."

My Delia looks up at him out of the pit of her troubles. Really, she looks *into* him, as though he is smoke or fog, her eyes surprised that a man stands above her, and it seems to me that she does not recognize his face.

NINETEEN

When I get back to the Wind Motel, it's after midnight. I try, but I can't get to sleep. I lie on my saggy bed thinking about what I did tonight and how it could have gone wrong. As the weird energy of my trespassing winds down, thoughts of accidents creep in, and pretty soon I'm shaking in a sick, cold sweat. In reform school I was fascinated by accidents. I read all the newspaper stories about them I could find. About the strange, crazy things that happen to people. One January in Chicago, a young man on his way to get married walked past a tall building just as a huge sheet of ice broke loose and fell. In Birmingham, an old woman went outside carrying a bag of garbage and was mauled by a raccoon. A nine-year-old boy on his way home from school in Orlando fell through the earth into a hornets' nest as big as a steamer trunk. These things fascinated me. I was trying to understand how bad things happened, why people died who shouldn't have. I was trying to understand simple ideas like should and shouldn't and deserving or not deserving. No nine-year-old boy deserves to fall through the surface of earth into a hell of ten thousand stings and die before he knows what's happening to him, or worse, after he knows.

For a while I didn't know why these questions fascinated me. Then I realized that I knew why and didn't want to face it. I needed to see myself as the boy who fell through the surface of life into another place, a place called Delia, where everything was different, and the good things were better than anyone knew in the world above us, and the bad things were worse than up there too. And it was stranger than that even: I was trying to see myself as a sheet of ice or a hornets' nest. If I could be both the end and the means, the accident and the thing that caused it, then I was not someone who had killed two people. Not exactly. I was just part of the big shape we see only dimly, the design, the weave in which we are all strands. It was a way of thinking that kept me from going crazy for a while.

When the first sunlight comes to my window, and I hear the already lubricated Widow walking and singing to herself outside, I'm tired. More tired than I think I've ever been. I have to go to work and act normal until I see Delia again. If she comes. If she decides to meet me. I lie in the space between light and dark, imagining her right now rising from her bed and reading my note again, this time with the understanding that comes with morning. I try to see her face as she reads, and how slowly or quickly she makes up her mind, to come or not to come.

Driving my Plymouth to the river, I see all that has changed since last I came this way, farmhouses torn down or let go to ruin, working fields overgrown with scrub oak and palmetto, tracts of green that stretched to the horizon cut through by the black excretion of the paving machines. And gone with the green is the tired, sun-beaten, barely-making-it feeling of the land. A machine-made prosperity has replaced Poor Old Nature. Not so many horses, but sleeker, finer ones. No mules anymore, and the few wagons I see are broken down in junk piles or full of flowerpots with signs nailed to them that say, *ANTIQUES EMPORIUM TWO MILES.*

Progress is not all bad. The perpetual-motion machine of turkey buzzards wheeling the high blue sky is gone, so I guess there's not so much death lying on the ground. Builders have staked out subdivisions. Electrical weather heads stick up among the broom sage and dog fennel, and sidewalks and driveways lie waiting for their houses. I remember when we lived in the wheat field in Omaha, how our house was the last human trickle drying up in a vacancy that seemed to roll on forever. Maybe this place will grow in good ways.

The sand road that leads to Widow Rock is paved now, and wider.

The place where people used to park, their tires beating down grasping vines and weeds, is a neat asphalt square bordered by creosoted railroad ties. There's a picnic table in a little clearing under some tall pines, and a trash barrel full of bullet holes. Some things don't change.

My Plymouth snubs its front tires against a tie, and I kill the engine and listen to its harsh echoes dying off in the windy trees. My heart fills with a dark joy when I get out of the car and smell the river. That wild spicy scent of a rushing road full of living things. I'm alone here and not sure if I'm glad about it. I stand on the warm asphalt of the little parking lot wondering. Has she been back here since the night Bick Sifford danced the rock edge and did not stay in the world? Has she relived that night here or elsewhere or not at all? So many questions. Who is she now? Is she the Delia I knew or some other one? And who am I? I kick the pavement, leaving a scuff mark. Should I wait here or climb up? Will I look more like a fool down here or up there if she does not come at all?

Finally, it's the river's wild scent and its voice like the far-off laughter of young girls on a summer night that makes up my mind. I climb.

The going is easier and less dangerous than it was six years ago. Root footholds and stair steps are shoed into the earth, and there are places where you can step off the path and rest. Halfway up, I stop to listen for the sound of an engine pulling in below. Nothing but the wind in the pines and the whisper of the river. She's late. She's not coming. My lungs burn with hard breathing, with disappointment, anger, then the old melting clemency forms in my belly, and I start up the path again. If she doesn't come, there will be a reason.

The tree door at the top of the white limestone shelf is much as I remember it, a circle of light ahead of me, wider maybe, the pine boughs a little ragged for the hands that have swung them apart to expose this natural surprise. And swinging them wide now, I see the vault of bright blue sky, feel the cool dangerous wind of this high place on my sweating face, and follow a trail of wet footprints on the hot white limestone to the naked woman lying out at the edge.

Oh, how she rocks me! Her footprints and remembering my own cut and bleeding boy feet wetting this rock as I ran toward Bick are the hardest shocks. But this dizzy, guilty feeling fades when she turns her face to me, and the blond hair that frames her pale cheeks swings thickly wet and dripping. "Surprised?" she asks in a voice that's warm, low, and tired.

Surprise she always was. Why did I think a house like an English castle and a husband like Temp Tarleton could change that? And she isn't naked, just wearing the slightest bikini I've ever seen in a disturbingly flesh-colored fabric.

She swings her long legs around toward me from where they hang out into infinity, and says, "I swam over from the other side. The path up here is still hard to find." She means the path I climbed in the dark after swimming the river naked to find my Delia with Bick Sifford.

I want so many things. I don't know what to do first, or say. My mind and mouth shut, and all I do is step toward her, looking down at her water-beaded face and dripping hair. I want to know how she's changed. So bad, I want to know what I've missed, the years of her that have passed without me. When she was sixteen and pale with black hair (she never tanned and never wanted to), she was all of the women in movies who don't get the man or don't want him. Now, she's tanned with blond hair from a bottle, but there's a joke hiding in this change. The blue eyes framed by the wet blond hair make fun of male dreams.

The silence stretches on between us. Her smile is cool and unafraid, and her eyes are dark blue. The makeup she wore last night has washed off in the river and her eyes are windows inviting me into the house of Delia. I remember what her eyes have told me. I've seen fun and carefree joy and quiet brooding and fear in them. And when we held each other, as we certainly should not have done, I saw in them a bridge for souls that called me over, and I sent Travis into Delia and accepted her into me.

She looks out across the gorge, that dangerous drop she showed me six years ago, telling me the story of the town's namesake, the

Widow Cray, who climbed this rock and jumped to her death because a man would not leave her alone. She says, "Travis, don't look at me like that."

"Like what?" I ask, but I know. We both know. It's my wanting. Then I say, "I didn't look at you, I only looked into your eyes." *You were younger than I am now when I knew you, and in those days I thought of you as grown. I asked you all my hidden questions, I believed all the answers you gave me. You were wisdom. I carried your secrets, and you carried mine, and for that reason I had to save you.*

Delia's limbs are filled out now. That loose coltish connection of bone and sinew, muscle and skin, that begs words like *gambol* and *loll*, is mostly gone, only a memory here and there, a dimple above the knee and a fragile narrowness at the wrist. There's a plenitude to her now that is almost ready to be called Mother. She was once all youth, all risk, all possibility, and now she is all garden wanting seed, and I am fighting an erection that will explode my worn old Levi's and reach to the tops of these pines that wave above our heads in the wind that pushes up cool from the river.

"You look good," I say. I try to keep lust from my voice. I want her to hear only the appreciation of a sculptor stepping back exhausted from stone. "Like I knew you would." And then I'm shy because my words have spilled out unplanned and they are far from the poetry I had imagined myself telling after the years of keeping her flame.

She turns back to me, the water drying on her face, a glowing ripeness in the skin she pulls away from the sun, and she seems annoyed. And I know it's because we are talking about her. Being the center of things was always necessary and always trouble for my Delia.

"You spilled your wine on purpose?" It's a cold question, and like a lot of things that have happened between her and me, it seems to have fallen on us out of the sky.

"To make someone stop asking stupid questions."

Shame is in the pit of my stomach so sudden and strong it almost bends me over. There's no lust anymore, only shame. I could tell her that the wine made me ask about her and Temp. I could say the questions seemed innocent at the time, but I remember creeping through the house she shares with Temp Tarleton and how the darkness, like the wine, seemed to permit anything. That's crime. There are a hundred ways to believe you've got permission.

"There's trouble between you and Temp."

She looks at me hard and long, then turns back to the deep, windy fall above the river. "That's not your business, Travis."

There. She said my name. There's a sudden rising in my head, and the straight line of the horizon tilts like the wings of an airplane speeding away from me. It takes me a second or two to recover, which I guess means covering up. Oh, the word of me, *Travis*, sweet from her mouth!

She pats the hot white stone beside her. "Come and sit," she says, and I remember how she invited a little boy into her bed at night when the storms came, that patting of the counterpane. *This is your place beside me. Take it.*

I walk over and sit close beside her, and she pulls her knees up to her chin and hugs them with her firm, perfect arms. I feel her beside me, I don't look. We have sat like this before, side by side looking away into the distance. I think she just wants us like this for a while, together and letting the past settle into the air and water around us. Then she takes a long breath, lets it out, and says, "Travis, I always expected you. I didn't know how or when, but I always knew you'd come back. It's wrong to ask why you're here, so I won't do that. I think I know why, at least some of it. If some of it is me, then I hope my part is good. I always wanted to be good for you."

I can't look at her, and I'm glad she's not looking at me. That's another way the novels are wrong. Eyes that might love or have loved can't meet when the biggest truth is told. I squeeze my eyes shut trying to stop the tears. I don't want her to see them. I want my voice steady when I tell her about the letters I wrote her, full of the parts of me that were hers. But I can't tell her, not yet.

I say, "What was it like, swimming across? Do you do it much, swim I mean? Like we used to do?"

She reaches up and shades her eyes, looks down at the river. "I guess not, Travis. I guess my river-swimming days were mostly over after you left."

"But you did it just now?"

"Yes, I did. I didn't know what it would be like meeting you up here after so long." She doesn't say it, but she means she wanted this meeting her way, not mine. That's Delia. The surprises were always hers until the last one, which was mine.

"I wish I'd seen you." I mean her swimming. How pretty that would have been.

She says, "You look good, Travis. You've grown up very well. Let me see you." She turns, and it's a family moment. She could be any aunt talking to a nephew she hasn't seen in a while. But this aunt says, "Take off your shirt and let me see those muscles."

Sure, I have them. I did a million push-ups and sit-ups in reform school and armed myself up a hundred times to the rafters of the gym, no legs. I wasn't the toughest kid at Bridgedale, not by a long way, but you don't look at me and see a pushover. I reach down and pull up my shirt, and wrestle it over my head and use the motion to dry my eyes. They're red I know, but not wet anymore when I toss my shirt away and sit there beside her bare-chested.

"Wow," she says, "look at you. Charles Atlas. Ain't nobody gonna kick sand in your face, kiddo."

And I remember how she called me Killer because I reminded her of Jerry Lee Lewis, and how, after Bick's death, she never called me that again. I'm blushing. I can feel the heat creeping up my neck because she likes the way I look. But I know she doesn't really want what an aunt wants, to see how a nephew has grown. She wants us equal. She always did. She wants the common ground you're on when your clothes are mostly off. It's hard to lie when you're like this. Maybe she knows this because she grew up around women covered in layers of stifling cloth, all poof and spoof and perfume, and even when their bosoms heaved and you could see their gorgeous ankles under those crinolines, you still felt miles away from the truth.

"Why didn't you answer my letters?"

She squeezes her eyes shut like they hurt. "I didn't get them, honey. Daddy took them and threw them all away. He never said anything, but I knew you must have written to me, and I knew he'd never let me have your letters."

"Did you write to me?" Maybe she's got letters hidden away. Maybe there's a Travis Book.

"Only in my heart." She lowers her eyes to mine now, and they burn into me, and I can see the tears forming. I don't want her to cry. I never liked it even though her crying first brought us together. I don't know what to say. I've had this talk with her a thousand times inside my own head, and it went one way and another. Sometimes I was angry at her (but we got over it); other times I was just sad for the past and happy for the here and now. Here, now, even in the sad power of her eyes, I can't help but think: *You could have found a way. Some way.*

"What did you do?" I ask, my voice low and cold. "After I left Widow Rock."

She stares off at the trees across the river. A cloud goes over the sun and the river gorge in front of us changes from white rock and brown water to gray and black. "I just got sadder and sadder," she says, "until I couldn't even get out of bed. It started right after you left, and it kept on until about the time I was supposed to start school, and so Mama and Daddy sent me away to a school for girls, a kind of prep school in Atlanta."

I say, "I went to a fancy school too, called Bridgedale."

She looks at me, confused, and I see that no one has told her where I've been. She and I could walk down the main street of Widow Rock right now arm in arm, and we'd just be aunt and nephew and no one the wiser. No one but my father to know I've been locked up for stabbing Jimmy Pultney.

She says, "Travis, you shouldn't have stuck that note in my hand. You could have called me some other way. It was a mean thing to do." She looks at me stern, the way she used to when I was a kid and she was just my aunt and not My Delia. It's the way she'll someday be with her own kids. And we both know the note reminded her of more than me. A note left in her car in her father's driveway called her to meet Bick Sifford the night he died.

"What happened to Grandma and Grandpa?" I pick up my shirt and put it on. "I didn't see them in the phone book."

I can see all the questions tumbling into her mind: How long have I been back? What have I done since my arrival here? How much do I know about the life she's living now? She says, "They moved down south like everybody else, Travis. They live in New Port Richey now. Daddy bought a little house on the river down there, right where it empties into the gulf. He mostly fishes all day and Mama cooks for him, and she has a little flower garden, and she volunteers at the local library, reading to the children." She tells me this in a kind of memorized way, just as she's told it before. Maybe she wants to keep them simple in her mind, her parents gone off to retirement like two cartoon characters, one holding a fishing pole, the other a library book. But I know they hold all the memories, especially Grandpa, things only he and I share. "What about your brother Lloyd? Is he happy with Eleanor?"

She hugs her legs tight and looks around as though someone might be hiding in the trees. All of the swimming wet has evaporated from her now, and I can see sweat starting on her forehead and at her temples. She says, "As far as I know, your dad's as happy as a male Hollister can ever be. He's doing very well, Travis. He's the local lawyer. Oh, there are others . . ." *Your husband included.* ". . . but he's *the* one. He's the war hero and the son of the sheriff who was the law back before there was a police department. He's general counsel for the box factory now, and he's making oodles of money in real estate. That's what everybody's doing around here." She looks down at her toes, and I remember how she used to wiggle them and then look up at me like she'd just discovered how they worked. I think of all the things we're not saying: box factory instead of Sifford Container and Packaging Company, for example.

"Nobody told you anything about me?"

She nods, her head still down.

"And you didn't ask?"

She looks up, defiance in her red cheeks and her cold eyes. "I couldn't. How could I? How much of that could I have opened up?" Her eyes go shy now. "Did you really go to a fancy school?"

I have to be careful now. I'm not bitter about the past. The thinking I did about means and ends did not make me bitter. Back in my accident phase, I decided that I hadn't earned bitterness. A sheet of ice is only ice. There has to be a piece of good in you to deserve bitterness, and mostly I have considered myself completely bad. But sometimes I can see it far off, the place of bitterness and anger. It glows red out there and sometimes it calls to me. I don't want to go.

So I straighten the ruffled smile that shapes my lips and compose a neutral face and say, "That was a joke. I spent six years incarcerated in reform school. When I left . . . you and went back to Omaha, a kid tried to kill me, and I stabbed him, but he didn't die, and the State of Nebraska didn't believe I was defending myself. They thought it would be best for me to stay away from other people for a while." *So they put me inside that fence with a lot of what were not entirely people.*

"I'm so sorry, Travis. So sorry that happened to you."

And she is. I see a deep sorrow in her eyes, though I don't want sympathy. Sympathy confuses love. I wave my hand at the past, at Bridgedale, like it was nothing. "I was lucky," I say, "in a way. The kid I stabbed didn't kill me, and I didn't kill him."

She shakes her head, sorry for me, and confused by what I've said about luck.

I try again: "After what happened, there was nowhere else for me to be. Some people said I got off light."

Delia stands up. She reaches behind her and brushes dust from the bottom of her bikini. A loving look comes over her face, and for a moment I see Grandma Hollister standing in front of me, Delia's inheritance of her soft caring way. She says, "But Travis, where are you staying now? Who are you with?"

This is hard for me. The habit of hiding is hard to let go. In reform school you are officially hidden away, and when you get out it seems that your natural home is the distance between yourself and other people. I could lie to her, and maybe I should, but we never lied to each other, and once you start it's hard to stop. I say, "I've got my own place. It's not much, but it's mine. I've got a car and a job too." I think of telling her that I saw her with Temp at Big Sam's. I watch her wide blue eyes taking this all in. It's like my words are waking her up. The meaning of all this—me back here—is like a loud noise in a room where she's been sleeping.

She says, "But how long have you been back?" For the first time she looks scared. Is she wondering what else I've done since I came home? She lifts her right hand to her lips, bites the nail of her little finger, catches herself, and lets it go. "Are you sure coming back is the right thing?"

Her voice is the sound of six years ago when she was scared of boys like Bick and the things they could make her do. I have to look away. I don't want her scared of me. I didn't come home to bring those boys back.

I reach out and put my hand on her shoulder, and I feel the deep thrilling life in her. I raise the back of my hand to her cheek and move it upward, just brushing the light between our two skins. I say, "I didn't come back here to hurt you. I—"

"But you could." She says it so fast, ignoring my hand hovering at her cheek. "You know that, don't you?"

My hand drops to my side. "Yes, I know it." Should I tell her I want her? Is this when I should explain how she can simplify her life? I don't even know what her life is, except for Temp Tarleton and the manor house magically transported from England. What are her secrets now? She must have them.

She steps toward me and extends her hand, and it stops an inch from my face. I can see the wet bitten spot still on the tip of her little finger, and I want it, that little dot of wet, just as it is right now. She says, "Travis, I knew you were coming. I felt you near. I saw you in a dream. That's why things aren't so good . . ."

She means the night at my father's house, the spilled wine, the sudden tears. "With Temp?" I say. *Ole Temp.* "With your husband?"

She looks at me, her eyes fierce. "All right, Travis, we've covered it now, haven't we mostly? There's been a lot of wasted time. A lot of people don't know things. There's a lot to be sorry about. So what's next? What are you going to do?"

Why not we, what are we going to do? I gave away a third of my life so far to save yours. What are you going to do with it? And do with me, since I still belong to you?

But I don't say it. I just stand there trying not to see beyond her to the place where bitterness burns with a cold fire. She waits for the space of ten heartbeats, then ten more, and then she says, "Goodbye, Travis," and turns toward the other path, the dangerous one. She'll have to swim the river again to find her car. She turns back. "Travis, don't summon me again with a dirty little note. I've had enough of men doing that."

As she disappears into the trees, a trick of light and shadow strips the skin-colored bikini from her, and she's naked. I say, "For now. Goodbye for now."

TWENTY

The walls of the barn are made of fire. Fire seethes and hisses from the old pitch pine boards and melts the tar paper that lines the cracks. Little rivers of black tar run down to the red clay floor and puddle there, catching fire. I'm trying to get out, and I know there's not much time. Soon the hissing snakes of fire that creep the walls will light the roof, and I'll be in a burning cage, dancing and running so that falling rafts of flaming wood and hay can't cover me. I make my way to the doors, the old wide double doors with rusted hinges glowing now with heat, and I try to push them open. They are never locked. Who would lock them? I push as hard as I can, with all of my strength and weight, but they don't give. I back up and charge, throwing my shoulder against them. I'm running in a rain of fire and the choking smoke of burning hay, tar, gasoline, old rags, and the oil from car parts strewn around on benches and shelves. And from behind me I hear a high shriek. A man is there, burning.

I turn. His whole body is made of fire, and he holds burning hands out to me, and I don't know what to do, and he screams again, a high wail that ends low and guttural in the back of a throat that is now only a column of flame rising out of a chest that glows like the belly of a stove in winter. The smoke is so thick I can't speak, but I tell the fire man with my eyes that I will get us out. I turn and throw myself against the doors again, and they don't give, but I can see through them. I've parted them with my wild charging, and I can see through the opening I've made, out into the cool calm night, and there is someone looking back at me. A face is pressed to the opening, looking in at what is happening. The face is mine.

I wake up standing at my little sink with my hands under the running water. Trying to cool them, I've made a mistake. I've turned on the hot, not the cold, and it burns. I look around, blinking in the dark, trying to keep the dream from coming back. Walking will wake me all the way, and the dream won't come back. I stand at the door of my tourist cabin looking out, shaking my burning hands. I step into the dark, dripping morning between my cabin and the Widow's dark bedroom windows, and I start walking in my underwear, going nowhere, just walking to stay awake, walking as far away from the burning barn as I can go. I raise my hands to my face and press them there, pressing and pulling at my eyes. I have to see Dawnell again.

"What you want, boy?"

The man comes around the side of the house fast in a half crouch, holding an ax handle in both hands and looking like he means to use it. He must have been out in the woods behind the house. I'm standing on his front porch now with one hand raised to knock. He must have heard me drive up in the Plymouth. I look around for something to use to block that ax handle if he rushes me. If he decides to split my head open.

We stand this way for a while, both of us leaning, him forward, me back, both of us half finished with something and not knowing what to do next. At least I hope he doesn't know.

I say, "I'm just here to see Dawnell. She's a friend of mine."

His face is covered with a two-day beard that looks like dirt, like he's just pulled his snout from a trough. He's wearing some kind of faded-green canvas coveralls that zip from the crotch to the neck, but the zipper stops just above his navel, and I can see one amber nipple set in a hairless chest as white as the belly of a catfish. He closes one eye like he's aiming a rifle and says, "Dawnell don't have no *friends*. She's too young to have *friends*." The way he leans on the word, we both know he thinks I'm here to carry his daughter off and grow her up fast. But for all her small years, that's the way she's always seemed to me, far more experienced than I am.

I hear feet scrape inside the house, and Dawnell's face appears in the dim beyond the rusty screen. A white oval framed in honey hair with a slash of cherry red that is her painted lips. She comes out cautiously and sees what I'm seeing, the man with the ax handle. She says, "Daddy, don't hurt the boy."

It's hard to tell what's in her voice or what the man is hearing. Some women can command men. Delia could always tell Grandpa Hollister what to do in one way or another because he loved her so much. Too much, I finally learned. This father, if that's what he is, doesn't act like he loves too much. He does a lot of *too much*, and by the look of his red eyes and blue-swollen nose, some of it is drinking, but tender love for a daughter doesn't seem to be in him.

He says, "Dawnie-ell, get on back in the house and leave this to me." He takes a step toward me. I look again for something, anything, to pick up, a thing I can use to defend myself. And now I see him better. He's lean and sinewy, and the hands that are white around the ax handle aren't shaking, but he's also about my size, and I'm less than half his age. Something I don't like and like very much starts to sing in the back of my head, starts to rumble out of my chest and into my arms and hands. It's a song about taking that ax handle away from him however I have to do it. It's a very old song about breaking bones.

A little table, hardly more than a stool, stands to my left on the porch. Like everything else here except Dawnell, it's rotting from neglect and abuse, but I see that I could sweep it up in my closest hand and block that ax handle. I see that I could swing it with both hands until it breaks into pieces or until I don't need it anymore. The man sees me looking at the table. He takes another step toward me. I smile at him. It's the crazy smile I learned when I was incarcerated.

Before I can snatch up my weapon, Dawnell shoves out through the screen door. She's wearing that same white dress, a red leather belt cinched so tight it threatens to cut her in half, and sandals the same red color as her lips and toenails. She stands between me and her father with a tired, embarrassed look on her face, and says, "Daddy, please." This man is no Grandpa Hollister. His only love is control;

she's what's left here of the wife he couldn't keep. I'm not saying he does things to her, not those things, but what I see in the way they look at each other is an old story. A girl who is her mama all over again and a father who's repeating what already didn't work. But I can see he's broken now too. There is something in that one word, *please*. She's said it to him before, and it means something only these two know.

His lean, dirty cheeks pinch down into a frown, and he makes fun of her in a high sneering voice. "Daddy, *please*." The ax handle swings down to rest beside his right leg.

I let the little table fade out of my side vision.

Dawnell turns her back to the man and faces me. She says, "You better go, boy." But she slides her eyes to the side, toward the woods, and I know what she means.

Behind her, her father says, "Who are you anyway, boy? Don't I know you? Ain't I seen you around here somewhere? Who's your daddy?"

I let him stand there in his own questions for a while, then I say, "I don't know who you've seen, sir. I've been around. And Dawnell is just what I said she is, a friend."

I look back at her and slide my eyes toward the woods.

She turns and goes back into the house without even a glance at the man with the ax handle. He says, "You're trespassing, boy. Didn't you see my sign?"

The truth is I didn't. It must be hidden, shrouded in vines like the entrance to this place. I would have ignored it anyway. I need to see Dawnell.

I get into the Plymouth and drive to the turnoff Dawnell showed me for the abandoned farmhouse, and I park where I did before and sit in the car with the radio playing.

The songs come from Birmingham and Dothan and Tallahassee and even Jacksonville sometimes, and they roll out of my tinny old radio and stream off into the pines and scrub oaks. I hear Jay and the Americans sing "This Magic Moment," and The Box Tops sing

"My Baby Wrote Me a Letter," and the Stones sing "Paint It Black." They're saying things in the songs now they didn't used to say. They're getting closer to the truth about love. It's a darker, stranger truth than I knew when I sat in my Aunt Delia's white Chevy and listened to the music of six years ago about Little Suzie and Handsome Johnny and let's go to the hop. I'm still listening for the truth about love, but not like I used to. Now I've read novels, and I've watched people I never noticed when I was twelve.

As I wait, I look at my hands, and I remember Dawnell's daddy's grip on that ax handle and my father's hands steering the boat. I think about what my hands have done, and how easy it would have been to let the old song of broken bones play, and pick up that table, and say to Mr. Briscoe, *All right, pig-snout face, what are you going to do with that ax handle before I shove it up your ass?* I'm sitting there in a kind of glorious evil stew of love music and violent reverie when Dawnell emerges like a puff of white smoke from out of the green leaves a hundred yards away at the end of a ruined cow pasture. She looks behind her, and even reaches back to adjust the branches and vines so that no one watching from where I am can see a pathway.

All the violence in me breaks like a wave over that one poor little deception of hers. I want to get out of my car and run across that field and take her in my arms and tell her that her father already knows about this place or can find it in ten of her sweet little heartbeats and it's only a matter of time until he comes here and when that happens she won't have anything. She'll be desperate like her mother, but too young to pack a pillowcase and run when the old man is asleep in his whiskey.

But I don't. I watch how she moves across the field from clump of weed to patch of grass, trying to avoid the bare earth where she might leave footprints. She finally looks up and sees me sitting behind the wheel of my Plymouth. She stops walking and smiles, and I swear she stands for a second in a pool of sunlight and reaches up and pats at her hair like an actress in a movie, some tough glamour queen speculating at herself in the mirror of a nightclub powder room. Only I'm the mirror. She's doing it for me, telling me she wants to look good for me.

I get out of the car and walk toward her, and we meet at the front door of the old house, and I can smell Dawnell's strong, cheap perfume and the moist, mushroomy odor from inside. She turns and takes my hand and gives it a light, warm squeeze, and then pushes open the door, pulling me in behind her. Inside the room, nothing has changed. In the middle, in the only empty space between the nook where her pallet and bookshelves are and the wall with the candles and pictures cut from magazines, she does a little spin and steps close to me, and this room is suddenly only the size of our mingled breath and her perfume and whatever burns from me that's left from my reverie of love and violence. She reaches her small hot hand up and takes the back of my neck, pulls my face down, and kisses me on the lips. It's not what I expected. I expected something actressy, overdone, stolen from a movie and rehearsed alone in this room. It's a sweet, brief kiss full of questions and reservations and a simple plea: *Don't hurt me, boy.*

I take the kiss and give her one back that I hope carries the right messages. It all happens so fast, and without physical hesitation, but I'm a thunderstorm inside. I haven't touched a woman, not this way, in six years, the night before my second venture into death in Widow Rock. And maybe that's not unusual. Most boys my age haven't touched women. What's unusual about me is what I've never told anyone, and never been tempted to tell, even in the bull sessions at Bridgedale when boredom and desperation could pull the worst truth or the worst lies from even the best people. What I never told is this: when I was twelve years old, I knew a woman, twice. It seemed like a miracle to me then, not just that I did it, we did it, but that anybody could, the entire act of love seemed so improbable, such a gift, and in my memory it still does. I did it with Delia, twice, and I never felt the need to do it again with anyone, though of course I've felt the urgencies all boys feel. But I waited. I hoped for Delia. I relived those moments with her a thousand times so that I would never lose them, never lose any part of any second of those two nights.

Now I'm standing in a hot, small room in a ruined house in the woods, a room full of girl things that remind me of Delia's room and those slow dreaming afternoons with her and her teenaged friends, Beulah and Caroline, and I'm holding in my arms this girl who wants so badly to be grown up.

Dawnell raises up her face to me again, her eyes closed, her cherry lips parted, and releases her sweet warm breath onto my face. She says, "Kiss me again, boy."

It's not easy, but gently I push her away from me. She holds onto me like a drowning girl whose rescuer is taking her back out to the deep water. And I say, "You can't do it this way. You can't make yourself happy this way."

Her softly closed eyes open. "How do *you* know?"

And suddenly we're at war again about who's the more experienced one.

I say, "I just know," but I'm confused. I don't half understand what I just said, where it came from. It seemed true to me.

She says, "I bet you've never even done this before."

I say, "You better *not* ever have done this before."

She says, "What do you mean?" but she knows what I mean. She turns away, her lower lip pouting down, and says, "You ain't my daddy, and you ain't my brother, so don't tell me what I can't do."

I say, "Thank God I'm not your daddy, from what I just saw. I haven't seen your brother, but I'm not hopeful I'd want to be him either."

She turns with an angry heat that surprises me. I've done something even I know never to do—get between a country girl and her family. I want to say I'm sorry, but I don't. She turns away again, still burning with her anger and her wishing we hadn't stopped. I know what she's thinking: Did I mean it when I told her father we were just friends? Don't I want her *that way?* Why am I here with her, if I don't want her that way? And I can't help being curious too, in a way that doesn't make me proud. I wonder if, young as she is, she really has done this before. Something more than spin the bottle, though God knows she'd have to walk miles with that transistor radio pressed to her ear to find a circle of kids her age to spin the bottle with, and the bottle would probably be half full of homemade whiskey.

Dawnell sits down on the little pallet like she did the last time I was here, and she stares into what little space there is between me and the wall. *Your turn*, her angry eyes are saying. I sigh, and my breath comes out with a shudder. I feel all the chemicals of anger and confusion flowing through the drains of my tensed-up body and out to whatever sea there is in me that disposes of them for now.

I say, "Is there room for two down there?"

She moves her eyes to me quick and angry, like a blue jay noticing something to eat in a nearby bush. She pulls her lower lip in from its pout. "I guess so, Mr. Big Disappointment."

I say, "You're disappointed now, but you won't be later when you think about it. And consider this later when you're thinking. Where would we be a half hour from now after letting nature take its course? We'd still be right here in this room looking at each other, or not looking, trying to figure out what comes next."

She smiles at me, and I swear it's almost a leer. "I think I know what'd come next." Of course, she means more of the same, and she's probably right, but I think she gets what I'm saying because the pout comes back, though not as big as before, and her eyes return to scanning the wall covered with James Bond and *The Man from U.N.C.L.E.*

I come over and sit next to her, and as I do I get a strange vivid memory of Delia patting the hot limestone of Widow Rock, inviting me to walk through the veil of those six years and sit beside her again. When I sit, Dawnell moves over, pressing against the wall. She reaches under the pillow and pulls out the pack of Chesterfields and the Zippo lighter. She shucks out two cigarettes, stabs one into her mouth, and reaches over with the other. She wants to put it in my mouth, something from a movie probably. I lean and let her do it. Her hand is so steady, and mine are warm and nervous. She lifts the lighter and starts to open it, and I reach out and take it from her.

"Let me do it," I say, and she looks annoyed for a second, but then she smiles, and I know what she's thinking: *Act Two, Scene Three: For the first time, the Man Lights the Woman's Cigarette.* My thumb flips up the cover of the lighter and then drops down on the little wheel that rolls across the flint and starts a fire.

I stare into the flame dancing in my hand, and I breathe in the heady vapor of the lighter fluid. I watch it so long that I can feel Dawnell growing impatient beside me, wanting Scene Three to end. I pull my eyes away from the flame and reach over and light her cigarette, watching its brown-and-white tip glow red and hearing her suck in the smoke and release her lips with a small sweet *pop*. I light my own cigarette, though a turning worm of nausea in my stomach tells me it's the last thing I need right now. I drop the lighter into her hand. She doesn't say anything, and finally I look at her. There are tears in her eyes.

I reach over and rest my hand on her shoulder. "What's the matter? Is it me? Did I do something?"

She looks at me through a blear of tears. "No, it's not you. It's just, this lighter, it belonged to my Uncle Bobby. He died young."

I should rise and leave this room. Start my car and drive as far as gas and asphalt will carry me. Spend the night in some nameless room in a town where I've never been before and no one knows me. Then rise in the morning and do it all over again. Instead, I put my arm around her. "Tell me about him," I say.

She leans into me and cries quietly, once or twice reaching up to snatch at the tears that roll down her cheeks. Her back where I touch her is hot as fire. I hold her for as long as she cries, staring at the wall of suave men in tuxedos whose knowing smirks never change. Finally, she bends and lifts the tail of my shirt and dries her eyes. She sniffles, then laughs the way people do when the feelings are over and it feels good to get beyond them.

She turns to me and says, "I was only six when he died. People always tell me I didn't really know him, but I swear I remember him. He had this wonderful car, a convertible, and he took me for rides in it. Would you like to see a picture of him?"

And again I know I should leave, but I know that if I do, I will never stop, at least not for long in one place. And where I stop, I will do harm. So I tell her, "Sure I would. If you want to show me. I don't want to upset you."

So she gets up and goes over to the bookshelf where she keeps her strange collection of high and low literature and pulls out the fattest volume, a copy of *Ben Hur*, and reaches into the vacancy, and pulls a cigar box from the space between the books and the wall. She comes back over and sits down and snuggles into me and opens the box, and the first thing we see is a faded black-and-white of a young man, maybe a year or two older than I am, standing beside a '48 DeSoto convertible. In the small, faded black-and-white photo, the young man wears baggy blue jeans, a white T-shirt, engineer boots, and a leather jacket. Most of the shots are about the same. The young man always stands with one hip shot out to the side, usually with a hand or both hands shoved down hard into the pockets of his jeans. He's trying to look tough, uninvolved, his mind elsewhere, but managing only to seem shy and hurt by the camera, what it's taking from him. Dawnell and I sort through all the pictures and some other things she has that remind her of him, a key chain he used and a small, black-and-white plastic human skull that once clamped to the steering wheel of his car so he could turn corners with one hand.

"Was he your mother's or your father's brother?"

She turns sharply and gives me a frown.

I say, "Your mother's. Did she look like him?"

She nods. "Some. She had hair like mine. He had black hair. But they had the same mouth and the same eyes. She loved her little brother. She's the one who took these pictures."

I look at the last of six or seven black-and-whites of the young uncle and try to imagine his mouth, his eyes in the face of a woman, Dawnell's mother. I can think of nothing else to say. Suddenly, I feel very tired. It's the weariness I used to get sometimes at Bridgedale when everything, the people, the rules, the very buildings seemed to close in on me, freeze me solid, bleed from me all energy and leave me wishing for death. I say, "You must have . . . loved him if he can still make you cry."

She closes the box and slides it onto the floor. "I just remember little flickers of things here and there, but I remember them so strong. And they come to me in dreams."

And I smile at that, my weird ruffled smile that recognizes means and ends, accidents and the things that cause them. I say, "What do you dream?"

"Good things. Sweet things. Warm things. I wake up feeling good when I dream of him, but sad too. I don't know, it's hard to explain." She looks at me as though I can explain. Because I'm older. Because I'm a boy. And the strange thing is, I could explain a great deal to her about her uncle. About boys his age who die young.

I try to think of what to say. Finally, it comes to me. I don't know if it's right, but I say it anyway: "I think your dreams are warm because you know that if he hadn't . . . left you, things would have been different. Better."

She nods again. She's thinking about it. She's connecting loose ends of memory and possibility in her mind, things that might have been different if her uncle had stayed in the world. A little smile comes to her lips, a glow to her eyes. My theory makes sense to her. And in a way I hope she will never see, it makes sense to me too, a kind of terrible burdensome sense that I will have to live with every day of my life. I have come back to Widow Rock to find out exactly what it meant that I did things nobody knows I did. To see how all of the vibrations went out and out and out to the farthest strands of the web, into the big design that we never fully understand.

Dawnell snuggles close to me, and I count heartbeats for a while. Eventually, she says, "I know where he's buried, but I've never been there. It's in the yard of a little church. It's too far for me to walk, and my daddy won't take me. It's called Mount Zion Free Will Baptist. Will you take me there?"

TWENTY-ONE

Dawnell Briscoe rolls down the window of my old gray Plymouth and leans her head out into the streaming wind. Her hair whips behind her, snapping at the back of her neck. Her eyes are closed, and the smile on her face is like those you see on Egyptian statues in the history books. *Serene,* I guess you'd call it. I can't see the Zippo because she's gripping it so hard, but I know she's holding it in her left hand. My radio is playing "Day Tripper." We're plowing through tiger stripes of buttery sunlight on the black asphalt that stretches ahead as far as you can see until it disappears into the throat of that pine tree canyon you never reach. I'm taking Dawnell to find the country graveyard where her uncle is buried. The Beatles sing, *"She took me half the way there now."* I don't know how far we're going, Dawnell and me.

We've been on the road for an hour now, lost most of the time, zigzagging through the pine forest northwest of Ebro. We've stopped twice for directions, at a gas station and a farmhouse. It seems there are at least three Mount Zion Free Will Baptist Churches out this way. At least that's what the country voices tell us, only they're not sure if the churches they've heard of are called Mount Zion or Mount Horeb, or Free Will, or just Baptist, or maybe Friendship Baptist. This could turn out to be a long hard day, maybe harder for me than for Dawnell, but I don't know. I look over at her again. The expression on her face hasn't changed. She loves the warm wind on her closed eyes, the way the wind whips her hair. She reaches her right arm out into the stream as far as it will go and flies her hand up and down like the wing of a bird. And she smiles that Egyptian smile.

I'm not sure what I'm doing here, only know that I have to do this for her, and somehow for the uncle who took little Dawnie-ell riding in his convertible and never saw her grow up. I think I can protect myself from the worst of this. I'm the driver, the guy with a car and time on his hands. We'll find the church, and maybe even the grave, and if we don't, we'll look for it another time, or maybe Dawnell will be happy enough with this day trip and stop looking.

My instructions from a blind man who sat in a ladder-back chair in the sun in front of a one-pump Shell station are to turn right onto a sand road exactly six-tenths of a mile from a place where he said I'd feel my tires bump across the Seaboard Coast Line tracks. That's what I do, and that's when Dawnell pulls her head into the car, opens her bright-blue eyes, and looks at me, serious, her pretty face in a tangle of honey-brown hair.

"Are we there?" she asks. She lifts the Zippo and holds it over her heart, covering it with both hands.

I say, "We'll find the place the blind man knows. That doesn't mean it's the right one."

She says, "It's the right place. I can feel it." She moves the Zippo down from her heart to her stomach where I guess she feels things.

About half a mile after we make the turn, a white church floats into view through the striping pines. Like so many country churches, it's a pretty little thing standing tall and proud on nine redbrick stilts with a space underneath for the cool air to move, and a redbrick path up to its porch, and a taller-than-usual steeple with a cross on top. You can tell it's not a working church anymore, but somebody still comes out here to care for the building and the patch of graveyard that lies at the edge of a two-acre clearing.

I cut my engine where the peanut farmers and turpentine workers used to park cars as old as mine or older, maybe even mule-drawn wagons. The smooth brown bed of pine needles tells us nobody has stopped a car here in a while. We stand beside the Plymouth looking out at the little graveyard. There's no lettering on the church that says *Free Will*, or *Friendship*, or which Mount we're on, or even that it's

Baptist, but that, at least, is a safe bet. I wait for Dawnell to start walking to the graves, but she just stands beside me holding the lighter and staring out at the three or four rows of stone markers, sunken at angles in the dappled sunlight and shade.

I'm thinking things to say—*Are you ready to go look?* or *Don't worry, if this isn't the right one, we'll keep looking*—but they stop in my throat. This is her moment, her place, she has the feeling in her stomach and the lighter pressed hard against it, and it's mine to wait and see what she wants to do.

Finally, she sighs and says, "I know he's dead, but somehow every minute I don't go over there, he's still the boy I remember who took me riding in his pretty car. Over there, he's just some long-gone thing in the ground." She looks up at me, and I can see she's as surprised by her own words as I am. I wish I could tell her what is long gone and what isn't, and how some things stay with you long after mercy should kill them. All I do is look into her eyes and nod, then I take a step toward the graveyard, hoping she'll follow.

We wander among the headstones, some of them cracked or split open, most of them very old. The newest ones are from the late 1950s. We take our time. By some unspoken agreement, we want this moment to have its drama. If there will be a discovery, it should not come too quickly. Dawnell walks ahead of me. I stay a step or two behind watching her stop, kneel, touch the stones, the words carved in them, then rise again and move on. She pauses at a half-buried, tablet-shaped stone dark green with moss and lichen and trails her fingers along the words *From the arms of mother to the arms of Jesus*. It's the grave of a child named Chloe Harden whose life was three years long, from 1918 until 1921. Dawnell rises and looks at me in sad wonder. "What do you think killed her?"

I remember a little history I read before nodding off in some classroom at Bridgedale. I say, "Maybe the influenza epidemic. The dates are about right. A lot of children died then." And it makes me think of my old theory, my fascination with accidents. It wasn't only newspaper stories I read about the strange, crazy things that happen to people, the sheet of ice, the hornets' nest as big as a steamer trunk. These things were in the history books too. This dead child lying at my feet is the perfect illustration of my theory of deserving or not deserving, of the accident and its cause. They called it the Spanish flu because it started in Madrid. It was spread around the world by the soldiers of World War I. The doughboys who returned from making the world safe for democracy brought it back with them and it killed two hundred thousand of their fellow democrats. Maybe this little Chloe at my feet, who fell through the surface of life into a place called influenza, saw something in her last delirium like what I saw in a place called Delia, where everything was different, and the good things were better than anyone knew in the world above, and the bad things were worse. My falling, when I was both the accident and the cause, left only two people dead. Is this something I can take strength and courage from, a matter of proportion? Or am I just kidding myself here in this place of peaceful death? *Chloe*, I think, as Dawnell wanders to another stone, *you and I are parts of the big shape seen only dimly. We are strands in the web. If in your delirium you saw something, I hope it comforted you.*

Dawnell finds it before I do. That was my plan. And if nothing was here to find, she would know that first too. I look up from Chloe Harden, 1918–1921, and there is Dawnell kneeling before the last stone in the last row of graves at the border of this churchyard. From behind her, I can see the hem of her dress falling across the backs of her calves and her feet in those scuffed red shoes splayed out in the grass. Her shoulders are curved in sadness or resignation, and she is reaching out her hands toward the grass at the base of the stone. I should walk over and stand above her. I know this, but somehow I can't yet. I know she is placing the Zippo lighter before the headstone, a simple act of giving. Of returning. She is putting something important in its rightful place and leaving something of herself here. I close my eyes and see fire, and I am kneeling in a barn at night listening to a radio softly playing a love song from a bench littered with tools and greasy carburetor parts. Gasoline fumes are sudden and strong in my nostrils. And there below me hang my hands holding the bright-silver Zippo with its dancing flame down to the place where gasoline has been poured. Another inch, another half inch and the rising fumes will marry the flame and my decision will be made for me. Did I decide? To this day I do not recall. I made many decisions climbing to the moment when I held the flame near the fuel, but I do not remember putting them together. I remember only the force of the explosion in my chest like the kick of a horse and then sprawling on my back in the dust outside watching the barn become a giant hand of flame clawing high into the dark heavens. A giant burning hand reaching up for the cold relief of night.

I hear a sob. I open my eyes to flood that night of flame with soft afternoon sunlight, and Dawnell, still kneeling, is turning to me. She says, "Don't cry, boy. Why are *you* crying?"

I'm not. I'm not crying. The sob I heard was yours.

I don't say anything. I can see the tears on her cheeks, two shining ribbons. I'm about to say, *It was you. Not me.* But I feel it then, cool wind on my wet eyes, a tear breaking and falling down my face.

We drive a long time without saying anything, and finally we find a little country restaurant and bar on a shady bank just below the two-lane bridge that jumps a creek. The bridge only has a number. Only the locals know the name of the creek, but enough of them come here to pull crappie and small-mouth bass from the tea-colored water to support this little eating place.

I settle Dawnell at a table out by the somber flow of the creek, and when I approach the woman at the counter, she slides her wide haunches off a stool and gives me a hard look. I guess she's defending the leaky Schlitz tap and three bottles of indifferent bourbon from an underage drinker. I purchase two Cokes and leave her a quarter tip. I set the Cokes down in front of Dawnell, wink at her, and say loudly, "Here you are, little sister. Now don't drink it too fast. It'll give you gas."

We sit in the shade of a tall willow that trails its branches into the cool creek and listen to the car tires that once in a while *thump-bump* over the bridge. A man and a boy in a skiff with a two-horse kicker go putt-putting by, pulling trolling lines. Their motor echoes under the bridge. I feel like an echo. Like breath blown into an empty bottle. I feel used up. Spent. It's as though pieces of me I've carefully arranged to keep my feet walking and my mind cranking away at the problems of daily life have been blown up and have fallen back to earth in a new and crazy pattern.

I haven't said anything to Dawnell since we left the graveyard, and she hasn't spoken to me. I think she's respecting my silence. And I guess I'm doing the same for her. I don't want her to ask me again why I cried at the grave of an uncle dead six years, a boy I didn't know. If she asks, I will lie to her, and I think it will be a good lie and she'll think enough of me to believe it. So for now, this quiet time in this quiet place is a good thing for both of us. And when I sneak a look at her eyes, I can see some deep peace in them I've not seen before. It's as though all of the wild chemicals that drive girls her age have mixed with the tears she shed and evaporated into that sunshine back at the little church that had no name, and she's fine for a while. Maybe not happy, but down-deep calm for the first time in a long while.

I'm almost finished with my Coke, and about to suggest we head back to her house and whatever waits there in the form of her father's anger and her brother's nasty nocturnal pleasures, when she surprises me. She says, "I'm leaving here now."

"What do you mean, *leaving here?*"

"I'm going away. That's what I mean. I don't know how yet, but I'll find a way." She lifts her chin an inch and tightens her lips to show me she means it, but in her eyes I see all of those miles I hitched from the Bridgedale School to San Francisco and then down here to Panama City and all the evil things that could happen to her out there on the road. There's fear in her eyes. She's afraid of what she just said because talking makes things real.

I try to calculate some words. I want to say, *No, you're not leaving here*, but I know it won't work. "What makes you think you can get away with it? The minute you're gone, your daddy will come after you, or send the cops after you, and they'll just haul you back and hand you over to him. Then you'll be a girl with the same father *and* a juvenile court record."

The chin goes up an inch higher, and the cool blue eyes get smaller and colder. "I don't care about no damn juvenile record, and if they haul me back, I'll just haul ass again." She looks out over the creek, the almost-black water flowing between sandy banks, then into the dark hollow under the bridge. "Anyway, my daddy didn't go after my mother when she ran away. He just drank whiskey and said good riddance."

I want to ask her what it is about seeing her uncle's grave that makes her want to run. Maybe it's just seeing how country people die and end up in holes in the ground it takes all day to find. I want to tell her it's how you live that matters, not how long or where you're buried when it's over, but maybe she already knows that. Instead, I say, "You don't know what's out there waiting for runaway girls. You think it's going to be like joining the circus or something, like they show it in the movies?"

Dawnell drinks the last of her Coke and looks at the big, hard woman behind the counter who hasn't taken her eyes off us since we sat down. Dawnell turns and throws her empty Coke bottle into the creek, then stares a challenge back at the woman. The bottle hits midstream with a big splash and fills about halfway, then starts floating toward that dark hollow under the bridge. The woman behind the counter only shakes her head and mutters something (*White trash*, probably). I watch the bottle disappear into the dark.

"Don't get mad at me," I tell her, my voice low and calm, "I'm just trying to help you see into the future. I hitchhiked from Nebraska to California, and all I found out there was a lot of road and not much home. If it's road you want, fine, but you need to know what it's like before you try it. Wouldn't that be better than getting into a lot of trouble, and *then* thinking about it?" I guess what I just gave her is the not-very-eloquent version of *Run in haste, repent at leisure.* I wish there'd been somebody to tell me this back before I did my own running away. Into the land of Delia. But just as soon as I think this, something in me sinks like that Coke bottle in the dark under the bridge. I know I wouldn't have listened.

Dawnell looks at me across two feet of trestle table. She's not thinking about what I just said. Not at all. She drops her chin an inch, then another, and the tightening around her mouth eases into a teasing little smile. She says to me, "I want you to kiss me. Right now. Right here." She glances over at the hard-eyed woman behind the counter.

I stand up and take my Coke bottle over to the bar and set it down in front of the woman who knows white trash when she sees it. I smile. She doesn't. She says, "Them bottles costs me two cent apiece."

I say, "And I tipped you a quarter." I go over and stand next to Dawnell and wait until she pushes herself up.

I need to get her out of here before she throws something else away.

I say, "I'll kiss you, but not here, not now."

She smiles, satisfied for now, and that's how I know she's not worried about hitting that road alone. She has plans for me too.

TWENTY-TWO

Rain drums on the roof of my tourist cabin. Gusts of wind whistle under the eaves and rush into the space above the ceiling with a sudden thump in my ears. There haven't been many storms this summer, not like my summer here six years ago. This is the first big one, pushing waves up the beach all the way to the sea oats in the dunes that protect the highway, swinging the neon signs that hang from rusty chains up and down US 98, banging the halyards against the aluminum masts of sailboats, and spinning torn-off shingles through the air until their corners disappear and they become circles. It's four in the morning, and I've been up for an hour riding this storm, listening to its angry voice. I'm not scared of what it will do to me. I don't own anything here, and I'm not hearing much damage to the Widow's property, but I know there are people in trouble somewhere nearby. I think about pulling on my clothes and walking out into the night looking for somebody to help, a car to push out of a ditch, an old woman's broken window to patch with canvas and boards. Tomorrow the whole town will stagger like a drunk after a bar fight. There'll be dazed citizens out looking for things and people that blew away. There'll be people looking for someone to tell about how lucky they are to be alive or about somebody who wasn't so lucky. The wind gusts under my roof again, pushing my ceiling down and giving my eardrums that weird little concussion, and then there's a space in the wind, and I hear it, the phone ringing out by the Widow's washhouse.

At first I don't believe my ears. Who'd be calling this place at four in the morning in a howling squall? I get up, pull on Levi's and a T-shirt, and go to my front door. It takes some strength to push it open against the wind. When I lean out, my face is instantly wet. And there it is, unmistakable. The phone is ringing in the pool of light under the shed roof by the single row of rusting washers and dryers. That's the way it is here. Just the one phone and a pad for messages hanging from a string. Everybody answers it, and when nobody's around, nobody does. The Widow won't answer it, ever. That's her policy. ("I'm not your social secretary," she says if anyone mentions it.)

I listen to it ringing, the sound loud then faint as the rain and wind rise and fall. I'm about to go back inside, towel off my wet head, and get back into bed, when I remember something. Something I never should have forgotten. I push my door all the way open, turn, and try to keep it from banging shut. Then I run through the slanting rain.

"Hello?"

"Travis, I'm scared. Didn't you know I'd be scared?"

"Yes," I say. "Yes, baby. I knew you'd be scared. I'm sorry I didn't come sooner."

I hear her sobbing at the other end. It's quiet, because I know she's alone somewhere in that big new house out in the suburb of international design, and she's hiding what she feels tonight from Ole Temp. From everyone but me.

"Delia," I whisper, my lips pressed hard to the phone, which smells like the breath of a dog. "Delia, where are you?" Maybe she's not in that big house. Maybe she's somewhere nearby and can come to me.

I still hear her sobbing—no, that isn't true for what I hear. It's a singing, and the notes are the ragged pieces of a broken heart. It's a moaning call from the last lost place, and it's a sound I've heard only once before in my life. That summer six years ago. Delia says to me, "Travis, do you remember?"

"Yes, I remember." She means the nights when the big storms came one after another, the nights I held her and tried to warm and touch and whisper the past out of her mind.

"That's all," she says now, and the storm around me seems to give up the worst of its bad intentions. "That's all I needed to know." She breathes a long, shuddering sigh into the phone. "Where are you?" I repeat.

"At home," she whispers, a catch in her throat. "I'm at home, but I wish I wasn't."

"I wish you weren't too." I should say I want her here with me. That's not the same as wishing she wasn't at home.

"We have to meet," she says.

"I'll come. I'll come right now."

"No," she says, tired, worn out like she always was when a storm was over. "Not tonight. Not here. I'll get in touch. I'll let you know." She lets her phone fall softly into its receiver before I can say, *Good night, my dream.*

My father says, "So, you see, it's not all green eyeshades and dusty law books. Once you've learned the law, using it in business is mostly common sense. The legal fraternity around here is pretty informal. We solve a lot of problems over lunch or on the golf course. It's not like what you see in the movies, all those dramatic confessions from the witness stand. Most lawyers do business. We write contracts, search titles, manage trusts. We work hard for our clients, but we don't cut each other's throats. We all have to live here, and we all benefit when business is good." My father holds a shiny metal construction helmet in his hands, and in front of him unrolled on a long conference table are some architect's blueprints. He's showing me the props of the big show in which he's an actor. And maybe, cautiously, he's inviting me in.

This morning we've had a tour of his office, later we're going to lunch at the country club. I've met a receptionist, a legal secretary, and some accountants and brokers who work for Lloyd Hollister, Esq. The people in this office speak quietly and confidently, move slowly, and wear a grave concern for their work and for one another. The shiny construction helmet (my father calls it a hard hat) is a souvenir from a recent ground breaking, a new subdivision called Loch Haven.

The name of the place and the date are painted in blue on the helmet. My father puts it down on the blue lines of the architectural plans and looks at me. Pride pours from his eyes. I smile, nod, withdraw my eyes from his, and look around at his office again. I need a moment to collect some words. His plan, I think, is to invite me to work here, just help around the office, to see what the law is like. After that, he hopes maybe I'll catch fire and go off to college, and then maybe to law school and come back and partner with him. I wonder if he knows what he's risking. I know some of his reasons for doing this. Eleanor has been at him, I'll bet, and his guilt about me is awake. Now that I've traveled east to the place where he lives, and not west to be with my mother, he thinks I've made a choice about him and he has to make one about me. But he must have his doubts. Any sane man would.

I turn and walk to his desk. It's an antique oak rolltop, more for show I think than real work, a very impressive old piece. In fact, just about everything here, from the amber glass and bright brass of the banker's lamp to the tall golden oak shelves with their rows of law books bound in green leather, to the old bloodred Persian carpet on the peg-planked pine floor, might have come from the pages of novels I've read about lawyers and businessmen. This suite of offices is on the second floor of the old mercantile, and we are standing now where once a block and tackle swung bags of rice and pallets of country hams up from the beds of mule-drawn wagons. I can see where, behind my father's desk, the new red brick has been feathered in among the old to close that old loft door.

I turn back to my father's expecting eyes and say, "It's all really impressive. I don't know what I imagined, but not this. It's . . ." I pretend to struggle for a word, ". . . glamorous." I look at him, shy. I can see it's not the word he expected, or wanted.

He goes to the phone, presses a button, and I hear a ring somewhere in another room. My father says, "Mary Beth, my son and I are going to lunch at the club. If anything comes in about Breckenridge, tell Alan to handle it until I get back." He checks his watch.

"That'll be about two o'clock." He cradles the phone and looks at me. "Hungry?"

I nod. "I could eat." I'm noticing how he seems to enjoy saying "my son," and how he's looking forward to showing me the country club.

"You'll like the food at the club," he says. "Usually these places have just passable food, but for some reason Quail Run does better than that." He raises his hand toward me, hovers it above my shoulder, letting me know that I should precede him through the door.

Quail Run is a big, brand-new place carved into some hill country northwest of Widow Rock. We stop in a parking lot so new the asphalt is soft in the noon sun, and when I step out of my father's white Sedan de Ville, I hear that cocky two-note call of a bobwhite. There's a covey in the pine woods not far from the long, low sandstone and stucco clubhouse, so I guess Quail Run isn't misnamed. I stand beside my father while he points out the first and tenth tees, the fairways curving off into the tall loblolly pines with sand traps as white as snow, the big practice green near the floor-to-ceiling windows of the dining room, and the driving range where some guys are hitting shots before starting their rounds.

On the putting green, a man about my father's age in pink slacks and a blue polo shirt with a club crest over the heart misses a ten-footer and drops his putter in mild frustration. Nearby, his pal in yellow slacks and a red polo strolls over. They squat and examine the line of the putt, frowning and gesturing like two catchers about to haul in fastballs from Bob Gibson and Sandy Koufax. Over it all, a high blue sky streams on to the four horizons.

My father is proud of all he surveys, and he tells me about his part in the making of this place. He's what they call a charter member, and that means certain privileges. One of these is the parking place where the new Cadillac rests, and I guess I'll see some of the others before we leave here today.

We tour the ballroom, card rooms, restaurant, and meeting rooms, but the locker room is the strangest thing. As you go in, there's a little cage where a smiling Black man sits polishing golf shoes and screwing in fresh spikes. The cage smells of shoe polish and solvents, and the sleepy smile on the Black man's face reminds me of smiles I used to see late on hot summer afternoons in the furniture shop at Bridgedale when the varnish fumes hung heavy in the air. My father's locker is in the first row nearest the shower, and his name is embossed on a shiny brass plate with a star next to it, signifying charter membership.

Just past the best lockers is the bathroom, and there's another surprise. The towels are cotton not paper, and the shelves above the sinks are stocked with hair creams, shaving lotions, powders, salves, aspirin, and even combs in a big jar of green antiseptic liquid. You don't have to bring anything with you when you come to this place. They'll even store your golf clubs for you if you like.

The men's grill is full of cigar smoke, green leather, dark mahogany, and the sound of spikes clicking on red Spanish tile. You can wear spiked shoes in here, but you have to take off your hat. The only women they let in are carrying trays of food and drink. My father takes me from table to table and introduces me as his son Travis "who's just finished school out west with his mother." I shake some hands, look into some speculating eyes, some of them warm and some cold, and I forget most of the names as soon as they're announced. It's funny how rich men say their names so triumphantly. They could be calling out victories (*Agincourt! Waterloo!*). Well, every victory is a defeat. You'd think they'd know that. I've never been able to say my name, except quietly. At least not since Bridgedale.

For reasons I can't explain, I order liver and bacon with grilled onions. I guess I want something grilled in the men's grill, and it's the only item on the menu that actually uses the word. I take a crisp little piece of bacon and some soft sweet onion with each bite of liver. The food is good. The subject of strong drink does not come up, of course. My father orders iced tea for both of us.

We make what I guess you'd call small talk for a while (how nice the club is, my father's handicap—he's a ten, whatever that means— how nice it was to meet Eleanor the other night and to see Aunt Delia again after such a long time). Mostly my father does the talking, and it's not as awkward as it might be. (I guess you don't succeed in business if you can't talk to people.) But I'm not just people, I'm his son. Shouldn't there be something more? Maybe he doesn't want to pressure me about working for him. Just wants to let me shrug off my old life for an afternoon and try this one on.

When my liver and bacon are almost gone and my father's chef's salad is a mess pushed all around his plate, and most of the other diners have drifted off to golf or back to work, my father reaches into the breast pocket of his suit coat and pulls out a thick envelope. It's wrinkled and worn, so it's been in and out of a few pockets before. He puts it on the table in front of him. He squares himself up in his chair and surveys the room, his gaze stopping at the big window behind me that lets onto the immaculate practice green. The envelope on the table is why we're here. I drop my hands into my lap and wipe them on my khaki chinos, my one pair of almost dress-up pants. I can feel my heart quicken in my throat and under my left arm. When my father pulls his eyes away from the big window behind me, he pushes the envelope across the white tablecloth. "Go ahead, son," he says, "open it."

My hand shakes when I reach for it. I pull it over to me and spill its contents.

The woman who served us comes to take my plate. "Mr. Hollister, would your son like more iced tea?"

My dad looks up at her and blinks. "What? Oh, uh . . . how about it, Travis?"

"No thank you, ma'am." My hand instinctively covers the little mound of paper.

When the woman is gone, I unfold the first sheet and begin to read. The English is simple, formal, almost childish. I read a little, then skip to the bottom. The letter is signed by H. Kobayashi, DDS, my mother's brother, my uncle in San Francisco. I shuffle through the letters. They start not long after I went off to Bridgedale. The latest is from only a year ago. One of the letters holds a small black-and-white snapshot of my mother standing in a backyard garden, holding the hands of two children, an older brother, a younger sister. I know the children. Their small dark eyes stare with bland trust into the camera as their hands rest easily in my mother's. But my mother's eyes are full of storms. I can see this even through the narrow, clouded window of this photograph. I look up at my father.

His eyes are back at the window where the bright summer light pours in from the practice green. He says, "The children belong to her brother, Hiroshi. She takes care of them. I've been in touch with him since the day she left me." He drops his gaze from the window behind me. "And I've sent him money to take care of her, more than she'll ever need." He waits for me to say something.

I don't. I just watch him, my hand resting on the pile of letters.

"Your mother lives a very simple life. It's about all she can manage. Read the letters. You'll see that Hiroshi doesn't tell me much about her. He just acknowledges what I send, thanks me formally, and tells me she is healthy and he'll let me know if anything changes. He's a good man, but he's Japanese. He never wanted Miko to marry me. Nobody in either of our families did. I don't think he blames me for what happened, and I don't really know how he feels about having his sister with him. She's an obligation, I suppose. As you know or you will learn, son, life is full of obligations. We either shirk them or do the right thing." Here, he looks at me, and I see that he has stumbled on the bumpy road of moral explication. What am I if not his obligation? He shakes his head, brings his hand to his eyes, covers them for a moment as though the bright light hurts, then lets the hand drop back to the table. "Sometimes," he says, his voice quiet in this room where the cigar smoke has thinned and we are alone now that the last foursome has sipped the last of their coffee or iced tea or scotch and gone off to the first tee, "life just gives us too much, and we—"

"I don't think I want to read them." I push the mound of paper back toward him. "You said they're mostly all the same, didn't you?"

He nods. The waitress approaches with our check. She stops as though it's raining where we are, or cold. She takes a step back.

My father waves her sharply toward him. She sets down a silver tray, and he signs the check with a masculine flourish. "Thank you, Agnes."

"You're welcome, Mr. Hollister."

We're alone in the cold. Am I supposed to say more? I watch my father's eyes as they harden. This is enough for him for one day. He's done what he set out to do.

In the air-conditioned Cadillac on the way back to Widow Rock, my father drums his fingers on the steering wheel, a thing I remember him doing when I was little. I liked it then. It told me driving bored him, and important things were going on in his mind. I used to think someday he'd tell me about those things. I watch the pines and palmettos stroke past as the two-lane blacktop swings through the shallow swales, up and down hills that were once dunes by an inland sea. The hill country, where the armies of wealth have taken the high ground, slips away behind us, and we find the flatness of old corn and peanut fields near the town. Just when I think we'll finish our return trip without speaking, my father says, "Son, did you know anything about where your mother was? Was what I showed you a surprise?" He looks straight ahead through the spotless windshield, carefully guiding the big car down the center of his lane.

I think about it. What should he know about me and my mother? Then I think, what the hell. "I went out to see her after I got out of …" I'm about to say Bridgedale, but why not call a spade a spade, "… out of reform school. I didn't have any money, so I hitchhiked out west. It took a long time. I was pretty tired when I got there, but I finally found her, and I saw what she was doing. Taking care of the kids, I mean. So I just … left her alone, I guess. I think that's what she would want me to do." I look over at him. "Don't you?"

He stares into the stippled sunlight that falls through the pines. Finally, he bites his lip and shakes his head. His voice is quiet when he says, "I don't know, son. I never figured out what your mother wanted." It's the first time I've ever heard my father say he doesn't know something. I'm sure he does it a lot. Any sane man would, but I've never heard it before.

"I knew." My voice is almost a whisper, because it's something I'm not sure I want to say. Then certainty comes, and a little louder I say, "I always knew."

My father looks over at me sharply. It's almost the way he looked at the waitress back at the club, just before he waved her over with the check. I look back at him, hard, the way I learned to look at a guy just before a fight starts. It's a thing in your eyes that says, *You may win, but I'll mark you.* My father, the old marine, recognizes the look I'm giving him. He nods, purses his lips the way he does when he's made up his mind about something, and turns back to the road. Up ahead is the first stoplight on the main street of Widow Rock.

And I'm thinking, *What do you mean? What did you always know about your mother?* The voice of my good intentions answers, *That she was like me. Lost out there in all that wheat so far from everything she knew and loved. That she had only us to love, and we weren't enough. That she wanted to go home, to fly on the wind like the spirits of her ancestors, back to Osaka. Even as a little boy, I could recognize exile.*

My father and I stand on the street in front of his law office. My Plymouth is parked not far away. He looks up and down the street at the people going in and out of stores and returning to business after lunch. He looks at his watch, then at me. It's his legal voice that says, "What does your afternoon look like, son?"

I tell him, "It looks like shrimp."

He's confused, doesn't get it, then he smiles. "Let me know when you get tired of shrimp."

TWENTY-THREE

I t's morning in the suburb of international design, and I'm standing at Delia's door. The last of the cool wind from the night before is blowing, and things look different out here in the morning light. The air is clear and the light so bright it penetrates the surfaces of things, revealing their inner life. You could cut yourself on the sharp edges of the trimmed hedges and the shaved grass at the curbstones. I raise my hand to knock, then notice the doorbell. It's a brass knight's helmet with a white plastic button in its center. I press it and hear six notes from inside (*God save our graaa-cious Queen . . .*). After that I hear nothing, but I imagine the silence beyond the thick oak door deepening and my Delia alone, her breath stopping in her throat as she wonders who is on the other side. Temp Tarleton opens the door.

"Hello, Uncle Temp," I say to his surprised face. He's wearing dark-blue suit pants, black shoes, a white undershirt, and holding a towel in his right hand. His brown hair is wet and flecks of shaving cream hang from his earlobes. He blinks his eyes and says, "Well, hello there, Travis. Uh . . . come on in. Your Aunt Delia's out on the patio finishing her breakfast."

I search his eyes for signs of resentment at my unannounced visit, but all I see is more of the surprise that opened the door to me. I follow him into the foyer and the living room. The shapes of things that menaced me in the darkness of my night visit are recognizable and safe now. We walk out to the sunny patio, to a table where Delia sits in a robe and slippers, with the litter of breakfast and a newspaper in front of her. She's facing the backyard and doesn't look up as we approach.

Ole Temp says, "Hey, Delia baby, look who's here."

She turns to me, her blue eyes wide then narrowing, her hand rising from the newspaper to pull the lapels of her white terry-cloth robe together at her throat.

Before she can speak, I say, "Uncle Temp, I hope it's not too early for a visit, but you did say you wanted me to come out to the house as soon as I could. I got a day off from work, so I ..." I look over at Delia and smile like a twelve-year-old in a grown man's body.

Ole Temp wipes his face with the towel, two swipes to both cheeks, missing the white earrings of shaving cream.

Delia frowns and says, "Temp ...!" pointing at her own right ear.

Temp says, "Oh, uh ..." and scours his ears. He looks at me. "I always do that. Sometimes I get through half a day before someone tells me I've still got the stuff on my face."

This little domestic masquerade gives Delia time to start breathing again. In the breezy voice of a suburban matron starting another busy day, she answers my question: "Travis, it's good you came. Have you had breakfast? Can I fix you something?" She gets up, still holding the lapels of the robe at her throat.

"Well ..." I look over at Temp.

He smiles generously. "Sure, Travis. Get your Aunt Delia to make you some of her scrambled eggs with cream cheese. She can whip some up in ..." He checks his watch as though he just remembered he had one. "Wait a minute. I've got to get out of here. Got to meet Miller and Harrison in twenty minutes." He looks at Delia for the kind of female sympathy a hardworking man deserves.

"Go on, honey," she says. "I'll take care of Travis."

I walk off to the end of the backyard and pretend to examine a bed of blooming pink begonias. Behind me, I hear Temp whisper his goodbye, and maybe the silence that follows is a farewell kiss.

When I hear his white Lincoln slide down the driveway of snow-white concrete and hum away into the sunny morning, I walk over and stand in front of Delia. I put my hand over hers where she still holds the robe tight.

She whirls away from me. "Travis, don't. Don't *ever* do that." Her voice is low, uncertain, excited. The words are my command, but the music of her voice is all about our past, what we know about each other, what we can never forget. We stand that way, separated by inches, looking into each other's eyes. Finally, she says, "Don't you want me to fix you something?"

"No," I say. "I couldn't eat anything here."

"But you could touch me here?"

"I just did."

"Well, don't again." She sounds more certain now, but only about this place. Not my touch. The phone rings inside. Delia lets go of her lapels, and the two parts fall away, and now I can see it, in the sunlight that strikes her chest, the rap-rapping of her heart in the soft flesh above her breast. She gives me a look that says, *Don't follow.*

When she comes out again, I'm sitting at the patio table. She sits across from me. "Travis, what are you doing here?"

I came for you. "I was invited. You heard what Ole Temp said the other night at my father's house."

"Don't call him that," she snaps.

"What?"

"You know what, *Ole* Temp. And don't call him *uncle* either."

"All right, if that's what you want, but he doesn't seem to mind. I think he likes it."

She just looks at me. Her face, without makeup, looks a little tired from the long night, and maybe not as magazine pretty as it would be with makeup in the soft light of a candle at a dinner table, but it's wonderful. Most faces are flawed in some way, and some say the flaws make the face, but Delia's is perfectly symmetrical, a harmony of lines and angles, curves and ovals. When I was a boy, I could sit and look at her for an hour that passed like a few seconds. I could do the same thing now. She's the allure of a precipice. You know it's dangerous to go to the edge, but you are drawn. And once there, you are pulled out toward the infinite, and when there's only one more step to take, you'd better pray that something or someone calls you back.

"Why did you marry him?"

"Because I would have gone crazy without him. I *was* crazy, and he saved me from it. Didn't you know that? Couldn't you see it? It was there six years ago. What you loved when I was sixteen isn't so lovable now."

I didn't expect this, but I know what to say. My eyes tell her even before I speak. "I still love you. I always will." But I'm thinking about that word, *crazy*. I hated the word six years ago when my mother crawled under the sink in Omaha and lay there with bottles of Lysol and Lux against her face singing songs in Japanese. Nobody said it, but I hated it all the same because I knew they were thinking it. When I went to stay in Widow Rock, the first person who said it was my Aunt Delia, and then she told me she was sorry and would never say it again. After that, the word lost its power. In all the years I sat with Dr. Janeway pretending to analyze myself, it never came to me that maybe Delia was my second chance. I couldn't save my mother, and then I met my Aunt Delia. So, I say it again, "Always. I will always love you. Tell me why you married him."

"Oh, Travis, don't you see he's safe? He loves me so much, and he's safe because I don't love him. I'm the only thing he's ever loved more than he loves himself. He thinks that makes us very fine. I'll never have to worry about losing him or losing myself to him, or what's left of me."

"Everything," I tell her. "Everything is left."

She rises and stands over me in the white robe, and part of me desperately wants to know again what is underneath it. I look at my own strong hands and know that I could take her into the bedroom where I saw her sleeping alone with the gold cross at her throat. She sees what's in my eyes. She says, "Travis, either I've got to fix you some eggs and you've got to eat them, and we have to talk like an aunt and nephew should, or you have to leave."

I stand too. My hands, my eyes, all of me wants her. I don't want scrambled eggs. "I'm going now," I tell her, my voice quiet. "But I'll be back. Remember the storm? You said we had to meet. This is not the meeting we have to have."

I walk over to the wide glass door that opens into the living room. When I open it, cold expensive air pours out into the warm morning. I stop and look back at her. She stands with both hands on the lapels of the robe. She knows what I could do.

"Goodbye, Travis."

"Goodbye, my Delia."

TWENTY-FOUR

I'm finishing my noon shift, bussing the last tables in Big Sam's acre of dining room, when Dawnell Briscoe walks in. She's wearing a *Go Gators* T-shirt and too-tight jeans, and carrying that cheap transistor radio pressed to her cheek. Her hair is pulled back into a ponytail, and she's wearing those red sandals that match the paint on her toenails and the usual slash of red lipstick. She drifts in looking half-asleep, dreaming to the music, her lips moving a little with the words of some song only she can hear. Fresh out of the bright sunlight, she stands blinking in the shadows by the bar, then saunters over to a two-top just past the little pulpit where the hostesses meet the crowd.

There's no hostess now. It's three o'clock, and everybody's gone but me, Emil, LeLe, and Jimmy Danes, the dishwasher. Dawnell sits, puts the radio on the table in front of her, turns it up so I can hear Mick Jagger singing "Get Off of My Cloud," and calls over to me, "Hey, boy, you got any shrimp left?"

The last overloaded bus tray rests on my right shoulder. The sweat of a long lunch shift is drying on my face, and my clothes are covered with the usual modern art: iced tea, cocktail sauce, beer, and French dressing. I set the tray down and walk over to her. LeLe, who's drinking coffee and counting her tips in a booth by the kitchen door, pushes herself up with a grunt and motors over in second gear. She looks at Dawnell, then at me, and says, "Travis, take that tray to the kitchen."

I just look at her. I don't take orders from her, and I keep out of range of those fingernails.

LeLe waits a count of three to see what I'm going to do, then she turns to Dawnell, looks her up and down, and says, "Missy, you're too young to apply for a job, and it's too late for lunch, so why don't you just take yourself back out the way you came."

Dawnell's eyes dial down to the size of burning blue gemstones. Hands on hips, she gives LeLe the same once-over she just got, only slower and hotter. She says, "Well now, missy miss, how would you like to just kiss my ass?" She wiggles in her seat to make sure LeLe knows she's not talking metaphor.

LeLe clamps her lips and shakes her head. "Road trash. Common road trash." The words come from the spaces between her locked teeth. She gives me a look that could boil a lobster and stalks back over to her coffee and her pile of singles and quarters.

I stand over Dawnell. The Stones are into the chorus. *"Hey! Hey! You! You! Get offa my cloud!"* She looks up at me, proud of herself for backing LeLe off. I say, "That was dainty."

She smiles, wiggles again, and says, "Sometimes you have to stand up for yourself."

It's hard to argue with that. In fact, it's exactly what I said to Dr. Janeway some years ago. I sit down across from Dawnell and turn off the radio.

She pouts in the silence, then smiles at me. "You look like you been working hard. I like that in a man."

I say, "You're confusing me. Am I a boy or a man?"

"That's up to you." She gives me the smoldering, femme fatale look she's seen in some movie. It's a pretty good one, actually. It burns into my chest and starts some fires. She reaches out and touches my arm with the tip of one finger. "I didn't really come here to eat. I'm meeting somebody." She looks over at the kitchen door. Jimmy Danes stands there in his dirty white smock and gray-checked trousers, wiping his hands on a bus towel. He shucks a pack of Marlboros and a silver Ronson out of his greasy pocket and lights up with a lot of flourish and snap. The *FUCK YOU!* tattooed on his knuckles tends to drain some of the Cary Grant out of the suave way he fires up a butt. Jimmy glances over at LeLe, who ignores him, then starts walking toward me and Dawnell.

As much as we can in a crowded kitchen, Jimmy and I have stayed out of each other's way since the night we had our altercation and he told me, "Later, shithead." He arrives for work in that junk '59 Ford of his, in a cloud of burned oil and loud country music and tends his steaming dishwasher with a look on his face that says he really belongs at the head of a column of guerrilla troops returning America to the true values of the Old South. The days go by. Once in a while, Jimmy gets a steam burn or a puncture from sticking his hands into a soapy tub of cutlery, and then you see it, that volcanic temper he holds back. He'll go on a screaming, cursing trip around the kitchen, holding his hurt hand out in front of him, daring anyone to get in his way or try to calm him down. Anyone except Emil. Emil can stop him, but usually doesn't. At least not for a while. He'll let Jimmy make one obscene, growling stomp around the kitchen, and he'll watch with a stern, concerned face. But once is enough. When the second round starts, Emil steps into Jimmy's path and quietly says something like, *That's enough, Jimmy. Now put a bandage on that and get back to work or go to Big Sam and make a claim for workman's comp.*

Jimmy stands in front of Dawnell and me. He gives me a *move or I'll move you* look, and then puts his hand on her shoulder like she's something he's owned for a long time. He says, "Come on, girl. The car's out back, and my boys are waiting."

My stomach lurches when she looks up at him, because sometimes she looks at me the same way. Like I'm a window into some future that can't be worse than what she's living right now. She stands up under the weight of his hand, and her eyes turn to me. I know what she wants. She wants me to stop this, make some declaration. The words don't have to be poetry. I could just say, *I thought you and I had a date this afternoon.* Or, *Wait here, I'll finish up and we'll go do something.* But it's anger that burns in me now, not love. I don't like being pushed into a corner, and I hate the stupidity of her using this asshole to push me. So I just smile at her, my eyes telling her she's making a big mistake, then I look over at Jimmy who has both thumbs tucked into his belt and both middle fingers hanging down in an unmistakable statement. The smile on his face has carrion in it. He's after roadkill, and that's what he figures Dawnell is. Something already dead he can scrape up and eat, tossing the bones when he's finished.

He says, "Did you want to talk to me, busboy?"

I can think of twenty things to say, all of them words from bad memories of arguments I've seen turn into brawls; snotty, bloody memories from Bridgedale that flare in my mind in the color of bruises. I just ignore him. I pick up my laden bus tray and head for the kitchen. At the swinging door, I turn and look back. Dawnell and Jimmy are moving through the rectangle of sunlight at the front of Big Sam's. Somehow I know she'll turn for a last look at me, and she does. She's still wearing her cinematic smile for Jimmy, but when she sees me watching her over my burdened shoulder, the smile quits and she looks like a child who's just dropped her ice cream on the hot pavement.

In the kitchen I put what's in the tray into tubs and bins, stand for a second or two stock-still in the middle of the room, then I punch the front of a refrigerator door so hard I leave four readable knuckle prints in the white metal.

Emil comes in from the storeroom with a clipboard in his hand. "The *hell* you doing, white boy?"

I'm standing there holding my hand, waiting for the pain to fade or deepen, in which case I've more than likely broken a bone. All I can say to Emil's disappointed face is, "Nothing. Don't worry about it."

He comes closer, dropping the clipboard on a countertop. "Boy, I *do* worry about damage to my employer's property. This is *my* kitchen, and I'm supposed to take care of things back here." His voice is all chief petty officer, but his eyes are already softening. He comes over and takes my hand in his. It's twice the size of mine, the skin long ago scalded to a thickly calloused gray. I try to pull away from him, yet I might as well be fighting a vice. He turns my hand one way and another and says, "Can you move your fingers?" I wiggle. He says, "Most likely you all right then." He lets go of my hand and looks into my eyes. "What's going on?"

I tell him, "I don't know. I wish I did."

"You punching my refrigerator because you don't know what's going on? Hell, boy, drink some whiskey, go to church, call up your mama, play the bolita, consult the tarot deck, go down to the welfare. That's what you do when you don't know what's going on. You don't go busting up other people's property."

He stares into my eyes. I look back at him out of pain that isn't from my hand. His eyebrows rise like black wings, and he nods. "Oh, I get it. You got the woman trouble, ain't you? Please tell me it ain't that little thing from out to Ebro. The one that come walking up the alley that night like she was onstage at the burlesque."

I guess my eyes are his answer. He nods again, sadly. I nod. "I've got to go," I say.

On my way out the back door, I hear Emil say, "Don't write out no check with your mouth your ass can't cover."

Out back, I fire up the Plymouth, speed down the alley pluming dust onto the lines of trash barrels and the loading docks. I don't know where to look. They could be anywhere. Maybe I can find them before Jimmy does too much harm.

I don't have to drive far. It's a little roadhouse about a mile off 98, south toward Mexico Beach. Jimmy's junk Ford with the Confederate flag in the back window is in the parking lot. Music throbs from inside, Johnny Cash singing about a boy named Sue: *"Well, it was Gatlinburg in mid-July. I'd just hit town and my throat was dry ..."* A red neon sign in the black-painted front window blinks, *BEER POOL,* and I remember that Jimmy fancies himself a pool shark, boasting about hustling hopeless tourists.

I park the Plymouth facing the highway and leave the engine running. I pull a dime out of my Levi's and use the edge to let the air out of Jimmy's rear tires. Then I stand in the sandy parking lot flanked by a couple of half-dead palm trees. I look west toward the gulf and take a deep breath. I close my eyes, and back there in the darkness the fires of bitterness spark on and start to burn. Another deep breath to blow all the smoke and grease of Big Sam's out of my lungs, to pull in clean fresh air to feed that fire, and then I push through the front door.

Jimmy's shooting pool under a cone of light at the far end of a long dark room. His back is to me. There's a little more light at the bar along the wall to my left, but not much. The walls and ceiling are painted black, the vinyl is red on the barstools and in the four booths opposite the bar. Dark and dirty, this place. A big rebel flag hangs above a mirror behind a beer tap tended by a big-bellied biker wearing a black death's-head T-shirt and a lot of cheap silver rings and chains. First I take a stool. Second I look for the rack where the pool cues hang. I don't want to be the only person in here without something to play with.

I order a draft beer. The bartender says, "You twenty-one?"

I say, "No."

He shakes his head like he's seen my sorry ass a thousand times before. He serves me anyway. "Don't tell nobody."

"Who would I tell?"

He seems to consider it, then goes back to a stool by the cash register and a copy of *Guns and Ammo*. I sip the beer, turn, and look at the dim nook where Jimmy yips like a small dog because he's just sunk somebody's hopes in the corner pocket. I don't see Dawnell, and I wonder if they've already dumped her somewhere along the road. *They* are the two country freaks Jimmy called "my boys." One, a short pale blond with the collapsed mouth of a toothless old man, is losing to Jimmy at pool. The other, a gaunt character with a black silk do-rag tied around his head, sits in the last booth watching the short hallway that leads, I suppose, to the toilets.

Dawnell appears, a flare in the dark frame of the hallway, blotting fresh red lipstick with a brown paper towel. She stops to watch Jimmy rack up another game. Without looking at her, he says, "Dawnie, I told you to sit down there and enjoy yourself with Dwayne." She looks at the boy in the booth. South of the do-rag, Dwayne is wearing a black T-shirt, a black leather vest with silver studs and Western-style fringes, and a big silver peace symbol on a leather thong. Dawnell hangs her head and sits across from him. He reaches over the table, takes her by the wrist, and pulls her around to his side, shoving her in next to the wall. I wonder if she took this ride knowing she'd be common property.

I close my eyes again. In the vast darkness, the fires have spread. The foreground is a long desert land of black, but the horizon writhes with livid red and orange flame. I drink my beer in one long, burning swallow, then walk fast to the rack of cues. I pick one for the thickness of its handle. It's an old bent thing. No true practitioner of the billiard arts would give it a second thought. I turn and face the table. Spread out over a difficult bank shot, one leg kicking in the air behind him, Jimmy looks up at the stranger, new worlds to conquer. When he recognizes what stands in front of him, he stops humping the rail, pulls himself to his full five feet ten, and says, "Busboy! When did you come in?"

I shoulder past the short man, who moves into the dark hallway where *EXIT* glows bright red. I look over at the booth. Dwayne is drilling his tongue into Dawnell's ear. I can't see her face, and I'm glad. Her small hands are pushing at him without much effect. I walk over and drive the sharp end of the cue into Dwayne's rib cage, hard. His squeal is high-pitched, "Aww! Shit! What the . . . ?" I hear the short man run the hallway past the restrooms to the back door.

Dwayne comes out of the booth like a yard dog from under a porch, no idea who I am or why I'm doing this to him. I drill the sharp end into his chest and say, "Stop, shitbird. Dawnell, you're coming with me." She looks at me, her white face smeared with lipstick and tears. There's just enough tough-girl pride left in her eyes to make me think she'll balk, but then Dwayne slaps the cue point out of his chest and reaches back behind him. He gives Dawnell a shove that bounces her hard off the wall. She sits down dazed. He looks back to see how she's taking it, and that's when I know I've got to take Jimmy down. I turn, whipping the cue with a sound like Arnold Palmer's driver bottoming out in a full-on swing, and it meets the thick end of Jimmy's cue just behind my right shoulder.

My cue shatters and Jimmy's stick slides down what's left, ripping across my already aching knuckles to the lump of bunched muscle between my neck and shoulder.

I reverse my grip on the stick, thick end out, turn, and lay it to the side of Dwayne's head. It's his raised forearm I get, but it's enough to sit him back down next to Dawnell with a look of recognition in his eyes. He spies the fires burning far away. I turn back to Jimmy in time to parry a blow, then shove the butt end of the broken cue into his throat, and that's when I hear the biker vaulting the bar with a sound like a growling dog. Johnny Cash is singing, "*I'm the man in black,*" and there's another sound, small and metallic, in all the melee of scraping feet, music, and hard breathing. It's the bartender cocking a long-barreled, stainless-steel revolver.

I drop the cue and raise my hands high over my head. Choking and clawing at his neck, Jimmy raises his cue in the air, his eyes full of pain and the delight he is going to know when he splits my unprotected skull. The bartender slaps the barrel of the revolver across Jimmy's temple so hard that his eyes are empty before his hands know to stop what they're doing with the cue.

Jimmy drops like so much wilted lettuce at my feet, both hands still holding the stick. I look down and his hands curse me: *FUCK YOU!* The bartender steps over Jimmy and sticks the gleaming revolver in my face. "You see this, kid?" His thumb taps the cocked hammer of the weapon. "*Never* hit a man in the head with a cocked weapon. It could go *off.*"

I nod. My voice is lost somewhere in that vacant country where the fires still burn. I find it somehow and say, "Yes sir. I will remember that."

He looks around me at Dwayne, who cradles his bruised or broken forearm, grunting, "Unh, unh." Tears run down his face.

The bartender says to me, "Kid, you get that girl out of here right now. You hear me?"

I take Dwayne by the hair, shove him onto the floor, grab Dawnell by the hand, and walk toward the front door.

In the parking lot, my knuckles are bleeding and my right arm is going numb, but I can still open the door of the idling Plymouth for Dawnell. I look over at Jimmy's flattened Ford. The short man sits in the backseat, his head barely clearing the windowsill, staring straight ahead. It would be funny if my shoulder didn't hurt so bad. I back out, taking my time now that a fast getaway isn't necessary. Before I shift into first and power out onto 98, I close my eyes, take a deep breath, and blow out the fires burning in the dark. Dawnell sits straight up beside me, her back not touching the upholstery, both hands on the dash, crying without a sound.

I reach over to put my numb hand on her rocking back, but she says, "Don't. I don't want *no*body touching me. Not anymore."

I take her the only way I can think of, out to her father's place near Ebro. But I'm not going to that house unless she tells me to. I'll take her to the abandoned house in the woods where she'll have her things around her, and I'll stay with her if she wants me to.

TWENTY-FIVE

We see the plume of black smoke in the sky a mile before we get to the turnoff at Dawnell's daddy's house. It rises up fast, hot and black, and then thins and turns east on the wind that blows from the gulf into the steaming pine forests. It's not more than a minute after we pass Dawnell's turnoff that we know the smoke is coming from the little house where Dawnell lives her pretend life. I look over at her. My stomach aches with acid from the aftermath of Jimmy and the bartender with the big revolver, and now the smoke in the sky and the certainty of its source make my hands shake on the steering wheel. Dawnell won't look at me. She's fascinated by the tower of smoke. Somehow the sight of it has dried her tears. She looks as numb now as my right arm feels from Jimmy's cue-stick thumping. I stop at the turnoff to the secret place where little things made Dawnell happy. I say, "Tell me what to do. Do you want to go in there, or not?"

I'm thinking maybe we can save something. I'm thinking probably we can't and trying could be dangerous. And there's a chance, small, that it's not the old house that's burning, just some brush or an old haystack. She looks at me for the first time since we left the bar. "Go ahead," she says. "I guess I want to see it."

I stop the Plymouth where I always have. Two men stand in what was once the front yard of the old house. A red kerosene can rests on the ground between them. In the roar of the flames, they don't hear my engine rev and then stop. Finally, one of them senses something behind him and turns. I can tell by his face that he's Dawnell's brother, but not by any resemblance to her. He looks like her father, the other man who turns and looks at me now, smiling, half his face painted a weird orange by the glow of the fire. There's a rifle leaning against the boy's leg and, watching me, he takes it by the barrel, tosses it into the air, and catches it by the pistol grip. He holds it with the butt on his hip like a soldier resting on the march.

Dawnell comes to life beside me. I don't have time to reach for her before she screams, "Noooo!" and throws herself out of the car, running for the window at the side of the house where her dream room is. The fire is clawing up through the center of the house and some of it is already consuming that little room full of things that will burn fast when the flames come, but the window and the outside wall of that room are still holding. I get out of the car, only a few steps behind Dawnell, and chase. She throws herself at the wall, clawing her hands up to the windowsill and trying to climb and push the window up all at once, and somehow she manages to get it cracked, then shoved up far enough for her head and shoulders to fit inside. And that's where she is when I grab her and pull her back, legs kicking and arms flailing, screaming, "Noooo!"

I trap her arms from behind in an imprisoning hug and whisper in her ear, "It's too late. It's gone. There's nothing you can do."

She fights me, wild as a forest creature, but I hold on with my eyes shut, until I begin to feel the strength seep from her limbs. I look down and see blood on my ankles where she's gouged me with those red, high-heeled shoes. When she's finally still in my arms, all whimpering sobs and hard exhausted breathing, I look over at the two men.

They stare with fascinated eyes into the red heart of the fire. Have they seen this before? How the timbers, squeezed by the terrible heat, bleed their sap in droplets that hiss as they fall, fire snakes exploding into flame? How the roof becomes vapor and the walls lean in and the floor sags under the weight of the falling bones of the house until it gives way and an enormous cone of red embers lies on the bare ground under the four brick props that held up the house? How the mortar in the little chimney beyond the old rotten kitchen splits and zigzag-cracks with a sound like pistol shots until a few bricks separate and fall away into the greedy fire?

When it's almost over, the brother's eyes, drunk with destruction, draw away from the fire, and he looks at me holding his sister, her head fallen forward now to rest on my forearms. He smiles like he recognizes me, or just knows what I'm doing, swings the rifle down from his hip to a position at midthigh, and ambles over to me and Dawnell. "Get your hands off her," he says, "you pogey boy." He's wearing greasy Levi's, flared at the bottom over high, scuffed boots with the mud-caked laces dragging. His bare chest, sweating from the fire, is muscled but oddly long and tubular, with a dark cross of man hair running up from the navel to the throat and from nipple to nipple. He wears a black-and-white-striped railroad engineer's cap pushed off to the side and a slow smile that says he's as much as I am even without the rifle that is not quite pointed at me. He says, "Dawnie-ell, you get away from him. Come over here to me." He stamps his booted foot like he's trying to scare a dog, and the muddy laces snap.

Dawnell just hangs in my arms. Her right cheek rests on my right forearm hot and wet with tears. I realize that her feet still hang above the ground, that I am using strength I may need to hold her up like this. Without taking my eyes off her brother, I lower my mouth to her ear and say, "Wait for me in the car." I let her down slowly until her dangling red shoes touch the earth and I feel control grow back up into her legs. She sniffles, wipes her mouth, and steps away from me, to the side at first, then back toward the Plymouth.

Her brother shakes his head with dark philosophy. He's a man who's just told his truth to the world for the last time, and his next message will not come in words. The father takes a step away from the boy, then another, but not toward Dawnell and my Plymouth. He's moving away from ground where something messy is about to happen. He wears the same ancient zippered, vaguely military nylon jumpsuit, the kind that fliers wore, and his gut and mealy white chest spill out of it beneath the black whorls of stubble growing down his neck. He takes a few more steps back, then to the side, and stands there curiously passive, his eyes on his son's back, then on me, and then back on the boy holding the rifle. I hear the car door open and close, but I don't look. I watch the boy.

Dawnell's father and I had our meeting on her front porch. He saw me edge toward the little table with the song in my head about bone marrow seeing the light of day, and he backed off. Now he's going to watch me and the boy, like two roosters in a pit, do what we have to do. I don't like the rifle, a Winchester semiauto .22 with a small black steel flashlight taped to the fore end, but I don't believe he'll use it on me. His brown eyes are mean, but they're pale and squinted too. They've spent too much time in the dark, sighting down that barrel at small things that can't shoot back. I'm guessing he'll kill a man, but not now, not yet, later. And a voice in my head says, *Dirty white boy, don't guess wrong.*

He takes a step toward me, raising the rifle six inches higher and drawing that black dot, the hole in the end of the barrel, twenty degrees closer to pointing at my belly. He says, "What are you doing with my little sister, pogey boy?" Then he shouts, "Dawnie-ell, you little whore!" and behind me in the piney woods a covey of quail takes wing at the outrage of his family grief.

I say, "You going to shoot me with that rifle? If you are, go ahead and do it. If you're not, put it down." I point at the ground. I look across the boy's bare shoulder, slick with sweat, at the father. I call to him, guessing, "Mr. Briscoe, you've already burned down a building that doesn't belong to you. Are you going to add murder to your day's work?"

The father looks at me, at the back of his son's head, at the pine trees that surround the place where the house is now a smoking pyramid of shrunken timbers. He says, "I wutn' worried she'd catch to them trees. Man owns them trees wouldn't like that. But nobody owns this here house." He looks out at the woods, the path shrouded in vines that Dawnell took the day she met me here. He says, "Sides, a man can burn down a whorehouse. Leastways he ort to be able to.

Ain't no jury court around here would convict a man for burning down a whorehouse."

The man's words give the boy back some of the evil courage mine took away from him, and he swings the rifle another ten degrees toward my middle. If he pulled the trigger now, the bullet would miss me in the precious inches between my left hand and left hip.

I point my bloody right hand at his face and say, "Put the gun down and let me get out of here. You don't want me here when the sheriff comes. That smoke can be seen from ten miles away."

The father says, his voice singsongy, "I *know* the sheriff. Know him *well*."

The brother says, "Pogey boy, you whored out my sister, and I'm gone kill you for it."

I say, "I never touched your sister." I look around the boy, finding the father's face in a white haze. It's my fatigue and fear and the pain in my shoulder. I say, "I told you, sir, Dawnell and I are just friends."

He sings out low and musical, "And I *told* you, city boy, Dawn-ie-ell don't have no *friends*. She too *young* for that."

My arm still out straight in front of me, my forefinger still pointing at the brother's face, I close my eyes and try to think. Back in the infinite spaces behind my eyes, I see the condition of things. My anger is all gone. The fires of bitterness are cold, blown out by broken pool cues and a biker's comically long-barreled revolver, extinguished by the draft from the flames that took away Dawnell's little world of candles and books and men in dinner jackets. I open my eyes, take a deep, tired breath, and walk forward, seizing the end of the rifle barrel. I pull it the last ten degrees, fit it into my navel, and say, "Shoot, goddamn you, or let me go."

I look into his eyes, expecting change and seeing none. I've never known terror like this—he is considering it. His left eye twitches, trying to close as it does when he lays his cheek on the rifle stock and sights, flipping on the flashlight to send a sharp white beam across the forest floor to the eyes of a fox or a rabbit, paralyzed in light. I watch the eye, and the tired voice in my head says, *If he closes it, you're dead.*

The eye doesn't close. Slowly, I unlock the black hole at the end of the barrel from the notch at the bottom of my torso where my mother once sent life into me, and I slide it ten, then ten more degrees away from me, toward the still-hissing, smoking pile of wrack that was Dawnell's boat of dreams. I start walking toward my car. I tell myself, *Don't run. Keep it slow. Don't shoot off your mouth. No parting words.*

I get in, start the engine, and back up, past where the father stands watching his boy make the end of this story. I hear the boy yell, "Dawnie-ell, you come *back* here to me!" There's a frustrated whine in his voice now, and I know that frustration can be more dangerous than outrage. In my mind's eye, I see him aim the rifle. It's one thing to let me go, another to let me take his sister. But I don't turn to look. I'd rather have the bullet in the side of my head than see the puff of gray smoke at the barrel end before my brain splatters the white dress of the girl cowering next to me.

TWENTY-SIX

I drive thirty miles straight to J. M. Fields, a discount store in Panama City. It's the kind of place that sells cheap everything, shirts and pants and dresses and shoes that look like the expensive ones and even have labels that mock those in the better stores. It's all cheap, but some of it is strong and will last, and that's what I'm looking for. I take Dawnell not by the hand, but by the wrist, and walk her fast across the parking lot, past the gaping gazes of matrons pushing shopping carts and dragging dazed children, past the eyebrows that arch above the tortoiseshell rims of sunglasses on the faces of tourists who forgot their suntan lotion when they left Dothan, and I take her inside, straight to the section marked *Misses*, where I start pulling shorts and jeans and blouses off the racks, shoving them into Dawnell's startled face, and I tell her, "There," and, "There," and, "This one too," and when she's loaded down like the world's most inept shoplifter, I take her hand and walk her to the little room marked *Women*, and I stand watching her bare legs under the swinging door of the booth with shorts and pants rising and falling on them.

She's about finished when I say, "Now hand over that damn white dress."

And she says, low and cool now that most of her fear and her anger have drained away, "Why?"

I want to say, *Because I said so. Because your weasel brother almost shot my guts out with his rabbit-killing tool.* But I take a deep breath and say, "Because it's not right for you, and it's too dirty to ever be cleaned, and you need some new things, now hand it over." She tosses the dress through the gap above the door, kicks out the tired, red shoes for good measure, and that's when I feel the hand fall heavy on my shoulder. I turn to the skeptical eyes and mercantile face of a trim, crew-cut young man in gray flannels and a cheap blue blazer and a name tag that says, *Bob Billings, Manager.*

Mr. Bob Billings says, "What's going on here?"

I say, "A lot's going on, sir. I'm buying some of your fine clothing for my little sister."

This rocks him back on his heels. He looks at the two shapely legs under the swinging door, sees a pair of denim shorts fall and, after a dainty sidestep, get picked up monkey fashion by some red-painted toes and lifted out of sight. "Oh," he says, "well, you're not supposed to be in here with her. This area is restricted to women only. You can wait for her outside."

I look at him thoughtfully. "But my mother told me to help her decide what to get, and to make sure what she purchases is . . . appropriate. I don't want to disappoint my mother."

"Well," he says, firm, "we'd be delighted to have your mother come in and help your sister, but our store policy is that you can't be back here."

"All right," I say, "I'll wait outside, but I'm afraid my sister may end up purchasing some garments that don't fit her correctly."

He turns to leave, shooting his cuffs and tugging down the lapels of his blue blazer to eliminate the gap where it drapes poorly at the back of his neck. Over his shoulder he says, "We'll be happy to let you return anything that doesn't fit, provided it hasn't been worn and you bring in your proof of purchase."

Outside the little dressing room with four booths, two women wait with garments hanging over their arms. They have been listening to our little drama. As I pass them, they look at me with eyes that say, *Good brother.*

I knock left-handed on the Widow's door and stand on her stoop in the bruising sun waiting for her to open it. I find that I look forward to seeing her face. She's not just my landlady anymore, she's the impresario of the vodka cure and a woman who thinks my father is a very interesting man. Probably the worst that can happen is that she will have me evicted before nightfall.

When she appears at the door, not in her yellow muumuu, but in a pink terry-cloth bathrobe and without a drink in her hand, she shades her eyes from the sun and says, "What do you . . . ? Oh, *Travis!* What can I do for you?" Her voice is low and thin. She tries to smile, but it's not working very well. Her right hand, the one that usually holds the tall, sweating glass of vodka and grapefruit juice, is shaking. She sees me look at it and stuffs it into the pocket of her pink robe.

I say, "I hope I didn't wake you?"

"Wake me? Well of course not, honey! It's the middle of the afternoon."

"I thought maybe you were taking a nap."

"I don't nap," she snaps, then raises her left hand in apology, and lifts it higher to her forehead, rubbing at the headache that must be starting hard. She peers up at the sun behind me, squints, blinks. "Come in for a minute, honey, and let me—"

"No, uh, no, I need you to come with me."

"Come with *you?*"

"Uh, yeah, just over to my place." I gesture at the twenty yards of sandy earth between her door and mine.

She looks back at her neat, cool cabin, up again at the sun behind me. "Well, all right. Can I come like this?" She means the robe, her bare feet. She wiggles her toes. Pink nails match the robe.

I say, "Sure. I mean it's fine with me."

She smiles shyly. I have no idea what she thinks waits for her in my cabin, but I can see she's strangely pleased to be crossing over in her robe.

The Widow is no more than a step inside my door before she throws both hands out in front of her as though to keep something big and moving fast from knocking her off the road of life. "Travis," she says, "I *told* you I will not tolerate . . ."

Dawnell is sitting on my bed with her legs crossed beneath her in a new pair of denim shorts and a white short-sleeved cotton blouse. She's wearing white cotton socks and a pair of no-brand sneakers. She's surrounded by plastic J. M. Fields bags full of the things we bought: we even stopped at the cosmetics counter on the way out and I picked out a tube of flesh-colored lip gloss. (She: "You can't even see this stuff!" I: "That's the point.") Dawnell looks her age now. The electric lipstick and rouge have faded from her face. When the red polish has all chipped from her nails, and if I can persuade her not to reapply it, she'll look like what she is, a child going on woman at not quite breakneck speed. She looks up from one of my novels, *A Separate Peace*, and smiles at the Widow. I wish I could say the Widow smiles back.

To the Widow, I say, "*Stop!* Just . . . stop."

Her eyes struggle with the changes that have taken place between her and me in such a short time. I've gone from Travis Flotsam, just another human container of unsavory history that floated up, dusty and disheveled, from US 98 asking for a place to sleep and able to produce in advance, just barely, one week's rent. Travis Flotsam turns out to have a daddy who is making a fortune in real estate and, consequently, driving a very fine automobile. The Widow has had to promote me up the social ladder from rags to possible riches. She likes riches, but she also likes clear categories, and she doesn't like the way I talk about my father and my family and wanting to be apart from them for the time being. Now I've just yelled, *Stop!* into the teeth of one of her well-practiced laments about what she will not tolerate on her premises. I've yelled stop, also, into the deep, damp, hurting hollows of her ten thousandth hangover, and now, by God, I'd better explain myself.

"Just . . ." I say again very softly, "give me a chance to explain. Then, if you don't like what you hear, you can . . . Well, you can do whatever you like, and I won't complain."

She draws herself up into the righteousness of freeholding property ownership, writs of eviction, and having the phone number of the sheriff's office permanently scored into her brainpan and easily retrievable. "Like *you'd* have anything to complain about," she mutters, her eyes sidling over to Dawnell whose bright smile is about to give way to the Pouts. "What are *you* doing here, young lady?"

Dawnell is about to answer. I guess the Widow would prefer to hear the story from her, owing to the theory that, woman to woman, she'll get a lot more truth, but I reach out and put my hand on Dawnell's shoulder and say, "Let me. Just this once."

I tell it all, from the beginning. How Dawnell and I met, what we've seen of each other these last few weeks, how it's all been chaste (Dawnell's aggrieved eyes tell me that her femme fatale is offended by this, but she manages to keep quiet), how I took her back from Jimmy and the Guerrilla Army for the Return of America to the True Values of the Old South (playing down the violence), how Dawnell can't go back to her father and brother because, and here I give myself some license to elaborate, "they are an older and younger version of the same deranged scum that no innocent young girl should ever have to see in a roadside ditch, much less live with," and I finish, simply, my eyes looking straight into the Widow's, my voice quiet, calm, west of begging, but well east of any certainty as to her decision: "Can she just stay here a few nights until we sort some things out?"

"*Here!*" The Widow looks knowingly around her at what is now Travis's Den of Iniquity: Virgins Deflowered, Reputations Ruined, Satisfaction Guaranteed.

I say, "Not here with me. No, no. I mean stay with *you*."

The Widow shakes her head slowly, presses a hand flat to her forehead, and feels herself the way you do a child who might have a fever. She says, "You two wait a minute, I need to go get something."

When she comes back a few minutes later with a tall, sweating vodka and grapefruit juice, I'm sitting on the bed beside Dawnell with a rehearsed expression of expectancy and hope on my face.

The Widow already looks somewhat revived. Has she slyly partaken of the cure, those frosty shot glasses, those little sin bullets, even before calculating the measure of this tall vodka and pink grapefruit juice? She sits at my little desk and looks at the two of us on the bed.

"My two little waifs," she says. She's already got a bit of a slur that makes Dawnell and me sound like two ruffled, four-footed creatures from the Russian steppes. I have more years than Dawnell, and the aching hurt where Jimmy's pool cue puddled the muscle that knits my neck to my shoulder, and the lucky guess I made about the feral brother with the rifle adapted for night killing, seem to me to constitute a passport into the same adulthood that wraps the Widow in wisdom, but I don't protest. Let's see what she has to say first.

"I assume," she begins, "that the two of you know a minor child can't just leave her parents, or in this case her father, ditch scum though he may be. It ain't legal. In order for you to leave home . . . What's your name, honey?"

Meekly: "Dawnell."

Honey. This is progress.

"In order for you to leave home *legally,* Dawnell, you'll have to either get your father's permission and find a place to live the law will approve, or you'll have to go to the courts and make some kind of charge against your father." The Widow's eyes go dark and small. "He ain't been messing with your britches, has he?" We all stop breathing and look at the floor. After a space, I glance over at Dawnell. Her face is the reddest I've ever seen it.

She looks up from under hung brows and says, "No, he ain't done nothing like that. But I hate living with him, with the two of them and no . . . privacy. They don't care how they walk around or what they say, and my brother called me a . . . a ho-urr."

The Widow shakes her head at the low meanness of it all, but I can see she's relieved. It hasn't happened yet, but that doesn't mean it won't. In her father's house, Dawnell is a morsel waiting to be eaten.

"Well, all right then." The Widow stands up decisively, but she wobbles a little at the knees and covers herself by staring pensively into her drink. "Get your things, honey, and go on over to my place. It's the first door straight ahead. We'll see what we can do about you for a few days."

Dawnell gets up and looks at me with pure simple hope in her bright-blue eyes. She smiles. Three times I've helped her in a day. I smile back, hoping my help doesn't go bad and knowing there are a hundred ways it can. Dawnell gathers up the plastic bags full of the things I've bought her. She stands at the door and looks back.

The Widow says, "Go on, honey. I want to talk to Travis here for a minute."

Dawnell quietly closes my door, and in a while we hear the Widow's jalousies rattle open and rattle shut.

The Widow looks hard at me and says, "How do you know they won't come here looking for her? Those two stinkdogs from the woods."

I look into her sad eyes and think about it. It occurs to me that I could flex my muscles a bit and say something like, *Well if they do, I'll be ready,* but that's crap and she'll know it before the words are out of my mouth. One of my arms is hanging half-dead. I might be able to handle the brother, without his rifle, but together the two dogs would make short work of me, and when they were finished, I'd probably have to watch them through bloodied eyes beating the hell out of Dawnell. If they left me with eyes to see. And there wouldn't have to be any violence at all if they came with the sheriff. It's like the Widow said, the rights of parents, even the worst ones, trump the desires of young girls and their somewhat older, ambiguously interested male friends. I shake my head, shrug. "I don't know it. They might come. I guess I'm sort of counting on them not giving enough of a damn about her to bother. At least not for a while, and maybe that will give me time to think."

She sniffs. "Give *you* time. She's sitting over there at *my* place now."

Suddenly, I'm feeling very tired. I reach up and touch the swollen contusion under my T-shirt. My right shoulder feels like a burning boil that's about to burst and pour the lava of anger all over me. It hurts like hell, or like how I imagine the punishments of hell will hurt when I get there.

The Widow squints at me, her eyes narrowing. She says, "My

Gawd, Travis, what *is* that?" She walks over and sits next to me, reaching out toward my neck. "Let me see." She picks at my shirt collar, but I shrug away from her, and even that hurts. She says, "Don't be silly. Let me see." Carefully, she plucks up my collar and peeks under it. "Good Lord, look at you. How did that happen?"

"I don't know," I say. "I was helping her . . ." I nod toward the door where Dawnell has just disappeared.

The Widow breathes, "Whew!" Then she says, "Well, somebody sure as hell didn't help *you*. Did her daddy do that?"

"No," I say, "it was before I got to her daddy." The bed under me feels good. Suddenly, I want to lie down and sleep for a long time. I want the Widow to leave.

She reaches down to the waistband of my jeans and starts tugging at my shirt. "Stand up," she says, firm now, in the voice they used at Bridgedale when they marched us around. "I have to look at you. Let me take off your shirt."

"I can take it off." But I can't. Not very well, anyway, with only one working arm.

The Widow puts her hands under my arms and pulls me up. "Come over to the sink." She walks me over, and I stand facing the tap, leaning on the counter while she pulls the shirt up and over my head.

"Ow! *Damn* it."

"I'm trying not to hurt you, Travis."

"Try harder."

I feel like I'm going to fall asleep standing up. She gets the shirt off me and gasps at what she sees. "Honey, you need a doctor. This thing is black as midnight. Your collarbone could be broken." She lifts her hand and hovers it above my shoulder but doesn't touch me. "Who did this to you?"

I'm not going to mention Jimmy Danes and his crew. I don't want her thinking about all of the forces arrayed against us. I say, "A guy hit me with a pool cue. I hope there's somebody taking care of *him* right now, because he sure as hell needs it." It sounds braggy, but it's true and saying it makes me feel better.

"Never mind that," the Widow says, "you need to go to the emergency room."

"It's not broken," I tell her. I know it's true. I've broken bones before, and when they break, you hear them snap. A doctor once told me it's called bone conduction noise. "Besides, I can't afford the emergency room. I spent all my money on clothes for her. Can you get me some ice . . . and some of *that?*" Her vodka and pink grapefruit juice sits on the counter next to me.

She considers for a minute, but I know I won't have to argue with her. She understands the medicinal value of alcohol. She pulls my ice tray from the fridge and cracks it open, takes a towel from the bathroom, and fixes me an ice pack. Then she hands me her drink. "Here, finish it. I'll go get myself another one and come back and sit with you."

I say, "No, please, I just need to sleep awhile. I'll lie down with the ice on my shoulder and see if I can drift off. Would you go take care of Dawnell?"

The Widow looks a little unhappy about not coming back to me, but she smiles again and says, "Sure, honey, don't you worry about her. You get some rest."

"Thank you, Mrs. Reddick."

She reaches out and draws the back of her hand across my cheek. It's cold from holding the vodka, but the gesture is warm. She says, "Honey, I want you to call me Sandralene. We might as well be on a first-name basis if we're going to be violating the Mann Act together."

In my dream the trash can in front of the J. M. Fields store tumbles over and Dawnell's white dress walks with no one in it, and then Delia is in it, with hair black like it used to be, not blond, and she's Dawnell's age, and we're riding in my car, but I'm not driving, Dawnell's young uncle is driving, smiling shyly and whistling with the radio, and I smell something on the warm air blowing through my open window. It's smoke, a strong acrid pine and tar odor, and I look out the window, and there's a high, black column of smoke foaming up out of the pines, and then I look into the front seat of my car and the driver is gone. No one is holding the wheel, and we're veering toward the soft wet shoulder and the deep ditch beyond, and Delia looks back at me with tears of fury in her eyes and says, "Do something, Travis! Do something!"

I wake up standing at the bathroom door with my useless right arm hanging, and my left hand frozen to the doorknob. I'm still half in my dream and the bathroom door is the steering wheel, and I'm trying to steer from the backseat, but the car is veering, veering. In the struggle, I shove my bruised shoulder against the wall, and the pain wakes me up the rest of the way.

There are bad dreams and bad dreams. The worst ones wake you up. There's a deep place in your mind where something lives that cannot trust the worst dreams to end while you are sleeping. Five or six times now, I've awakened walking, far from my bed, trying to use the world to wrench me out of sleep.

I touch my aching shoulder and go back to my bed in the dark. The ice in the towel has melted all over my sheets and pillow. I throw the towel at the kitchen sink. I open my front door and breathe the night air, warm, watery, and smelling of dew on sea oats, the Podocarpus bushes that border the Widow's walkway, and laundry detergent from the washhouse. There's a light on in the Widow's cabin. Somehow, I know it's Dawnell. It's one in the morning and the Widow, with all she drinks, can't withstand sleep this long, even if she does nap and lie about it.

I shut my door quietly and slip barefooted across the sand to the window, hopping to avoid the clumps of sandspurs. I think about it for a while. If I knock, and it's Dawnell, we'll talk and who knows what then? I have to be careful now with everything I do. So many things are going on now, so many strands that make the web, the big design I can't yet see, may never see. I've told myself the lie that I'm the designer. I've spun the threads—Delia, my father, Ole Temp Tarleton, Emil, Dawnell, the Widow—and I am winding them together in a way that catches something, something that signifies. Something called the rest of my life. But the thought is never far off that all I'm catching in the web of my design is Travis Hollister. Travis Flotsam. Travis Criminal. Travis Paralyzed. Travis Dead.

I hear a faint singing through the lighted window glass. It might be the radio playing low, the way I once heard music drifting, a sinuous night mystery, from Delia's door across the hallway, to my bed where I lay trying to understand love. Believing that somehow the truth of love was in the songs my Delia listened to and loved. But this is not the radio. More listening instructs me that it's Dawnell singing to herself in this new room in a strange woman's house (she has no idea yet how strange). I move closer to the glass, and I get the melody, a floating word here and there. It's a song from one of the new British groups, Chad & Jeremy: *"Trees swayin' in the summer breeze, showin' off their silver leaves, as we walk by."* It's a sweet, sad song, full of the moment when autumn seizes summer in its cold hands, and all the world knows it in one way or another, and, though summer and autumn are two kinds of delight, the change, the fact of the change itself, is terrifying. It's not a song I thought I would hear Dawnell sing.

I reach out and tap softly on the window, and the sweet, small voice inside ceases, and we are about to spin another thread of our lives. Dawnell swipes aside the white cotton curtain and thrusts her face so close to the glass I'm afraid she'll break it. Her eyes are late-night wide and wild. There's no fear in them of what might be at her window. With a mixture of kindness and regret she recognizes my face, a few feet below her sill. Was she expecting Chad & Jeremy, the two russet-domed British choirboys, or is the regret because I bring back her past just when she is settling into new digs.

I jab my thumb up twice and mouth, *Open the window.* Her lips go *Oops!* and she tugs until the window lifts from its painted bed and rises a few inches. The blessed cool of the Widow's air-conditioning bathes my face. I whisper, "Is she asleep?"

Dawnell shrugs. "I think so. Once in a while I hear her snoring. That's weird, a lady snoring."

I'm thinking, *That was no lady. That was a drunk.* But who am I to think, *Vodka drinker, walking dreamer, midnight window tapper?* I start with the obvious: "How are you doing?"

Dawnell's face gets serious and she rolls her eyes. "Pretty good," she says. "But I can't help wondering what Daddy's doing right now. And Ard. What they're doing and all, you know."

In her soft wide eyes and her pensive tone, there are equal parts of plain curiosity and a little girl's longing for the family circle. It doesn't surprise me. What surprised me was that she got into my car when I told her to, back there at the burning house. That she went through the show at J. M. Fields without putting up a serious fight for her red shoes and the white dress. Somewhere along the way, I heard the proverb *Never get between a country girl and her family*—not, at least, with anything in your hand but a diamond ring.

"What do they usually do?" I whisper, looking up at her glowing face, her gem-blue eyes.

She thinks about it. "Right about now Daddy's falling asleep in his chair in front of the TV with an empty bottle of Heaven Hill on the floor beside him, and Ard's out in the woods with his gun. I'm in my room playing records or reading or something, you know." She's painted herself back into the family circle. She looks long and hard into my eyes, and it seems that what she just said sputtered from an idling mind while her eyes explored mine.

I blink, look off at the row of forty-watt porch lights that mark the domiciles of the drifters, shrimpers, lost tourists, and paper mill shift workers who live at the Wind Motel. Beyond the row of lights there's a tall stand of Australian pines, and their boughs, smelling of swamp tang, swish and hush in the night breeze. My eyes dig around in that far darkness for a few seconds before returning to Dawnell. I say, "That's his name, your brother? Ard?"

She's says, "Yeah. Ard." Nothing strange about this to her.

"What's it short for?" I ask.

She looks at me like I just don't know up from down. She says, "Nothing. His name is Ard."

I shake my head, smile. I don't want her to think I'm making fun.

I never want to do that. In the big design of things, who's to say that "Travis" makes any more sense than "Ard." But I think, *It's got to be short for aardvark. Surely.*

I look up at her. She's resting her chin now on her folded hands, tired, I guess, of fitting her eye to six inches of open window. The cool AC bathes my face. Dawnell, I know, is nobody's fool, though it suits her sometimes to play the role. I say, "What are we going to do with you now?"

She takes my words as a mild insult, then turns them into another slow, knowing smile that's all woman. She says, "Who's this *we* you talking about? You and her?" She rolls her eyes back at the bedroom behind her. The snoring widow, Sandralene. "Or you and me?"

I just shake my head. It's too late at night. I don't know why I'm standing here. Maybe it is just to wake up from a bad dream. I look off into that deepest darkness where the only proof of the Australian pine boughs is their soughing, hushing, pushing on the night wind. I say, "I've got to go back now. You get some sleep. Turn off the radio. Turn out the light." My voice, trying to be firm, sounds thin as air.

I reach up and press my left forefinger to the screen, two inches from her chin. She puts out one finger and meets mine. Mates it. A strange heat.

"Night," I say.

"Night, boy."

TWENTY-SEVEN

'Ve never seen Emil like this.

Saturday night is coming like a freight train. The rising rush and noise of the dining room seem to make the building rock and swell. Emil's muttering to himself under his breath and walking the line of his bubbling, smoking fryers and using his knives and spatulas with quick angry motions. He asks me, "You the reason I ain't got no dishwasher?" He looks at me like I better not lie to him, like we're on one of his navy ships, and he'll throw me overboard if I prevaricate. *No mendacity.*

I look into his big dark eyes where his anger burns. "Yes sir. I guess so."

He stops what he's doing, wipes his hands on the first of fifty white bus towels he'll use tonight, and walks over to stand in front of me. He bends down and looks into my eyes, and I can smell his shaving lotion, Bay Rum, and his minty breath. He says, "You guess so, huh? Well, you my dishwasher now. Get back there behind that machine and learn what you got to learn before it gets any mo' busy out there." He walks away, turns back. "You get a fifty-cent-an-hour raise and no tips. It comes out just about even."

I can learn it. I've watched Jimmy Danes do it for weeks now. There's some danger to it, and not just sticking your hands into soapy tubs of knives and forks. The big dishwashing machine uses superheated water under pressure and, if you're not careful, you can steam the skin off your hands or face.

The night rolls on, and I learn. Emil doesn't look at me with approval for the fast study I've made of dishwashing. He doesn't look at me at all. I know he's not just mad about being shorthanded. I'm his protégé, and he's pissed off at me because I've gotten myself involved in what he calls "redneck drama." He talks about it often enough, all the things that the uneducated, the drunken, the drugged-out, and the uncareful youth around here do to shorten or scar their lives. I feel sorry for Emil because he liked me and trusted me and I let him down. I even feel sorry for Jimmy, a little bit. He's the second Jimmy I've done bodily harm. I stabbed Jimmy Pultney in self-defense, and I shoved a pool cue into Jimmy Danes's throat to save Dawnell from the group activity that was surely coming to her. I went to jail for the first effort. Now, pushing racks of lard-congealed plates into the steaming maw of the big machine, it comes to me that I could go back to jail for the second, if things go wrong. Why didn't I think of that before I let the air out of Jimmy's tires and walked into that bar? I don't know. I just don't know. If I had thought about it, would I have done anything different? In my head, as I stack dishes, I hear what Dr. Janeway would say: *Travis, you could have gone to the local law enforcement and told them three delinquent boys ran off with an underage girl and meant her no good.*

"Yeah, yeah, yeah," I'm saying out loud, "and I'm an outsider here, and the local law enforcement, in the form of a bag of grits with boots and a pistol, was a delinquent boy on his last birthday. He probably used to raid crab traps with Jimmy Danes's daddy."

I'm talking to myself too loud. Emil looks over at me. He's muttering under his breath too, and we're two fantastical stammering figures, Vulcan at his forge, huge and angry, and me, some half-human, sweating, apprentice boy with a man's body and the moral nature of a donkey. Emil shakes his head and drops a handful of floured shrimp into a fryer (he can pick up a perfect twelve-count without looking nineteen times out of twenty).

The night rolls on. Busboys come and go giving me the evil eye because the waitresses are cursing them for more forks. A waitress rushes into the kitchen carrying a bus tray because we're shorthanded. She drops it, *Whack! Splash!* in front of my big, hissing, thumping ma-

chine and doesn't bother to sort the contents for me. Another waitress comes in with a tray, stands with her hands on her hips, reaches
up and flips sweat from her brow, and gives me a piece of her mind.
It's a slimy thing, her mind. "Yeah, yeah, yeah," I mutter. "Everybody's
name is motherfucker."

When it's all over, and I've left five pounds of my own body in
sweat on the duckboards with all the rest of the grime, I do Jimmy's
job and my own too, without being asked. I clean the machine for the
next day, help sweep out the dining room, restock the waitress stations with clean flatware, and take out the garbage. I make six trips to
the trash barrels in the alley, each one a slip and slide past the shooting gallery of Emil's eyes as he sits on the loading dock smoking and
drinking from his little silver cup. On my last trip, a little dizzy from
fatigue, weight loss, and the pain in my shoulder, I walk head down,
not wanting to meet his eyes. I'll give the dining room one more look
for anything unfinished, and then leave by the front door, sneaking
past the light from Big Sam's office and the crank and whirr of his
adding machine.

"Get yourself one," Emil says in a tired voice that's nonetheless
sure of being obeyed. I look up at him. He's holding out the pack
of Camels, one already shaken out for me to pinch. "Go on in the
kitchen," he mutters. It means I can join him in a silver cup of white
shine. I pluck the butt, lean to his palm-cupped lighter, and walk inside for my thimble of divine compensation.

I drop next to him and smoke, pluming my gray exhalations
beside his in the still night air. He says, "You know Jimmy's in the
hospital?"

"No. What's hurting him?"

He looks over at me, sharp, suspicious. "You don't know?"

"I know it could be any number of things, some of them I did to
him."

"Well, he's got a concussion, a bad one. He went home the other
night from a bar, and they say he collapsed and stayed under so long
his boys decided to take him to the emergency."

I take a deep breath, blow it out with a load of relief. "A big biker did that to him. Hit him in the head with the barrel of a handgun. All I did was poke him in the throat with a pool cue."

Emil looks down at his Camel, his gray, burn-scarred hands. He spits a shred of tobacco out into the alley with more than necessary force. "He's damn lucky those mean little shits he runs with didn't just let him lie there till he died." He looks over at me. "You pretty good with a pool cue? In a scrap? In a cut-and-shoot dive by the county hard road? Is that your thing, boy? That what you been so quiet about all this time?"

"Not that good," I say. "Just lucky with a pool cue, and quick to take the high ground." I pull in a big drag of the good, sweet Carolina tobacco smoke. "There were three of them," I tell him. "Before you start writing me down as a sucker-punch artist, you might consider that." My voice sounds a little big-man to me, and a little aggrieved too.

Emil lets me have the first smile of a long night. "I guess your nuts ain't so numb as I thought they were, colonel." He holds his Camel out at arm's length, admires the ash, the glowing coal inside. He says, "I seen men die in battle. Don't think I'm impressed by roughy-toughy boys with pool cues, or any damn pissant bikers, either." He looks up at the clear black sky, the band of bright stars that fans across it. He looks over at me again. "Them boys gon' be coming for you now. You know that, don't you?"

I look down the alley, then up at the vast, clean, burning field of stars. I try not to show it. I think I'm doing a pretty good job, but what Emil said scares the shit out of me. The idea of being creeped by Jimmy and his gang of fuck-ups. Coming around some corner late at night and finding them there, smiling, waiting for me with tire irons and bicycle chains. My hands are shaking, so I rest them on my thighs, palms up. *Relax,* I tell them. There's a feeling on the floor of my belly like a fast elevator to the top of a tall building just started with me in it. Without looking at Emil, I say, "I was in a correctional facility out in Nebraska. For six years, starting when I was twelve. I took a bayonet my father brought back from the South Pacific and stabbed a kid who lived next door to me. The kid shot a steel-tipped arrow at me, twice. The first time I ducked, and it went right through my hair, cut my scalp, I can show you the scar. The second time, well, there wasn't a second time, not completely. When he put the arrow on the bowstring, I stuck the bayonet into his arm, right here." I raise my left arm and point at my right shoulder, where the pain and stiffness from Jimmy's cue are coming on again after the heat and struggle of the night's work. "I stuck the bayonet in him right here. Cut all the nerves, I guess. He never could use the arm again. That's what they told me, but when I got the medical news, I was already in the shade. That's what they call prison. *Spending some time in the shade.* I used to tell the guys in Bridgedale that I didn't give a shit . . ." Emil winces at my cussing, even in the middle of a story like this one. ". . . about the guy's arm. He was a worse asshole with two good arms. I did the world a service."

It's a long story, a version of something much longer I'm not yet ready to tell. I'm a little out of breath with the way the words rushed out of me after being held inside so long. I can't say it feels good, but it doesn't feel bad either. Not yet. I look at my Camel. It's burned down to the tips of my fingers. I toss it away.

Emil silently offers me another, lights it for me. He says, "So that's what you ain't been saying all this time. I knew it was something." He thinks about it, about me. He sips his whiskey with a little "Ahh," and follows it with a quick suck of smoke. He says, "And that's why you took Jimmy Danes to the woodshed. You got the habit, and you can't lose it?"

I say, "No, at least I don't think I got the habit. He was . . . Jimmy was hurting somebody, and I had to make him stop."

"Ohhh," Emil says, "that little girl." It's not a question.

I don't say anything. I know there's more coming from him.

Emil looks up at the high, cold field of stars. He sweeps his eyes across the whole dome of sky, from one end of what we can see to the other. He says, "You know, kid, all my life in the navy I tried to accomplish one thing, just one thing. You got to train young men, make them do their jobs as well as they can, up to a certain standard, and in most cases that ain't hard. The worst ones wash up out at Great Lakes, and the ones that make it to the fleet are more or less ready to learn, and for the few hard cases that slip through you got ways and means, if you know what I mean." He drags his eyes out of the stars, makes two fists, and looks at the gray scarred knuckles. "But train them, make them work up to a decent standard, that wasn't the most important thing to me. What I tried to do with the best of them was get them past the waterfront, past the first line of bars and whore-houses they hit when they left the ship."

He glances over at me, our eyes meet, and I can see he's giving me the best he's got, his philosophy.

"You know, kid," he says, "the slogan used to be, *Join the US Navy and see the world,* but most of these kids, even some of the best ones, they'd go to the most interesting ports in the world and never make it past that first bar and whorehouse on the waterfront. I used to tell them, *For Jesus sake, you're in Spain, you're in Italy, you're in the Phil-ippine Islands, Japan, get into the country, go to a museum, see the forest, the crops, the mountains, the monuments, meet the real people.* But most of them, even the best of them, would come staggering, crawling, hanging between the shoulders of two buddies, back from that first bar and whorehouse, with those silly-ass grins on their faces. I used to look at them coming aboard ship, look at them with the whiskey shakes and green at the gills in my galley the next morning, and say, *You know, whiskey's the same wherever you go, and believe it or not, pussy's the same too, even if it does come wrapped in different colors of skin and speaking in strange tongues, but architecture, forests, crops, museums, they change from place to place, and you just pissed away your chance to under-stand that and most likely picked up a dose of the clap in the bargain. Well, maybe next time.* We'd be under weigh, the ship rolling under our feet, and some of these boys, green at the gills, trying to scramble eggs or fry potatoes with whiskey puke knocking at the back of their throats, is wondering, I hope they was wondering, if they'd ever get back to Subic or Rota or Heraklion again."

He looks over at me, and I nod, and nod again, trying to show him I've taken the message. But he just shakes his head, flicks his butt onto the wet sand of the alley, and shoves himself up with an "Oof" of weariness. He's not just tired from a Saturday night in Big Sam's kitchen, he's tired of me, and of all the young men in his memories who came staggering back from that first night ashore, that first street of red neon and loud music and bargain humanity, and who missed so much.

I push myself up too, using just my left arm. I don't want Emil standing above me like that, looking down from so high. I want to tell him more about me, about how stabbing Jimmy Pultney was not just self-defense. How it was about my summer in Widow Rock, and Delia and two boys who died there, Bick Sifford and Kenny Griner, and how I felt so pushed around and so dealt with and so hopeless and helpless so much of the time, except when I was with Delia, and except when I understood that I could help her. Helping her, the bad, crazy ways I did it, was really what Jimmy Pultney and Bridgedale were all about. I came back from that summer full of something that had to come out, and Jimmy was just unlucky enough to be there when it did.

I want to tell Emil I'm different now. I'm looking for a new way to live. I'm helping someone again and trying to do it right this time, and she's not a whore, though this is the second time today she's been called one. I want to tell him I heard what he said. I want to understand his philosophy, use it in my life. He thinks Dawnell is that first street of neon, and he doesn't even know Delia. He thinks I haven't seen the forest, the town, the mountains beyond that first street, and maybe he's right. That's part of what I've got to learn.

We've hired a new dishwasher, a long-faced, quiet old man named Carl, who's done the work all his life and seems as resigned to the hiss and moan and sudden spurts of steam from the machine as he is to the threadbare khakis he wears and the Prince Albert tobacco he slowly rolls into cigarettes with twists at both ends. When Big Sam's goes dark at midnight, I see Carl walking off down US 98, a tired, shambling ghost dematerializing into the night.

I'm back on duty in the dining room bussing tables and stocking stations. It's one thirty, late in the lunch hour, and I'm doing my job in a daze of sweat and speed and confused daydreams of possible futures when I see Delia and two other women being seated by a hostess in a booth near the front. She's wearing a short lime-green silk skirt and a matching blouse, pearl stockings, and her hair is done in what I've heard called a flip. She looks a little bit like Mrs. Kennedy, and so do her two companions. Their colors are fruity, bright yellows and greens and plum. The two women are flushed and excited (God knows what they've escaped to be here today), chatting away, glancing around the dining room to see who's here, and throwing their wrists up limp in front of their eyes to ogle rings and bracelets and manicures. Delia's doing a pretty fair imitation of her friends, but there's a concentration in her face as she surveys the room. She's looking for someone. It doesn't take her long to find me. I'm standing iron straight at the back of the room, a full bus tray on my shoulder, sweat, ketchup, and beer soaking my collar, trying to keep my face from opening for her in a way that everyone will see.

We look at each other. A kind of electric burn forces a red flush up both of our necks, and we turn away quickly. When I look back again and take a step toward her, she shakes her head in a way no one but me can see, *Don't,* and turns back to her two friends.

The three have a long lunch. The dining room is clearing out when they finish. I've been in and out, but never close to them. Another busboy covers that part of the dining room. I've stolen looks at them, at Delia. I've watched the way she tosses, then pats her blond hair, lifts her drink to her mouth, forks her salad to her parted lips. I've counted their drinks, whiskey sours, and passed close to the waitress serving them to see what she ordered, what they all ordered. The two women are now smoking cigarettes, their hands like the heads of swans on long white necks, dipping and turning in spirals of smoke. Delia watches the smoking, the coffee disappearing sip by sip, with what seems to me impatience.

Finally, the three pay their bill, passing it around, tittering over the total, and piling money from all of their purses in the middle of the table. They get up to leave without a backward glance at the dining room. Delia walks out last, her head slightly down, her hips making rhythm, and her fancy-shod feet crossing over a little with each stride. It seems to me that if I got there quick, I'd see her footprints still releasing smoke in a straight line to the door.

I stand at the back of the dining room in a dream of confusion. Did she come here only to look at me that one time and let her eyes say, *Don't?* Did she come here merely to eat and chat with two friends, and was seeing me a surprise, a pleasure, an annoyance? A busboy moves toward the mess of Delia's table, and I wake up.

Quickly I cross the dining room and step in front of him, begin to clear the table. There must be something here. Something for me, a message in the way her knife and fork are laid across the plate, something written in lipstick on a carelessly crushed napkin. The other busboy stands behind me frowning, then shrugs, moves on, plenty of work to do here. I've cleared the table, found nothing, my mind full of empty spaces and crowded rooms where voices whisper about betrayal and longing. Then I look down at the green leatherette cushion where Delia sat, and I catch the wink of something bright. I bend and pick up a gold key ring. Car keys.

A hand grazes my shoulder. Delia says, loudly, "Oh, thank you. I guess they fell out of my bag. Wouldn't get far without them." I spin, and she smiles at me, the full brilliant Public Delia Smile. She takes the keys from my hand, drops them into her purse, fishes for a five-dollar bill, and presses it into my palm. "Thank you, young man," she says publicly. The few diners who are left, sun-stumped tourists in T-shirts and flip-flops, three road workers who have been repaving a stretch of highway, blink at our little exchange and go back to pinching the tails off their shrimp. Delia leans inches closer to me and says, "When do you get off?"

Stupefied, I look at the clock on the wall back by the kitchen. "In about thirty minutes."

"I'll be in the parking lot." She smiles at me, our old secret smile, then turns and burns the dining room to the ground with the beam of that public smile. She walks away so sweet, like the rolling swell on a morning tide, and everyone in the place watches her leave.

TWENTY-EIGHT

At two o'clock, I hurry out to the parking lot, and there's Delia's car, a light-blue Dodge Barracuda convertible, and I stand looking at it, thinking, *Perfect*. It's cool, fast, low to the road, and you can pull down the top and feel the wind in your hair at night when the weather cools. Hot exhaust fumes shimmer above the white sand behind the car, and I hear a soft throb of music, and I know she's in there with the AC and the music flowing, and her secret smell, like a drug, fragrant around her, waiting for me. I can't see her face. There's a glare on the light-blue hood of the Barracuda, but I can make out a blond glow through the smoked-glass windshield that blends with the sun pool on the hood.

I walk over and pull open the passenger door, lean in. A man with long oily hair in a flowered Hawaiian shirt and white duck pants sits with a woman's head in his lap. He's stroking her brown hair. Her bare feet are in my face. The radio plays "Dream Lover," Dion and the Belmonts, an oldies station. She lurches to her elbows. The man says, "Hey, damn it . . . what? . . ." but I've already closed the door, muttering, "Sorry, sorry . . ." wiping sweat from my forehead, and looking around the parking lot. I turn in a quick, dizzy circle and see a hand waving from a car in the shade of an Australian pine over on the beach side of 98. An electric window rolls down and Delia dips her head out the window of a new, black Chrysler Imperial. She fits her arm out next to her face and waves again. The Barracuda powers out of the parking lot behind me, heading south in a twister of dust. I start walking.

When I open Delia's door and slide onto the cool gray leather, she looks over at me with worried eyes and says, "It was getting weird in that parking lot, so I moved over here." The radio is playing "Kind of a Drag" by the Buckinghams.

"Weird?" The sweat is cold on my face in the powerful stream from Delia's AC. I pull my shirtsleeve over and wipe my forehead. I look back at Big Sam's lot—a few cars, dust settling where the Barracuda scratched away, traffic flowing by on 98.

She looks out at the highway, the brilliant white beach beyond the low dunes mounded with russet clumps of sea oats. "I mean empty. I was beginning to stand out." Her voice is small now, she looks back at me, appealing.

"Okay," I say, "sure, that's fine." I lean back and let my hot neck touch the cool crest of the bench seat. "Nice car," I say under a breath that smells like shrimp. Maybe this is better for her than the Barracuda. She's from the Town and Country set now, a suburbanite, a member of the country club. I try to conjure from novels I've read what a woman like this should drive, the young wife of a successful attorney. I seem to remember big conservative cars, comfortable but powerful enough to race if she needs speed, agile enough to slip smoothly between a speeding gasoline truck and a dawdling jalopy on the Long Island Expressway. But she has to be able to meet the commuter train from Grand Central and stow in her big trunk the luggage of weekend visitors from the Upper West Side, driving them up winding roads through forests of birch and fir to the rambling Colonial house in picturesque Tarrytown.

Delia starts the car and says, "I want to see where you live. You'll have to give me directions."

I close my eyes. For some reason, I can't get out of my mind the guy with the long greasy hair tangled in red Hawaiian blossoms and the tired, sad woman on his lap. I shake my eyes open and say, "You came here because you want to see where I live?" I reach out and turn the radio dial from Tallahassee to Jacksonville, the Big Ape. The Righteous Brothers are singing "Soul and Inspiration."

Delia smiles big and false. It's the phony smile she has to use at sorority meetings and cocktail mixers at the Quail Run Country Club. She says, "You're my nephew, and I love you, and of course I take an interest in you. Now come on, show me where you live." Something's coming, more than a casual drive to take an interest in me.

It occurs to me that in all of the nights at Bridgedale when I lay under a blanket with a flashlight and her picture (actually the best approximation of her face I could find in the magazines I ravaged), and in all of my slow-drag days in the furniture factory, lathing spindles for chairs, and in the classrooms and the cafeteria, in all those zombie days and hot furtive nights, I never thought much about who Delia would grow up to be.

Of course, I knew she must change, and passing images of her visited me. Sometimes she was a pert young nurse, dedicated to healing, working long nights in a hospital as somber and silent as a nun's cloister, or she came to me as a hippie girl, a strange new possibility of mixed appeal, a bandanna'd, long-haired, sun-smiling, zori-sandaled singer of folk songs about the wretched of the earth, but always spanking clean and ethereally pure, and always moving on down that highway when attachment threatened her poetic independence. Sometimes I allowed her to be a scholar, though the actualities of education beyond college were vague to me and even college was only a staccato blur of images from 1940s movies, hopelessly dated, that had flickered onto the screen in the Bridgedale gymnasium. My Scientist Delia was always seeking a cure for strange wasting diseases in bright pools of light in basement laboratories surrounded by gleaming instruments and bubbling retorts. Athlete Delia was a tennis star, noble in her amateur standing and pure in her abstinence from alcohol, tobacco, and the company of persons who partook of these vices. I never saw the common theme in these brief imaginings, probably because they were brief, and because I did not want to. The theme was "Delia the Isolate." Delia the seeker on a lonely path, a path that could someday intersect my own. Delia and Travis meeting in some future where the theme changed from isolation to love.

I look over at her as she drives to my directions, finding the seedy, weedy neighborhood where I live, near the water, but too close to the noise and oily odors of Wilson's Marina. The radio plays the hot songs of the summer, "Hanky Panky," and "Good Vibrations," and "Devil with a Blue Dress On," but I see who Delia is now, a country club wife, the Mrs. of an attorney named Templeton, a luncher with chattering friends, the driver of a fine and high-class automobile.

"Turn in there." I point at the rusting tin sign drooping from the limb of a water oak, the black block letters: *The Wind Motel . . . Vacancy*. There's a place where the word *No* can be slid into brackets before *Vacancy*, but the brackets have rusted away, and there is always a vacancy.

We roll to a slow, purring stop in the oystershell lot, and Delia switches off the ignition. The big new engine whispers out its fires.

"You sure you want to see it?" I ask, smiling at what I guess will be her reaction when she does. Horror.

She doesn't open her door, just looks around at the off-beam cabins on their short stilts of crumbling concrete block, their skimpy porches with shadeless sixty-watt bulbs. Delia brightens, "Of course I want to see it." She opens her door and gives me a playful, Old-Time Delia face: *Let the games begin.* "Take me there," she says in a high and breathless voice.

I get out and stand on the hot crushed shell. The Widow's old Ford Fairlane is gone from its usual spot. Years of spilled oil draw the approximate shape of what is under her hood. But the Widow is just one of my problems. Where is Dawnell, the other one? Is she off with the Widow looking for the world's best cheap manicurist? But that is unkind. Dawnell, the Widow, and I are a family now, strangely combined, but growing fatefully closer.

I think of telling it all to Delia, how I have washed up here on this shore of redneck drama with an underage girl whose father and brother want to cut out my heart (and with Jimmy Danes getting stronger every day in a hospital bed, dreaming of my death), and with the Widow, spy and scold turned benefactress and keeper of the vodka cure. What would Delia think of the story? Of my entanglements. Surely she'd give a soft and knowing laugh and tell me, *Travis, my good young nephew, you can't get through life without entanglements. You just have to try not to let them become stranglements.* Delia, the Delia I remember, was always one for making up words, laughing at their sounds, wondering at their constellations of meaning. As we walk quietly past the Widow's cabin, I cross fingers on both hands and even cross my eyes, hoping that Dawnell's face does not appear at the Widow's jalousie windows.

At my door, I fish keys from my Levi's and say, softly, "Here we are. A man's tourist court is his castle." I wonder if she gets my jest. Delia lives in a castle.

She looks at me quizzically and says, "Why are you *whis*pering?" She looks around us. "Oooh," she whispers behind my shoulder as I knee open the damp stuck door, "you're not allowed to have . . . *female* visitors, are you?"

As we cross the threshold, I say, "Well, the rules are sort of on a sliding scale around here, but . . . it's discouraged."

Delia moves past me, into the center of the room, looks down at my plate of potato chips sprayed with Black Flag. Three dead cockroaches nestle among the chips. One of them wiggles its legs faintly. Delia whistles, low and long. "Well," she says, "this place has its charms." She turns and looks at me. "Where does a girl sit?"

I glance around. As always, there are only two choices, the bed or the chair at my little desk where I strain and grapple with the Delia Book. I'm the writer, at least some of the time, so I take the chair and point Delia to the sway-backed mattress.

She tiptoes toward it, and settles, knees together, back straight like a pledge at a sorority tea. She lifts a finger and crosses her lips. "We still whispering?" The fun has overtaken her face, and it's a good thing to see. It takes me back years, to those two bedrooms upstairs in Grandpa Hollister's house, hers and mine with the stairwell and the hallway between, and the bathroom overlooking the backyard.

I remember her visiting my room, and then later, me visiting hers. I remember how necessary it was then that so little distance separated us, how sweet at night to know she was close, to hear her breathing, or the radio she had fallen asleep to, caressing the darkness with dreamy sound. I remember how we comforted each other, and how Delia's friends, Beulah and Caroline, visited, and how we all lay around Delia's room through the hot afternoons. I was the boy from far away accepted into their world of squealing laughter, and sudden exasperated tears, and gushing confessions unregretted because the rule, never violated, was that secrets were kept in Delia's room.

I look at Delia, grown up now, some heavy age on her, the owner of eyes that have already seen too much, and I see that she is remembering too. And memory has made her younger while it was making me older. I see the years rise and fly from under her eyes and the corners of her mouth, and she smiles, soft and slow as she once did swimming with me in the river or rolling down the car window to mix loud rock 'n' roll with the warm wind that whipped her black hair around her face. *And hold!* We are timeless. We are back there. The trouble has not yet started. *And hold a little longer.* And like a rushing wind before a storm, like a rip current that takes your feet from under you and sweeps you out past the markers before you can wave at the shore, time comes to us again.

I watch the shock of its return, the hours, the days, the years, return to Delia's face. I see her pulling herself back, blinking, from that inner sight of her old room, of the four of us lounging in the heat in the music in a languor that only Elvis and oak boughs rubbing fevers beyond the window screens and youth that never fades confer. She smiles at me, so sweet, still so young, and says, "Travis, how did we ever hurt each other so much?"

Before I can think of what to say, her eyes see something monstrous coming, not from the past but from the future, and she raises her hands to cover the sudden tears. I rise and go to her, sit next to her, and pull her close. I touch her hot wet cheek with my own, and then with the back of my hand. I have no words. I can only hold her, trying to be again what I was before the trouble started. I can feel it in her shoulders, in her shuddering breathing as she sobs, then subsides:

it is better I am here than not here. But I can feel also that these are not just the tremors of old sorrows, they are warnings of new ones to come. Delia has cried many times like this, and she will do it again.

When she finishes, when she is sufficiently aware of herself to be aware of me and to resent me a little as anyone would who has come apart in front of another, she shrinks away. I let her out of my hands and retake my seat at the writer's table. It's a long time before she looks at me. "How *did* we?" she says, her voice rushing, urgent. *How did we ever hurt each other so much?*

I have my answers. You do not spend six years thinking only about one thing, your brain alight with questions, without finding answers.

"Travis," Delia says, still the urgent whisper, "*how?*"

"You never hurt me." I don't know where the words come from, but I know they are true and all I need to say. It was I, Travis Hollister, the boy from out of town, the poison poured into warm sweet milk, who did the hurting. *And so, why have you come back? To hurt more or to heal?* It's the question I have not yet answered for myself.

Delia raises her hand, wet with tears, palm flat out toward me, as though to stop what's coming. "Don't you *see*, Travis," she says, "don't you see I did hurt you? How I *used* you?"

"Used me?" I want to appeal to her. I want to fall to my knees in front of her and seize her in my arms, bore my face into the warm bowl of her belly. "Used me? You didn't use me. I helped you. The others, they wanted to use you." Bick and, yes, even Griner. I remember Bick's funeral, how Delia and I concealed what we knew, and how we learned that only Griner, Kenny Griner, the town hood, the misunderstood boy with a good heart, only Griner knew or might guess what had really happened to Bick. I remember how Delia and I knelt at my bedroom window at midnight watching Griner's hot rod slip through the pool of streetlight at the corner, a love song drifting from his radio, and how I said to her, "He'll never leave you alone now," and Delia, my Delia, said, "I know."

By a force of will I did not know I possessed, I stay where I sit, and I try to keep the lostness from my voice, "You never used me. I wanted to help you. God help me, I *wanted* to do what I did. I *had* to do it."

She shakes her head, tired, sad. "Poor Travis," she says. "My poor, poor Travis. You took the fall for me." It's a phrase from movies about gangsters and their molls. It doesn't belong between us.

I shake my head violently no. Bick took the fall, one hundred fifty feet to the rocky riverbed.

Delia leans toward me, her eyes beseeching. "Listen to me, Travis. I need you to listen. It matters to me for you to understand this. It's all I have now, to save myself. For you to know and to forgive me."

I shake my head again. I want to put my hands over my ears, but I can't let her see me do that. I say again, "I helped you. You needed me. You couldn't have made it on your own."

Like a grown woman speaking to a slow child, like someone pressing a lesson into a brain that can't keep up, she says, "Travis, listen to me. Don't you know, couldn't you see I wanted Bick and I wanted Kenny too? I wanted them both, and a girl like me wasn't supposed to do that. There just wasn't any way for a girl like me in a time like that to want them, to have the world know I wanted them." She clenches her fists, shakes them in front of her, closes her eyes. "But it's worse than that. I *didn't* want them. I knew I was too young for what was happening to me, not ready for it, too young for what had already happened. I was afraid of them and of myself and of what would happen to me, of what had already happened to me. But that was the quiet voice, the one that said no."

I nod at what she is saying now, at some of it. "You see? You didn't want them." It's hard for me to say what comes next, but if not now, when? "You wanted *me*. I proved that to you. Remember what we did?"

She knows what I mean. And Delia, the wife of an attorney, for whom such things are now legal, expected, unremarkable, frequent, blushes. We are remembering the night I came to her bed, not long after Bick's funeral. I took her in my arms, and we did what only love makes happen, and then I knew I could not stop helping her.

Delia's eyes grow hooded and vague with the recollection of our nights together, only two nights, but a life to me. "Yes," she says, her voice like the plucking of the strings of a lost mythical instrument, "I loved you, my dear Travis. I loved you in every way a girl can, and in ways I shouldn't have. God help me, on the last day I live I will be sorry I let myself do that to you, but . . ."

"Not *to* me," I whisper. "*With* me. You . . ."

She holds up her hand, squeezes her eyes shut, stops my voice with hers: "But I did it, we did it, and yes, it was sweet, so sweet, my dear, dear Travis, but it was wrong, and I knew it then, and I know it now, and somehow, no matter what has happened to you, no matter why you've come back here, you know it was wrong too." She looks at me, her face thrust forward, her nails digging into her thighs, her eyes begging. "Not that we loved, but that we loved like that." Still begging, she says, "I love you now, so much, my dear, sweet Travis, but I've come here to ask you to let me go."

She raises her hand again to stop my voice. A sickness grows inside my chest, a weary sickness I have never felt before. Not when I was taken away in handcuffs before the whole neighborhood after I stabbed Jimmy Pultney, not in my darkest night at Bridgedale when the faces I had scissored from magazines blurred and faded and I could no longer see Delia's true face. She raises her hand to stop my words, and I find that I have none.

"I can't send you away, Travis. I can't make you go away. I can't bring myself to do anything more to you. I've done too much already. There's too much to live with already. But I can ask you, beg you to let me go, to stop loving me that way, so that I can get on with the life I have and you can make one for yourself." She gets up and moves to the door, wiping first one hand then the other across her cheeks to clear the last of her tears. She's leaving. This is the way she will have the last word. There is so much more to say, but now no more time.

I get up and go to her, take her shoulders in my hands, pull her away from the door. "You can't go out like that." Even in the middle of all this, I care for her reputation, how she will look now to anyone beyond this door. Her eyes are afraid of me, wide with resistance. I loosen my grip on her. "Just wait here," I say. "Don't go yet." I go to the sink and moisten a towel with cool water and return to her and touch it to her inflamed cheeks.

She lets me, and then she takes the towel from me and applies it herself. "Thank you," she says. "Thank you, Travis."

Ten minutes later, she comes out of my bathroom snapping her purse shut. The fresh makeup on her face makes her look almost right, almost as though she has not gone to the hell of memory, witnessing both the past and the future here in this dirty little place. I'm sitting on the bed, looking down at my resigned hands. Twice before I've seen her in the new Florida of my second life, and twice we've parted with the same words (*I will see you again*).

Now I don't know. I can't put her through this again, though any closeness to her is goodness to me, even this hell of memory and wanting. I tell her, "You should go now. I'll walk you to your car."

She says, "Oh, honey, you don't have to . . ." with a flip of her wrist, a hand delicate but strong. It reminds me of her lunch, her two companions back at Big Sam's. She's crossed back now into that world, and this one must seem to her very dirty indeed, a place to be leaving soon. I go to the door, open it for her, and we step out into the strong midafternoon sunlight. I shade my eyes, and Delia searches her beige leather purse for her sunglasses. When she puts them on and looks at me, they are a barrier. It is as though we never crossed the threshold behind us, never spent time together in my little room of dead insects and living memories.

Delia says, "Well . . ." There's a catch in her throat, a last small throb.

I repeat my offer: "I'll walk you to your car."

We start down the crushed-shell walk to the parking lot where her black Chrysler sits baking in the sun. The Widow's Fairlane pulls up in a white cloud of oystershell dust, slides to a halt, creaking on its shot suspension. The Widow's door opens and Hawaiian music pours out (*"Tiny bubbles . . ."*). The Widow gently places her feet, one then the other, in purple espadrilles, onto the white shell. Then the passenger door opens and out swing the tanned legs of Dawnell Briscoe. She's wearing the shorts and blouse I bought her and cradling an armful of new purchases, parcels and plastic bags. The two get out, talking and laughing, steady themselves in the harsh sunlight, then look down the walk. They see Delia and me coming at them.

I don't know what to do. All I've got left are my manners, and I'm not sure of them in this mixed company. Dawnell starts walking fast toward me with that slow, knowing smile on her face, then she double-takes Delia and slows down. The Widow has walked only a few steps and already looks winded and sun-stunned. Well, heat like this slows everyone, not just those who drink too much grapefruit juice. Delia takes my arm in an auntly way as our two parties are about to collide on the narrow path. Dawnell walks up and stands in front of me, her hands drooping with their bright burdens.

Delia says, "Travis, introduce me to your friends."

Before I can open my mouth, Dawnell looks at Delia and says, "You're *her*, ain't you?"

Delia bends a little at the waist, smiles, equal to the social requirements of the moment. "I'm . . . *who*, honey? What did you say?"

Dawnell guns Delia with spurts of fire from her gem-blue eyes. Then she's on me with that hot glare. "She ain't *made up*. You told me she was invented. She ain't invented. She's real. I know it's her, that Delia."

What can I say? I am found in a lie. The Widow has caught up with us and gives Delia her professional property owner's smile and me a look that speaks of a desperate need for the cure. I say, "Delia, this is my landlady, Mrs. Reddick, and this is a friend of mine, Dawnell Briscoe."

Delia shakes hands with both of them. Sandralene Reddick pulls it off with some aplomb, stopping herself just short of genuflecting to the money Delia represents. Dawnell takes Delia's hand, looks down at it, calculates its worth, and gives it back decisively. We all stand there in the pouring-down sun. It's too hot to be social anymore.

"Well . . ." says the Widow, "it's sure nice to meet you, Mrs. Tarleton. My goodness, it's hot. I'm afraid I have to . . ." She glances at the doorway of her little cabin where important business awaits.

Dawnell just stands there until the Widow puts a hand flat to the middle of her back and gives her a gentle push. The Widow starts her moving well enough, but after two steps Dawnell digs her new white no-brand sneakers into the oystershells and turns. Biting her lower lip, she nods at me like she has finally recognized something for what it is. "You!" she says. And one more time, "She ain't made up."

Beside me, Delia touches the powder and rouge she has recently applied to her right cheek. "Travis, what is your friend talking about?"

I put my hand in the middle of Delia's back and start her along too. "I'll tell you all about it. Come on. You've got to take me back to Big Sam's before I lose my job."

Delia looks back over her shoulder at Dawnell standing there, feet wide apart, purchases dangling from both hands, lips in a pout. Delia says, "What did she mean, I'm not made up?"

"I'll explain it to you. Come on. Let's go."

Dawnell says, "He *writes* about you," as though "writes" were "murders" or "rapes." And maybe it is, I am thinking as I guide a confused Delia toward her car. Maybe it is.

TWENTY-NINE

'm lying in bed in the dark with the back of my wrist over my aching eyes. The radio is playing low, the Beatles, *"Close your eyes and I'll kiss you, tomorrow I'll miss you."* Somebody knocks. The knock is quiet. I think of ignoring whatever's out there, just lying here quietly until he, she, or it gives up and goes away. I try for a while. There's another quiet rapping. I get up and open the door to the Widow's well-cured face. She follows me in, and I lie back down on the bed. She closes the door, and it's black dark, but I figure she owns the place so she knows the layout. I'm exhausted from the long lunch shift, the afternoon interlude with Delia, and a busier-than-usual evening trade.

The Widow stands there in the dark. I can smell her perfume and the vodka cure. "Turn on a light if you want to," I tell her. She doesn't say anything, and I hear her mules slide across the floor and then feel my saggy mattress lose another six inches to gravity.

She moves, and I know she's resting her elbows on her knees and her face in her hands. If she's not going to talk, I guess I have to. "How is she?"

"She's mad at you, of course. You lied to her."

"Did I really? What do you know about it?"

"Only what she told me."

"Well, consider the possibility that she has no idea what she's talking about."

"All right, I'll consider it. Why don't *you* tell me what she's talking about?"

I exchange one wrist for the other across my aching eyes. Come to think of it, there is not much of me that doesn't ache after two shifts at Big Sam's. Nights, after work, if my mind empties for a second, all of the noise and smell and rush of Big Sam's snaps on like a bad movie in the theater of my skull.

The Widow says, "Well?"

It's all too complicated to tell, especially right now, after Delia. I say, "Can we talk about it later?"

The Widow's voice is cold and firm in the darkness: "We'll talk about it now if you want that girl to sleep another night under my roof."

So, it's blackmail. Coercion. Enforcement. I begin the story: "What she ... what Dawnell means about *ain't made up* is that I wrote something, a diary, a memoir, about ..."

"A mem-*what?*"

"A mem*oir*. It's a type of writing you do about yourself, about your life. I wrote something about the woman you met today. She's my aunt. Delia ..."

"What's so interesting about your life that you got to write about it?"

I can tell the Widow is intrigued. Maybe her interest can reach beyond the obvious and the prurient, possibly even as far as the finer points of how a twelve-year-old boy's scrappy diary became a rewritten, reconsidered ... something. Not a fiction, but not quite a true account. I have settled for myself the question of truth about me and Delia—there is none, there is only a stream of sensation, pleasurable, necessary, and profound. What I will do with the writing, I do not know.

The Widow is interested in my writing and in me. And I can tell she likes Dawnell, though she disapproves too, in the way that only an aging reprobate can disapprove. And she has seen Delia. Who wouldn't be intrigued? She wants to know why I write about Delia. I can't tell most of it, of course, but here in the dark, at the end of a long hard day, it feels right to tell some of it.

"A memoir only has to be interesting to the one who writes it," I tell the Widow, "at least at first. And then later, if the writer wants to publish it, it has to be interesting to other people." I sound like something my English teacher back at Bridgedale occasionally mentioned, *pretentious*. It's a thing to be avoided. But what am I pretending to be? I've never told anyone I'm a writer, except when I had to, when something dangerous had to be covered by a lie. The Delia Book was never for anyone but her and me. Dawnell stole her way into it, and I still don't know how much she read. Apparently it was enough to recognize Delia in a pair of sunglasses. And with blond hair, not black.

"I've never had a writer living here before," the Widow says in a contemplative tone. "You should have told me what you were up to. I can tell you all kinds of stories for your . . . mem*wore* or your storybook, or whatever. You don't live in a place like this as many years as I have without picking up some whoppers, I'll tell you."

"Tell me," I say.

"Well, let's see, there was the time I . . . Hey, wait a minute! I'm not telling you. Not tonight. Tonight, you're telling me. Now what about this Aunt Delia of yours. Why is little Miss . . . Why is Dawnie over there so upset about what she read you wrote about your aunt?"

Dawnie? Dawnie-ell? Why can't anyone say the girl's name right except me? I reach out and give the Widow's shoulder a brief squeeze. "You like her, don't you? Dawnell?" When I touch her, her ample buttocks rock against my thigh, and there's a sharp drawing of breath that makes me sad. How often does she receive anything from a kind hand? We sit counting heartbeats in the dark for a space, then I say, "Don't you? I think you do."

The Widow says, "All right, I like her. Underneath all that paint and fakey tough-girl act, she's really a sweet little thing. Which is why I want to know what's going on between you two, starting with what's got her so upset about your writing."

So the sidetrack I have built finds its way back to the main line. I shift my weight a little in confusion and frustration. I don't want to talk about this. How do I know I can really trust this lush with a heart of gold? I've seen her send grown men down the road with the imprint of her mules on their sorry asses. Big mean pulp-wooders with loaded gun racks in their rambly pickups and pints of cheap whiskey sticking out of their hip pockets. She makes short work of road trash and nonpaying customers. She'd have me out of here in two shakes if I didn't show up every first of the month bright and early with my sweaty hand full of fives and tens.

I start into it, worried about where it will go, choosing my words carefully: "Not long after I moved in here, I met Dawnell late one night when Big Sam's closed. She was walking the streets alone, dressed like, well, like you wouldn't want her to be, looking for a guy she said she knew. Well, I knew him too, and he's no damn good, so I brought her back here and let her stay the night with me, to keep her out of trouble."

"You *didn't*. An underage girl at the Wind Motel!" The Widow turns, and I feel the wind from her open hand before it hits me on the upper arm. *Smack.* It's a punishment, but it's kind of playful too. How things have changed! I hate to think what she'd have done if she'd caught me that night with Dawnell.

"I'm sorry."

"No you're not, but go ahead and tell me the rest of it."

"Well, that night she got up while I was still asleep and read some of what I wrote about my aunt, and later on, when she and I, I mean Dawnell and I, got a little bit involved, she got angry, I mean jealous about it. That's all."

"That's all? How involved?"

"Not that much. Honest. I swear."

"You swear! I'll bet you do, on a stack of Trojans, you little beast!"

It's hard to read the Widow in the dark. As far as I can tell without seeing her face, her eyes, she's three things: protecting Dawnell from me and all other male interference, intrigued by my story, and giving me more credit for amorous experience than I deserve.

I reassure her on points one and three: "We haven't done anything, I swear. And I don't own any Trojans, you can search me if you want to."

She turns and digs her fingers into my ribs, tickling me in the dark. "I'll search you, all right. I find out you been . . . *at* that girl, I'll search you good." I can't make myself laugh at being tickled. I never have been able to. The Widow withdraws her fingers and says, "Well, how *do* you feel about her?"

I wish I knew. I say, "I like her, but not as much as she likes me."

"Well," she takes a deep breath, and I can't help thinking about her large melony breasts rising and falling in the darkness, "that's an old story, isn't it?"

"I guess so."

"Well it is, you can take my word for it. What do you plan to do with her? She can't stay on here like this forever. What about her family? What about school starting in another few weeks?"

I've thought about all of this, but thinking hasn't got me anywhere much. For now, I'm just glad that Dawnell is away from her father and brother and wearing some appropriate clothes and laughing with the Widow. Either it has to go back to being like it was, or I have to figure out something.

"I have to figure out something."

"I guess you do." The Widow pushes herself up with a wheezy breath. She moves to the door in the dark. She stands there, and without seeing, I know she has her hand on the knob. "You're a strange one, you are. You know that?"

I don't answer. *Not the first time I've been told.*

"If I was a few years younger . . ."

The heat creeps up my neck, spreads to my scalp. She's just said what we've both thought about, I guess. I try to think of an answer. *My life's a little too complicated already.* All I say is, "Sandralene?"

"Yes, honey."

"Thank you, I mean for all you've done and all."

She takes another big breath, exhales vodka and a sweetness that is, I suppose, the reason she drinks so much, the thing she has to keep back within herself so the world won't take advantage. She says, "That's all right, honey. You get some sleep." She opens the door, and I see her outlined in the soft light from what is now Dawnell's bedroom. She pauses with one foot across the threshold. "I just can't figure out why she'd be so jealous of your aunt."

She quietly closes the door.

I wait twenty minutes or so and then get up and pull on some Levi's, a T-shirt, and tennis shoes. I peek out through my door, and it's just like the last time. Dawnell's window is lit, and I can hear the music drifting out, soft and beckoning, from under her open sash. It's Sam Cooke. *"That's the sound of the men working on the chain gaa-aaa-aang!"*

I tiptoe over into the pool of light that falls from her window onto sand still warm from the heat of the day. I reach up and scratch her window screen with my fingernail. The music doesn't stop. No face appears. I see no moving shadow on the drawn blinds, but I know she hears it. She's in there listening, wondering what to do about me.

I scratch again, and the blinds go up, and there's her oval face in a nimbus of honey-brown hair with light streaming through from behind. She lifts the sash and, though it's only a scraping of wood, to me it sounds like the collision of two beer trucks. I put my finger across my lip as Dawnell leans closer, tilting her face at the ten inches of open window. She comes into focus now, closer to me, the high, flushed cheeks and the scoops below them, the pink bow of lips, the gem-blue eyes, and the forehead oddly lined where too-early burdens have come to live.

She puts a finger to her lips too. "Shush, yourself. She's sleeping." She folds her hands prayerfully against her cheek and closes her eyes, then makes a fair approximation of a snore, *"Skeeee! Whooo! Skeeee! Whooo!"*

It's too loud, but I have to laugh anyway. I push my face up into the air-conditioned air that pours out and ruffles Dawnell's hair. I say, "Can you sneak out? We need to talk." Something tightens hard in my stomach.

Her face darkens with seriousness and craft. She bites her bottom lip. "I don't know, that front door is a mess of noise, and there ain't no other—"

"Push the sash up a little more and unhook the screen. I'll help you down."

She looks at me with all of a country girl's experience. Accidents can happen, but craft takes over, and she glances back at the door of her new bedroom, at the house beyond where the Widow sleeps. She lifts the sash another eight inches. Pretty soon her feet appear above me, and I reach out and take one in each hand to reassure her as she shinnies out and down. I let go of her feet, take her waist, and lower her the rest of the way.

We stand beneath the window in that pool of light, our bare feet on warm sand, and I say, "Let's hope this is still open when we get back."

She looks up at me out of blue gems gone dark and says, "Who says we're comin' back?"

I take her hand and we tiptoe through the dark village of the Wind Motel. Only the porch lights people have forgotten or were too drunk to turn off still burn, with mad constellations of insects wheeling around them. At the far end of the property we pass through a wall of tall Australian pines. It's hot and calm down among the trunks, but a strong sea breeze makes the tallest branches swish and sway. I know the path and pull Dawnell along behind me by the hand, our bare feet thumping on beds of needles and pressing through the sand.

When we reach my fishing spot, the moon slides from behind a cloud, and we can see the long, creamy seawall shooting straight off toward Wilson's Marina, and the thick mangroves that claw their roots into its foundation. The tide is low, the air smells of rotting seaweed, salt, and solvents used in fiberglassing. I help Dawnell down from the seawall to the place where I wade in to go fishing. We stand at the waterline, cooling our feet in the Gulf of Mexico.

After a while of playing our toes in the water, one foot lifted then the other, and neither of us talking, she leans toward me and touches first her cheek against my arm and then the rest of her, a flank, a hip, and a calf that swings out and hooks my shin.

I clear my throat. "We have to decide what to do."

"I know." She sounds tired and older, not actressy like I expected.

"Mrs. Reddick is right. Your daddy won't let you stay away from him forever. He could be looking for you right now."

I expect some of the usual Dawnell Briscoe bravado, something like, *Well, let him look,* but she says, only, "I know," and leans in closer to me, squeezing my arm with both hands as though she's cold. I wish I'd brought my windbreaker. She has her head pressed against my arm and her eyes shut as though she's afraid I'll disappear, or this water will rise and take her away, alone into the dark. I encircle her with my arm and pull her closer. It occurs to me that I have not thought much, and we have not talked at all, about what *she* wants. Really wants. Where and how she sees herself living five or ten years from now. I bend down and hover my lips above the warm crown of her head. I've been helping her, or so I've told myself. Now it's time to ask her: "What do *you* want to do? Do you want to go back with your daddy?"

She doesn't look up, only nestles close. "No," she whispers. Only that. I wait. Nothing more. I hold her, and she shivers, and I can feel the little tremors in her back where my hand rests and even in her calf that still hooks mine. "What do you want to do?" She lifts her face to mine so quickly, so fiercely, that we almost collide, a bruise of lips or noses. The look in her eyes here in the moonlight is so plainly despairing, so plainly disappointed, that shame rises from the tight place in my belly and flames my face.

I breathe out long until I am empty, but the sickness stays there deep inside me. I look out as far as I can see, past the faint green phosphorescent gleam of the breakers at the mouth of Wilson's channel, out to the darkest dark where the sky and the sea meet indistinguishable. I say, "There are things about me you don't know."

"I know that," she says. "I'm not stupid." She waits for me to speak again, and when I don't, she says, with resignation, "Scared, but not stupid."

In the darkest dark out there, where the deep water starts, a shade of blue that even in bright sunlight is almost black, something waits for me. The darkness in me yearns for it, must join with it someday. I know this as surely as I know that the innocence I hold in my arms will soon evaporate into the fierce sunlight out on those godforsaken swampy acres an evil father owns and an evil brother hunts. Unless

I do something about it. I make myself speak: "I've done bad things. How do you know I won't hurt you?"

"You won't," she says. "I know you, and you won't. I know what you did. I read about it."

I draw breath and say, exhausted, "Men and women hurt each other. They have to. It can't be any other way."

I feel her neck stretch, her head rise along the muscle of my arm, as she realizes what is finished, what is new. She whispers into the muscle of my arm, "I know that. I know it. Every girl knows it. But there's hurt and hurt. You're not a bad man."

And there it is. Could there be two simpler words, good and bad, two words more impossible to understand? The question is, who am I? A good man or a bad one? I turn to face her, untangling her from me, and, taking her in my hands, I feel her shiver. I pull her to me, wrap her in what warmth I have left. I say to her upturned face, "Maybe I can be what someone good believes I am. Maybe that's what faith is. Hoping something is there, wanting it to be."

THIRTY

I'm idling into the parking lot at the Wind Motel, my old Plymouth humming reliably under me, when I see the Widow standing at the window of a green and white sheriff's car, talking to the man inside. She moves aside, glances back at me, and I see his face. He's a deputy I've noticed around, cruising 98, netting speeders with a regretful, patient look on his face, drifting past the bars and restaurants around closing time, watching the last-call crowd for signs of lethal impairment. He's lean with a long, tanned face and dark eyebrows that grow together above his nose. The kind of slow-moving man you don't mess with because you figure he's saving his speed for something important.

I get out of my Plymouth, keeping my distance until I know what's going on. I stand at my car door in my reeking restaurant clothes looking across the roof at the Widow and the deputy, and then I hear the Widow's jalousie door rattle open and then close, and Dawnell comes walking up the oystershell path with all of her bags of J. M. Fields loot dangling from her hands. I start walking fast toward the deputy's cruiser, but Dawnell gets there first, and I watch as the Widow puts her hand on the back of Dawnell's neck, then raises it to the crown of her head, bends and kisses her cheek, then opens the back door of the deputy's car for her. I walk faster, then I run, and I'm pulling open the deputy's back door when the Widow steps in front of me.

"Don't, honey. I tried talking to him. There's nothing we can do. Her daddy got a straining order on you."

I look into her tired, sad eyes and see that she's been at this thing for some time, and she's just about reached the limits of her civility. Inside the car, Dawnell sits facing straight ahead, her rigid back not touching the seat behind her, her plastic bags of goods arrayed on either side of her bare knees. I edge around the Widow. She sighs and steps back as though I'm about to undo all the good she's done. I try to open the door, but it's locked.

The deputy puts the cruiser into reverse and backs up until his face and mine are six inches apart. "Kid," he says, "we've been patient with you. Her daddy wants you locked up for statutory rape. Mrs. Reddick here says you've behaved yourself with this young lady, but I wouldn't push it any further if I was you." He waits for me to say something, give him the excuse he wants to put me back there with Dawnell, and for a crazy second or two I think that's what I want. To be back there beside her, even though we'll end up in different places.

Somehow, my better judgment intervenes, and all I say is, "Yes sir." I use my old Bridgedale voice, servile, craven, and mocking. I hate it, but it's tactics. The deputy backs up, a ruffle of oystershell dust skirting his fenders, and starts forward. And I run. I run alongside the car, my head bent down to look in. Dawnell looks at me, her eyes as big blue as I've ever seen them, tears on her cheeks. I say, loud, through my running breath, "I'll see you. Don't worry. I'll do something." I kiss my hand and slap it to the glass in front of her, and she's staring at the print of my promise when the deputy guns the cruiser away.

I walk back to the Widow. She reaches up angrily and rakes the wet from her eyes, two big yanking motions that leave them dry but red. I stand in front of her. "Rape?" I say. "Statutory rape. How can they . . . ?"

"Oh quit," she says. "They'd have to prove you did something to that girl, and I don't think your daddy'd let that happen. Not if he's any kind of lawyer at all."

I don't tell her what kind of lawyer he is, or that this is not the first time I've been in the kind of trouble that brings police cars. We stand in the parking lot watching the white dust settle where the cruiser turned out onto the hard road. Dawnell's on her way back to her father and brother, and somewhere in a judge's office there's a re-straining order, which I know means I'm supposed to stay away from her. "Rape?" I whisper.

The Widow takes me by the muscle of my arm. "Come on, honey. Let's get out of this heat."

She leads me to her cabin, and inside, at her kitchen table, she sits me down and sets the tray of shot glasses in front of me. She pulls the bottle of vodka from the freezer compartment of her Frigidaire. It's the cheapest vodka you can buy anywhere within fifty miles. The blue label says, simply, *VODKA*, and the fine print explains that it was manufactured from orange peels in Auburndale, Florida. If you sip, squint, and roll it around the back of your tongue, you just can get a glimmer of the burned-orange smoke that hovers in the air for miles around the big juice concentrate plants. The Widow pours us two shots. I swallow mine quick, and I'm all right until I close my eyes and see Dawnell's face peering at me through that rusty screened door back at her father's house. I reach up and press the heels of both palms to my eyes.

"Take it easy, honey," the Widow says. "You wanted to do the right thing."

I try not to, but I can hear in her words the relief she feels. Things are back to normal now at the Wind Motel. I pour myself a second shot. The Widow draws back and looks at me, somewhat affronted. She is the high priestess of the vodka cure, and she does the pouring. I say, "She can't stay out there."

She finishes her first shot and pours another. "Don't go out there, honey. That would be stupid, and you're not stupid."

I look at her with the first fierce fumes of the cure misting my eyes. "What should I do then? If I'm not stupid?"

I reach out to pour my third, but she covers my hand with hers. When I withdraw it from the bottle, she moves the blue label out of my reach. Her eyes tell me to calm down, the afternoon looms long and full of possibility before us. "Pace yourself. What's your hurry?" She looks into her shot, back up at me. "You can do one of two things, the way I see it," she says. "You can forget about her, for a whole bunch of reasons, all of which make a whole bunch of sense, or you can just ... wait awhile, and let things calm down a little, and see what happens. Throwing a little *time* at the problem could be just the right thing. The girl's father calms down a little. The girl grows up a little. The straining order has a time limit. Did you know that?"

I didn't. I look at her blankly. None of this appeals. Anything could happen to Dawnell now that she has been with me and the bad ones have taken her back.

I walk into Emil's kitchen for the dinner shift. My hands are shaking as I grab a fresh apron from the hook by the door to the loading dock. After the Widow and I took five sin bullets each, those frosty shots of no-name vodka, I went back to my cabin and dropped to the floor and counted off seventy-five bleary, belly-sloshing push-ups, counted until I pushed myself through euphoria, to nausea, and finally came to earth in the land of exhausted emptiness. I crawled into my bed dripping sweat and slept until it was time for Big Sam's.

My hands and arms shake as I take up the first bus tray of the day, load it with knives, forks, and spoons, and start for the dining room. What makes me shake is not weary muscles complaining of abuse, it's knowing what I have to do but not knowing exactly why. It's a strange place to be, on the road to inevitable with no map.

The hours come and go, and the diners appear at the door of Big Sam's full of greed and anticipation and they leave full of shrimp and with that look on their faces: too much too fast. I work in a dream of anticipation, hauling trays and dodging curses, watching the clock, and avoiding Emil's eye. Once or twice as the night rolls on, he looks out through the curtain of heat from his line of smoking fryers, cants his hip to the side, and watches me come and go. He knows something's different, maybe wrong.

When it's all over, and the dining room is dark, and the last of the slack-bellied legions of calories is out the door and down the road, I walk out to the loading dock. Emil's sitting there with the usual rewards, smoke curling up from the corner of his mouth and the little silver cup resting on his knee. "Join me, colonel," he says.

"I can't tonight." My voice sounds strange. The long butcher knife I have stolen from the rack where Emil trims steaks and prime rib sticks up the back of me, cold under my shirt. I'm walking stiff and careful when I leave him there, smoking and thinking. I turn back through the kitchen, not the way I usually go, and start toward my car, parked out front. Emil calls from behind me, "Night now!"

I call back, "Night."

I test the gleaming blade with my thumb, slip the knife under the seat, handle out where I can reach it fast without looking down. I tell myself it is only security, a last resort. I will not use it, but it would be stupid to go without something. I have no plan. I will go and see what happens. Perhaps tonight is only a reconnoitering. I know where the house is, but have only been in the front yard, on the front porch, and only in daylight. Dawnell said the old man falls asleep drunk and the brother goes out creeping the woods with his lighted rifle.

As I clear the outskirts of the city, increase my speed, rumble down the first canyon of pine trees, I look up at the sky. It's a half-moon night, light enough to see among the trees, but not dangerously bright. I open the vent and let the rush of air cool my sweating face. *Have you thought this thing through carefully enough?* I have not thought it through at all. *Shouldn't you stop and think now, plan? Why not just pull over to the side and rest, think a moment?* No time. No time for that. A few words come to me from English class back at Bridgedale. "The pale cast of thought." Dr. Janeway always told me that successful people (by which he meant not criminals) thought before they acted, weighed their options, did not repeat unsuccessful plans. *Is that what you are about to do? Your hand on a knife again?* I don't know. It's a precaution. Stupid to go without something to a place where they have things. *A butcher knife is not just a thing.*

I slow down, but don't pull over. The wind from the vent is sweet and cooling, though it can't dry my hot wet face. If I get Dawnell back again, we can't return to the Wind Motel. We'll have to run away, and that means leaving Delia, maybe for a long time. *I didn't come back here just to leave again with a wild girl from the woods who doesn't know a finger bowl from a flowerpot. I came for Delia.*

Dr. Janeway is pulling on his cold pipe the way he always did, his cheeks hollowed in, his eyes peering at me like I'm an ancient manuscript of mild interest in a language he knows all too well. *Pull over and think about it*, he says. But there's a light in my eyes, bothersome. It shoots down from my rearview mirror. A car coming up behind, fast. I didn't see it back there. The long straight road behind me was empty. *You were thinking.* Must have pulled out from a side road. The car shoves up close, lights on bright, and then pulls out to pass in a rush of unmuffled engine and red primer–splotched metal. I want the car to pass, pull ahead, leave me alone here again on this long straight road through the pines. *Primer? Confederate flag in the back window?*

Jimmy Danes's old Ford brakes in front of me in a blur of burning rubber, red taillights, and boy howls from open windows. I can't count the wild tongues that wail from the Ford, but they're enough to make the hair on my arms rise to the old electricity of fear. I brake hard, stop inches short of Jimmy's rear bumper. The howling, hooting boys explode from doors that swing wide, and they run at me from all directions. I try to throw the Plymouth into a U, but it's hopeless. The only way out by car is running Jimmy down, or the boy, Dwayne, who wore the black bandanna and the fringed leather jacket back in the biker bar. Dawnell's brother, Ard, runs past my window, grinning, to block my backing up. The last face I see before I reach down for the butcher knife is the short man, pulling aside the red and blue curtain of the Confederate flag in Jimmy's rear window and looking at me out of blank eyes above jaws that mull, toothless.

I sit in the Plymouth, engine running, foot gunning the flathead six as though its life is mine. For a second, I see myself doing it, backing up fast, my tires chewing at Ard's feet and legs, his face hitting with a wet smack against the bulbous differential joint between my rear tires. Then I crank the shifter and dig out with Jimmy's face setting down my hood like the sun of stupidity it is. But a deep breath blows out of me hard, sweeping away this dream, leaving the hollow-ness of understanding. And my hand grips, then drops the butcher knife. *Maybe you can take this beating? Maybe better that than hurt someone again?*

Jimmy stands outside my window striking something against his palm like a man with a tool, considering how best to apply it to the job at hand. My eyes slip from his face, down to the thing itself. It *is* a tool, a big grinning crescent wrench, cranked open wide for maxi-mum effect. I look up at Jimmy again. His long greasy hair has been shorn by doctors, and a spot just above his right temple has been shaved. Big black stitches pucker the skin there, and the scalp around them is obscenely white. Jimmy says through bitten teeth, "You better get out, busboy. We got a word to say to you."

I look over my left shoulder. Ard stands at my rear bumper hold-ing something too. It's not the rifle, I can see that. Dwayne, the one whose arm I bruised or broke with a pool cue, stands at my passenger window, looking in like I'm something on television. I reach down and cut the engine, leaving us all in a terrible quiet I know will last only until they beat screams from me. Hearing the engine stop, Ard and the other boy come around to my door. I open my throat, fill my-self with a last long, unpainful breath, and unlatch the door. Jimmy will try to hit me, for the sake of symmetry, right where the biker hit him, and he will do it before I get my feet under me. I kick the door out, flinging him back, step inside the arc of his bright wrench, and bring my right hand up hard, between our two chests, under his chin. My knuckles hit flush and break teeth. They are all on me.

I can't see what Ard's holding but know it has a black friction-taped handle, and it's so heavy he can't swing it with one hand. It hits my back between the spine and shoulder blade as I grapple with the fringed vest, and things break all through me, bone, blood, and organ. I can't get breath, any breath, and I'm down in front of Jimmy who spits blood and teeth into my face, screams, "FUUUUUUCK!" and brings his knee up to crush my nose. Without breath, almost without strength, I have enough mind to dip my head and take Jimmy's kneecap on the forehead rather than the nose. The force takes from my brain the neural equivalent of breath, and I go down in a ball, under a rain of feet and fists, with sense enough only to pull my face down to my knees and clasp my hands across the back of my head. As sleep approaches, so does a tall man. I feel the thumping, stabbing, pounding, cursing becoming increasingly abstract, each hit not a feeling but a word, and I know this is not a good thing. Then I hear something different.

At least I think I hear it, for now I am at the borderland between actual hearing and the invention of things. This thing is a wild, high keening, as of the deepest sorrow, or the most intimate pain. Slowly I unfit my bruised and swollen fingers from what is left of my face and, raking blood and mucous from my eyes, look up. The tall man stands over me. He holds two things in his hands, two limp things, and he shakes them. He brings them together in front of him with such violence, such force, that they lose all animation.

I rake at my eyes again, look up, and Emil stands above me holding Jimmy Danes in his left hand by Jimmy's bare testicles and, in his right hand, Jimmy's crewman, the boy in the fringed leather vest, by the long greasy hair. Again, Emil bangs them together, grunting with the effort, but with no more effort than I have seen him use to haul two ten-gallon tubs of lard from a high shelf. Dwayne's face strikes Jimmy's bare buttocks with a smack for what I can see is not the first time. Jimmy, clearly getting the worst of this, screams the scream I heard back there, miles away. I push myself up, elbows first, then knees under me. Emil throws the bandanna boy against the side of my car, denting the hard old sheet metal like it was tinfoil. He looks down at his free hand, then shakes a hank of ripped-out bloody hair from it. He shakes Jimmy a last time by the testicles and throws him, pants flying around his shoe tops, into the ditch. Jimmy splashes, screams, moans, and then lies still. I can see now between Emil's spread legs, Ard lying coldcocked on the warm asphalt, blood pooling from the corner of his mouth. Beyond Ard, I see a car, headlights on, a vague figure standing by the passenger door in a corona of light. The figure moves forward now with halting steps, and I see purple espadrilles, a yellow muumuu, two still-shapely ankles. The Widow. Sandralene Reddick.

Emil kneels in front of me, but I fall back, lying spread-eagled, feeling the warmth of the asphalt leech into my flesh where Ard's sap separated rib from spine. I look up into the high night sky, but only for a moment. Emil's face intrudes. "How bad is it? Can you walk? We need to get you out of here. Hell, we all need to get out of here 'fore somebody comes along."

I try to speak, but my lips have swollen shut, and soon, too, will my eyes. I manage to whisper, "Thanks, Emil."

"Quiet, colonel. Let's get you out of here." He sounds genuinely annoyed. I feel his big arms nudging under me, and then I'm lifted, the pain in my back shooting my limbs out stiff and pulling a cry through my swollen lips. I hear Emil mutter to himself, "Easy, easy." He puts me in the front seat of my Plymouth, but not behind the wheel. I hear him shout, "Mrs. Reddick, you drive my car, follow me!" Emil moves away then, and I hear him dragging limp Ard off the asphalt onto the shoulder of the road. Then Emil is behind the wheel of my car, and firing up the flathead six, and wheeling us into a U-turn. I hear the Widow troubling with the shifter in Emil's big black Lincoln.

I reach up and pry my right eyelid open and the last thing I glimpse before it slips bloody shut again is the short man pulling aside the red and blue curtain of the battle flag of the Confederacy, seeing Emil at the wheel of my car, and, pale, haggard, and rubber-lipped, letting the curtain drop.

THIRTY-ONE

'm sitting on a steel bunk with a bucket between my knees and my head in my hands. The room is about twenty by twenty with tiered bunks along two walls, seatless steel toilets at the back, and bars across the front. The reeking pallet under my haunches is stained with vomit and urine. A man's feet dangle to my left. His ankles are swollen, the skin gray with heavy callouses and red with ruptured capillaries. A pair of sneakers have half rotted off his feet, and they smell somewhere between skunk musk and sun-ripened, roadkilled armadillo. On the bunk across from me two Black men play a card game they call Tunk. They play for matches torn from a book and then torn in half. The matches stand for cigarettes, and somebody's going to pay up in goods when they get out of here. Over in the corner, two college boys, the only people in here more scared than me, stand huddled together. They both wear starched, short-sleeved oxford cloth shirts, Bermuda shorts, and sockless Weejun loafers. One of them has a ripped ear, the lobe torn loose from the side of his head. Blood runs down his shirt all the way to his expensive alligator belt. The other boy has a weeping gash below his left eye and a nose swollen the size of a plum and about the same color. They both have bloody knuckles and bits of oystershell embedded in their scraped knees. You can read on them the progress of the encounter they had with a couple of shrimpers from Apalachicola. It started out as a fair fight in a bar down in Mexico Beach, but they got tossed into the parking lot by the bouncer and some patrons who wanted peace and quiet, and things weren't fair after that. In the parking lot, all the college boys had was a red Pontiac Bonneville. The shrimpers had a

Ford pickup with tools in the back, ax handles, bolt cutters, and the like. The fight was short. I didn't have to read the progress of the fracas in blood and oystershells, because last night at four o'clock when the two boys came in handcuffed, their blood was still up and mixed with Early Times and Coke, and they told everybody in here the story. They were about finished when one of the two Black men now playing cards said from a top bunk, "You two little turds better shut up and let me sleep, or I'm getting down off of here. You understand me?" Not a peep after that, and now it's morning, and the two college boys are quiet, cold, and leaning on each other in the corner.

I haven't said anything. I've been puking into this bucket every so often. I asked for it, the bucket, when the deputy, the same drawn, patient man who took Dawnell away, came to get me from the Wind Motel at three o'clock after some passersby scraped Ard and Jimmy and Dwayne off the asphalt and took them to the hospital and they told about how I waylaid them out there on the highway, me and "two or three big niggers." That's the word going around the county lockup. When the jailer handed me the bucket, he said, "Boy, it's good you asked for this. You be cleaning my floor with a toothbrush if you didn't."

My head won't clear, my eyes and lips are swollen, my back feels broken, and I keep throwing up and getting these shakes, convulsions that wrack me out stiff and tremble my limbs, and then comes the nausea. I want to sleep, but I know I shouldn't until my head clears better.

Emil tried to take me to the hospital last night, but I wouldn't let him. He almost did anyway, yet I talked him out of it. I told him I'd be all right if I just had some time to rest. If I went to the hospital, there'd be too much explaining to do.

When the deputy knocked on my door at three o'clock, I let him in, and he looked me over before he handcuffed me. "Do you want medical attention?" he asked me.

"No," I said, "I just want to—"

"Then you refuse medical attention? Is that right?"

"Yes sir." Nothing in my voice but tired and sick.

The convulsions wrack me again, and the nausea comes, and I dry heave into the bucket. One of the two Black men playing Tunk looks over at me, frowns, shakes his head, and goes back to the game. He'd like to come over here and slap me silly for making ugly noises and smells, but he's holding back because he's getting out in a few hours, when everyone in here, I've been told, will either make bail or go to the morning court for a fine or sentencing.

Keys rattle in the door at the end of the corridor, and the jailer, a big redheaded man with small pale eyes, huge hands and feet, and a voice so low and vibrant it sounds like a noise from the bowels of a diesel engine, walks down the hallway slapping his key ring against his thigh. Emil walks behind him. He's wearing his black suit with the thin white pinstripe, gleaming black shoes, a white shirt, and a dark-purple bow tie. The two stop and stare into this cell. "There he is," the redheaded jailer says, nodding in my direction. He looks at his watch. "You got ten minutes." The jailer walks back down the corridor, unlocks the door, and leaves.

Emil approaches the bars. I push the bucket away with my foot, wipe my face on my sleeve, and get up with the concrete floor pitching under me. Carefully, I walk to Emil and stand in front of him, holding myself up by the bars. I look into his still, speculating eyes. I try to smile, but that hurts. I say, "Thanks for coming to see me, Emil."

He says, "I didn't come to see you, colonel. I came to see him." He looks over my shoulder at the man on the top bunk, the drunk with the swollen feet and rotting sneakers. "How are you, Albert?"

I turn carefully and look at Albert. He rouses himself from a mumbling stupor, focuses eyes so bloodshot they seem to seep red, and waves like he's throwing something away. "Good, good, Emil. How you?"

"I'm fine, Albert." Emil's eyes fasten back onto mine. He says, "All right, now I've seen Albert."

"You've seen . . . ?"

"I couldn't tell the bulls I was here to see you. That wouldn't be good for me at all. Albert's always in here." He looks around the pen, lowers his voice a little more. "They gon' charge you with something, maybe just disorderly conduct, maybe felony assault." He raises his hand to what little outrage I can muster. "I know, I know. They got it all backward, but the fact is you were on your way to violating a restraining order, and they don't like that."

Again I try to speak.

Again the hand. "Now, Mrs. Reddick is making your bail, so you'll be out of here sometime today. When you get out, you and I have to talk. Either you did all that damage by yourself, or somebody helped you, and if it was me helped you, some of these rednecks around here ain't going to like it very much. Do you understand what I'm saying?"

I shake my head, think about it. Some light breaks into my cracked skull. To me, Emil is Vulcan, God of fire, lightning striker in the heat and fury of the kitchen. But who is he to men like the big redheaded jailer with the keys and the huge hands and feet? I remember that Emil has always seemed a little smaller to me the few times I have seen him away from Big Sam's. Small minds, white minds, legions of them, have made him smaller still. I see now in his eyes that he is not just angry at me for dragging him into this, but also plainly afraid. That even in his clean pressed clothes, and in his body the size of a telephone booth, and in his dignity, he is only a few words, a misstep, a casual mistake from crossing over to where I am and becoming what I am right now. Incarcerated again. Again a felon.

I thank him again. He nods solemnly. I say, "When I get out, we'll talk. We'll plan something. I'll tell them it was . . ."

He looks at me closely, a slow, sad smile coming to his lips. What was I about to say? *I'll tell them it was me alone on that dark road against Jimmy, Ard, and the boys.* It won't work. I'm willing to take the fall for Emil, but it won't work. He helped me, and now he's in trouble too. We look at each other for a space, each of us digging far into the other's eyes, searching for the future there.

Finally, Emil says, "All right, colonel, take care of yourself for a few more hours, and then you be out of here."

He turns and walks off down the corridor, and I hear him knock three times politely on the metal door. The keys rattle on the other side.

A little before noon, when I'm the last one left in what they call the drunk tank, the Widow comes with the papers to get me out. All of my overnight companions have been called out. I've watched them get up, groaning and stretching, and follow the redheaded jailer. I've watched the bottom of my bucket, too, slowly filling with bile, and then a blood-flecked, clear substance, battery acid. The phrase "internal injuries" keeps crawling into my head. I push it away and wonder why I'm last to get out of here. Is this some message to the trashy white boy who enlisted three Negroes to gang up on Jimmy and Ard?

The Widow, quiet and flustered from her visits to the bail bondsman and the sheriff's department, drives me home in her oil-stewing, rump-sprung Fairlane and puts me to bed at her place, where I lie slipping in and out of warped and slanted dreams, visiting dark and sometimes luminous places where strange creatures beckon to me from floating cocoons of haloing light. The Widow comes and goes too, offering me hot tomato soup, cold orange juice, a ham sandwich, and sometimes sitting with me and stroking the parts of my face that can bear touching. She brings me ice packs when I can hold them, but they often slip from my hand. Sometimes she holds them to my face, or tells me to roll over and cools the big black bruise along my spine. "Sweet Jesus," she says the first time she sees it, "what hit you, a truck?"

I manage, "I don't know." I hear her laugh under her breath at my bent-brain nonsense, and then I remember the Widow was there when Emil came, and I understand how it must have been. How it was the Widow, cured by vodka, who went to Big Sam's. How it was Sandralene Reddick who told Emil what she thought I might do, and asked him to come with her looking for me. Two strangers chasing the trashy white boy through the night.

* * *

I lie in the Widow's guest bedroom for three days, and on the third morning, she comes in, touches my hand with the tips of her fingers until I start awake, then groan with the pain of moving. She says, "Travis, honey, you have a visitor."

I mutter, "Who?" thinking maybe Emil, and with that thought come all of the complications of the talk Emil said we would have, and then I think maybe my visitor is Dawnell, but how is that possible? I hear footsteps out in the hall, and my father steps across the threshold.

The Widow, on tiptoes, peers at me over his shoulder, and says, "You can sit right over there. I'll just leave you two alone to talk."

My father's eyes take me in, and he winces with the shock of it, looks back at the Widow's disappearing footsteps, then at me again. "My God, son, what happened to you?" He drags a rattan chair with a red-and-pink-flowered cushion from the corner, drops into it, and then catches himself as he sinks into the poof and hiss of hibiscus blossoms and bamboo shoots. He's half lying back at an undignified angle, and his immaculate gray suit coat is wadded under him. He hitches forward, perching, adjusting his coat.

Watching this, I try to compose an answer to his question: *What happened to you?* I'm six years old again, pumping home on my bike to beat the dark. I'm a little boy standing at the back step, leaning my Schwinn against the flagstones, reaching down to pluck bullhead stickers from my pant cuffs, and composing an alibi for my father, the story of why I am home after the sun has gone down.

But it turns out I don't have to plead my case. My father presses a thumb and forefinger to his eyes and says, "Never mind. I know most of it, at least the general outline."

Ah yes, I'm thinking, *of course.* Attorney Lloyd Hollister has contacts at the sheriff's office. His father, my grandfather, an old fisherman now in New Port Richey, was once the sheriff of Widow Rock.

He looks at me again, more carefully now. "Have you been to see a doctor? Do you need one?"

I reach up and touch my face. The motion makes my back seize.

My fingers play along the contusions and swellings that have subsided somewhat now. "I don't think any of these need stitches, do you?"

He looks not at my wounds but into my eyes. "I don't know, son. I'm a lawyer, not a physician."

But I'm thinking, *You saw plenty of this in the war, and worse. You know what needs a stitch and what doesn't.* My father presses his eyes again, as though he feels a headache coming on. "Would you like some aspirin?" I offer. There's a bottle of white pills, a pitcher of water, and a glass on my bedside table.

He looks at me sharply, like I might be smart-assing him, but he sees I'm not. Sees that I've become a friend of the aspirin bottle.

We just sit for a while, my father rubbing his eyes and thinking. His son, I am trapped in a bed, sinking lower and lower into a white snow of counterpane and lassitude. Finally, he says, "Travis, what do you want? We've all waited for you to tell us. I've . . . made offers to you, and I've meant them. I've asked your Aunt Delia if you've said anything to her. I know you two were close that summer you stayed in Widow Rock."

I say, "What did she tell you, Aunt Delia? Did she tell you anything?"

"No, son. She said you'd had some pleasant visits together, talked about old memories, but you hadn't opened up your heart to her."

"Is that what she said?" I try to keep a neutral tone, but the comedy of his description of me and Delia is almost too much. Almost makes me bust a bitter laugh that will surely break open whatever has healed inside me.

He looks at me, curious, in a funk of confusion and some resentment. Why won't a boy with reform school in his past, a mad mother, years of lost time, no prospects anywhere else, take him up on a solid-gold offer to become an attorney's apprentice? I could string him along. I still don't know how I feel about him, and probably never will, and this lonely, unfinished feeling for the man who ought to be the closest to me in the world tempts me to cruelty, though I don't give in. I've got a surprise for him. "I'll tell you what I want. I want to get out of here. Will you help me do that?"

He looks at me for a long time. His legal mind sifts possibilities; he can't help that. How will it be for Lloyd Hollister, Esq., that his son came home and went away again? What will people say? What will he tell them? What will Eleanor think? Will I still be his only son and heir, or will I be written off, disowned, like I once was when he didn't write to me for four years? But these siftings are all of a practical nature, more or less. What I really want to know is this: does he ask himself how he will feel after I disappear? I can't guess the answer. I hope so, and I hope not. Who knows better than me what it is to carry a burden of sadness about the people you love.

My father shifts uncomfortably in his sober gray suit on the ridiculous riot of Hawaiian colors. He says, "All right, Travis, if that's what you want. How can I help you?"

I try to push up out of the bed, but I fall back into it, and it knocks the breath out of me. When I get air back into me, I say, "I want to take something with me when I go, and you can help me with that. At least I think you can. I'll let you know when the time comes. It won't be long now."

"All right, Travis, son," he says, "you let me know." He stands with difficulty, finally tall and straight, always the marine lieutenant. The day he dies, he'll be whispering, *Semper fidelis.* He leans down over me, his handsome, somber face looming close, covering me in shadow and the smell of his aftershave. I'm a boy again, in a house in the Nebraska wheat fields. It is evening time. My father leans down to kiss me good night. I strain up toward him and offer my cheek, but he does not take it. He kisses me on the lips and says, again, so moved that his voice cracks in his throat, "Let me know when it's time, and I'll do what I can."

After four days in the Widow's guest bedroom and three more in my own cabin, with no lifting but some walking to stretch my legs and to work the stiffness out of my back and release the poisons from what's damaged inside, I am not as good as new, but I am serviceable with prospects for light work and clear thinking. My mirror shows me that

I will have some permanent reminders of a night on a dark country road, but I will not have a face from which my fellow man will turn away in disgust. In lighter moments, I think of myself as some men are described in novels, "craggy" or "rugged." I receive a letter from the court. I am to report for an arraignment in two weeks. An arraignment, I learn from reading the local newspaper, is a proceeding to determine how I will be charged.

My father calls to offer Temp Tarleton as my attorney. It strikes me as interesting that Temp, the man himself, does not call me, but such are the ways of fathers and the men who marry their sisters. My first words to my father about this are, "Why do I need an attorney?"

There is a silence on the line, during which I realize that my innocence (in the sense of stupid, not guiltless) is being indulged. At length, my father says, "Son, it wouldn't be a very good idea to show up in court without representation. Judge Bryant might see it as an indication that you aren't taking what happened very seriously. And why not accept Temp's help if he's offering it to you? You won't have to pay him."

How matters conspire! Ole Temp now my savior!

I tell my father I'll think about it.

"You'll think . . . ?" He is more than exasperated. I hear him breathing some patience back into his chest. I imagine him sitting at the showpiece antique rolltop in the office lined with golden oak shelves and green leather-bound law books. Quietly but firmly, he says, "Well, don't wait too long, son. Temp will need some time to prepare."

Jimmy Danes is in the hospital again, where he has had a ruptured testicle removed. It's a simple procedure, I am told, and with one ball in good order, Jimmy can procreate at will. It's a dismal prospect. Ard Briscoe, Dawnell's night-crawling brother, has a glass jaw. One blow from Emil's fist laid him out on the asphalt for the duration of the night's conflict. The pool of blood I remember issuing from his mouth was nothing more than the result of a split lip. His injuries are minor, though now surely he knows he cannot cherish dreams of a career in the prize ring. Dwayne, the boy with the do-rag and the fringed leather vest, got off pretty lightly too. Aside from the divot of hair Emil yanked from his scalp, and a mild concussion from imprinting his skull into the sheet metal on the left rear fender of my gray Plymouth, he is fine, if you define the word in a very limited way. I haven't worked for a week, my money is running out, my job at Big Sam's may be gone, and the Widow, despite a lifetime of swearing never to do it, has granted me an extension on my rent.

One night late, eight days into my recovery, I park in Big Sam's lot and walk not through the dining room but around to the alley, past the rows of trash barrels to the loading dock. Emil is sitting in his usual spot, smoking a Camel and drinking a silver toddy. I resolve myself out of the gray mist that creeps down the alley this time of night and stand in front of him. "Can I come up?"

He gives me a look of mock nonrecognition, then pretends to compromise his standards. "Sure. Hell, why not? Come up here and sit with me, colonel. Old habits die hard, and especially bad ones."

I sit with him and accept a Camel and the flame from a kitchen match, pulling in the sweet rich smoke I've missed during my convalescence. Behind us, through the office window, we hear Big Sam crank his adding machine and mutter to himself about the mysteries of numbers. I wince at the sound. "You think he'll take me back?" I have to get some kind of grubstake together to pay off the Widow and set me up for what I plan to do.

"You want some of this homemade?" Emil shows me his empty cup.

"Sure," I say, and take his cup in with me for a refill.

When I sit again, and we sip and appreciate, he looks me over with a critical eye. "You looking better. A little better."

"You think I'm gonna be pretty again?"

"You never was pretty."

"Women used to say so."

"Will you *listen* to the man, now!"

"So, how have things been around here since I been gone?" Emil knows I don't mean frying shrimp and bussing tables.

He shrugs, sips, tokes, blows, and looks back over his shoulder at the light that falls at the side of the building from Big Sam's window. "Big Sam's been putting his head together with some of them boys from out to Ebro. And I wouldn't say his attitude toward me has been exactly cordial."

I don't understand this. Out to Ebro is where Dawnell lives. Roughly. And who would Big Sam know from out there? And why not be cordial with the best fry cook and kitchen manager in a hundred-mile radius? I guess Big Sam knows everybody. I turn to Emil, tap his shirt pocket for another Camel.

He pulls the pack, shakes one out. "You getting pretty familiar, ain't you?"

"What do you mean about Big Sam and the boys from Ebro?"

He regards me, chin down, neck stretched back skeptical. He blows streams of smoke from his nostrils, like an angry bull in the Sunday comics. He looks back out into the mist that drifts through the alley.

"Emil?"

"Come on, boy!"

"Emil?"

"You never heard of the Invisible Empire? The Klan?" His voice is small now. His shoulders hunch down, and maybe he shivers a little. It's that getting-small again.

We finish our cigarettes. I guess he means Big Sam is negotiating with the Klan. Trying to cool them off. I wonder what Big Sam said to the boys from Ebro when they all put their heads together.

Emil stands up, and I hear the cartilage in his knees creak. He stretches, throwing his head back, and says, "Well, it's about time to . . ."

A car noses through the mist from the south end of the alley. A big white Pontiac, no more than a few years old. The radio's playing. It's an old Hank Williams tune. *"Why don't you love me like you used to do? How come you treat me like a worn-out shoe My hair's still curly, and my eyes are still blue."* Nobody drives back here late at night. The car stops opposite us, the engine running. We're standing, looking down at it, and I can't see much. There's a haze of cigarette smoke inside. The driver's hammy forearm rests on the windowsill. It's covered with fine, reddish hair. They're probably tourists, lost, looking for directions. The driver turns toward us, but all I can see beneath the bill of a faded blue ball cap is the fat red tip of a nose and two hairy ears. The near back door opens and the short man gets out. The grip of a fist in my stomach eases as the comical chewing mouth comes toward us above no neck, stumpy legs thrusting out to the sides like Popeye the Sailor Man. The short man looks up at me, an unlit cigarette pinched between his loose lips. He's wearing one of those light-yellow, see-through nylon shirts Cubans like and carrying a can of beer. He reaches into his pants pocket and pulls out a cigarette lighter.

I look over at Emil. Did he see the little man that night staring at us from the backseat of Jimmy Danes's car? Emil doesn't seem to recognize the rubber face, the small, buried eyes. He leans over, about to say something.

The short man slashes the beer can at Emil, once, twice. Up and across. Crotch to face. Shoulder to shoulder. I smell gasoline and hear a *flick*. The man throws the lit Zippo at Emil's chest. In a reflex that happens even before Emil knows what's been done to him, he catches the lighter rather than slapping it away. *WHUMP!*

The short man spits the cigarette and runs. The Pontiac's V-8 whines, tires digging, a shout, "Now you ain't so big, nigger!" warps around the corner. Emil is dancing beside me with a cross of flame down his chest and across his arms. I throw myself at him, into the searing flame, embracing his chest. He thinks to push me away. I feel his big arms strain at mine, then he knows what I'm doing and beats his burning arms on my back until I hear the flames go out behind me. Our faces, our eyes, are inches apart, and the heat from his face burns mine. I reach up and beat his hair, his cheeks, with my open hands until they go dark, and nothing is left but the reek of petroleum.

We stand like that in each other's arms for a space, then Emil pushes me away and, moaning, "Lord, oh my Lord," runs inside to the big sink by the dishwashing machine. Following, I watch him splash cold water on his face, chest, arms, into his eyes. I reach down under the cold stream and throw handfuls of water at him, then I run to the refrigerator and bring back a cake of butter. It's what I've heard to do. I pull at his shoulder, feeling the heat in his flesh. He looks at me, wild. "No, no, I don't want that. Get me to the hospital."

THIRTY-TWO

Big Sam takes me back. He has to. We're so shorthanded, Big Sam's the cook now. It's no fun in the kitchen with Emil gone and Big Sam behind the fryers, his fat middle wrapped in a spattered apron, his arms covered with flour up to the rolled shirtsleeves, his lips muttering about how the whole place is going to hell as the smoking fryers pop boiling lard onto his hands. The lore is that Big Sam used to cook and do it well, back when his mama and daddy owned what was only a shack, and Big Sam was just back from his sojourn on the Gator gridiron, still wearing a brace on his bum knee, and still dreaming of coeds, frat parties, and rich boosters from Jacksonville who slapped you on the back and stuffed greenbacks into your shoulder pads. Back then, Big Sam was a dream with a fried shrimp, a hush puppy, and a simple tossed salad. But he's been out of the heat too long, and every day that passes teaches him how much he needs Emil.

Nobody knows if Emil is coming back. I've been to the hospital twice, but they won't let me see him. The nurses say the burns are not as bad as they looked, second degree mostly, but he's caught some kind of infection, and it's gone to his lungs.

Once, I asked LeLe if she knew what was going on. "Is Big Sam saving Emil's job until he gets out of the hospital?"

We were standing at the back of the dining room. I was stocking silver at LeLe's station. She looked at me for a while, eyebrows arched and one corner of her fishy mouth hooked down. Finally, she said, "You think Big Sam'd spend eight hours up to his ass in hot lard if he was going to replace Emil?" She took a step toward me. I stepped back. She hissed, "You little shit, you're the reason all this happened."

I hated hearing it from her, but she was right. I didn't make Jimmy Danes do what he did, or Emil, or Dawnell for that matter, but I could have left bad enough alone, and I didn't. There's a sick sad feeling in me because Emil's hurt, and it's my fault.

The next time I go to the hospital, the nurse behind a desk at the crossing of two corridors tells me they've just brought Emil down from intensive care. She says, "I'll let you have ten minutes with him. We don't want him to get too tired."

When I come into the room, Emil's asleep, cranked up almost to a sitting position in a bed that bends in the middle. His face is turned toward the window. A little clicking sound comes from his throat with each breath. I look him over. A white dressing like a skullcap covers the top of his burned-bald head, but I can see places at his temple where the black hair has started to grow back in. One of his eyes is burned and drips yellow medicine down his cheek. There's an apron of bright-red skin at his neck, disappearing into the collar of his green gown. Both his hands are wrapped in gloves of gauze with yellow oozing through. I pluck a tissue from a box on the bedside table and touch it to his cheek, absorbing the seeping there. Emil groans and throws both hands out in front of him, batting, swatting, pushing an imaginary Zippo away from him. His eyes are still closed through most of it, but when I reach out and take one of his wrists, he wakes up. His eyes are wide and scared for a moment, and he doesn't know who has him in hand, but at length he takes in my face, and an apologetic smile comes to his lips.

"Colonel! What you doing here?" His voice is thick and raspy, but the old life is in it.

"I just dropped by to see how you're getting along."

"Well . . ." he holds up his hands in front of him, turns them, ". . . how'm I doing?"

"The nurse says a lot better."

"Lying women. It's a world of lying women out there, Travis."

He chuckles low in his throat. "Just kidding, son. You know I love women."

"I know you do."

"That's right, you know it." He tries to wink at me, but it doesn't work. He just doesn't have the equipment. I look away while his stuck, lashless eyelids slip open again. "So, how you doing, anyway?" he says. "Let me look at you. Uh-huh, uh-huh, you looking good. All healed up there. Everything turning out all right now?"

I say, "When are you coming back to Big Sam's, Emil? We need you there real bad."

He looks out the window, at the trunk of a palm tree that slips up into the sky, its crown of green fronds higher up, decorating someone else's window. "I don't know, colonel. I don't know. You say you think Big Sam wants me back?"

"Wants you back? Big Sam's doing the cooking himself just to hold the position for you. He'd give you half the franchise if you'd come on back this afternoon for the dinner shift. Hell, the people who have to eat what he cooks would come get you right now if they knew where you were."

"Well, you tell 'em not to come today. I ain't ready yet." He lifts his hands and looks at the yellowed gauze. "But soon, soon." He looks away at the window again.

Two gulls bank into view, wheel up into a stall side by side, using their webbed feet as flaps. They drop out of sight. I stand with my hands on the cold metal bed rail and look at Emil's shape under the sheet. He's smaller again. The small white minds have shrunk him down. I wonder if he'll go back to Big Sam's. I wonder if he'll even stay in Panama City. Who will he be now, even if he's king of Big Sam's kitchen? Can he be Vulcan again for a few more years, or will he be the Black man who was cooked by the Klan?

Sticking his head out of the kitchen to look at the acre of people chewing like bovines in a pasture, Emil will know that one of the men who turns from grazing to stare back at him could be the one who drove the Pontiac that night, or could know a man who knows one who said, *You should have seen that nigger jump with the fire on him. Talk about burning a cross? We put it right on him.*

Emil's still looking out the window. Or maybe he's fallen asleep. I whisper, "Emil, I'm sorry."

After a long space, he says low, firm, "It ain't your fault, son. It's just the world. The way it is. Like I told you, some people never learn. You try to teach them, but they never learn."

He can't look at me. I wish he could because this might be our last time to see each other. Maybe it hurts him too much to turn his head to me. I clear my throat. "Emil, I'm getting off the ship, so you might not see me for a while. I promise you I'll get past the waterfront. I'll see the forests, and the museums, and the buildings, and I'll meet the people."

He doesn't look at me, but he lifts his hand and holds it out to me. Gently I take it in both of mine, cupping my palms under it like it's an ancient holy book.

Emil says, "You do that, son, and you'll make ole Emil proud of you. Now get on out of here and let me rest."

He lets me hold his hand for a second or two more, then he takes it away and lowers it to the sheet.

I'm tiptoeing out of the room when I hear him say, "Travis, it's over now, son. You understand me? No more. It's over."

He's telling me I can't go after the short man. I turn and look back at him. His eyes are closed, his face slack. He looks asleep or dead. It's as though the words came from someplace else, from the very air.

Temp Tarleton and I meet to talk about my impending court appearance. His advice to me, delivered with a chuck to my shoulder in his bluff fine fellow way is, "Travis, let me do most of the talking. If the judge speaks to you directly, keep it simple. Don't get mouthy, and don't complicate things."

Temp's strategy (I'm sure it's my father's too) is to leave Emil out of things entirely. Jimmy and Ard have shot off their mouths all over the place about me and "two or three niggers." Their manhood can't abide their getting ass-whipped by just one Black man. (I only got in one punch.) The sheriff's department, my attorney Temp Tarleton, and the wagging tongues of the town have all been asking Jimmy and Ard and Dwayne, the third crewboy, to describe the Black men who helped me assault them. Shouldn't the identities and whereabouts of these two (or three?) miscreants be, uh, ascertained? And this is where the tale of a certain night on a dark and lonely road gets so murky that Jimmy and Ard and Dwayne are becoming the subjects of some healthy suspicion.

The pot boils for a few days after Temp and I have our meeting, the town takes a sober look at itself, Black and white people stare at each other across the middle ground of their mutual self-interest, the local newspaper publishes an editorial about how what happened to Emil is a slimy throwback to the days of Jim Crow and a stain on our community it will take years to wash away.

In this improving climate, Temp Tarleton asks for a meeting with the judge and the county prosecutor *in camera*, which means behind closed doors, and tells these two august gentlemen the story of that night on the road to Ebro from my point of view, how I was jumped three-on-one, and Emil, who happened to be driving by, came to my rescue. Temp even offers up a surprise witness, a local woman of excellent character and standing in the community who has, heretofore, in view of her reputation and her, uh, standing in the community, chosen not to come forward. (The Widow will testify if she has to, but would rather not.)

The result of this meeting is that the judge and prosecutor agree to put their heads together, a not entirely ethical but locally fairly common practice, and see what they can do about the matter. Which means, Temp tells me as we sit over coffee in the Po' Gal Cafe in Widow Rock, "Boy, you are almost out of the woods. I'm betting we can count on, oh, say, nothing worse than disorderly conduct and a modest fine."

Temp picks up the tab for our two coffees and his jelly donut, and we walk outside. He is wearing a blue summer-weight suit, black Weejuns, and carrying a black leather briefcase that reflects the morning sunlight like a mirror. He chucks me on the shoulder, which hurts me in several places, all of them owing to Jimmy Danes and his crew. Temp says, "So, Travis boy, looks like you dodged the big bullet."

I smile my gratitude and say, "No, Temp. We both know you dodged it for me."

"Well, hell, man . . ." he says, the Southern male's standard averment about your obligation and his largesse. Temp smiles and rocks back on his heels: This is just a small corner of the larger canvas of noblesse oblige. He looks off into the morning sun, squints, reaches into his suit pocket, and pulls out some slick aviator sunglasses, all the rage now. He says, "You know, Trav boy, that cook, what was his name . . . ?"

"His name is Emil Bontemps."

"Right. Anyway, that cook got you off as much as anything else did. After what happened to him, nobody around here wanted to see this thing go any further. Folks wanted it buried." He jabs his clean legal thumb emphatically at the pavement to signify burial. Deep. He glances around at his fellow citizens going about their morning business. Traffic flows, stores are busy, the new drive-in teller window at the Orange Bank is strangled with cars, a woman in a beige suit at the realty office is changing *House for Sale* signs in her window. Temp says, "God knows we don't want the kind of trouble around here they had over in St. Augustine." His face is confidently grave.

I nod in agreement, then shake my head, *No we don't. We certainly do not.* But I'm thinking how complete a victory it was for the Invisible Empire. A couple of their foot soldiers got some hurting, and one of them lost a testicle, but they sent their age-old message, and they got away with it. The sheriff won't be looking very hard for the short man and his confederates.

I hold out my hand to Temp, and he takes it. We shake, and it's a good, firm, friendly one. He says, "Well . . ." looking at his watch.

I say thanks, again.

He takes a step away, another, rocks forward and back on fine black leather. "What are your plans now, Travis? Lloyd said something about you leaving? We sure don't want you to do that."

"What does Delia say? What does she want me to do?"

Temp does not find the question strange. He pushes his aviators up onto his forehead and looks off into the middle distance thinking about it. "Aww, she hasn't said much, you know, but I know she'd be real sad if you didn't stay around. She's real fond of her nephew Travis."

"How is she doing?"

"Oh, she's fine." But he blinks and reaches up to thumb the glasses down again, taps them to the bridge of his nose. I've put him on his guard. From behind the blued glass, he looks into my eyes, wondering what I know.

I say, "Well, if I do leave, you know I hope you and Delia will be very happy together. I know you will."

"Well thanks, Travis. A fellow always needs the good wishes of family. And don't you worry. Me and ole Delia are fine, just fine."

We shake hands again, and he turns, perched on the curb, leaning out into the traffic, waiting for his chance to run.

THIRTY-THREE

My father and I have met, and I have told him what I want. The afternoon when I lay in the Widow's guest bedroom and he came to see me, just before he bent to give me a father's kiss of blessing and farewell, I told him there was something I wanted him to do for me. Later, when I explained to him what I wanted, he resisted, so I played what I thought was my trump card. I told him that in exchange for the favor I was asking, I would give up my birthright. I had to say these words with some suppression of irony. I have never really believed myself to be entitled to anything from my father. The moment when I took the bayonet he had used honorably on Guadalcanal and drove it in rage and frustration into the flesh of Jimmy Pultney, I forfeited any right to an inheritance from my father save for the brains and a certain stiffness of the spine he gave me at birth. But, suppressing both irony and desperation, I played the card.

My father looked at me for a long time, and then he agreed. I know he did not agree because he liked the bargain I offered. He can only have been amused by my reference to a birthright which is only mine anyway by the most tendentious of claims. He gave in to me finally, I think, out of the simple goodness of his heart and a small measure of his own self-interest. When he did, I told him, "Please give anything that might have come to me to Delia's children."

And now we are driving through the night in his new white Cadillac, our faces bathed by the green glow from the instrument panel. The pine trees in their dark canyons seem to lean over us as we pass, their limbs whispering of night secrets. The two poles of my father's headlights ram as solid as yellow steel down the asphalt, revealing ferny ditches, fence posts, the bright-red eyes of possum and raccoon. We haven't spoken since he picked me up where I left my car in the parking lot at Big Sam's, but ours is not an uncomfortable silence. I think we've said what we have to say. My father is a man of his age. He grew up in the cruelty of the Great Depression, left it for the cruelty of a great war, and came home full of hope to make a family with a woman he had no hope of ever knowing. By his lights, given his gifts and limitations, he has done his best, even by me. I think somewhere in the core of him, he knows the offense that keeps a distance between us is more mine than his. Our lips have touched, and that is all we need, will ever need, it seems to me now.

I tell him, "There." The red coffee can nailed to a fence post. "Turn there."

We slow and my father turns, then stops at the hanging curtain of vines that obscures the drive. I look over at him. He looks at me, shrugs, and pushes the big blunt nose of the Cadillac through the clinging, scraping vines and on down the winding two-rut path through the cypress trees to the dooryard. We get out and stand on either side of the car. The moon has just risen over the tree line to our right, a fine full moon, the color of milk laced with blood. A harvest moon, but what kind of harvest?

The yard is puddled. Rotting cypress stumps, sawn off at sharp angles, jut from black groundwater. Ruptured machines, big and small, lie all around, oil and grease running down their metal sides and pooling on the ground beneath them. My father looks at all this spectral wreckage in the moonlight. Disdain twists his lips. "My God," he says, "no wonder she ran away from here." It's not much of a compliment to me, but I let it pass. We start walking for the porch where the bare light bulb that hangs from a braided wire warms its buzzing choir of bugs.

Just before we reach the porch, I look to my left and see, thirty yards away, a figure, slender in dark clothing, making for an aperture in the dark wall of trees. Something long and black swings at his knee. He stops, turns back toward us, turns on the flashlight affixed to the barrel of a rifle, and paints me in light. I smile into this deadly light. The flash snaps off, and Ard Briscoe steps into the trees. "Out of my life forever," I mutter, glancing at my father, who, standing on the porch holding his briefcase, did not notice Ard's light.

My father squares his shoulders and looks at me. His eyes say, *Ready?* I nod, and he knocks and calls, "Hello the house!"

We hear, "Come on in!" neither high nor low, without inflection save the faint warble of alcohol. We walk into the long hallway of the old shotgun house, my father first, then me. We turn right, into a large room, into the low-slung light of old fringe-shaded lamps, the smell of tobacco, whiskey, dogs, leather, wet denim, and the pine-cinder breath of a cold fireplace. The house isn't as bad as I thought it would be, and I lay this good surprise to the care and industry of Dawnell, who is nowhere to be seen. Her father sits in a rocker near the hearth with his hand resting on the head of a dog of indifferent breed, somewhere between beagle and pit bull terrier. The dog's chin rests on Mr. Briscoe's knee, and its eyes roll from adoring the man's face over to us with little curiosity and none of the protective instinct of either breed. Dawnell's father pushes the dog's muzzle away. He holds a smeared water glass half full of whiskey from a bottle on the floor. I can see from the heavy weight in his eyes that he has filled the glass more than once tonight. "Well, here you are," he says, "the lawyer and his shirttail boy."

He is wearing a white cotton shirt under a pair of new blue denim overalls. One of his suspenders covers some red stitching, somebody's name written gas station style above the shirt pocket. He sets the glass down on a table near to hand and takes the bottle by the neck (the brand is Heaven Hill) and holds it out toward my father. "Have a toddy with me, Lawyer Hollister."

My father looks at the bottle, the man, the bottle, and surprising me not for the first time tonight says, "All right, thank you. Where's a glass?" His voice is calm, decisive, neither avid nor reluctant.

Mr. Briscoe, whose first name I still do not know, says with a flip of the hand that caressed the dog, "In the kitchen thar. Send the boy."

My father looks over at me, but I'm already on my way. In the small kitchen, as neat as I now expect, there is an old hand-crank pump, disconnected from the earth under the house, and near its red-painted head, a spillway leads to a porcelain sink and a tap. On a drainboard, several clean glasses rest dripping from a recent washing. I pick one, turn to leave, noticing in the corner an old wringer washer, the altar of years of someone's sweaty worship and legendary for the accidents that happened: hair, hands, even breasts caught in the turning rubber rollers.

Out in the big room, I hand my father the clean glass, and he steps forward, takes the bottle from Mr. Briscoe, pours himself two fingers, and passes the bottle back. Mr. Briscoe watches all this with a sad smirk on his face. Nobody thinks to offer me anything, and that's fine. The less of me that is noticed here tonight, the better.

My father takes a liberal drink of his whiskey, appreciates it in his mouth, swallows it, and says, "Good. Thank you." He pulls a ladder-back chair from over by the hearth, sits, and rests his scuffed leather briefcase on his knees. He sets the glass of whiskey down on the wide-planked heart-pine floor. "All right," he says, "Mr. Briscoe, these papers say that you agree to sell all of this land, four hundred and thirty acres, from the Old Morgan Road on the west, not including the county's easement of course, to the east side of Cattlemen's Creek, and there, of course, riparian law requires not an easement but a guarantee of reasonable access to water for those downstream. You are selling this property to me, or more properly to the Hollister and Tarleton Development Corporation, for the sum of $170,000. Everything here is in good order, just as we agreed it would be. In front of my son here, I advise you to have these papers examined by your own attorney before you sign them, but you have indicated to me that you choose not to do that."

Mr. Briscoe takes a drink of whiskey, looks off into a gloom only he can see, and says, "One lawyer's enough. Any more and I'd be paying you to take the land."

My father unscrews the cap from his gold Sheaffer fountain pen and offers it and a thick sheaf of papers to Mr. Briscoe's shaking hand. Mr. Briscoe looks at the white parchment, looks up at my father, over at me, here to witness and to gain, and takes the pen.

He looks at the pen, hefts it, an impressive item his eyes tell us, an instrument of power. He drives a big machine called a bombardier into the swamp, a tractor that can swim and drag huge cypress logs back here to his sawmill, and yet, his sad eyes tell us, this golden pen is stronger. It can take away his land and the trees that stand on it, and replace them with the abstraction of money. It can even take human flesh away from him.

He takes the papers my father offers, looks at the lines where he is to sign. He rests the papers on his knees where the dog's head has left its warmth, he rests the golden instrument on top of the papers, and he takes up his whiskey and he drinks. He nudges the bottle with the toe of his sodden boot, and says, "Drink some more with me, Lawyer Hollister. It ain't every day I sell away my daddy's land." The man's eyes swell red with tears. The water rises, brimming but not falling.

My father reaches down for the bottle at the man's toe, adds some to the unfinished portion in his glass, and raises it to his lips. He drinks, mulls, swallows as though it is water, says, "Good. Thank you. And congratulations. One hundred seventy thousand dollars is a lot of money."

Mr. Briscoe's eyes suddenly snap tight and dry. He has drawn his tears back into a head full of cunning. "I could of got more for it. You'll sure as hell make a lot more from it than I did. You with your golf course, and your swimmin' pools, and Lord knows what else."

My father looks into the man's eyes, resting the whiskey glass on top of his briefcase. "Mr. Briscoe, you are welcome to rethink this if you like. Nothing is settled until you sign. I can come back another night when you are more certain."

The man's eyes dial down small and dark. He bites his front teeth together, and his lips disappear. The flesh of his cheeks is white, and sweat forms under his nose. Slopping whiskey, he sets his glass on the table and snatches up the paper and pen again. "God*damn* it," he moans, "a good man don't have a chance in this world. Not a single goddamn chance in this whole wide world." He looks at my father and, for the first time, furiously, at me. He signs. He shoves the papers across to my father and they land disarrayed atop the briefcase. My father gathers them, gives Mr. Briscoe his copies, and carefully puts his own away. Mr. Briscoe takes up the whiskey glass again and glares off into the farthest, darkest corner of the room, his face like that of a schoolboy who has been punished for something he did not do.

My father fastens his briefcase, careful to secure the old-fashioned brass buckles. He screws the cap onto his gold Sheaffer and puts it away in the breast pocket of his black suit. He stands. Mr. Briscoe sits, looking up at him, the victim of a fountain pen. My father says, "Well, all right then, it was a pleasure doing business with you, Mr. Briscoe." My father bends, extends his hand for a shaking.

Mr. Briscoe only looks at it. Then he looks at me again with the purest murderous hatred I have ever seen, and he calls out to the air above his head, "Dawnie-*ELL!* You come on out here!"

My father and I look down the long shotgun hallway where a door cracks open and a shaft of buttery light falls out onto the pine floor. Dawnell steps out and looks at us like some small forest creature seeing sunlight after a long hibernation.

"Come here, girl," her father calls. She bumps the door open with her shoulder and steps out into the hall. All of her J. M. Fields bags hang from her fingers. She is wearing a plain white cotton blouse I bought her and new jeans. The white no-name sneakers. No makeup. No jewelry. Her honey-brown hair is pulled back into a neat ponytail. "*Here*, girl," her father says. Lying by the hearth, the dog looks up at him expectantly.

Dawnell walks down the hallway and into the big room where my father and I wait near the front door. She comes and stands in front of us. She looks only at me.

Her father squeezes his eyes shut tight like a man who can't bear to see something done to his own body. He says, "You go on, girl. Just go on." The cheap theatricality is thick and sickening, but I remind myself that he must be feeling some kind of anguish.

Dawnell's smile is like the sun rising after a long, cold night alone in a dark wood where wild things stalk and catch. She steps over to me, takes my hand, and we turn and walk out. The last I see of her father, his eyes are still squeezed tight, his face raised to the ceiling. It's a face from old Bible illustrations, an Old Testament prophet, Daniel in the Lion's Den, but there is no light on him and the only lions are in a bottle. His hands press the deed of sale to his knees. The old dog, nails clicking on the pine, is on his way back to resume their communion. My father says nothing more. He turns behind Dawnell and me and follows us out into the moonlit night.

In the car I say to him, "Are you really going to build a golf course, you and Temp?"

He looks off down the dark canyon of pines, pines he owns now, pines I never knew belonged to Mr. Briscoe. After a while, he sighs, taps his fingers on the steering wheel, and says, "I don't know, son. I might just hold onto the property for a while and see what happens to the market out this way." Is this his way of telling me he paid too much?

Dawnell sits in the backseat listening carefully, her eyes bright and her chin tilted to the side. Once in a while, I turn and give her a measured smile.

My father continues with his ruminations: "That fellow may live to regret the day he sold this land, or maybe I'll live to regret buying it. I paid the market price. You never know what the market will do." He doesn't sound the least bit worried.

I shake my head, push out a breath held so long it has turned to lead in my chest, and take a big pull of the fragrant night air that rushes in through the vents. I can't imagine having $170,000 to use in this way. But I don't mention it. I want my father to think I understand such things, appreciate them with a certain sophistication.

Just before we get to Big Sam's where my old Plymouth waits, I reach over and put my hand on my father's shoulder. The last time I will touch him in this world. I say, "Thank you."

He looks over at me, smiles his careful, sober lawyer's smile. He looks in the rearview mirror at Dawnell, sitting up on the backseat surrounded by all her cheap loot. His eyes rest on her for a while, speculating, maybe blessing. Then he looks back at me, and without a hint of reservation, he says, "You're welcome, son."

THIRTY-FOUR

Dawnell and I drive to the Wind Motel. I keep an eye on the streets, alleys, the sidewalks, anything that comes up behind me. No one has seen the short man since the night Emil was burned. According to the lean, patient deputy who handcuffed me and took me to jail, no one remembers seeing him in any of the places where I saw him. No one seems to know him.

When we get to my cabin, I carry Dawnell's loot inside. With the door closed and the world locked outside, we stand and look at each other. She says, "All right, you bought me, now what you gon' do with me." She puts her hands on her hips, all big girl now that she's away from her daddy and her brother.

I step to her, take her in my arms. "You need this for starters," I say quietly into the soft hair above her ear. I feel her grow quiet in my arms, then grow down and grow up at the same time. She's not so much the big girl anymore, pretending she's ready to pay me back for delivering her from her father's hell in the woods, and she's not so much the little girl either, lost in an embrace. I pat her back. "You're all right now," I whisper.

She breathes into my chest. "Yeah, I think so." I try to let go of her. She holds me. "Stay here with me?"

"I have to go talk to Mrs. Reddick. Tell her we're here."

"Stay," she says, holding me. "She knows."

I hold her for a few moments longer, rocking her a little, then I reach back behind me and loosen her hands. "I'll be right back." I move over to the desk and turn on the radio, and I'll be damned if it doesn't happen, like it does maybe one in a million times. The song is an old fifties tune I love. Maurice Williams and the Zodiacs. *"Oh, won't you stay-yay-yay, just a little bit long-ger-ruur-ruur!"* I stand there smiling in the memories, smiling at Dawnell, and after a while she smiles back. She closes her eyes and dreams into the music.

"Go on," she says. "Go talk to her."

I cross the sand yard between my cabin and the Widow's and knock on her jalousie door. It opens immediately, and there's her pale face, close, and her big soft body throbbing with worry. She must have been standing there waiting for me to come. Now that I'm here, she goes shy. She steps away from the door and sits at the little kitchen table, pulling the lapels of a pink terry-cloth robe together across her chest. Her hair is wet at the temples, and I can smell soap and steam from the shower down the hall. I stand over her, waiting for an invitation to sit. I feel the shyness coming over me. I look around the kitchen. There's no glass of vodka and grapefruit juice, fresh or otherwise. Everything is clean and neat and put away.

I say, "Did you have a good shower?" My face flushes hot with the stupidity of it. I'm no good at these things. Who is?

She looks up at me, still pinching the lapels of her pink robe together. "She back?"

I nod. "She's over there waiting for me. I told her I needed to talk to you. Do you want me to bring her over?"

She gives me a bleak look. "Hell no," she says. "She's yours now. Keep her where she is." *Keep her.* I wince at the finality of it, the grim look in the Widow's eyes. She turns away, lets go of her robe, and holds her hands out in front of her, examining pink nail polish. She says to the wall, "I hope you know what you're doing."

"I do too." What else is there to say? I glance around the kitchen a little wildly, wishing I hadn't come here. Then, something settles in my chest, my head, and I feel it all go away, all of the bad, the sad, and the crazy. The hunted and hunting feeling of the last few weeks. I know it's not gone forever, but it's gone for now. "Let's drink to it," I say in a bright tone. "What do you say? Let's drink to my knowing what I'm doing for once. Just for once." I go to the refrigerator and take the liberty. I stand in front of the Widow with the cold-steaming blue label in my hand.

She tries to stay on in the Land of Grim, but she can't. My eyes, the grin on my face, the stupid things rattling out of my mouth just cancel her passport to the Land of Long Faces, and she busts out in a giggle. I hand her the steaming blue bottle and sit down across from her as she rises for the tray of shot glasses. She says, "All right, you little fool, but let me pour my own liquor."

She sits down again, not bothering much about her robe, the flesh rolling, trembling, and settling pleasantly as she arranges the little glasses and pours.

"Sin bullets," I say, when the two glasses rest brimming in front of us.

"That's what you call them?" She gives me a girlish smile, sniffs, and thumbs the end of her nose where the laughter has left an itch. "So, what to?" she says, fitting her glass into the curve of thumb and forefinger, ready to toast.

I think about it. I don't want to ruin the moment with anything too serious. Finally, I say, "Can you bring yourself to toast the three of us? Our good health, long life, and happiness?"

Her eyes go a little somber. She looks down at the shot glass as though it will tell her. She looks up at me again and smiles bravely. "Yes." She looks over at the wall, and through it to my cabin where Dawnell waits. Doing what? God only knows. The Widow raises her glass. We touch them and pour the cold burn down our throats, and the Widow's hand is on the bottle even before her empty hits the table.

When she finishes pouring, I say, "I'm not going to have to think too hard about what the second toast will be." I look down at my glass, look back up at her under hooded brows, my best please-don't-kick-this-dog look.

"Oh-oh, what's this about?"

I raise my glass. "Here's to landladies who give markers for back rent."

She kicks me with a bare foot under the table. We touch glasses and drink. She's pouring again. She takes a deep breath to mix air with the fumes and says, "I never do that . . ." to give me a scare, then, ". . . but I'll make this one exception . . ."

I lean toward her, accept my third, feel the cool curve of it in my hand, and say, low, "I'll send it to you. I promise I will."

She rears back and gives me her tough-gal look, the one that says, *I've seen this sorry show coming down the road before.* I wait, looking into her eyes. She looks away, looks down at her glass, then reaches up and wipes her eyes with the back of her hand. "Don't you do this to me. We're having a happy time."

I lean back. "Sorry."

We touch glasses again, and she says, "You can forget about the money, sweetheart."

We drink, and I say, "No, I'll send it. A debt is a debt."

She reaches for the bottle again, but I put my hand on her wrist. "I owe you more than money."

"Oh shut up," she says. She pulls her robe together now, and says, "Look at me now, I'm falling apart."

I stand, look at her through the bent truth of vodka and love. "You look beautiful," I say.

She stands and comes to me, into my arms. I hold her as she presses her warm, soap-fragrant cheek against mine. She leans back, then in, and kisses me once, hard. She pushes me away. "You won't get around me this way," she says, touching her hair, my cheek, then giving me a hard but playful slap on the shoulder. She steps back. "Get out of here. She's waiting."

Dawnell and I are on the road in my old gray Plymouth with everything we own in the backseat and the trunk. It's not much. We're traveling light of necessity. Especially light in the wallet. The flathead six is running smooth, and I'm not pushing her. I never go over fifty-five, because the old engine starts to complain a little when I do. We just crossed the bridge to Panacea, Florida, heading south on US

98. It's a tidy little fishing town, shrimp boats bumping against the docks waiting for their crews, a gas station, a tourist court, some small clapboard cracker shacks, and a café called Mom's Kitchen. And way off to our left the blue water meets the blue sky in a hazy tremor.

We left the Wind Motel just at sunrise, early enough to get away before the Widow was stirring. I figured I had said my goodbyes, and I didn't think she wanted to see the last of Dawnell.

Dawnell and I walked our last tour of my little home to make sure we weren't leaving anything behind, and I carried the last plastic bag of odds and ends, one of them the Delia Book, out to my car. I opened the door for Dawnell, who looked at me like no one had ever done such a thing for her before, her eyes full of surprise and a satisfaction she wasn't quite sure how to repay. I started the Plymouth, took a last look at the place where I had lived for three months, whispered to myself, "Goodbye, Wind Motel. May the weather treat you well and the cockroaches reside elsewhere." I put the Plymouth in gear, backed out, and then heard a high, breathless call, "Waiiiit!"

The Widow was running down the white-shell path, holding the flying hem of her pink robe together with one hand and the top with the other, which also held a brown paper sack. Her hair was all pushed out of shape from the pillow, and her eyes were wide with the usual *Where am I?* morning look. I stopped, but she went to Dawnell's window, not mine. Dawnell looked over at me, grim, and I nodded to her to roll it down. She did, and the Widow thrust the paper sack in at her. "I made you egg salad sandwiches and sugar cookies. You can stop and picnic along the way." The Widow touched a hand to the side of her head, plucking at the matted hair. She said, breathless, "I knew you'd get an early start."

I looked over at her, about to say a flabbergasted thank you, but she reached inside the car and grabbed Dawnell by the chin, pulling her face to the window. She gave Dawnell's cheek a big motherly kiss, the first she's had in many years. Dawnell gave in to it with a sweetness that surprised me. The Widow let go of her, and the two of them looked at each other in fierce female conspiracy. The Widow said to

Dawnell, "You take care now, honey. You hear me? And if you ever need anything, the phone number of the Wind Motel is in that paper sack." Their eyes were locked, passing messages I can never hope to understand, things that go all the way back to the first book of the Bible.

The Widow pulled back, gave me one last fierce look, and then she was gone, running back up the shell path, looking right and left to make sure none of the shrimpers and pulp wooders who live at the Wind Motel were gawking out their windows at her.

There are speed traps along this route. In small towns the cops love to bust someone who's not local. I'm taking care. I'm taking care of more than my speed. I look over at Dawnell. *Keep her.* She's riding along with her forearm resting on the window, her head thrown back, gazing out at the morning countryside, the wind playing in the wispy hair at her temples and on her forehead. I say, "Hey?"

She looks over and says, "Hey?" then looks back at the sunny road coming at us at a manageable speed. As far as I can tell from looking at her, we might as well be driving across town, not straight into the rest of our lives. I want to tell her, *It won't always do that. The road. It will come at us too hard, too dark, and too fast sometimes, and we won't know what to do. We'll just have to do our best, and hope, and sometimes rely on the kindness of strangers, as the man said in a famous work of literature, but let us not be strangers to each other.*

I don't say anything to her. Not right now. Let's just ride for a while, enjoy the sunshine, the cool wind, the prospect of an egg salad sandwich and a sugar cookie in a few more miles on a blanket spread under a tree by the Gulf of Mexico. Anyway, she probably knows. She probably knows all that about the hard road, and hope and the kindness of strangers. If she doesn't, my telling won't do any good. She'll have to learn it with me as we go along, two students in the school of life.

There are things I could tell her. Some would say *should* tell her. About my part in putting two young men under the ground forever. If I told her, what would she do? I can't guess and probably won't know until I do tell her. If I ever do. Is it cowardice that I haven't told her? Is it some kind of cruelty or a sick joke that we have started this journey together, me knowing what I know and Dawnell riding along in ignorance? I have wrestled with it. I've had my theories.

Back at Bridgedale, my theory of accidents was a kid's dodge, nothing but a way to get me off the hook and let me live for a while until I could invent something better. In those days I thought that if I was just something bad that happened to other people, no different from a hornets' nest or a sheet of ice, then bad things just happened and I was not to blame, nor could I blame the people who had done things to me. When Dawnell and I stood by the water that night at Wilson's Marina, and I asked her what she wanted, she looked up at me with angry eyes that told me how ignorant I was, eyes that said, *I want you. You are good enough.* Nothing more.

When she did that, I invented the theory of hope. It holds that faith is really hope. That we never really believe Jonah was swallowed by the whale, or that Moses parted the Red Sea, or that Christ died for our sins. We just hope these things happened, especially the last one, and for most of us hope is enough, a way of seeing how things should be. Our hope designs the best possible world, even if it's impossible here and now. If Dawnell can put that much hope in me, believe I'm good enough, then why can't I hope to be the good she needs?

That is what I am doing now. I am driving south on a highway of hope with a girl-woman on the seat beside me, into the rest of our lives.

Last night, after I left the Widow, after our three shots, two toasts, and one sweet kiss, I went back to my cabin for the last night there and lay down on the saggy bed. I said to Dawnell, "Come and put your head on my shoulder."

"That's all?" she said.

"That's all," I said. I turned out the light.

She crawled in beside me, laid her warm, tired head on my shoulder, and said, "Are you all right?"

"I'm fine. I feel very fine, and I hope you do too."

She said, "I feel pretty good. It's nice to be here with you like this." She rocked her head like she was plumping a pillow, fitting it just right in the swale between my shoulder and collarbone, where I suppose it will lie for a long time to come. She sniffed twice and said, "You been drinking."

I said, "Yes, Mrs. Reddick and I had a celebratory goodbye snifter." My word choice goes straight to hell when I've had a few.

Dawnell got serious. "You don't do that *too* much, do you?" She has every reason to wonder. She's a girl whose daddy crawls into a bottle every night.

I said, "I don't know. I hope not. We'll see."

She lifted her hand to my forehead and touched me like I might have a fever. She held her hand there for a moment, reading me, then she put it back across my chest. "You're all right," she said. Then she said, "I love you."

The words sailed from her throat, her lips, to the highest part of that dark little room, and exploded like fireworks over us. What was I to do? There'd been no preparation. I had thought we were miles, maybe years from this declaration. I said the only thing that she could possibly understand, given what we had to do: "I love you too."

An hour or two later, it rained. I was lying there awake, listening to Dawnell's quiet breathing, smelling her hair and her candy breath, feeling her hand suddenly make a fist on my chest when she needed a fist for a fight in her dream. I had heard the thunder coming, but it seemed far away and not big, so I was surprised when the storm broke so violently over the Wind Motel. A hard rain and a mean wind tore at the trees, raking the palm fronds together, throwing gritty water in sheets against the windows. Lightning banged loud and close, filling the room with sudden white light. Dawnell stirred, moaned, and I whispered, "It's all right, just some rain. Go back to sleep." She settled, her breathing eased again, even as the storm brought more violence. I lay there idly thinking that if the storm blew this house down, at least it wasn't my house anymore. All my worldly goods were packed in my Plymouth, waiting for an early morning start. *Just one more night, old house,* I whispered in the empty vaults of my brain. And then I heard it.

Outside in the rain, there under the cone of light at the washhouse, small but insistent, never ceasing, going on and on, the phone ringing.

THIRTY-FIVE

got up as carefully as I could, lifting Dawnell's head and sliding the pillow under it. I knelt, waiting beside the bed until the waves calmed again over her disturbed rest.

The wind cried when I opened and closed the door. I ran in nothing but underwear to the washhouse where slanting rain spun and swayed the bare light bulb above the rusty old machines. I picked up the phone, water pouring down my face and into the foul-smelling receiver. "Don't be afraid," I gasped. "I'm here."

"Oh, Travis, my Travis. I'm not afraid. It's a miracle. I'm not."

I stood there numb, shivering, dizzy with fatigue and lack of sleep, my beaten body stiffening under the pelting rain. I didn't know what to say to her. *Not my Delia. Not anymore.* Hot tears broke from my eyes. I pushed the receiver away from me, out into the noise of the storm, so that my gutted sobs could not cross the distance to that house in the suburbs where somehow she had managed to call me without Templeton Tarleton knowing. I sobbed, then cried, then I heard her voice, far away, and I didn't know how long she'd been waiting for me. I pulled the receiver back to my ear, as ". . . Travis, are you there? Are you there, my darling?"

"I'm here. Sorry. It's raining very hard. This connection is bad."

"You sound upset, Travis, honey. Are you all right? Did the storm scare you?"

"No." What could I call her then, except another man's wife? A woman who had asked me to leave her alone to live the rest of her life as best she could. "No," I said. "I'm all right. It's just . . . a bad connection. I'm glad there is . . . a miracle. How did it happen?"

There was a long silence. I heard her blow a ragged breath like static on an old radio, like the sound that sometimes came from the speaker in her old '54 Chevy late at night when the stations in Dothan and Tallahassee went dark and she and I were racing home from some teenage mischief.

She breathed long and deep again. "I guess, I guess it's just time for me to grow up and not be so scared anymore. Everybody has to do it, don't you think?"

She really wanted an answer. What did I think? Can you grow out of fear, make it go away with age and responsibility? I hope so. It's exactly what I am trying to do. The miracle sounded so fragile, but I had to give it affirmation. I said, "Yes, I do think so. That's exactly what I think." My chest filled with the thrill of a sadness as dark as this night, as heavy as the world. I gave my sadness to Delia in the only way I could: "I'm glad the storms won't bother you anymore. Now I can—"

"Oh, Travis, I know. I know. Temp told me you're leaving. I'm so sorry you're going. I'll miss you so much."

"I know," I said, my voice dead flat.

Even connected as badly as we were by wires flying this storm, she heard it. The dark thrill of sorrow in my voice. "Oh, Travis, I'm so sorry." She was crying. "So sorry it all turned out this way."

"No, don't be sorry. It's turning out good. Better than I thought it would." I could hear her mastering her tears at the other end. The rustle of tissue, some wiping, sniffles, a deep thick suck of breath.

"Let me tell you some news, Travis."

"News?"

"I'm going to have a baby. I just found out yesterday."

My mind went black like a room where someone has shot out the lights. There was a sound between my ears as of a great dynamo seizing, shuddering to a molten zero with a dying moan. From a long way off I heard myself saying, "Congratulations, Delia. That's wonderful. It really is. It's what you've always wanted, isn't it, you and Temp?"

She was listening carefully to me, reading my tone, and I was glad of the storm, past its zenith but still full of bad intentions. "Yes, I guess it is, Travis. We've been trying for a long time." Her voice got sad, small, and young again. "You know how it is with me. You're the only one who knows all I've been through. I was afraid I wouldn't be able to . . ." She couldn't say the rest of it. But I could.

"I always knew you would, and you'll be a great mom." For a second I mourned the swelling of that belly, those coltish ankles, the plumping and stretching of Delia, beautiful Delia. Then the dark thought passed, and I saw her in a sunny backyard chasing after some determined, giggling little Temp Jr., a hank of damp hair flopping in her eyes, and, *Oh no you don't, you little scamp!* bubbling from her mouth. It was a good sunny visit to the future, somebody's dream.

"Well . . ." She sounded tired, but it was sweet, the exhaustion of confession and farewell; morning after the dark night of the soul. "Well, I knew you'd answer the phone, somehow I knew. And I was so worried we wouldn't get to talk before you left. I'm going to miss you so."

"Me too. So much."

There was a long time then when we only listened to each other breathe. What messages there were in our breath! Finally, she said, "Take care of her, Travis. I know you will."

So, my father told her. I wonder which version it was. Did he say simply that I'm leaving with Dawnell, or did he give his sister more? Did he tell her that someday an investment of his will go right and her children will be rich? Did he tell her that getting the complication of Travis out of his life and out of hers was part of the deal? Knowing my father as I do and knowing also that Delia could complicate his life as badly as I could, I suppose that he gave her the simple sunny version. *Oh, you know how Travis is. No grass grows under that boy's feet. He's off to further adventures.* He had to tell her something, and it had to be a story she could tell to Temp, his business partner in the Hollister and Tarleton Development Corporation, and it had to be a story that Temp could pass on to friends on the first tee at Quail Run if the need arose. You can't spend $170,000 on land of questionable value and not explain yourself to the family.

"I will," I said. Now that Dawnell had been mentioned, it was all over. "Well, goodbye," I said, and once again, "I'm glad you weren't afraid of the storm."

Delia breathed sweetly into the phone. "I'm so glad too, Travis, my dear, dear Travis, and it was you who made me not scared anymore. I couldn't have done it without you."

So, I had helped her. Again.

"Goodbye, sweet boy," she said.

"Goodbye," I said, "Delia," and cradled the phone.

When I lay in my saggy bed again, and lifted Dawnell's head back into its place on my shoulder, she whispered, grog-headed, "It rained. Where have you been?"

"The phone rang. Go back to sleep."

"Who was it?"

"Nobody. Wrong number."

Around noon, Dawnell and I stop in a little place called St. Marks, just a few miles off the highway, right on the water. There's a small restaurant, a weathered but warm place called Posey's, but we can't afford to eat there. I go in and buy two bottled Nehi root beers from a skinny girl in biker leathers, and we look for a place to spread our blanket under a tree near the water. We find a vacant lot between two cracker shacks, with a trail snaking through the tall Australian pines toward the water. There's no *Keep Out* sign, only a rain-bleached Realtor's notice: *For Sale. Okay,* I think, *so we are a couple of prospective buyers.*

I nose the Plymouth into the sand under the shade of a pine and get out. When I unlock the Plymouth's trunk, Dawnell is there beside me. I lean in for the blanket, but she shoulders me aside. "What are you doing? Let me." I sidestep, rock back on my heels, and smile. *Ah! The division of labor.* Fine, fine with me. I stand there in the cool shade stretching the kinks of a long drive out of my limbs and watching her slender, tanned arms reach in for the blanket, then roll it onto her hip.

I pop the caps off the two Nehis on the car door latch. A pleasant, patient voice inside my brainpan says, *You'll have to get a real opener, maybe a regular entire picnic basket to use as you roll along.* I stoop to pick up the two bottle caps. No littering. I follow Dawnell along the serpentine sand trail toward the *flap-flap* sound of the surf.

We are lying side by side on the blanket, sipping the last of our tall Nehis, the scraps of our sandwiches attracting ants nearby, sugar cookie crumbs on our chests. "It's nice, isn't it?" Dawnell says. "Our first meal together." She's getting heavy-eyed, sleepy, and pretty soon she'll want to put her head on my shoulder, and I'll want her to. I look to my left. A patch of sunlight is inching toward us across the bed of pine needles. In about ten minutes it will invade our shade, but I figure Dawnell can sleep before it does. I let out a big breath, wiggle my bare toes, listen to the water *flap, flap, flap* on the marly sand of this shallow estuary. I take a deep breath of clean late-summer Gulf of Mexico air.

In a few minutes we will rise from here, shake the sand from our blanket, pick up our scraps, brush the cookie crumbs from our clothes, and walk back to the car. We will drive back out to 98, turn right, and head south again—but why? Where are we going? And on what? We have an old car, the clothes we stand up in and a few changes, about sixty dollars, and one industrial high school diploma between us. In about two weeks, somewhere, Dawnell has to start school. Where will we live, and on what terms? I've thought about this with what time I've had to think, between going to jail and visiting Emil and helping my dad buy land and slipping out of town with Dawnell. Leaving Widow Rock, Panama City, Big Sam's, my family, Delia, means more to me than just putting distance between places and people. It means starting over, new, becoming somebody else as much as that is possible.

But who will Dawnell and I be to each other in the eyes of the world we will have to manage every day? We can't be boyfriend and girlfriend and live together, not unless we are very careful and very lucky. I've decided that in the face of the world's curiosity, we will be brother and sister. But this is only part of it. We have shared only one kiss: it happened that first time in Dawnell's fantasy house when her lips, lifted to me, took me by surprise. In my English class at Bridgedale, we read *The Romance of Tristan and Iseult*. On a journey, the two (he, a knight sworn to protect her, and she, the wife of his king) lay down to sleep in a forest. As a pledge of fidelity to his king and a symbol of his honor, Tristan placed his naked sword between them. I have decided that Dawnell and I will sleep that way until . . . I don't know what will change it. The age of consent in the State of Florida is sixteen, but who knows where we will go or what law will govern us. I have made myself this promise. My sword will lie between us until the time when we both know what our love is, and that we share it. It's the best I can think now, the limit of my understanding. Dawnell says that I bought her, and it's true in a way, and I know she thinks she bought me with promises of reckless love, but that is not true. Yes, she bought me, but not with her body; she did it by becoming the promise of my redemption.

At Bridgedale, I heard that it's not hard to change your identity (*Hell, man, what do you think "alias" means?*), get the ID cards, and licenses, and certificates that say you are someone else. Maybe we can do that. I think I want to try. I don't want to be Travis Hollister anymore, and I don't think Dawnell wants to be a Briscoe. I think she'll agree. We'll have to take it one step at a time, use our wits, take care of each other, and be resourceful. What is America if not a place where you can write your own story?

As the warm air moves across my face, and my eyes close, I see us driving a long, narrow road into the deep piney woods to a small house owned by an old country woman, recently widowed. We stop and introduce ourselves as brother and sister Smith or Jones, and Dawnell hangs her head in sadness as I explain the deaths of our parents in a terrible flood or auto crash, and that we are looking for a place to rent so that I can get a job and we can start a new life far away from those sorrowful regions where our past was lived. The old widow is skeptical at first, but my boyish charm and Dawnell's tears win her. She takes pity on us, and we rent a small cabin in the woods, and things begin for us. I find a job. I am not afraid of work. I am smart and original if not well-educated, and I work my way up in the business, and before long . . .

"Wake up," Dawnell whispers to me. I sit up and wipe the sweat from my face. "You were having a bad dream. You were shaking and moaning. I wanted to let you sleep, but . . ."

My mouth feels gluey and tastes rank. My shirt sticks to me where Dawnell's head has rested on my shoulder. The sun has invaded our patch of shade. I shake my head, clearing my thoughts. "I'm sorry. Did I scare you?"

"No." She smiles and looks at me with concern. The hair where she has rested her head on me is stuck wet to the side of her head. "But you scared yourself."

It's a bad moment for us. I am the older one. I am supposed to take care. *Keep her.* I am not supposed to be scared. I close my eyes and will this moment to pass. We have a long day ahead of us. We have to find shelter before night falls. I say, "Don't worry. I wasn't scared. It was just a dream. We better get going, don't you think?"

She gets up, brushes sand from her knees, stretches, yawns, says, "Yeah, we better."

She takes my hand and pulls me out to the water. The surf has receded while we slept. The water is maybe thirty feet farther out into the marsh. We stand there holding hands, swishing our bare feet in the warm waves.

Dawnell reaches up and fits her warm little hand to the back of my neck and pulls me down. She kisses me soft, full on the lips. "Don't worry," she says. "It'll be all right."

I look down at her blue eyes, her lips still parted from our kiss, and her simple faith.

And I believe her.

Acknowledgments

My thanks to librarian Jamie Gill for help with research, and to the Pretenders, Dean Jollay, Jack Vanek, Gale Massey, and Luis Castillo, and to Ann McArdle for commentary. Your insights made this book better.

Thanks also to the MacDowell Colony where much of this book was written.

Thanks again to my literary agent, Ann Rittenberg, for many years of thoughtful and patient guidance, and to the brilliant crew at Akashic Books for making me a guest at the best address in New York.

And finally, as always, a loving thanks to Kathy, the best reader of all, whose instincts for what to keep and what to kill are always right.